BOOK ONE IN THE LEGACY SERIES

The Rise to Power

David Francis

Clovercroft Publishing

The Rise to Power
Book One of The Legacy Series

Published by Clovercroft Publishing, Franklin, Tennessee

Cover Design by Debbie Manning Sheppard

Interior Layout Design by Suzanne Lawing

Edited by Gail Fallen

Printed in the United States of America

978-1-940262-16-1

To my family:
Delisa, Mary Anne, and Alexander

ACKNOWLEDGEMENTS

Tammy Kling: Author, Writer and Advisor
Kim Biggerstaff: Personal Editor
Dawn Herring: First Edit

****

Gwendol Bowling for Advice and Content
Julia Bowser for Content
Nicolas Cook for Inspiration

The Legacy
"A Story about Dreams that Come True."

The Legacy is a saga that derives its story from the previous age of Atlantis. Cartius, who was challenged by the climatic change in the earth's temperature, was doomed to die. In spite of his use of extremely advanced technology to divert this reality, nature had her way. He had the opportunity to go with his father to a star system named the Pleiades and live at a higher level of dimension. He chose to die and reincarnate again. Before Cartius dies, he leaves his teleportation chair to Orga, his faithful servant.

After thousands of years, the chair gets rediscovered in the new age and finds its way eventually back to England. It is highly revered for its seemingly magical powers, which no one has yet understood scientifically.

Cartius is reincarnated as James Bannerman and is the son of the Ninth Earl of Penbroke. Upon the death of his father in 1958, he is elevated to become the Tenth Earl. It becomes his mission to unlock the mysteries of the chair, which had been held under lock and key in the East Wing of his estate. The chair is later referred to as the throne and is designed and decorated with the most brilliant of gemstones.

In addition to the vast inheritance he receives, he continues to build the Merchant Bank and Shipping Empire to meet the demands of the modern age to come. The books are and will be written as follows:

Part I: *The Rise to Power*
Part II: *The Temptation for Greed*
Part III: *The Justification for Injustice*

This saga takes the reader through to the new millennium and beyond. The evil intrigues of human nature and the beauty of the enlightened is clearly defined along with intense, gripping, love affairs and marriages. *The Legacy* is a series of books written about a family whose roots go back to 1704.

The books depict how a family and the temptations of life can lead us astray. This story, however, stands as a proclamation to the very fact that if a family can respect its heritage and forefathers, any person can rise from the most modest of places to become an example to humanity and a legend to be upheld. Apart from the beautiful aspects of spirituality, these books are intended to open our minds as to what is really out there.

It is the belief of the writer that a family is a small nation, and if we have the right principles in the family, then we can truly evolve as a great nation. The wealth of a nation is, after all, its people.

October 27, 1977

Angels sing as they bring,
A package to unwrap.
No finer thing, can they bring
So put it in your lap.

Untie the blue-red ribbon,
And lay the white cloth down.
Now look at what lies hidden
Inside the box face down.

Can you see the light
That emanates so bright?
This planet comes from heaven
Just like the number seven.

Pull it from the box,
And set it on a rock,
For this is the beginning
Of your greatest shock!

Now take another look,
For this will write your book
About a plan to be
That man will live to see.

Can you see it now?
It's not so far away.
Remember you took a vow,
For here you are to stay.

PROLOGUE

He stood on the terrace in front of his magnificent home. It would be hard to leave after all these years. It was mid-afternoon in late summer, and the sun was beginning to drop in the sky. Many had already left years ago, but those who had such a hand in the development of their civilization could not leave. They had worked too hard to make their island the great capital of their nation.

However, nature has her own way, and in the end, they were at the mercy of her power. Yes, she moved slowly, and despite all the warnings she had surely given them, they somehow believed that with their technology, they could avoid the inevitable destiny they were about to witness.

The world was changing. He could feel the threatening vibrations of the polar ice caps cracking as they melted into the oceans, the ensuing waves slamming against their island shores. In spite of the distance from the poles, their island, which now would be above the Tropic of Cancer in the eastern region of the Atlantic Ocean, not far from the gateway to the Mediterranean Sea, was in imminent danger. The oceans were rising, as were the daily temperatures. The world was warming, and change was coming.

Soon this civilization and technology would be lost. He had chosen to stay and die. He knew that moving away to a new land and working all over again to create what they had here on Atlantis would take many generations. Their efforts to divert the rise in seawater by drilling through the ocean bed and filling the cavities that lay beneath the earth's mantle were in vain. The volume of seawater was now so immense that their island was doomed.

He looked around and wept at all the lost hopes and dreams.

The huge crystal towers that dominated the skyline transmitted vast amounts of energy throughout the Atlantean Islands. Their towers, with their pyramid partners next to them, produced all the energy needed to run an advanced way of life. These amazing generators, which harnessed sunlight and the electromagnetic fields of the earth, advanced their culture to a way of life that created no air pollution. The dangers lay in their radioactivity and damaging light waves. The contaminated vats had to be buried in the vast colder wastelands of the North American continent.

The center of the earth had been a beautiful oasis, a temperate climate, which allowed all of them an abundant way of life. Ice covered almost half the planet. The North Pole stretched from what is now Greenland to Kansas in North America, and the South Pole stretched from beneath South America to Sao Paolo, Brazil, and covered the continent of Australia. All this was changing, and their islands would be overcome by water. The vast continents of North America, Africa, and Europe would start to emerge, and new opportunities would take place. However, their technology would be lost. The amount of knowledge and power that they had gained could not be given to anyone, and so those things would die with the people; the new world would have to take the good and find its own way.

Cartius had given his teleportation chair to Orga, his faithful manservant, to take to the new land in Northern Africa where Atlanteans had already built a great pyramid. This strategic place, which lay in the center of the earth's land mass, was being developed by the Atlanteans for the survival of their knowledge and a future in the new world that was to come. Others had chosen to go to Central America and start over there. Cartius's wives, family, and some friends had also left and waited for him to come and join them. He couldn't leave, though. It was too much. He would stay and die and then return when the new world was advanced enough for him to live his way of life again.

CHAPTER 1

PENBROKE COURT

It was autumn. The golden leaves of the season had unhinged themselves from their summer mooring and laid a fine carpet of colors across the lawn of Penbroke Estate.

James awoke early. He'd had trouble sleeping, as he had a lot on his mind. He'd passed his entrance exam to Sterling Heights in Scotland, and today he had to pack all his suitcases for the upcoming winter term. At thirteen, he was excited about leaving prep school behind and attending his new boarding school, but he was bothered that he'd missed being in the A stream by 2 percent. He planned to make it up during the school year, and he felt sure he'd be in the top stream for academics by the end of summer. He was concerned that he had disappointed his father, but his father had not made a big deal about it; he'd simply said he thought James would improve once he was settled in his new boarding school.

James got dressed and then headed down to the small breakfast room off the kitchen to have an early breakfast. As usual, his father, Collin, was already up and was sitting at the table reading the morning newspaper.

"Good morning, young man. You're up early. Got a few things on your mind, I bet." Collin knew exactly what it was like to go to a new school, particularly Sterling Heights, as he'd been a student there himself.

Still bothered that he had let his father down, James said, "I think I've got a good plan, Father. It bugs me that I missed the A stream by two points, but I'll make it up this year, I promise."

Seemingly unconcerned, his father replied, "I know you will. A little catch-up won't hurt you. Those exams can be the luck of the draw. It seems they test you on the very thing you don't read up on." His father put down the newspaper, and changing the subject, said, "I've got something important I want to do with you today, so I'm glad you've made an early start."

Intrigued, James asked, "What are we going to do?"

"I think it's time we had a little history lesson on your ancestors."

"Okay, Father. I look forward to it." James was excited. He had always wanted to know more about past generations in his family. He was particularly interested in the history behind what was known as the East Wing, a part of the estate that was kept locked at all times. The children had never been allowed to enter the wing and see what it contained, hence James had always been fascinated by it.

"Finish your breakfast while I make a few phone calls, and then come join me in my study."

"Yes, sir."

James sat for a moment thinking about his father, whom he idolized. Though his father looked stern, James and many others knew that beneath his aristocratic countenance radiated a kindness and warmth. His eyes appeared to be always smiling, and he had a heart as big as a lion. He was a man of few words, but what he had to say was of value. His staff respected him, and he had a knack for helping people help themselves. He was a tall, good-looking man with a strong, sharp nose and kind, sympathetic blue eyes that had a way of penetrating a person at first glance. He had an air of authority about him, and he knew how to talk to people in a civil manner. He had a shabby elegance to his conservative taste in clothes, preferring to wear his tweed jacket and shooting cap. He looked the part of a gentleman farmer and preferred this form of dress to his business suit. Now in his late forties, he had experienced enough of life to run his estate and his vast global business empire with ease. James thought his father's only fault might be the fact that he had chosen James's mother as his wife. The two were so different, and James couldn't understand the attraction.

Just as James was thinking this unkind thought, his mother walked into the room. In her late thirties, she was an extremely attractive woman, with stylish blonde hair and powerful blue eyes. She had not come from aristocratic blood, but she made up for it with her haughty manner. In her twenties, she had been an entertainer and singer. His father had met her at a show and fell madly in love with her. He had whisked her away from the bright lights of London to the countryside of Penbroke. James felt that she probably hated the place from the first time she saw it. Even all these years later, she constantly complained about the dampness and how she could not wait to return to their second home in Mayfair, London.

She greeted him in what he considered her usual cold manner. "Good morning, James."

He met her coldness with his own. "Morning, Mother."

Close behind his mother were his two sisters, Rebecca and Felicity, known as Becky and Flick. Becky was twelve, and Flick, ten and a half. He and Becky got along well; they were alike in many ways. He found Flick to be extremely annoying; she was constantly interrupting him with her tricks and antics.

As his mother and sisters sat down, Claudia, the children's governess, walked in. James was extremely fond of Claudia and returned her bright smile and friendly greeting. Claudia had been with the family for about two years. She had initially been hired to administrate the finances of the estate and help His Lordship with the management of the farm. Now, she also helped look after the children during school holidays, a necessity brought on by their mother's penchant for spending her time in London rather than at Penbroke.

Claudia had an accounting degree from Cambridge. She was in her late twenties and a good-looking woman. Her hair, dark brown and long, was usually swept off her face and held with a clasp behind her head. She had large eyes, brown and expressive; petite features; and high cheekbones. Before coming to Penbroke, she'd had plans to get married, but her boyfriend had met with an accident. Why she hadn't found another love, nobody understood. James's father had been suspected of having an easy eye for her, but no one ever saw anything questionable occur between them. Because his mother was often absent, both physically and emotionally, James had transferred his affections to Claudia, who he felt better filled the role of "mom" to him and his sisters.

James figured his father was probably done with his phone calls, so he excused himself and headed to the study. He knocked on the open door and said, "Father, here I am."

"Good. Let's go into the main hall. I'd like to take a look at the different paintings and tell you about your ancestors. You're going to be a man soon, and it's important that you understand how I got to where I am in life and what will be expected of you one day."

He followed his father into the main hall where the paintings of the eight earls of Penbroke were hung. His father stopped in front of the first painting. "This is the First Earl, Arthur E. Bannerman; he's the man that started it all. After his battles in the War of the Spanish Succession, he was knighted by Queen Anne in 1705. He built Penbroke Court, and from the money he received from the Crown, he invested in what was known as the South Sea Bubble. The South Sea Bubble was a plan by the government and a group of businessmen to raise investment so that ships could venture to South America in search of gold and silver. It was well known that the Spanish were getting rich off their finds. In a number of cases, British ships raided the Spanish ships and brought the proceeds back to England. These so-called buccaneers were well rewarded by the Crown for their efforts. The investment grew at such a fantastic rate that the shares went through the roof, so the First Earl sold out and made a fortune. This turned out to be a wise move because shortly after, in 1720, the whole thing crashed and fortunes were lost."

They moved to the next portrait, and his father continued. "In 1730, he passed this great inheritance to the Second Earl, who took the money and started the company we have today called Trans Global Shipping. He started slowly, but by the end of his life, he had accumulated twelve ships in the fleet. He concentrated all his efforts on shipping goods between Hong Kong and London."

His father motioned toward the next few portraits saying, "For the next earls, it was a tough and demanding business. The ships that were built had sails and were not powered as they are today, and the high seas were a place where maritime law had very few rules. Pirates could highjack a ship, or sailors could go missing with a ship and never be seen again. Building a trusted team and making the pay above average for the captain and his immediate staff was critical to success. Weather played an important role, and many ships were lost to storms. In those days, there was no Suez Canal, so all the ships rounded the South African coast. The time it took to get from Hong Kong to the London docks could be up to four or five months, depending on the weather. So, you see, it could take nearly a year to load and unload a vessel and complete a round trip. The business grew slowly until the late 1800s, when the steam engines improved enough for ocean-going vessels. It was then that the business started to mushroom."

They moved along to the portraits of the next group of earls. "The Sixth Earl, knowing the slow growth of the shipping business, started Bannerman's International Bank in 1838 to invest in different enterprises to create a greater return. He eventually moved the offices from Tilbury docks to Threadneedle Street, where they are today. The Seventh Earl was much like the First Earl. He had a great pioneering spirit and traveled on many of the vessels we had at that time. He did much to build the fleet. He also brought back the artifacts that we have in the East Wing, which I will explain more about later. The Eighth Earl, your grandfather, saw the beginning of the new steamships, and it was during this time that the business started to really grow, almost overnight. As the Ninth Earl, in my life, I have seen enormous change. My father and I worked hard to increase the number of ships, and by the 1930s, we had a very profitable banking business as well as a shipping line. So, as you can see, we've come a long way from the battlefields of Europe to the present."

"Father, I've also read that the French and the English were busy traveling the North Atlantic to America. Why didn't we get involved with those trading routes?"

"We wanted no part of that situation. It was hard enough getting around Napoleon and his blockade in Europe at the turn of the 1800s. French war ships were abundant, and they thought nothing of taking our British merchant ships that were arriving back fully laden from the Far East. We made many night runs through the Bay of Biscay and had to watch for pirates and independent buccaneers who were also eager to take us out. On some of our ships, the ones where we had valuable merchandise, we had cannons on the lower decks. They were used on many occasions to ward off would-be profiteers who were ruthless in taking out any vessel they presumed to be weak or unarmed."

"What did you do about the loss of ships at that time? Was there insurance?"

"Lloyds Insurance started in 1688, primarily to insure the ships for the slave trade. It was then we could insure our own ships, and that's why we have a large part of our capital in savings with them today; both our businesses go back a long way. Peter Hawthorne is a shareholder for Lloyds in our bank, and he sits on our board of directors. Before that, we tried to insure people's merchandise ourselves, but they had to pay a stiff price or just take the risk. As we built our reputation, we earned more trust, and that was the foundation of the goodwill we have built for the business we have today in London and around the world. Many books have been written about the shipping line as well as the heritage of the earls of Penbroke. I'll give you a couple to take back to school with you. They make good reading for those times when you are alone with not a lot to do."

"Thanks, Dad, for telling me all this. I look forward to carrying on the Penbroke name as the Tenth Earl someday."

"I know you'll make us all proud, my boy. Now, I want to share something else with you, but it's of a more sensitive nature. Let's go back to the study where we can sit and talk."

Curious as to what kind of sensitive information his father would want to share with him, James anxiously followed him back to the study. As they walked in, his father said, "Close the door and sit down."

The log fire was crackling loudly. The study wasn't large in comparison to the other rooms in the house, but it was personal and stacked with heavily bound volumes of the Earl's favorite books. His father was a great philosopher at heart, and much of James's profound thinking was owed to the time he spent with him.

"James," began his father, "you are old enough now to know a few more things about our history." James listened closely as he watched his father push tobacco down into his pipe. "I know you've always had an interest in the East Wing. Since a child, you've almost instinctively known that something special existed there."

His father paused to take a long pull on his pipe, and James waited anxiously for him to continue. "It was written by the Seventh Earl, to whom you show such admiration, that whoever became the Tenth Earl of Penbroke would unlock the secret to the collection of his precious artifacts collected in India, the Far East, and Africa. The collection consists of rare stones, gems, crystals, papyri scrolls and writings, which at this moment are not understood by any of the world's most famous historians, museums, and the like. There is believed to be some special knowledge, information yet to be discovered for mankind. It would appear that the scrolls define esoteric knowledge yet to be deciphered, and the stones form some mystical component in accessing this knowledge. Whether your grandfather knew the Tenth Earl would be born in an age that would have suitable technology to decipher these mysterious findings or that the Tenth Earl would have some hidden faculty that would allow him to unravel the secrets of these artifacts is not clear."

His father looked into the fireplace; he appeared to be trying to decide what more he should reveal. "I don't intend to take you into the room until the Christmas season. The reason I have these things locked away is obvious—for their incredible value to the world. I personally believe that they hold the key or some strange link to another consciousness. The reason I say this is that apparently, the Seventh Earl became extremely eccentric in his later years. It was as though he could not only write about the past, but he could somehow glimpse the future. You will find all his writings quite illuminating. You can imagine that in 1850, people thought he was out of his mind."

James was amazed at what his father was telling him. "Father, this sounds absolutely fascinating, I have yearned to know about these artifacts. I feel that maybe I can unlock the mystery."

"Now, hold on, James. First things first. You have a big year ahead of you, and I don't want this to distract you from your more important duties at Sterling. I just want to whet your appetite for your future interest and development."

"Yes, Father, I know. And I thank you for trusting in me to share this!" James was careful not to push his luck. After all, he had learned more about the East Wing in one hour than he had in his entire life. The mystery—what a challenge! It was something that would keep him excited for his return.

His father, pleased with his enthusiasm about the family history and the mystery of the East Wing, said, "I think that's enough history for now. Let's have some fun before you have to head off to school. How about if we go down to the stables and ride that horse of yours? I want to see how competent a rider you're becoming."

"Sounds great. I'll meet you at the stables after I change."

James changed into his riding gear and began the walk to the stables. He was struck by a feeling of sadness at the thought of leaving for school. He knew he would miss his father and his home, and he stopped for a moment to look back at the house and surrounding gardens.

He loved this place. He felt he had somehow known it before, but he couldn't explain why. He could almost imagine the very atmosphere when the First Earl walked over the threshold for the first time.

The house looked Greco-Roman in design. Later, this style would be known as Georgian, but it had been built prior to that era, in the reign of Queen Anne. The house, or more correctly, the court, had been named after the village it surrounded. The estate encircled the little village of Penbroke, and it too continued to be a part of the main estate. Vast columns cascaded around the exterior of the house, which sat upon a plinth over-looking the crashing waves of the North Sea in the fair coun-ty of Lincolnshire. The estate consisted of several thousands of acres with three farms. One was dairy, another was for crops, and the home farm cultivated more specialized produce for the vegetable market. The wood and lake areas' primary purpose, apart from shooting, was for walks. The prized asset had always been the horse stables that housed polo ponies, hunting horses, and racehorses.

Realizing his father might be waiting, James began walking again. It was difficult to see the stables quietly nestled below the copse, as the house stood at the summit of the property. He scampered across the open lawn and past the East Wing of the house that jutted out like a finger from the main house. The East Wing was actually separate. To reach it, one had to climb down steps from the parading veranda toward what appeared to be a miniature single-story version of the main house. James was excited at the thought that in just a few short months, he would get to see what mysteries the East Wing held.

As James approached the stables, he was greeted by Joe, the stable hand. "'Ow are ya ta-day, Master James?" Joe, at seven-teen years old, had been with the Bannerman family all his life. His father now managed the dairy farm, and ever since James could remember, Joe had worked at the stables.

Out of breath from the run over, James said, "Oh, fine, Joe; thanks."

His father arrived at the stable yard. "Well, my boy, are you ready to ride that horse of yours for a change?"

"You bet!" James was hoping he could get Smokey over the breakwaters on the beach and impress his father.

Joe brought Smokey out for James and then another horse, Foxy, out for James's father. Foxy quickly jumped sideways as a flurry of leaves blew up through the stable yard. Her fiery mane and tail also picked up in the wind, and her head nearly pulled the halter rope out of Joe's hands. "Easy now, girl, easy," said Joe reassuringly. "This mare's ready for a good gallop. Yeah, you're ready for a good gallop, aren't ya, girl?"

Foxy's muscles bulged; there was not an ounce of fat on her. At five years of age, she stood seventeen hands high. The excellent ingredients of her Anglo-Arab bloodline gave her the right balance between speed and stamina. Between the whites of her eyes and the impetuous stamping on the cobbled courtyard, James could sense the immense power in her limbs. Smokey, a dark gray gelding, stood fifteen and a half hands high and gave James all the challenge he needed for his level of experience. Smokey's heavy stature and shorter legs clearly contrasted with the aristocratic bloodline of Foxy.

They mounted their horses, and then James followed his father down the hillside path to the beach. The low tide gave them plenty of room to ride on the beach, and the way Foxy pranced sideways took all of Collin's strength to hold her back. With the sand now firm and hard, the wind blowing hard across them, it took him a full hundred yards to get her galloping in a straight line. God, she had speed! And she had won her share of races to prove it. She had been trained as a show horse for dressage events at the White City in London.

Foxy had taken off so far ahead of Smokey that James's vain attempts to ride jockey style, with his feet locked into the straps above the stirrups, made no difference. It didn't matter, though, for he had only one thing in mind before he left that beach—he must jump that breakwater. He imagined himself riding into battle like the First Earl of Penbroke, charging toward the battlements.

"Now, Smokey, we're going to do it, boy. No stopping. We're going. Hell or high water, we're going over." He corrected his feet back into the stirrups, sat back sharply into the saddle, and with a little help from his riding crop and a good firm kick from his heels, they were off.

They were about fifty yards away and nearing a full gallop, then thirty, twenty, ten, and "Ally–uppppp," shouted James, and they cleared the breakwater. He was astonished. Foxy's explosive speed must have woken up Smokey. James just couldn't believe it. For over two years he had patiently waited for this moment, and he had enough falls and bruises to prove it.

At that moment, his father and Foxy burst past again. "Well done, James, well done! I'm proud of you, my boy! You'll ride at Aintree yet!"

"Hold on, Dad. Gotta go one more time. I have to prove it's not just luck."

"Okay. Go for it."

James wielded Smokey around and galloped back about seventy-five yards. He started to take another run, with his heart pounding. *We must do it. It can't have been a fluke.* Then, they were at thirty, twenty, ten, and then over the breakwater again. They sailed over easily, Smokey loving the attention.

"That's enough for one day, my boy. Let's take 'em back to the stables and let Joe give 'em a big feed of bran mash. Next holiday, we'll go hunting!"

"I'll look forward to that, Dad." James was proud of his day's outing.

Once they were back at the stables, James said goodbye to Joe, who wished him luck at his new school. His father had left to head over to the office to check on some things. He walked back up the driveway to the house a little slower than he had gone down. He didn't want to have to go back to school with its rules, restrictions, and confinement. Penbroke would always be his home, his haven, and his life. Leaving felt like being torn away from everything he loved best. However, his disappointment was offset with knowing he would get to see the East Wing upon his return at Christmas.

CHAPTER 2

STERLING HEIGHTS

The train journey to Scotland seemed to take forever. James never forgot his father taking him to the station. It was painful, and he would miss the time with him, but his eyes, yes, his eyes, were smiling. It seemed that his soul was at peace. At last he had the chance to talk about the East Wing and share something he must have believed in deeply, however incredible.

Still, James had to get it out of his mind. He had to work hard at school, and work hard he would. No Penbroke had ever flunked at anything. His family was built on guts from the first day the First Lord stood on the battlefield. Whatever his road, he knew faith and courage would prevail. Empires could be built only with this kind of character—there was no other way.

After getting off the train in Edinburgh, James met up with a bunch of new boys. They were surrounding a tall, thin man holding up a yellow wood plaque with "Sterling Heights" marked across it in black.

"Your name, boy?" asked the master with the plaque, recognizing James's yellow-and-black quartered cap.

"Err, James Bannerman . . . sir." All the other boys looked around at him.

"Now, let me see." The man looked through the list. "Ah, yes, you're Lord Penbroke's boy, aren't you?"

"Yes, sir."

"Well, lord or no lord, you're all treated the same here." He cast his eye on the smirking faces of his other attendees.

"Yes, sir," James replied again.

"Alright, you scrawny lot, time to get into the bus, and I don't want a bloody word out of one of you. Well, don't just stand there—get to it, boys!" James could see the summer holiday was definitely over.

The coach made its way through the winding roads to smaller roads that led to a small town at least fifty miles north of Edinburgh called St. Andrews. The town was quaint, but it was hard to see any life in the twilight hours of the day. When they left the town and headed out into the countryside again, they took a hard right down a small lane, and there in front of them stood the awesome walls and fortress entrance to Sterling Heights.

"Now, boys, when you get out of the coach, I want you to follow the matron to the common room, where you will have your name called, and there the headmaster will make himself known."

The boy next to James started blubbing his eyes out. Poor little chap looked wretched, his cap over to one side, holding onto his satchel, clutching it as if he held the crown jewels. Another boy overheard and leaned over and yelled, "Hey, sissy, you know what we do to little beggars like you that blub their eyes out?" The scared little boy stared back, horrified. The other boy continued, "We beat the living daylights out of their beastly little bodies until they can't see straight. I know what happens because my older brother is here, and you won't want to meet up with him!"

James interrupted forcefully, "You lay one finger on him and I'll knock your brains out. Then you won't even be able to think whether you are here or anywhere for that matter."

"Yes, we've all heard about His Lordship. Strong boy, are you?" The other boys laughed. James turned around and belted him with a pounding punch to his gut. The other boy then grabbed James's cap and kicked it down the aisle of the coach.

"Why, you brat," said James. Within seconds, the two were scrapping like maniacs on the floor of the aisle. The other boys were fixated, intensely watching what they thought to be a great start to the new school term. Things had been quiet on the journey up; everyone was reflecting on the past holidays and naturally apprehensive about the new school year. For them, this altercation was great stuff; it broke up the mood and gave everyone some entertainment.

The bus came to a grinding halt outside the front entrance, and then James heard the master shout, "Bannerman! You little bully. Get up! Get up, now. Stand outside away from the group, and I'll deal with you separately. If there's one thing I hate, it's a bully, and you can be sure I'll personally beat you with my slapstick, and that goes for the rest of you. I'll beat any one of you if I catch this type of behavior again. Do I make myself clear?"

All the boys gave a resounding "Yes!"

The boys timidly filed into the common room behind the matron. James stood trembling at the entrance, waiting for instructions. "Well, Bannerman, I'm going to teach you a lesson you'll not forget. You'll report to my study at eight o'clock this evening after the headmaster's introduction. Now get to the common room."

The matron came out and took James by the hand. "Watch this one, Matron," warned the master. "Got the devil in him."

"What have you been up to . . . err . . . " began the matron.

"Bannerman. The name is Bannerman, miss."

The matron, to his amazement, wasn't beautiful but had an attractive manner. He wondered why a woman like her would be stuck away in an all-boys' boarding school in Scotland. She had to be in her late twenties, with long blonde hair down to her shoulders and strong, dark blue eyes. She had a good figure and was not much taller than James. What an inspiration for the male teaching staff. Somebody had to be dating her, that was for sure, and that's probably why she had chosen this position—to be close to that significant other.

"Well, Bannerman, don't you have another name?"

"Yes, Matron, it's James."

"Now tell me what really happened," she said mischievously.

"Matron, if you can believe me, it's not my fault. You see, this boy—I don't know his name—was about to hit another boy, who was next to me. This boy was crying because he was homesick. I stepped in front and hit the attacker, and, well, the rest escalated from there. This boy did say he had an older brother, though." James was anxious, not wanting the news of his behavior to be reported to his father.

"James, I think I know who this boy is, and his brother is known as a bully. I think with a little word dropped into Mr. Caldwell's ear, the housemaster on the bus, I might be able to have him give you another chance."

"Oh, Matron, I would be so grateful." James thought that he and the matron were going to get along fine.

"Now run along; otherwise you'll be late for roll call."

James ran down the hallway to the common room. He remembered the school layout from his previous interview and visit with his father, and he was glad he knew where the room was. He quietly sneaked in behind several boys and frantically asked them their names so he could find his place in the line.

The headmaster entered the common room, and there was absolute silence. The headmaster was wearing a long black cloak over his elegant dark blue suit. He sported an old Oxfordian tie and a mortise board on his head. The mortise board had a gold tassel attached at the center that hung over to one side. He was a man in his mid-fifties, with fine features. He had strong, piercing eyes, was strict but soulful in countenance, and possessed a certain charismatic air. He patiently looked around the room at his anxious new pupils. His quick pace to the front of the room demonstrated a man who liked things to happen quickly. Behind him stood a large flaming log fire. The Scottish evenings at the beginning of September were beginning to get colder, and the fire gave a warmer presence to the moment.

"Well, Mr. Caldwell, have you taken roll call yet?" he asked firmly.

"No, Headmaster. May I have your permission to proceed?" It was interesting to James to note the degree of humility demonstrated by Mr. Caldwell after his display of authority on the bus.

"Yes, please continue. We must know if everyone is present."

Monotonously, Caldwell reeled off the names of all the new boys. As he did so, there was a moment of comic relief to ease the tension. The log fire was crackling so loudly that one spark flew out and nearly caught the headmaster's cloak. He quickly stepped aside to the quiet chuckle of everyone.

All were present, so the headmaster introduced himself and started his welcoming speech.

"My name is Mr. Burke. I welcome you all to Sterling. I have been headmaster here for the past ten years. I have seen a lot of boys pass through with excellence, and some with less. For you boys to get the best out of Sterling, I want you all to feel at home. This place, for the next five years, is as much your home as it is ours. Here at Sterling, we pride ourselves on providing a friendly atmosphere. Yes, we are strict, but discipline has no meaning without team spirit and respect for one another. You will soon learn that we all have nicknames, don't we, Mr. Caldwell?"

"Oh, yes, Headmaster, most definitely." Everyone laughed as they wondered what Mr. Caldwell's nickname was. James thought that Coldy would be an appropriate nickname, as it went well with the climate of Scotland.

"Each of you has hailed from some of our country's finest prep schools. When you leave the common room, you will find which house you have been assigned to, and more importantly, the level of class you will be placed in. For example, our students who passed an entrance exam with an A or better average will be placed in the A stream, those with a B or better average will be in the B stream, and the rest will be in the C stream. If a pupil works well and improves his average, he will be graded annually and have the chance to change streams. The same will be true for those whose performance drops. Apart from our keen accent on academic ability, our primary focus is to develop young men into gentlemen. Can anyone give me the definition of a gentleman?"

The boy with whom James had the fight stuck his hand up.

"Well, what's your name, boy?"

"Petersen Minor, sir."

"Ah, you have a brother here."

"Yes, sir."

James now knew his name and couldn't wait to see what his brother was like.

"Well, go ahead."

"A gentleman, sir, is a person who is born into a higher position in life and has the authority to give orders to those who are of lesser standing. A gentleman must learn to speak well, excel in his education, and be an example to those who are less fortunate."

"True. Quite good. Anyone else?"

James decided to put his hand up. "Well, what's your name, boy?"

"Bannerman, sir. Bannerman."

The headmaster turned to Mr. Caldwell for a moment. James thought he was checking him out, as he was sure he knew who he was.

"Well, Bannerman, according to Mr. Caldwell, your conduct on the bus wasn't very impressive." Everyone snickered. "Perhaps you have a chance to redeem yourself."

"Yes, sir, absolutely."

"Well then, let's hear it."

"A gentleman is a man who should put people at ease from all walks of life. His example should demonstrate the ability to unite rather than divide in order to find the best in all of us." James knew this in his sleep, having had his father constantly remind him of the fact that along with having privilege comes responsibility to one's fellow man.

"Very impressive. You've been well taught. I would, however, add that manners maketh the man." Again, a small ring of laughter wafted around the room.

"Here at Sterling," the headmaster continued, "we want to produce a citizen who is not only a credit to his family and to his fellow man but to his country. Leaders are what the world lacks, but it takes time to build leaders, so remember the best leaders are gentlemen. Well, boys, it's good to see you are all here. I wish you success and happiness on your journey at Sterling Heights. I now hand you back to Mr. Caldwell, who will finish by explaining all the facilities available to you."

Caldwell went into great depth to explain everything, and how, when the other boys arrived tomorrow night, each one of them would be expected to make a speech at the supper table, or more precisely, on the supper table. James and the other boys were dreading this. Apparently, all the masters would leave, and it would be time to see how the character of each new boy could stand up to the old-school tradition of being roasted, having buns thrown at him, and being generally heckled. Every new boy had to go through this pointless initiation and stand the test of character evaluation.

However, for James, that was still a night away; at the moment, he had to contend with Mr. Caldwell.

"Bannerman, I want to see you in my study immediately."

James quickly checked on which house he had been assigned to and his class stream, and then he wound his way through endless corridors, having to ask numerous times the direction to Caldwell's study. Finally, he arrived at the foot of the winding staircase of a turret that led to the oak door of his study. A brass plate on the door read "Thomas E. Caldwell, Housemaster of Pemble House." He nervously knocked on the door and waited for a response.

"Come in, come in. Don't hang about in the corridor; you'll get my room cold and drafty."

James entered the room and waited for the master to speak. The master was stooped over his desk, trying to get his pipe stoked. After a moment, he said, "Quite a performance on the bus. I think you need a little reminder, don't you?"

"Well, sir, with every respect, I believe I need an opportunity to explain myself before you pronounce judgment."

"Ha!" he belted. "I liked your explanation of a gentleman, and as for what happened, Matron has already informed me. I just thought you needed a little shake up because whether you're right or wrong, Bannerman, you can't go around punching people. It's barbaric. We would have no order in a boarding school community if boys were allowed to behave like this."

"No, sir. I completely understand. My intentions were well founded, but my behavior was incorrect."

"Good, Bannerman. I'm beginning to like you more. Time will tell if you have substance. I know you're a boy of privilege, but that's all the more reason to not make yourself obvious. People that have something in life are a target. Learn to walk always with your cap in hand to start with, and learn the people that surround you. It's not easy, I admit, but it's necessary, particularly for you. Your father is well admired for his contributions to our country, abroad, and to this school. You have a great tradition to keep up. People like you must set an example to others. God gave you a wonderful start to your life. Make sure you show your gratitude by honoring His ways. Well, that's enough for now. So what stream are you in?"

"The B stream, sir. I missed A stream by two points, sir."

"Well, I've no doubt you'll turn that around. A little fight to succeed never hurt anyone. So you know what house you're in?"

"Yes, sir. Yours."

"Good then. Now that we've had a moment to understand each other, I'm going to work hard to help you, but no more nonsense, okay?"

"Yes, sir. I appreciate your kind consideration of my blunder, and it won't happen again, sir."

"Good. Then off with you. Get some supper in you and find your dormitory before somebody else bags the best bed," the housemaster said with a smirk.

"Yes, sir. Goodnight." James flew out of the room, realizing his extreme luck. He thought that maybe the master wasn't such a bad old grouch, but he was thankful for the matron. He now knew she had the ear of the school, and what a pleasant task he was going to have trying to know her better.

James's first night was a cold one. The beginnings of the northeast winds and no heating caused him to dress warmly and get tough. The next morning, the bell blasted at 6:00 a.m. on the dot. The prefects stood in the corridor and ran the boys in single file to a cold shower.

The classroom block was in separate buildings and set away from the different houses. The main building—the old fortress—was where all the administrative staff worked and the headmaster resided. The various houses—Pemble, Sedgwick, Dumfries, Birkenhead, and Kipling—were located on different parts of the campus. The five houses were seriously competitive in sports and other areas with each other. Pemble had been named after a previous headmaster, as were all the other houses, and James had to find out all the various traditions that were peculiar to his house. Mr. Caldwell was the housemaster, and it looked as though he would be stuck with him for the next five years. Each house had its own housemaster and matron. The A, B, and C streams had always comprised a mixture of the houses, so academic excellence, although revered by the house, was gained as a whole regardless of a boy's house.

Walking to the classroom block after breakfast, James met up with the boy he sat next to on the bus. "Hey, thanks, Bannerman, for sticking up for me on the bus yesterday. I'm not normally like that; it was just a bad moment. Peter Lloyd's the name, by the way."

"Hey, no problem. It all worked out, thanks to the matron."

"What do you mean?" asked Peter.

"Tell you another time; got to find my class. See you later."

It turned out that Peter and James were in the same house and in the same class, with none other than old Caldwell as their teacher for the first class. The class was math, James's best subject and one he knew would be necessary if he were going to run a bank one day

By the end of the day, Peter and James had become great friends, and they were not looking forward to the arrival of the older boys. That afternoon, the buses started streaming through the gates. Supper began at 6:00 p.m., and then the fun would begin. After their meal, all the masters and prefects exited, leaving the new boys to the mercy of the old boys.

One of the seniors got up. "Well, what have we got here? A bunch of scrawny little fags, I think." The older boys all started laughing. They had all lived through the same ritual and always enjoyed seeing what the new boys would do.

"So, which one of you little beggars is going to go first? Who has the guts or the stupidity?"

Against tradition, James had organized five of them to get up on the tables at the same time. They scampered up on their respective tables simultaneously.

"You can't do that," shouted the crowd. "It's against tradition."

"Why not?" James asked. "Do you really want to be here all night listening to a bunch of new boys one at a time?"

"He's got a good point," said one older boy. "Let them do their thing, and if it's good, we'll set a new tradition. What about it, lads?"

"Yeah, give 'em a chance!" agreed the others.

James started out with his speech. "Boys of old, and in the wonderful tradition that is Sterling, please take the time to listen to our humble presentation. It is my opinion that it's possible to teach old dogs new tricks!"

A great jeer went up, and words like "cheeky little blighter" rang in James's ears.

James had Peter lead off, giving him the opportunity to regain his composure after the incident on the bus, and then the rest of the boys joined in:

There was once a team at Sterling,
That lost its balls one day.
Surely a reason to pray,
You see . . .
The seniors had lost a great prize,
To a school that was half our size.
Our team was shredded to bits,
Which we would describe as the pits.
They showed us up to be mutts!
So now we must kick their butts.

At this point, everyone became hysterical, and the whole room began throwing everything from buns to lemonade to cutlery. The boys ducked and continued:

The loss you sustained was treason,
And gives us all a reason,

To get back what you've lost,
At a terrible cost.
Surely we shall retrieve,
And allow us all to believe,
THAT WE CAN AND WE SHALL WIN AGAIN!

The whole dining room was in absolute bedlam. The older boys had lost last term to Harrow in rugby, an absolute disgrace to the normally outstanding team. A loss was acceptable, but to be beaten 37-0 was humiliating.

Prefects and housemasters came running into the room to see what all the noise was about. "By God, Bannerman, your life is going to be living hell round here!" yelled one senior.

"I couldn't care less. Just take on someone your own size first," shouted James, enjoying the challenge.

"That's enough, Bannerman," said Mr. Caldwell firmly.

On the instructions of two housemasters, the school captain's voice echoed throughout the dining hall announcing that supper was over, and all the boys would be confined to their respective houses and dormitories immediately.

It took James a full term to adapt to the strict environment of his new school. The older boys viewed him with suspicion, but with time, he knew he would gain their respect. He was starting to make friends, but he viewed his titled position as an impediment or barrier in getting to know school friends in the way others did.

CHAPTER 3

THE EAST WING

James had made good use of his first term and now looked forward to the Christmas holidays. His father had bought him a new horse for the hunting season, and he couldn't wait to get home and go riding. James managed to talk his father into sending the chauffeur to pick him up.

Rodney, the chauffeur, arrived at noon on the dot. The car silently made its way down the winding roads onto the main highway. Rodney was mostly silent for the seven-hour journey. They stopped for a small snack at a local pub when they crossed the border into England, and James was glad to eat a decent meal for a change. He didn't know why all schools were absolutely incompetent at cooking an edible meal.

As it was now almost Christmas. It was dark when they coasted up the driveway to the main house. James's mother demanded to see him first. Claudia directed him to the drawing room, where his mother waited. "Darling, how lovely to see you." His mother was well dressed, as usual, smoking her favorite brand through a long cigarette holder.

"Come and sit down and tell me how life is treating you at your new school."

James thought she had as much interest in Sterling as he had in one of her London shows, but he respectfully brought her up to date on all the details, at least the ones he felt were pertinent to the moment.

"We're all so very proud of you, James. We've heard nothing but good things." He raised his eyebrows, wondering what premeditated purpose was on his mother's agenda.

Claudia brought him his supper on a tray. Obviously, this was serious stuff warranting this amount of one-on-one time with his mother.

"Now, I want to explain to you your father's health. He's not at all well. Ever since you left, he's been rambling on about showing you some artifacts, relics in the East Wing. He couldn't wait for your school term to end. The problem is, he's not well—"

James butted in. "Mother, what has Father got? Why is he not well?"

"Well, James, it's not easy to hear. He has cancer, and the doctors give him less than a month or two before he passes on."

"Why has no one said a word to me? This is outrageous! I should have been told!"

"No, you shouldn't have been. There was nothing you could have done, and besides, you need to have all your concentration on your school work." He thought his mother had a point, even though she sounded so practical and cold.

"So, when he goes rambling on about these stories of the East Wing, you must realize that he's heavily medicated. The last thing I want is your head filled with all this rubbish when you have a duty and responsibility to do the very best you can in all sectors, from education to sportsmanship, at Sterling." His mother leaned back into the sofa, clearly having said precisely the information she wanted to impart.

James was polite in his response. "Yes, Mother, I do understand. I will take it all with a pinch of salt and spend an hour with him on the subject and no more."

"That's the spirit! I knew you would understand. I just want the best for you, James. Your future is so important to me." She kicked off her high heels and smiled. She had accomplished exactly what she wanted, for now. However, James didn't buy for a moment that she had his best interests at heart. "Finish up your meal and go see your father. I know he's anxiously awaiting your arrival."

James finished his dinner and then went to seek his father. James wandered through the great hallway toward the main entrance and then up the double-tiered majestic stairway toward his father's bedroom. James knocked firmly on the door.

"James, my boy, come on in."

James was shocked to see how frail his father had become. The fine stature of the man was being destroyed by the ghastly force inside his body. "Good to see you! Heard good reports from that school of yours. Keep up the good work."

"Yes, Father." He watched his father lean over to grab his glass of water from the bedside table, his hand shaking heavily. James just couldn't believe the difference in him between now and the time he'd left for school.

"James, tomorrow morning, I'll have Rodney get me up, and we'll go down to the East Wing. How about that? Something you've been waiting for, eh?"

James became excited. "Father, thank you so very much. I am really excited. This is the best treat I could dream of."

"Think nothing of it, my boy. You are going to learn a lot tomorrow, so run off and get a good night's sleep. You've had quite a day. Oh, and by the way, don't let your mother distract you if she should happen to talk about the room. She would never understand. Whatever I teach you, you must keep it to yourself. There will come a time in your life when you will be able to discuss these things, but only with like-minded people."

Even though his father was frail, James could see him light up as he talked about the room.

James could scarcely sleep that night being so filled with anticipation. At eight o'clock sharp, Rodney was knocking on his door. James was ready to go and join Rodney and his father for the walk down the long corridor and outside to the East Wing. Rodney took the large brass keys and unlocked the main master lock. James noticed that there were also several smaller, intricate circular locks with combinations. He figured these locks must have been added later. They had probably been added to ensure the safety of the room's contents. To James's astonishment, the door shot up vertically about twenty feet and was about fifteen feet wide. It was at least eight inches thick, carved out of solid oak, and it operated more like a portcullis than a door to a room.

Once in the entryway, Rodney opened a smaller but still large double-oak door with another large lock. As they entered the room, James froze, astounded at the brilliance. Not only were the ornaments and artifacts stunning, but the size and magnificence of the room was breathtaking. He could see that at one time, it had been a vast ballroom, probably for hosting events on a magnificent scale. The outer perimeter of the room was lined with numerous tables bearing all sorts of artifacts collected by the Seventh Earl and previous ancestors. The room was at least 75 feet wide by 150 feet long, with a galleried staircase from which onlookers likely once enjoyed events. A platform stood up on the far side of the room, probably the place where bands had performed. In the center of the room rose a huge glass dome. The ceiling height had to be around forty feet, and the glass dome extended out at least another twenty-five feet. The glass dome cast light onto a beautiful inlaid marble floor. The diameter of the dome was around thirty-five feet, as was the marble floor below it.

Beneath the glass dome and sitting upright on the marble centerpiece floor stood a magnificent throne. James had never seen anything like it before. The back of the throne was mounted with huge colored jewels, seven in number, all placed vertically and aligned equidistant from the center. At the head of the throne was mounted a crystal crown, and a huge crystal ball sat over the crown, which lay directly over the seat, so anyone sitting on the throne would be directly below this incredible work of art. The crown was encrusted with gold and interlaced with other jewelry, which gave color and richness to the crown.

James was fascinated by the throne; he had never seen anything like this before. It was not a traditional throne from any of the history he had been taught or seen. The throne appeared to be something from the future or another civilization. It baffled him completely. At each side of the throne were two beautifully cut crystal angels about six feet high that held a crown over the top of the throne. The symbolism of these two exquisite angels holding the crown made the throne look like a place of reverence. Whoever sat in this seat would be within sight of the divine creator, and somehow, someone from above would have placed authority upon the chosen candidate.

In front of the throne, directly and centrally underneath, stood a fountain. It stood around six feet high, was carved out of gold, and emitted water three hundred and sixty degrees through four beautifully carved fish with angel wings. The fish, also made out of gold, a sprayed the water into a huge carved granite circular bowl, which was dark green and black.

Words were not apt to describe the spectacle that stood before them. James's thought was that this was a sanctuary of the divine. As the morning sunlight started to increase through the glass dome above, James sensed a strange, ethereal uplifting feeling.

He looked around and noticed that Rodney had left. He felt

a sudden urge to sit on the throne in order to experience what it would be like to be seated on this supreme seat of authority. His father just stood there with a smile as he watched James take his place beneath the crown.

As he placed himself upon the lavish purple velvet-covered cushion, James felt the energy. The seven stones behind him seemed to be conveying extreme energy into his body at the various points they touched, and the crystal crown held by the angels shone what could only be described as a force of light so radiant that he thought his head would explode. Within seconds, he was staring into an abyss and felt as if he were in a swirling vortex. It seemed to suck him out of his body, and he had the sensation of traveling at a speed that was close to terrifying. Then, he found himself in a calm, serene environment on the shores of a brilliant blue ocean, where he was sitting in the sand.

Suddenly, a dog ran up to him and started licking his face. For a moment, he thought it was his St. Bernard, Bonza, but it wasn't. The dog motioned him to follow, and so he did. Where was he? What was this place? As he followed the dog, he saw a modest small house, not unlike a home one would see on holiday in, say, the Caribbean. As he approached, he realized it was no ordinary place. It shimmered with a glow, and as he got closer, he saw people moving about. They weren't walking, though; they were somehow gliding or floating just above the ground.

A man with fine white hair approached him and called out. "Cartius, welcome. It's been a while since we last met."

James looked around him to see if there was someone else the man might be talking to, but it was definitely him he was referring to. The man wore a long white robe and dressed like what James imagined the Greek or Roman people did long ago. "My son, it's so good to see you in your new life and to observe how you're doing. Come sit here with me under the shade of this cypress tree. I have much to tell you."

"Cartius, why do you call me that? Where am I? How did I get here?" James was concerned and started to be afraid. He was in awe of his surroundings and intensely curious. *How did this happen*, he thought. *Did I die traveling through the vortex?*

The wise man, unconcerned with his apprehension, began, "You were my son on Atlantis and a fine one at that. I was always so proud of your drive and ambition, a busy little bee always trying to discover new ideas and ways! In this lifetime you've accomplished something that hasn't been done since your great-grandfather, the Seventh Earl, over one hundred years ago. You've crossed part of the galaxy to a different star system. It's actually the next closest system to yours, named by your people as the Pleiades. We live on a planet nestled between a double star system, which gives us constant light, although there are periods when our planet goes through what we call twilight hours as the two suns cross each other."

"So you mean I'm not dead; I'm on another planet?" James asked, wondering for the hundredth time if this was a dream.

"No, you are not dreaming, and you're more alive than you've ever felt." James was startled. The wise old man could obviously read his thoughts. He continued, "In fact, this reality is even more real than your own. Have you not noticed that we are communicating, yet we are not talking? We use thought transference here. It's not necessary for us to use words. Our language is different from yours, yet from your energy and feelings, I can understand your thoughts, and you can understand mine."

"Wow," said James. They were talking without speaking, and yet it was so easy, a child could do it. "Please tell me what is happening. Why am I here? How did this happen?"

"That throne came from your home on Atlantis, the civilization before your present one today. So you are the reason that throne exists in your world today and hasn't been lost on the islands of Atlantis. From your throne you sat on, which, I might add, is set in a very critical location, we have created a vortex so that your spirit can travel to other parts of the galaxy.

"Your body right now is still in that room sitting on that throne. Your father is still gazing at you, and he suspects what is happening, but he is not quite sure. He will be anxious to hear of your experience. Anyway, it's time we discussed the reason you are here."

"Yes, but I want you to explain: the throne exists today because of me. I don't understand. I need to know…"

"First, remember that 'please' is a very good word. Manners are the essence of civilization and one of the basics of the divine structure you and I live within." He took a long pause and sipped on some herbal drink, and then he attempted to explain matters in a way James would understand.

"I will now call you James. On Atlantis there were many such chairs, or thrones, as you now call it. Atlanteans were much more advanced than your civilization is today. You had your servant carry the throne to Egypt; he also accompanied your wife, which is the sole reason it has survived all these years. It's no accident that it was brought back to England by your great-grandfather, the Seventh Earl." The wise older man looked at James knowing he had a thousand more questions, but he wanted to continue with what he knew to be more important.

"My name is Czaur. I am what you would refer to as a master, that is, a person who has the power through the divine to change reality, but only if it meets with divine approval. I am an instrument, so to speak, of an energy that is much more powerful than you could ever imagine. This energy created our universe and everything in it. The other inhabitants of this planet and I live in what you would call the fifth dimension. Let me explain. You live in the third dimension, of positive, negative, length, breadth, and height. Your earth is a place where a balance between positive and negative has created what you would refer to as matter.

"In this world of yours, the positive is the creative force energy, and the negative is its opposite. Yet, between the two, a reality is created so that you can touch and feel and see what you believe to be tangible objects. This is a world of time—past, present, and future. So, you see everything in terms of what happened in the past, what is happening now, and what will happen tomorrow, the future. Understand so far?"

"Yes, absolutely."

"Then I'll continue. We on this planet have advanced beyond conflict and warfare; in this way, our energy has increased. We understand the absolute senselessness of the territorial need that is derived from your animal body. You have the power to transform yourself with the very source of your existence and with the spirit that resides in each one of us. It will take time for Earth to reach that goal. The animal in man strives for survival and independence, which elevates to territorial power.

"That need for control to define and substantiate the ego can lead to separateness, which ultimately leads to conflict and war. The answer lies in achieving balance and working to unite above the desires of a misplaced ego. Your world is one in which the Law of Karma presides. In the words of your Scripture, 'Do unto others as you would have them do unto you.' I will not teach you this now, but I will give you time to think upon everything I am telling you."

But James was hanging on his every word. "Please continue," he pleaded.

Czaur smiled at James's hunger for information, and he proceeded to feed him some more. "The purpose of your life's journey, for which you have been chosen, is to bring harmony and balance. Think well before you act, for mistakes keep bringing you back to the reality you are in to relive the wheel of Karma. You will gain the wisdom you'll need from the very special inheritance you will receive. I'm not referring to material things but to what you are striving to attain from this room you are in.

However, it will not simply be handed to you. You understand that the essence of the divine is about personal growth, and you will be tested by many forces. In order to lead people to a better way, you must be the example, and that can only be achieved by overcoming challenges. We don't speak of negativity in our world because there is no such thing. Negativity is just the result of bad decisions and wrong choices, where people lose their way and start to live in a world which you would call hell."

"Are you saying that there is actually no such place as hell?"

"Why would the divine create such a place? It is not intelligent or spiritual. It's a manmade illusion, a place where people and souls have lost their way. It has become a belief system, even for the Church, as a means to enchant the congregation to fear. It's the need to support the Church in order to protect everyone from evil. There is only one thing in life to fear, and that's fear itself."

James could imagine trying to tell most of his friends and family what he was hearing. They wouldn't believe him for a moment.

Reading his mind, the old man said, "I know they won't believe, but it's the truth. The one thing that binds this universe and all creation is love."

"Then why does God allow this to happen?"

"I was wondering when you would ask me that age-old question."

"Well, is it not justified? After all the unspeakable things that are allowed to happen on our planet, surely even to the most intelligent of beings, this must surpass all logic."

"Yes, but it's freedom of choice. People often start out with the most admirable of ambitions to build a world, family, or business with the finest intentions and end up falling far shorter than their expectations. Along the way, they get sidetracked with many temptations—more money, sexual endeavors, and most of all, power. The history books are filled with the stories of fallen heroes. No one person does it all; it's an upward connection between people to excel. Demonstrating a good example for people to follow helps to not only balance the planet's ecosystem but increase the energy of everyone toward a much better way of life."

"So what happens to all those so-called evil people when they die?" James asked, skeptical of what he was hearing.

"When they pass on, all souls go to the fourth dimension, or the astral plane as it is referred to. This is a place you go when you sleep at night. There are both good and what you would call bad souls there. For example, your 'ghosts' that people sometimes experience—these are souls that have not moved on. They only connect with their life on Earth, and for many reasons—guilt, shame, or complete non-belief—in the afterlife, they hang around for sometimes hundreds of your earth years. However, in the end, no one actually dies. Will these souls have to go through a serious transformation that can separate their identity from what they have become? Yes, but only when they are ready. No one is forced. The divine has reasons not to interfere in an individual's soul journey.

"Unless there are very special circumstances, the divine will not interfere with the development of a species or civilization once it has begun its journey. To do so would alter reality as you know it in a very cataclysmic way. Something as drastic as a polar shift of the earth's axis or complete climatic change would only be considered as a last resort to eradicate a society bent on its own self-destruction."

"This is heavy stuff. I need to think all this out. You have given me a lot of answers, and I am eternally grateful. It all makes incredible sense, for if no one dies, ultimately we all have the possibility of eternal life." James breathed a sigh of relief.

"Not just possibly, but absolutely. Don't doubt the words of your Scripture for a moment. You are a part of the divine, and in whatever form you may be, you exist forever, as hard as that is to understand in your dimension. Remember well the laws of physics that work to explain the basic building blocks in your dimension. We all live in a universe of energy; there is no more or no less in this amount of energy—it just changes state. You are an intrinsic part of that energy.

"You will change state or form, and when you die, as you call it, you will become spirit. As there is evolution for the body you inhabit, so there is evolution for the soul. On your planet, the medium of exchange is money, a physical form of trapped energy that can be used to achieve various objectives. In the world of the spirit, our medium of exchange is energy, and the more advanced a soul is, the more energy that soul will have. The increasing of our energy is a highly evolved subject where souls merge to become a oneness, and this is how our universe works in its most basic form. The process is similar to the way in which atoms form to become molecules."

With an air of authority, Czaur concluded with, "I believe you have had enough instruction for now. My dear boy, I know you're anxious to learn more, but I think it's time you returned."

"Yes, but I have two more questions to ask you. Please explain why I can't remember my life as Cartius, your son, and what is your level of existence in the universe?"

"I will, but first you must understand that as we knew each other in the previous civilization known as Atlantis, you must study what remains in your texts. Atlantis was a string of islands that lay in the Atlantic Ocean; it was covered over as the seawater rose at the end of the last Ice Age, around 10,000 BC. We were extremely advanced, technologically; we could generate huge amounts of energy through crystals and sunlight. We stored this energy in vats; we also used pyramids to store energy from the electromagnetic fields of the earth. With this powerful energy, we discovered the ability to propel ourselves to different parts of the universe. Of course, there were those who used this power for good and those who didn't. The misuse of this energy had resulted in the planet's change in temperature. Too many experiments were conducted as the water rose that were harmful to the CO_2 levels in our atmosphere. Those who wanted military power over the planet helped destabilize the planet's environment with their experiments. As the polar ice caps started to melt due to the earth's warming, our string of islands became immersed in water.

"The cultures such as the Mayans, the wise scholars of Egypt, Persia, and so on are all remnants of Atlantis. Some decided to stay and continue with a new age, but I decided to leave. The islands were completely covered in volcanic ash and seawater. Finding them today would be nearly impossible with the present technology, but proof of their existence does lie below the pyramids in Egypt. A lot of our knowledge has been lost through the centuries, but the technological age you are about to move into will rediscover all these things.

"This knowledge will be held back until your planet has become more spiritually aware. If you read the notes of the Seventh Earl, you will find that the throne he found in India derived its beginning on Atlantis and was used by the monks for what you have just done. The knowledge got lost over time, and for years, no one knew what it was: it was just worshipped. However, adepts of the monastery understood the alignment of the seven chakras at the rear of the throne and began to understand the real meaning of its use."

"I've heard about Atlantis but thought it was just fiction. So how is it that I can't remember that?" asked James.

"It is possible to remember your past lives, but in most cases, the soul wants to concentrate on the present. The past can sometimes prevent a soul from advancing. It is more important to focus on the now, so there is a natural veil of forgetfulness. One doesn't want to become too preoccupied with past errors. A new life is a new chance. You know within your soul the script you have been a part of writing for this life. In each life you carry forward the lessons you have learned and the skills you have mastered. The present is about new challenges and mastering skills that you may not have mastered in past lives. On Atlantis you didn't want to leave Earth and start out a new life. You believed somehow that with the technology we had at that time, this cataclysmic climatic change could be halted or reversed."

"So, I died?"

"Yes, but you chose to go back to Earth. After many lifetimes, you believed that Earth could have a future with a special destiny for mankind. That's why you're here, so that I can guide you to a hopefully better ending than we had on Atlantis."

"Amazing." James realized that he had so much to learn and research to do.

"We returned to help the earlier civilizations get started but were very strategic in the information we gave. We knew many of the lesser-evolved souls were not ready for too much knowledge, and we were cautious not to create one culture to be more powerful than another. The earlier ancient Egyptians were far more advanced in spirituality than your planet is today, and much of that spiritual knowledge got lost. The pyramids of Egypt are much older than most people think. This will be realized when your scientists and geologists discover ancient writings in the hieroglyphics, and technology can gauge the dating of various artifacts and stones."

"This makes a lot of sense," said James. "The earth and its people had to take their own direction and evolve as the Atlanteans had done. Only this time with a more successful spiritual awareness to come."

"Precisely. You're going to do well; I can see that. In simple terms, we are a planet similar to Earth; we have evolved as souls and live at a higher level of energy. I shall elaborate on this subject more deeply when we next meet. We live in a dimension where our energy level is to a point where food like herbs, fruits, and vegetables is taken for cleansing and pleasure. Here we have an energy level that sustains us, and with sleep, we are renewed with this energy, a little like filling your car with gas," he said with a laugh.

James laughed too. It was a pleasant relief after such an intense encounter.

"And in answer to the last question, there are seven dimensions in the universe, even though there are subdirectories of those levels. The sixth is the angelic level, and the seventh is the divine." With that, Czaur got up from his chair and motioned James toward the beach to the point where he had arrived.

As they walked, he explained, "I will not be seeing you for the next several years. You must concentrate on your schoolwork, and when you are ready to start your career, we will visit again. I will be watching you, and there will be times you will feel my presence. Always remember the power of prayer, as all prayers are heard. Maybe they are not answered in a way we would like, but always in a way that's for our own good."

As James stood upright on the spot where he had arrived on the beach, he felt the kindness that his master had shown to him, and the feeling of love for him on his future journey. He looked out at the beautiful ocean beyond the soft white sand, and then a vortex swirled around him, and within an instant, he was back on the throne in the East Wing.

As he awoke from his trance, he gazed around the room. He found his father still looking at him with the same gaze he'd had when he left.

"How does it feel to sit on that magnificent throne?" As his father asked him the question, he realized that although it felt like he had been gone over an hour, hardly any time had actually passed.

"It was incredible; never have I experienced anything like that before", James said, a little dazed.

"Well, did you feel anything?"

"Yes, I did." But James, still perplexed, didn't elaborate.

"I don't expect you to feel something right away, but I know there's an energy when you sit there. Even I have experienced that," his father said, looking a little disappointed.

"There's definitely an energy. How long was I gone, Father?"

"Gone?" he said, astonished. "Why, you just sat down there a few minutes ago. You didn't go anywhere, at least not to my knowledge. I could see you taking it all in, so I let you enjoy the moment."

This confirmed James's suspicion that time had almost stood still. He started to laugh. "So, only a few minutes have passed since I sat on the throne?"

"Yes, only a few moments." His father became curious at his question. "So, you did feel something? I knew you would. So tell me about it. I want to hear everything."

He began to tell his father about everything that he had experienced, and his father's eyes went glassy with amazement. "This is astonishing, James. I knew this would happen. It's just like the Seventh Earl's travels—wonderful, wonderful stuff! It happened to me when I sat on the throne, but when things started to energize, I got up because I felt dizzy. I didn't have the courage to stay there and experience what you just did. Maybe it wasn't meant to be, as the Seventh Earl said it would be you."

His father walked toward an old oak desk sitting at the far end of the room and nervously rummaged through his pockets to find a key. "Aha! I have the key!" He opened the front drawer, and from inside, he pulled out an old notebook. "This was your grandfather's. All the information you now need to understand your experience is in those notes. Guard them with your life, and take your time to read these notes thoroughly. Many of the answers from your visit will start to make even more sense. It took us years to find this notebook. It was hidden away in the attic with his personal effects. I brought it down here and locked it away so no one would get their hands on it. It's these notes that, when recited, had him almost institutionalized. No one would believe him. Now in today's world, maybe we are a little more open-minded. Not that people will understand, but they will think they're just the imaginings of an old man. You'll find much to educate you there, James. I must say, I took my time, but after hearing of your experience now, I can see how he had such a rough time with all his family and friends."

James saw a look of sadness cross his father's face as he said, "It's time we got back to reality, so let's lock the place up and return to the main house. I'm sure everyone is wondering where we are."

It was past mid-morning, and James knew his mother would be wondering what he was up to, so he planned to just tell her a roundabout story with a measure of truth. His father was tired, and Rodney saw him back to his room. James heard his echoing voice as he walked away. "Well done, James. We'll talk later. Go see your mother. And look after those notes; remember what I said."

James found his mother, and after a few brief words, he headed back to his room, anxious to read the notebook. He threw himself on his bed and began to read.

> *In the year of our Lord, May 14, 1854*
> *To the enlightened reader of these memoirs, I bestow upon you the gifts of my journeys to the Far East, India, and to the southern continent of Africa. Together with these findings goes the knowledge of my experiences with my divine master Czaur and the great knowledge that he has entrusted unto me. I know I live in an age that is not blessed with untraditional thought, especially in holy and religious matters. I write these words in the hope that one day, someone will realize the value of these artifacts, not only in the material sense, but more importantly, in the spiritual and philosophical sense.*

James eagerly turned to the next page.

After twenty years of traveling to many parts of the distant world to learn the different beliefs and religions of other cultures, which was fortunately allowed to me by our many financial interests, I now cannot help but arrive at the distinct conclusion that mankind has yet to understand the amazing opportunities we have on this planet we call home. Science, religion, philosophy, and spiritualism are all joined together. Somehow, this entire universe is connected, and yet I have so little proof to validate my beliefs.

James thought that these memoirs were written by a man far from being crazy. A little eccentric maybe, but not crazy. He read about all of the Seventh Earl's challenges in bringing the jewels and the throne back to Penbroke, as well as the immense amount of money he spent altering the East Wing, to the outrage of his family and friends. He read about the many journeys to the Pleiades and his great-grandfather's conversations with Czaur. One particular description caught his attention.

It was dated Sunday, June 12, 1859.

I took an early breakfast and wandered down to the East Wing. Many matters were pressing, in particular the alienation I was receiving from not only my immediate family but from all those around who knew me. I felt a deep loneliness and the need for comfort, so I decided to seek advice from my beloved master.

Being close to the summer solstice, the sun was bright, and I knew that the light in the Throne Room, as I like to call it, would be particularly strong as it beamed down through the glass dome. This would be an excellent time to transport myself to the star system beyond. When I arrived at my usual place on the beach, there was my old friend there to greet me. We talked at great length about the journey of our planet and the many things that would come to pass—the birth of the automobile, the collapse of the US Treasury and the financial woes of the 1890s, the First World War, and the beginning of a new age of unparalleled technology.

I learned how people would start to drift from the strict religious beliefs of the Victorian era and focus more on materialism and financial power. Wealth that was previously held only by monarchs and nations would become accessible to the man in the street, and because of some of the suppressive ways of the previous era, man would experience a newfound freedom. Great achievements would be possible. There would be a new belief in self and what the new world had to offer. Adapting to this new world would not be achieved by the old-age methods of religious indoctrination but by embracing the adventurer and the buccaneer for their vision.

Women would have the right to vote, and the old, traditional family system would change to one where women and children would speak out more. The old-fashioned father of the house would have his hands full unless he shifted his traditional beliefs. Overall, this was not a bad outcome to a hungry nation of people looking for opportunity and advancement. However, the danger of worshipping the god of materialism and money would prove to be a serious challenge.

As for my own circumstances, Czaur implored me to be silent. He reaffirmed my need to write my memoirs. He assured me that three generations from my time, there would arise an earl that would understand the value of what others had laughed at and scorned. In response to those who thought I was one step away from "Bedlam," he suggested that I tone down the rhetoric and use the advice and knowledge I had been given, rather than try to explain the source and the way I had received this knowledge. He told me to think upon this knowledge as a certain intuition and leave it at that, for he assured me the time would come when all this knowledge would be appreciated. His words greatly healed me, and in hindsight, I wish I had followed a more cautious path. However, in my excitement, I wanted to share the fantastic revelations I had received with the world. I lived to learn that timing was everything.

James's mind was absorbing all the astonishing prophecies that had come to pass, by what he read. That afternoon, and all day Saturday, James could scarcely put the notebook down. He realized he was reading extremely good advice. With this kind of knowledge, he would have to be careful as to how he behaved in the future.

CHAPTER 4

THE WILL

After a good night's sleep, James awoke to the sound of the cockerel making his early-morning serenade. It was Sunday, which meant church. They would all have to put on their best dress for the occasion. The Bishop of Lincoln would be giving the sermon, so they knew as a family they would have to befit the occasion with the usual flair. It was a chance for the women to get dressed up and the men to look their best, especially those who were of countenance and standing within the community. Out came James's tweed suit, cuff links, and other accessories. He was used to it by now, but at the age of fourteen, he still had yet to appreciate being choked at the neck with his Windsor knot and wearing his shiny lace-up shoes.

After breakfast, they all congregated in the front entrance while Rodney was sent to fetch Father for the service. James was confirmed in his faith, Church of England, by the bishop, and since it was now the school holidays and getting close to

Christmas, the bishop would expect his presence at the eleven o'clock service.

Suddenly, Rodney came dashing down the front stairs, yelling like a madman. "Come quickly, Mas'er James. His Lordship has locked his door, and I can't hear a sound!"

Anxiously, his mother said, "James, go quickly. It could be urgent!"

Probably overslept or is in the bathroom, James thought hopefully as he tore up the front stairs and down the hallway. He reached the door and began to knock. "Father, Father, are you up? We're all waiting on you for church." He didn't hear a sound. He yelled out again but got no response. "Kick in the door, Rodney. Something is wrong. He had to have heard that."

"You won't kick that door in easily, sir. It's got one hell of a lock on it."

"Then let's blow the lock out with a gun."

"I don't know. That's not safe."

"Yes, it is. I'll run down to the gunroom and grab a pistol."

"That's dangerous, sir!"

His mother came up behind him. "James, what are you doing? I swear that boy is out of his mind. I want to know what you are doing."

"No time to talk. Tell you later." He ran down the hallway and into the gunroom. He smashed the glass window on the locked cabinet, grabbed his father's favorite pistol, loaded a couple of bullets, and ran back. After two heavy blasts from the gun, the door burst open. He charged into the room, only to find his father in front of the bathroom door on his knees clutching his heart.

"My God, let's turn him over on his back; get some brandy, alcohol, anything to try and stimulate him. Mother, call the doctor immediately." James thumped away at his father's heart, but to no avail. "I'm losing him. It's no use. I think he's gone."

His mother heard his words as she came back into the room.

She cried, "Keep trying, James! The doctor will arrive soon."

The tears started streaming down James's face. He knew it would take a miracle to save his father. The doctor and ambulance arrived, but after ten minutes, it was too late. They could do nothing to revive the helpless man. In spite of all the effort, the doctor shook his head and said, "Countess, I believe he's gone. There's not much more I can do other than have him taken in the ambulance for a final diagnosis and autopsy."

Devastation settled over all who were present. James realized that his father had obviously tried to get up to go to the bathroom, but as he was still not dressed, he didn't think he planned on going to the church service. James suddenly felt a warm sensation all around him. As tragic as the moment was, he had the sense that his father was in safe hands and was relieved to escape his slow death with cancer. No one spoke as they filed out of the bedroom. There would be no church service this Sunday for the grieving family.

James spent the rest of the day in a slight daze, wandering aimlessly around the estate, thinking of all the memories he and his father had shared. It just wouldn't be the same without him. He asked, "Why, God, why? Couldn't you have given him a few more years?" He didn't understand.

He arrived at an old five-bar gate that overlooked the paddock where the horses were quietly grazing. Staring into the small pond in the distance, he mounted the gate, sat atop it, and started to reason. It was at this moment that he felt a distinct presence. It was as though his father and Czaur were sitting on either side of him on the gate, although he knew that was impossible. However, in spirit form, he supposed a physical body didn't define a presence. Slowly, words started to flow into his head. "James, your father is with us now. He will wander the estate and the places he has known until his funeral has passed and the lawyer has read his will. When he feels at peace, he will depart to our way of life. Your father has chosen his path. He lived a full and blessed life. He has helped many, as was his duty, and now he goes to rest awhile before taking on a new challenge. Do not fear for him, for he will be watching over you, as you too have much to achieve. After certain events have been addressed, which is normal when a person such as your father passes away from your world, you have to get right back into your studies. It's your future, and time must not be wasted." Then the presence was gone, and he saw all the horses suddenly look up as if something flew over them. Moments later, his dog Bonza came running down the lane and jumped up against the gate, nearly knocking James off his perch. These signs confirmed Czaur's presence. James, understanding the message that he should not dwell on the past but see the good in it, jumped off the gate and slowly meandered back to the main house.

****

Father's death caused quite a commotion. Rebecca and Felicity were called home from their respective schools, and James had to delay his return to Sterling. Mother was in a state of panic, and all the staff members were extremely anxious. The positive aspect was that his father was greatly loved by so many people who respected his kindness and wisdom. He was a legend, and he would be missed by his family, his friends, his staff at Penbroke Court, and his thousands of employees around the world.

The day of the funeral was one never to be forgotten. James's father was so well known that even some members of the Royal Family were present. The Prince of Wales paid his tribute, and the Queen sent her condolences. Lords from all over England attended the funeral at Lincoln. The Bishop of Lincoln had carefully prepared his speech and brilliantly articulated the lifelong journey of his father. Becky and Flick were obviously not themselves, and the Countess looked lost, politely shaking people's hands with a distant gaze. Though he thought she gave Father a tough enough time when he was alive, James could see that she actually missed him. He believed that his mother realized the enormity of responsibility that would now be placed upon her shoulders, and she was feeling insecure. The one person who was more devastated than he could have imagined was Claudia. Obviously, there was more to that story than anyone knew.

After a few days had elapsed, and the funeral was behind them, James and his mother made the journey to London to see the lawyers. Sir Thomas Ringstone's offices were magnificent. The heavily wooded paneling and studded leather chairs all helped to display an image of refined yet aged opulence. The firm of Ringstone, Ringstone, and Farley started in 1860. James's family had been clients since at least the early 1860s. The firm's expertise was unrivalled with the knowledge of the family's history and affairs. Sir Thomas was at Sterling with James's father, so James knew that whatever they would be told would be accurate.

As James and his mother walked into the office, Sir Thomas himself greeted them. "Come in, come in, Phillipa. What a business. So untimely, never mind, damn fine man. Loved you all so much. Do sit down. James, I hear you are quite a young man these days, doing well at Sterling. I'll have to tell you some old stories about some of my and your father's antics."

"Err, yes, sir, definitely. I'd like that," James replied with a curious interest. His father certainly hadn't told him any stories, though maybe his young age had something to do with it.

Sir Thomas sat down at the head of the conference table and peered over the top of his half-rim eyeglasses. He was dressed like all people in the city—immaculately tailored pinstriped black suit, a blue shirt topped with a detachable white collar, and his favorite varsity tie from Oxford. In a serious tone, he began, "Let's get down to business." He motioned to his secretary to bring in coffee and biscuits.

Sir Thomas began, "Countess, your husband, knowing of his condition, had plenty of time to think out his estate, so I will skip the formalities, for we all conclude that he was of sound mind. To be sure, he had a full test conducted by a doctor as to his sanity, and I have the documentation to verify this fact. This is his wish, and being the organized man I knew him to be, and all of us knew him to be, he desired no friction amongst the immediate family or those he may have named in this will."

Sir Thomas then began reading the will. "I, the late Lord Penbroke, Ninth Earl, declare this to be my last will and testament. I bestow upon James, my only son and heir, the same title as his predecessors. The following are to be named the trustees in this will and must execute my wishes without fail unless a unanimous decision exists, because certain changes have taken place in the dynamics of the economy, in the event of death, or in the event of an unforeseen, uncalculated change. The trustees are as follows: Countess of Penbroke Phillipa Bannerman is trustee pro-tem until James is twenty-one years of age.

"Sir Thomas Ringstone is trustee pro-tem until my son and daughters, namely Lord James, Lady Felicity, and Lady Rebecca, reach the age of twenty-one. Sir Thomas will remain advisory trustee to James until he receives his inheritance on his twenty-first birthday, and while my daughters will have the right to make decisions as trustees when indeed they become of age, my son James will have the casting vote."

Sir Thomas paused, looked around the room to make sure there were no questions, and then continued reading. "To my son, James, I bequeath my entire estate at Penbroke Court and my shares in Bannerman's International Bank to be held in trust until the age of twenty-one. My wife, Phillipa, will oversee Penbroke Estate. During that period, she may derive an income that is in keeping with the money she now receives and is known through our accounting firm of Minyards and Weinstock. To my wife, I bequeath the Mayfair property in London to do with as she so wishes along with those accounts and personal investments held in my personal name at the bank. James will reserve the right to keep his mother in a manner according to her past. To my daughters, Rebecca and Felicity, I bequeath the sum of one million pounds each and properties adjacent to the estate as marked out on my map or payment of the fair market value at the age of twenty-one by my son. It is my intention to keep the estate farmed as a single unit. In this way, the estate can be financially viable. On no account can they sell these properties to an outside source. My shares in my business, which control 61 percent of my banking interests around the world and the investments so listed, I bequeath to my son, James. Any income derived from my shares in the bank will be held and invested and provided by Sir Thomas to James at the age of twenty-one."

James could tell the temperature in the room was rising. Sir Thomas, sensing the mood shift, said, "There will be plenty of time for discussion at the end of this will, so for now, I would appreciate it if everyone would keep their composure, until after the will has been formally read."

Sir Thomas then went back to reading. "To my secretary and confidant, Claudia, realizing that she may or may not be needed, I bequeath the sum of one hundred thousand pounds so that she will have a certain freedom for her devotion and loyalty."

Upon hearing this, Countess Phillipa could not contain herself. "That little bitch. I might have known better, flaunting herself around your father. I should have had her fired ages ago. Men! They are so gullible and easily manipulated."

"Phillipa!" interjected Sir Thomas. "Contain yourself. Your son is present. We can have any conversation you wish after this meeting has been adjourned."

He then finished the reading. "And finally, to the staff at Penbroke Estate, I bequeath an equal amount of one thousand pounds to all persons who have been in my employ for a period of ten or more years as a thank you for their loyal services."

Sir Thomas then looked up and said, "This concludes the main distribution of the will. As to more precise details, they can be discussed later, individually, or I am happy to answer any questions you may have now. I do caution you, though, not to express any undue emotion. The subject matter will have to be left until the contents of this will have sunk in." He sat forward, smiling, elbows on the table, ready to answer any questions. "Yes, Phillipa?"

"If I understand the will correctly, I get the London property and then I am left at the mercy of James's will, while that little bitch Claudia walks off with one hundred thousand pounds in her pocket. Is this all I get, all the thanks for being his wife after nearly twenty years?"

"Phillipa, you do have the money from His Lordship's personal accounts and investments. Also, you have the running, so to speak, of the estate for the next several years, and in view of your son's excellent progress, I hardly see how he would not have his mother honorably treated. Anyway, those conversations will be between the both of you at the appropriate time, and I can let you know what His Lordship has held in trust for you."

"Sir Thomas, it seems hardly fair. If I had divorced His Lordship, I think I would have been a lot better off financially."

In a condescending tone, he replied, "Maybe so. However, I hardly think that with your London property, which will only increase in value, and a generous allowance from His Lordship's estate in addition to what he's left you financially is hardly something to sneeze at." Sir Thomas then asked, "Anything else?"

"Yes, sir," James said. "What actual authority do I have over matters at this present time?"

"Not a lot," answered Sir Thomas indignantly, as though he thought James was lucky enough to inherit what was tantamount to almost everything at the age of twenty-one.

"I see. So what if, for some reason, my mother decides I'm

not fit to run the estate, or for that matter, the business?" Not trusting his mother, James felt it was an important question.

His mother butted in. "James, why in the world would I do that? You would have to be a very stupid young man to believe that I would do anything to jeopardize your father's will and that of my own son. You are the son and heir and are already the Tenth Earl. This is a proud tradition and one that will be honored without question."

"Well, there you have it. Well said, Phillipa." Sir Thomas regained some respect for the Countess. "Well, if there are no more questions, I believe that concludes this meeting." With a sigh of relief, Sir Thomas cordially shook James's hand as he walked out of the conference room. His mother was chatting feverishly behind his back to Sir Thomas. James didn't trust the situation. He felt his father was a little too trusting, and leaving his mother to handle the affairs of the estate meant that anything could happen.

Though concerned, James realized that with time, Sir Thomas would see that the will was carried out to the letter of the law; otherwise, he knew his father wouldn't have chosen him. They were school pals, at least, and his father had given him an enormous amount of business. James just had to stop dwelling on the nagging doubts.

They arrived back at Penbroke around four o'clock, in time for tea in the drawing room. His mother flew in through the front door yelling, "Where is Claudia? Where is she? I want to see her in my study immediately."

One of the cleaning staff replied, "I'll find her right away. I believe she's at the farm office as usual, My Lady."

Their mother continued shouting all sorts of abuse as a frightened Claudia, shivering from the wrath of his mother and the cold, damp weather outside, arrived at the front entrance. This poor soul who had done absolutely nothing wrong was now going to be lambasted by the Countess.

"This way, Miss Claudia," said Rodney as he ushered her into the study.

"There you are," said the Countess haughtily. "Well, shut the door; I've got a lot to say to you before we part company!"

James cringed at the thought of this very polite, good-looking woman being ripped apart. It wasn't enough that she had probably had many sleepless nights fretting over her future and the sad loss of their father, whom James knew she loved and admired with all her heart. With the relationship between his mother and father slowly deteriorating, and his mother spending so much time in London, it seemed only natural that his father would seek out the affections of someone else. Where was the harm? He would never have changed his life. He loved his wife too much.

The Countess continued, "Well, you've been left one hundred thousand pounds in His Lordship's will. What have you got to say for yourself?"

"Err . . . "

"Come on, I've not got all day. I'm listening."

"I don't know what to say, Countess. It's a complete surprise. How very kind and considerate he was."

"Kind! I bet he was. What kind of favors did you provide to earn yourself that kind of money—more money than most people see in a lifetime?"

Claudia, stunned at the accusation, forcefully replied, "It's totally unexpected! We never ever did anything inappropriate ma'am. You have to believe that!"

"Inappropriate?" the Countess asked curiously.

"Yes. He loved you, not me. I gave him comfort and companionship when he needed it but nothing more. He missed you so much when you would go off to London. He believed you hated this place, and he blamed himself terribly for not being with you in London. All he wanted to do was be at your side—he just had so much to take care of."

Phillipa sat silently for a good while. Then, totally out of character, she burst into tears. The memories of her early days when he'd swept her off her feet all started crashing back into her head. Now the good times were gone forever. "Oh, he was a good man. How could I have ever thought otherwise? It's so important to a woman's pride that the man she married still loves her. I know you're telling the truth. It's so like him. Our interests just grew apart with time, and I so wanted those days back, but his heart was here. After he organized his business, he ran most of his deals from here. I know you must have been a great personal asset to him, and of course he needed someone like that."

The children sat munching on their biscuits and sipping their tea while listening to this performance.

"Ma'am, you must know he did nothing but talk about you in a way that a man who loves a woman does."

"Oh, Claudia, I've been so wrong. Too much time has passed, and I have not recognized the valuable secretary you must have been to him. It's all just been too much lately. So forgive me. I know I would find it hard to replace you, but I wouldn't blame you if you left."

"Countess, it's been a shock for all of us, but I love my job, and I would serve you or any member of your family with the same dedication I showed to His Lordship."

"I'm so glad to hear that. Let the night pass, and then we can all move forward."

"Good night, Countess. Please know I'm here if you need me." Claudia quickly exited the study.

Phillipa sat in her study for a good hour, thinking about the unnecessary jealousy she had shown. Her husband had loved her with all his heart. How could she have doubted that? She faced the fact that she was the one that had not shown the appropriate affection.

CHAPTER 5

THE COUNTESS AND
HER FUTURE

With all her children back in school, the Countess had time to think, and think she did. Phillipa knew that Claudia was an excellent administrator for all the estate's many needs, and she too had a competent staff and farm manager to exercise all the facets of running the estate. Between Claudia and Arthur Ludgate, the farm manager, the Countess knew she was in good hands. She would now be free to go to London more often and for a longer duration than in the past. She had only really spent time at Penbroke because of her husband, and of course, all the social engagements she enjoyed hosting. However, hunting, shooting, and fishing were not her favorite pastimes; in her younger years, she had reluctantly participated and had become knowledgeable enough to talk with the neighboring gentry, business associates, and those socialites who often visited from the city, but she much preferred living in the city.

Now that her husband had passed away, she felt she had to

do something with her own life. She had to think about her own future. At thirty-nine, she was still a very attractive woman. As a dancer, she had a good athletic disposition; although not tall, she had nicely proportioned legs and an above-average bust line. Her face, though it could appear stern and severe, was extremely magnetic and captivating when she enjoyed the company of the person she was with. Her large, powerful blue eyes, retroussé nose, nicely flat and pretty ears, and long blonde hair would be appealing to any man. She had married an older man, but who could avoid the temptation of marrying a man so eligible as His Lordship. His upper-crust disposition, warmth, and good looks made them an attractive couple. They were often the subject of gossip in many newspapers and tabloids. Phillipa loved the attention, and she knew where to go to get that attention.

She had been brought up in a modest family, but she was well educated, and her natural good looks were a passport to the stage. Before she met her husband and was swept off her feet, she was planning on pursuing an acting career, having held many small parts in London playhouses. She considered London her real home. Thus, after seeing to all the pressing matters of the estate, she summoned Rodney to drive her to London, where she would carry out her plan for the future.

As soon as she walked through the front door of her Mayfair home and dismissed Rodney, she picked up the phone.

Authoritatively, she said, "I would like to speak with Sir Thomas Ringstone."

"And who may I say is calling?"

"Countess Phillipa." She thought using her first name might sound a little friendlier.

"Yes, of course. One moment, Countess."

After a brief pause, Sir Thomas came on the line. "Phillipa, how in the world are you? What a pleasure to hear from you."

"Yes. Well, I know you're a busy man, but if you have a moment to spare, I would very much like to talk with you."

"No problem at all. I'll cancel my three o'clock appointment, and we can discuss anything you like. How's that?"

"Since what I want to say is of a more private nature, would it be too forward of me to ask if we could possibly go out for dinner this evening?"

He hesitated, then said, "Even better. I'll pick you up at seven, and you can take all the time in the world to discuss whatever is on your mind."

"See you at seven, then?"

"I look forward to it, Phillipa."

Phillipa hung up, half jumping with delight. She felt like a schoolgirl again, but she knew she must hold her enthusiasm in check, for it had not been long since the passing of her husband.

Phillipa nervously awaited Sir Thomas's arrival. She felt as if she were going out on a date and kept trying on different dresses until she found just the right look—sexy but not too alluring with a higher-than-usual skirt line, high heels with an extended height, and some well-chosen jewels from her lavish collection. She looked stunning, and she knew it. If he weren't impressed by how she looked, she thought, he never would be. Sir Thomas was a very eligible bachelor himself, having inherited the law practice from his father and the long line of Ringstones. He was educated at Sterling and was well understanding of the standards of nobility and British upper class apparel and behavior.

The doorbell rang, and Phillipa, her heart beating fast, ran down the stairs to open the door. Sir Thomas greeted her. "Well, good evening, Your Ladyship, and how beautiful you look this evening."

"Oh, Sir Thomas. Flattery will get you everywhere. I just threw on something at the last moment. I need to go shopping. I'm sure I look hopelessly out of date to all you city socialites."

"Not at all. You're totally in keeping with the latest fashion and good taste, if I may say so."

They walked into the back drawing room where she poured him a glass of his favorite malt liquor. "Just a quick drink before we head out, don't you agree?"

Sir Thomas chose his words carefully. "Wonderful. It's been a while since I've visited you and your late husband here. I can see that you have made all the right choices for household decorations, which only a woman can do."

"I know you're probably just like my husband. He had little or no interest in these matters and much preferred to be out on the estate than hanging around here, so someone had to do those things."

Sir Thomas moved across the room to look at a framed picture on the table. "Good lord, that's an old picture of Collin and me at university. Oh, those were the days. He was in his last year, and I was just beginning, but he was a blast to be with—terrific sense of humor."

"So it is," said Phillipa as she joined him to look at the picture. "How young you both look, and handsome, I might add." She had an almost flirtatious look in her eye.

Sir Thomas was a tall, handsome man who had been married once before, in his earlier years. He had been single for quite a while, and he now looked at Phillipa, wondering whether she may or may not be a very fortuitous future partner. Thomas was about six foot three, athletically built, and kept himself in shape by being an avid squash player. He belonged to all the right London clubs and had contacts with all the right people. His hair was slightly receding and was brushed straight back with a little extra length behind the neck, giving him a younger, more dashing appearance for a man in his forties. He was impeccably dressed in a polo-neck sweater and blazer, which gave his normal professional persona a more relaxed and appealing boyish look that Phillipa was quietly admiring.

They went to what was both their favorite restaurant in Knightsbridge just behind Harrods' department store. There they could be at a private table where they could discuss whatever Phillipa had in mind and enjoy the best cuisine. They first discussed all the normal trivialities about health, friends, and acquaintances, and then Phillipa got down to business.

"I have some questions for you regarding the reading of the will. I know that I have custodial rights over the estate and can hopefully count on your experience and support. I also know that the children are far too young to understand these matters. I have to let you know I am very concerned that I only have a limited amount of time to, in a sense, get my house in order for myself and try to make the most financial benefit for my own wellbeing."

"My dear Phillipa, you have absolutely nothing to worry about. Collin has left you in the best hands possible. You do have some income from the estate and the remaining amount of savings from Collin's private affairs—"

She butted in, "But I have no idea what I have in cash reserves, and that makes me very nervous."

"Yes, I can understand that, but you obviously don't know what Collin has left you in the way of his personal finances."

"Well, between trying to understand the will and what is part of the bank is not easy. I don't want to end up penniless when James becomes twenty-one, so I must do everything I can now to enhance my personal position."

"I understand. I'm not able to give you the exact amount, but Collin left in the bank around two million pounds in his own personal cash and investments, which the bank will diligently manage for you. That's a fair sum of money. If managed wisely, it can grow and leave you in an extremely fortunate place over the next seven years. Let's see, James will be twenty-one in 1965. I see no reason why with your personal allowance from the estate, all expenses paid, this amount can't double by the time James reaches twenty-one!" Sir Thomas had a perplexed look on his face, wondering how more fortunate a woman could be.

"Yes, I understand that. It's more than I actually surmised from reading the will, but I still have all the costs and upkeep of my home in Mayfair."

"But you have more than enough income to support your home. You have no mortgage."

"But the taxes are exorbitant!"

"Yes, but well within the budget you can afford. Let's be honest. I don't think that property is going to go down, and in the next seven years, should you have the need, you can always sell or lease."

"You're right. I feel so much better now, just talking to you. I can't tell you how much you put my mind at ease." As Phillipa spoke, she was quietly dreaming up another scenario. Sir Thomas was a man she felt she could get along with well and one day possibly marry, in which case she could live at his very palatial home in North London, and as he said, sell or rent her home if it were a burden.

"So, Phillipa, don't worry. I will make it my personal task to see you are well cared for. After all, I am a director at the bank and a shareholder. Our families go way back, and in an absolute worst-case scenario, I know James would never see you wronged. Don't underestimate that boy of yours. I think he will go places; he seems to have an uncanny intuition for such a young man. Of course, Collin had great foresight too, but I don't know, that young man of yours might surprise you."

Phillipa was flattered that he was going to take a personal interest in her.

"And Phillipa, you can't rule out the possibility of meeting someone else. You are still young, very attractive, and an heiress. I think you're going to have to be very wise in your choices."

She laughed, thinking he sounded rather fatherly. She crossed her legs in a provocative manner and teasingly said, "Someone like you, perhaps?"

Sir Thomas turned bright red. "What? Me? You've got to be

joking. You're far too eligible to marry a humdrum lawyer like me."

"Nonsense. You're a very good-looking man, and it's time you settled down. Haven't you had enough of all those girlfriends?"

"Phillipa, I scarcely get time to go out with anyone. I work all the time."

"That's what they all say. No, it's time you got yourself a good woman. After all, if you can take the time to see me at such short notice, you can make time, and no doubt you do, to date. You're just not in love!" She sounded quite flippant and teasing and enjoyed him trying to wriggle out of that one.

"I must say, Phillipa, this is the first time I have had one-on-one company with you, and as crazy as it sounds, I think we would get on quite well." He began thinking of the possibilities.

Phillipa was delighted with his response but thought it best to let things go no further on this date. She would leave her design for another occasion. She had tweaked his interest just enough to let the door open slightly, and she was going to see if her game of chess would work. He would now have to make the next move.

The evening had been a success, going just the way Phillipa had planned. She mustn't be too hasty, though. Her worries had been put to rest for now so she could sleep and plan her next strategy.

CHAPTER 6

SCHOOL DAYS

James was looking forward to the summer holidays. A full year and a half had passed since his father's death, and life had been strange without his presence, especially at Christmas. His father's death had deeply affected James's outlook, and he was maturing and preparing to be the man he would have to be in the future.

Over the different holidays, he had spent a lot of time reading the Seventh Earl's notes and increasing his knowledge about all the amazing experiences. He realized that he had to keep this knowledge to himself, although he felt somehow that his father was with him. He now had a deeper sense of awareness of life and the afterlife. *There are guides that help us in the day today, and we just have to become more aware and listen to what we're being told and led toward,* he thought. It was like having another family that was always there. In a quiet moment, thoughts would pop into his head, and he knew from the extra energy he felt that these thoughts were coming to him as guidance.

He had become great friends with Peter Lloyd. They shared the same interests and decided that they would meet over the holidays. Peter's family was involved in the motor racing industry, and he had invited James to drive his go-kart as an introduction to the sport. Peter's father had his own private track, where he raced all types of race cars, and his machine tool factory had been a large force in supplying body shells for many of the Formula One race cars. His father had been a successful race car driver in his day and now devoted his time to high-precision machining, engine development, and aerodynamic designs for body shells.

One Sunday afternoon just before the break, Peter and James decided that after catching up on their homework, they would go for a bike ride. The nearest town to the school was St. Andrews, home of the famous golf course and the place to check out the local talent as far as girls went. There was one cafe called the Coffee Pot near the town center where young students hung out and got to meet peers from other schools. There they could play their favorite songs on the jukebox. Peter and James parked their bikes and walked in. The place was busy, but they spotted one table left on the far side of the room. A cute, young Scottish lass came up to their table and asked them what they would like.

"Oh, just a Coke," said

"The same for me," replied James.

The girl was around seventeen years old, and she knew the boys were from Sterling. She enjoyed teasing them with a flirtatious look. "I can tell from your accents you're certainly not from here."

"Oh no, you're absolutely right. We're from France. Parlez-vous Français?" asked Peter.

"Away with you. Neither of you are French!"

With a twinkle in his eye, James said, "Oh, yes we are. Our parents got so fed up with us that they left us here until we graduate. So we've now learned English. We sound like natives. From all the rain you get in England, we've lost our tans. So you see, we're starting to really think we are English. We can see why you're confused."

"Well, I never! If you come here a lot, you'll just have to teach me a few words."

Peter replied, "We can certainly do that, and we can teach you a lot more than words. The French are famous for many things like . . . well, I'll leave that to your imagination." They all started to laugh.

"I'm going to get your Cokes before you lads start getting too cheeky."

As she walked away, a voice clamored from the other side of the room, "I say, is that His Lordship over there? I think we've got some unfinished business. Guess what? I have my brother here to help me out."

"Oh God, not him again," said Peter.

"Let me handle this," replied James. He raised his voice so his assailant could hear him. "Well, it's a good thing you've got your brother with you. You need backup because the last time we had an altercation, you were, to the best of my memory, pathetic. It doesn't run in the family, does it?"

There were over twenty people in the restaurant, and they all began laughing. "You won't get away with it this time, Bannerman. We'll teach you a lesson you won't forget." The two brothers got up from their table and swaggered across the small dance floor in front of the jukebox.

"Now, Peter, here's your chance to show this coward what you're made of, and as for his brother, he's only a year-and-a-half older, so I'm going straight for his legs to get him down on the floor." James wanted to shut them up once and for all. He'd had enough of their bullying. They needed to be taught a lesson, and now was the time to do it.

"What? In here?" asked Peter apprehensively. "We'll get

thrown out!"

"Too bad! We're going to put an end to their bullshit." He turned to the brothers and said, "By the way, what do you call yourselves? I never did get your names." He knew they were the Petersen brothers, but he wanted to give them the impression he didn't know who they were in order to diminish their puffed-up egos.

"What's it to you?"

"I like to know who I'm fighting. Otherwise, I just won't fight."

"James, stop sparring with them. We are going to be in enough shit as it is," said Peter.

"For what it's worth, our last name, and that's all you little beggars need to know so you can well remember us, is Peters-en."

"More like cowardly bullies that throw their weight around on younger boys," taunted James.

The entire Coffee Pot crowd was on its feet laughing at James's outrageous comments and courage. A lot of them knew whom these Petersen bullies were, and they absolutely hated them.

"Go get 'em, Your Lordship," shouted several people in the crowd.

At that moment, the owner appeared on the scene to watch.

"Well, aren't you going to stop them?" asked one of the staff members.

"Hell, no. Let the lads have at it, as long as they don't break nothing, mind you."

The fight began. James had a few tricks up his sleeve. He threw himself low on the older brother, like he was making a rugby tackle. The older boy fell forward and landed flat on his face on the dance floor. James, who was extremely agile, had both of his legs on the arms of his opponent and was planted firmly on his back so he couldn't wriggle out.

"Give up, or I'll start beating your head to a pulp."

"Screw you! I can break this lock," he cried out in desperation.

"Okay." James stretched out the older Petersen's arms to their outer extremity and started to pull them back. He knew Petersen was overweight and lacked the agility to get out of his hold. With one sharp jolt, he proceeded to stretch his arms upward and backward, putting the boy in great pain. Then James dropped his arms, thumped the side of his head, and then picked up his arms again and started the same procedure.

"Want another?"

"No! No, you got it. I give up."

"First, you tell your brother to lay off Peter."

"Yes, yes," he said.

"Now, I'll tell you, if I find you being a bully to anyone at our school, I will come after you and your brother with a gang, and you're going to regret it for the rest of your school days. Understood?"

"You got it, you got it," he cried like the coward he really was.

The crowd applauded. James had become a local hero. The Petersen brothers silently collected their things and left the Coffee Pot, feeling disgraced.

Peter, collecting his breath, said, "Wow, James, you really put a move on that guy. How did you learn those moves?"

"When I was a young kid, the stable boy used to rag with me when I was not riding. He taught me a lot of tricks and helped me to toughen up. I was having trouble in prep school with guys pushing me around and making fun of me. He was tough on me, but I learned a lot.

"Joe told me that someone like me with a position in life would get picked on, so I needed to learn how to defend myself so people would respect me."

"Can you teach me? I need to learn a few tricks too. I want to hold my own. That younger Petersen nearly had the better of me."

"Don't worry. He won't come around taunting us again."

The young waitress came up to the table to congratulate the boys and brought them more Cokes and biscuits. She told them the owner said it was on the house. "You'll be a fine catch for some young lady one day—brains, good looks, and you know how to take care of yourself. Can I ask your name?"

"Yes, sure. This is my friend Peter, and my name is James. Thank you and your boss for your generosity. Much appreciated. May I ask *your* name?"

"My name is Tania, but everyone calls me Tani. I work here part-time to get some extra pocket money. I'm going to boarding school not far from here."

"Really? An all-girls' school?" James's interest increased, thinking she may know some girls nearer to his age.

"Yes. I'm sure there are some cute young girls who would love to spend time with you when you can get away from what I have heard is a very strict school."

"You're right about that, but hey, we're here today, so who knows?"

Peter and James savored the moment of their success and played some of their favorite music on the jukebox. They also enjoyed their hard-earned refreshments.

By the time James and Peter arrived back at the school, the word was out, and everyone, especially the older boys, looked at James in a very different way.

Mr. Caldwell passed them on the way to their dormitory and had some choice remarks. "So, I hear you've been up to no good again, Bannerman. What have you got to say for yourself?"

Apprehensively, James replied, "They started it, sir, and I thought it was about time they were taught a lesson."

"Well, that you did, and not on school grounds. However, we can't have everyone having punch-ups in the local cafe, can we?"

"No, sir, and it won't happen again," James said apologetically.

"By the way, off the record, good job," Mr. Caldwell said as he walked away with a smirk on his face.

****

James was on his way to breakfast one morning when he circled by the hall table in the main entrance to see if there was any mail for him. Sure enough, there was a letter from his mother. He opened it, and out dropped a five-pound note that she always sent. She was good for some things, he thought. He shoved the letter in his rear pocket and ran off to breakfast before he was too late.

Later, after a hard day of studies, he remembered the letter he had stuffed in his pocket and pulled it out to read. It opened with "James, how are you, darling?" and continued on with all the usual things mothers say. Then she dropped a bombshell. She and Sir Thomas would be arriving at the school the next weekend to talk with his housemaster about his progress and to take him out. She had already made the arrangements. She would be flying up from London with Sir Thomas, and they would be staying in St. Andrews.

He thought, *Wow, why with Sir Thomas? What is that all about? Sir Thomas is single. I wonder if something is going on there.* It had been some time since his father died, and he knew his mother was entitled to a life, but *Sir Thomas?* James had always thought of him as a rather suave city type, but then again, that could appeal to his mother, though it was quite a different choice from his late father. On the other hand, he was a Sterling boy, an executor of the estate, and on the board of directors at the bank, so it seemed logical that he would come. It was a chance to get to know him better outside an office environment. He would see the visit in a positive way and hoped this could be an opportunity to get to know a man who would one day play an important role in his life.

With their visit, James realized he would get a chance to show off his prowess as a bowler in the upcoming cricket match against Malvern. James and Peter loved cricket. He was the opening fast bowler for the senior colts, the under sixteens, and Peter was his trusted wicket keeper. They would practice for hours after school in the nets, working out techniques and all sorts of intimidating strategies to alarm the would-be batsman. The upcoming match on Saturday would be a test of their skills and a chance for Phillipa to see how her son was progressing. Not that she knew anything about the sport, but if he could get a few batsmen out, it would at least show some measure. Sir Thomas could always have the job of trying to explain all the intricacies of the sport to her. After all, this was a first. James couldn't remember the last time his mother attempted to watch anything. If they put on a good show, then who knows, she might be inspired to come another time.

Sir Thomas and Phillipa arrived Friday morning, as they wanted to have meetings with both the headmaster and Mr. Caldwell, the housemaster. That evening, they took James out to dinner at the Old Course Hotel at the famous St. Andrews Golf Club, where they were staying. Nothing but the best. His mother could enjoy the spa, and Sir Thomas was determined to get her out for nine holes of golf on Sunday.

Phillipa said, "James, we are very proud of your progress so far. It appears that you will be in the A stream next year, so you are doing all the right things to get to Oxford."

"No, Mother. Cambridge."

"Why Cambridge? Your father and Sir Thomas went to Oxford. The family has a history there. They would be disappointed. It's been a tradition."

"I understand all that, but on a practical note, Cambridge is much closer to home, and Oxford focuses more on the classics. I want to focus on business and the new world. It's the future of our banking, where things are headed, and I must learn all I can to that end." He was clearly a young man well advanced for his years.

"If I may, Phillipa," asked Sir Thomas.

"Yes, please do, Thomas."

"James, I think I agree with you for what your future holds. I think your choice is a good one. Like you say, Cambridge is closer to home. I think, in today's world, it may be a better choice, not that Oxford did the rest of us any harm." Sir Thomas paused, trying to understand the direction this young man was headed. "Since your father has passed on, I notice a distinct difference in you, James. I know that was a painful experience for you, as you were so close. My only advice is don't become too serious. You're still a young man, and I hope you enjoy these days as best you can. When you enter business life, as you will, then it can be all work and no play. So my advice to you is, of course, work hard, but make the very best of these years because they won't come again."

"Well said, Thomas. I couldn't agree more." Phillipa took another sip of her champagne.

James was silent, though he liked what Sir Thomas said. They were good words, and he appreciated them.

"Well, let's go forward to dinner," proposed Sir Thomas. James followed what he had come to realize was a new couple. It was a strange experience, seeing his mother with another man, but it was just another thing he would have to adapt to. At least she was there, and that meant a lot to him.

"It won't take long for me to decide what I want," said James, looking down the menu.

"And that is?" asked Sir Thomas.

"A bloody good steak. That school food is terrible. I spend all my pocket money eating out whenever I can. Otherwise, I would waste away to nothing."

They all laughed. "James, you are much thinner, but remember you're growing, too," said his mother.

"I know, but that's why I need food."

Sir Thomas advised, "Enjoy these days while you can eat and eat and eat and not put on one ounce. Of course, with all that bowling you're doing, I'm sure you burn it off. Can't wait to see you in action tomorrow. When does the match start?"

"First thing after lunch, which will be two o'clock sharp. I have to be there an hour before."

The rest of the evening was pleasant, and James had a good chance to get to know Sir Thomas better. He liked his drive. He was different from his father, who was much better suited to the estate even though he had a great financial mind. Sir Thomas had that energy that city people who are successful have, and that's what he would need one day for the job he wanted most of all.

****

It was two o'clock on Saturday, and the two captains went out to look at the wicket and condition of the ground. Malvern won the toss and chose to bat first. James was happy because he knew he would be the opening bowler and have a chance to show off his skills to his mother and Sir Thomas. He had studied all the styles of the bowlers and practiced plenty, and he knew that with his mother's short attention span, there would be no way she would stay to watch the whole match, which would last until six. In fairness, he knew that she had never seen a cricket match in her life, but at least Sir Thomas was there to educate her on the basics.

After the field was organized, the two batsman made their way to their respective wickets, and James started to walk away from the wicket. He began polishing one side of the ball on his trouser leg, which was the traditional method used by a fast bowler to swing the ball. The bowler, depending on whether he wanted to in-swing or out-swing the ball, could throw the shiny side on either side. James had something else in mind for this batsman. He wanted to bowl what was called a bouncer or bumper, meaning a ball that is pitched a little shorter than normal. The ball shoots up in an unnerving way to obviously intimidate the batsman and induce him to make mistakes.

James walked back at least twenty paces. His mother couldn't believe the distance he walked back from the wicket and asked Sir Thomas, "Is that normal to be so far back?"

"It's farther back than I would go, but I don't know what kind of bowler your son is, so let's wait and see."

James took off like a rocket, and by the time he was able to propel the ball from the right side of his body, he was at his fastest, jumping in the air while bringing his arm over the right side of his body. The ball flew out of his hand and landed exactly where he wanted it. The ball then shot up, just missing the batsman's face and going into the hands of his faithful friend Peter, who was the wicket keeper. The batsman was indeed shaken up, and the crowd roared with "Wow!" It was amazing to watch a boy of nearly sixteen years of age propel a ball at such high velocity. James had a smirk on his face. He knew he had unnerved the batsman, and yet, he had some other tricks up his sleeve.

Sir Thomas shouted, "By God, the boy can deliver a ball! Never seen such pace on a young man. I certainly wouldn't want to be on the receiving end of that delivery. The boy is quick. He's going to be a valuable player for the school—that I can assure you." Looking astonished, he asked Phillipa, "Where did he learn to bowl like that?"

"I've no idea," she replied in amazement. "I know Collin spent a lot of time teaching him, and he was a good bowler at prep school. I never really watched him, and like you, I think he looks very intimidating. I might say, I'm very proud of him," she added, realizing that the people around her were recognizing who she was, and she liked it.

James continued to bowl with intensity and ferocity, and the wickets did indeed tumble. By tea time, which was normally at four o'clock, he and his other bowlers had got them all out for 115 runs. James had got six batsmen out, out of a total of ten wickets. They all made their way to the pavilion to munch on their well-earned sandwiches and drink lemonade with their guests from Malvern.

"James, what happens now that you've got them all out?" asked his mother.

"It's our turn to bat, and I think we should be able to make more than 115 runs, and if that's the case, it will be a win for the team." He then asked his mother anxiously, "So what did you think of my bowling, Mother?"

"I'm no expert on the subject, but to me you looked extremely intimidating, and I would be terrified to stand at the other end and face anything being hurtled at me with such intensity," his mother laughed.

"So, it was good?"

"Of course it was good. I had no idea you could bowl like that."

Sir Thomas slapped him on the back and said, "Your father would have been overjoyed to see what an excellent bowler you've become. Keep that up and you'll be playing for the first XI in no time. There's a lot of people here noticing your talent. It won't take long, mark my words."

"Mother, I know it's tea time, so it's okay if you take a break and go back to the hotel. It's going to be a while before I bat, so don't feel you have to stick around."

"Darling, how considerate of you. Yes, I will go, but we'll see you for dinner, I hope. Thomas is trying to get me out for a round of golf tomorrow morning."

"Yes, Mother, but I have to be back here by nine o'clock."

"Thomas will be by later to pick you up."

They said their goodbyes, and James headed off to finish the game with his team.

CHAPTER 7

THE SUMMER HOLIDAYS

School was out, and the term was over. James couldn't wait to take a long, overdue break at Penbroke. Over the next two and a half months, he had a number of exciting things planned, particularly further reading and understanding of his great-grandfather's notebook, which he had safely locked away in his bedroom.

The first thing James did when he arrived at the main house was to go to his bedroom to see that all his things were as he had left them. He immediately went over to his small writing desk to look for the notebook, and to his amazement, he couldn't find it. He wondered where it was. Who would take it? The girls, maybe, but then they knew nothing about the writings. The staff, maybe? There was Rodney, but he would never go into his room. No, it had to be someone with an interest in those notes. He sat there thinking for a while and then started to become very frustrated. Who would want that old book?

Who knew about its existence and would even care to read such an old book without some knowledge of its origin? Then it hit him—his mother!

Now he became even more frustrated, as she was in London, as usual, and he didn't want to alert his mother over the telephone. He would just have to wait until she returned, which he knew would be that upcoming weekend. As angry as he was, he would have to wait until he could get her by herself and then broach the question. She must have gone through his room while he was at school and found the book. But why would she even be interested in it? She had always thought everything to do with the East Wing was a lot of superstitious rubbish. She was the only person that would have guessed that he had hidden the key in his drawer under his old gymkhana trophy that he'd won when he was jumping his pony at a local show.

Then it occurred to James that Claudia might know. At that moment, he heard the gong ring for supper. A snack had been prepared in the small dining room off the main kitchen, and Claudia, as usual, was seeing that he had a good meal before retiring for the evening after completing the long journey home. Becky and Flick were not home yet. They were arriving Friday, so James thought this would be a good moment to ask Claudia. Hungry, he hurried down the main staircase. Claudia had fixed his favorite meal, some fried eggs on top of baked beans on toast and a glass of milk.

"Good evening, James. It's so nice to see you. I bet you're excited to be home for the holidays. I made sure to cook your favorite meal, so no complaints, please."

"Thanks, Claudia, I appreciate it. You don't know how long I've waited for a decent meal like this." James noticed that she was prepared to eat with him, which he liked. She would keep him company, and they could catch up on all the latest news.

Claudia, as usual, had dressed smartly for the little supper they were going to have together, as she was looking forward to talking with James as much as he was. She always took pride in her appearance and liked to appear attractive after her day's work.

"James, tell me all the news. I want to hear about your school and the progress everyone says you're making," she said as she pulled her chair up to the table.

"A lot has happened apart from having a few fistfights, which, I might add, were very necessary. I have excelled in my cricket and will be in first XI next year, which is a great honor, and I managed to get into the A stream. Peter and I have become very good friends, and I'm looking forward to spending some time with his family in Banbury. I found a great little place to hang out in the town of St. Andrews. At least it gives us a break from being on the school campus. It's also a good place to meet some girls!"

"Girls! Be careful, James. Someone in your position will have plenty of opportunity, so go easy. I know some local girls may be attractive, but remember to look for girls with a similar education and background. You wouldn't be the first young man to get himself into trouble." She spoke with an air of protectiveness, and James liked that she cared for his wellbeing.

"Oh, come on. I've got to have some fun. I understand what you're saying, if that's what you're implying."

"I know your mother and Sir Thomas are proud of your progress, and so am I. After all, one day this place will be yours, and you have a lot to look forward to, but it's also a lot of responsibility."

James looked at her, still wondering why someone so attractive hadn't found anyone yet. He felt the urge to ask her about her personal life. "Claudia, how are things for you? Are you all work and no play, or do you have a boyfriend?"

"Me? I don't have anyone in particular. I go to the local pub with friends, and I get chatted up, but I just haven't met anyone in particular. I miss your father's company. Not in a wrong way, mind you; he just had such an understanding of life, and I felt so attached to him that it's taken me some time to get over his passing away, frankly." Claudia realized James was becoming a grown-up to ask such a question. She liked the intrusion, and in a way, felt closer to him for his concern.

James had felt all along she had an attraction to his father, and he didn't mind in the least. He thought they were very suited to each other in spite of the age difference. She continued, "I suppose if I was going to meet someone, I would have to move closer to London or a larger city. I love my work here too much. I would miss you, the family, and all the people on the estate. So for now, I'm content. Someone will come along when the time is right, but for now, I'm happy to be the way I am."

"I'm glad you like it here. I know we'd all be lost without you. If ever you do decide to leave, please give us plenty of warning so we can train someone else." James paused for a moment and then cautiously said, "Claudia, not to change the subject, but something is bothering me a little."

Concerned, Claudia responded, "What is it?"

"I had locked away in my room a notebook that was given to me by my father, and for the life of me, I don't know where it's gone."

"James, the only person I know that would go to your room outside the cleaning staff is your mother, but why she would take a notebook of yours, I don't know." She added with an air of suspicion, "I do know that your mother is worried about the estate, and that the running costs are at the moment above its earnings. Your father had the business acumen to run the estate profitably. The shareholders at the bank won't help. They are saying that the estate must pay its own way or be subsidized by your mother. They think the financial affairs of the estate should be of no concern to the bank. Of course, your mother does have the help of Sir Thomas, but he's unfortunately of the same viewpoint." Claudia started to collect the plates from the meal and then said, "I'm sure your mother will put you in the picture this weekend, as these are things you must now be aware of."

Something was just not adding up for James. He was frustrated that he still didn't know where the notebook could be.

"I'm sorry about your notebook, James, but perhaps you put it somewhere else and forgot."

"Don't worry, it will turn up. I'm sure there's an explanation." James knew full well where he had left the book. He just couldn't figure out why his mother would want a notebook she believed was complete rubbish.

****

His mother arrived with Sir Thomas unexpectedly on Saturday. His sisters, who had arrived on schedule the day before, were in the kitchen preparing a meal for the whole family. Everyone would be present, and the family could exchange all the news from their respective schools and plans for the summer. Becky was excited about her new school, as she had passed her exam to Benenden, a leading girls' school, and Flick was excited because she would soon follow in her footsteps and they would be together. The girls had spent most of their days at the same school. They got on well, and with the passing of James's father, it was seen as a positive sign.

The dinner gong sounded, and everyone was dressed for the occasion. Becky had grown a lot taller. She was now fourteen and was starting to have the appearance of a young woman. Flick, well, she was still young. Becky wore a chiffon purple dress with a hint of makeup and a wafting scent. James could tell she was already very aware of the opposite sex. His mother and Sir Thomas entered the room together, having enjoyed a quiet cocktail before the meal.

"It's wonderful to see you all," said his mother, appearing a little apprehensive that the children and the staff were noticing that she and Sir Thomas were on quite intimate terms. "I have some wonderful news to share with you all. Sir Thomas and I are thinking about getting engaged. I would like for all of you to receive him as a person your mother truly admires and who has the very best interests of this family at heart."

They were all silent. James had figured this was inevitable. His sisters looked quite taken aback and weren't at all sure of how to receive a man after their own father had not been long departed.

Sir Thomas then began, "Children, although two of you are approaching adult age, you have not known me for long, and due to the very close relationship I enjoyed with your father, I realize this may come as a bit of a shock. But your mother and I have known each other ever since your father and mother got married. As you know, your father and I were at school together, and I know that he would only want the very best for her and all of you. I can assure you that I will do everything in my power to carry on where your father left off. It will take time for all of us to get to know each other, but I am anxious to do that and hope you will receive me in the same way." Sir Thomas took Phillipa's hand in an act of consolation, and she complimented his kind words with a smile.

The room now had a harsh silence, and then Flick burst into tears, got up from the table, and ran out. Becky, in an effort to comfort her, followed, after the nodding approval of her mother. They both knew the news would not be taken easily at first, but life had to go on.

"James, how do you feel about this?" asked Sir Thomas, looking very concerned.

"Sir Thomas, I did have a chance to know you better at the time you came to my cricket match for the weekend, and frankly, the fact that you were my father's friend and make my mother happy is enough for me. What's happened has happened, and we all have to move on and make the best of the life in front of us." He knew his mother well enough by now to know that nothing was going to change her direction, so he needed to play her game in the best interests of his future.

His mother left the room, and within ten minutes, everyone was back at the table. During that time, Sir Thomas and James talked further, and James picked up enough of a hint about the state of the farm's finances to confirm what Claudia had told him.

This was the first time he saw his mother openly hugging and kissing the girls. It was good that she was giving them reassurance, and although neither had much to say for the rest of the meal, James was glad that they at least had the good manners to see the meal through. After an enjoyable roast beef dinner, with apple pie and ice cream, James was happy to leave the table. Then his mother and Sir Thomas invited him into the drawing room for a further discussion. *Here we go*, he thought. The girls were allowed to leave and unpack their cases in their rooms.

Coffee was brought to the living room along with a bottle of Sir Thomas's favorite malt whisky. His mother finished off her champagne, and James was invited to have a beer. He accepted with delight, having sneaked one or two before with his schoolmates.

His mother began, "James, I know you are about to start your school holidays, but as your guardian, I must bring you up to date on the affairs of this estate. Then you can focus on spending some time off from school and enjoy your summer as you should."

James looked at her with interest, half knowing what she was going to say. "You see, the farm just doesn't pay its way. Since your father passed on, it's been very difficult for Claudia. The farm manager has had a tough time filling his shoes. He does not have your father's experience in the business sense and is not equipped to deal with the finances in the same way your father was able to do. So, Sir Thomas and I have come up with what we believe to be a plausible solution for putting the farm back on its feet again. Although Sir Thomas is your guardian in respect of the investments you have at the bank, I too am your guardian when it comes to the affairs of the estate."

"Well, Mother, what's your plan?"

"I know you won't like this, but I want to sell all the artifacts in the East Wing. Those artifacts are priceless and would refurbish a lot of those old run-down cottages on the estate, which in turn would bring a good rental income to support the farm."

"Mother, I know you have little or no interest in those artifacts, but the simple fact is, I do."

"Then what's your solution?" asked his mother, becoming angry. She had to have known this wouldn't be easy, but she wasn't about to put one penny of her own money into trying to preserve the estate, and James knew that.

James pondered for a moment and then said, "What if we opened up the East Wing for viewing to the public? Those artifacts could never be found again. Any price we could get would never be enough. They belong to this family. They were given to us, and we must do everything to respect and preserve that tradition."

"Thomas, how would we raise the money to improve the farm cottages then?" She struggled to contain her frustration.

"James has a point. I'm sure I could talk to the bank and our shareholders. They would have to take a lien through the bank on the value of the assets in the East Wing, and I'm sure with a good business plan, we could raise enough money to refurbish the East Wing. The income we could derive from this would renovate the cottages and should more than support the loan," said Sir Thomas. He leaned back into the sofa, smoking his long cigar and taking another good belt of his malt whisky.

With enthusiasm, James said, "We need to find someone who truly loves the work that the Seventh Earl did on his voyages to the Far East . . . his writings, his notes . . . this could be a spectacular museum. People, I know, would be interested in those historical pieces. If people line up at the Tower of London to see the crown jewels, why would they not come to Lincolnshire to see what we have here?"

"Good point, James, but we would need car parks and a whole staff. Big ideas take plans and money. However, the idea has merit, and I for one am extremely interested." Sir Thomas paused, seeing the possibilities. "If we sell and market this possibility, it could be a huge revenue producer for the estate. After all, if you sold the artifacts, what would you do with such a vast building as the East Wing?" he asked, turning to Phillipa.

"I don't know. Sounds like a flash in the pan. The thought of all those people coming to this private estate doesn't excite me in the least, but if it can be put together and it can save the downward spiral of income for the estate, I can live with it," she concluded, then got up to leave the room.

"Mother, before you go, I have a question for you," James said, having waited the whole evening for this moment.

"Yes, what is it?"

"In my room, I had a notebook from the Seventh Earl given to me by Father, and I notice it's not there anymore."

Sheepishly, she replied, "James, yes, I have it. I just wanted to know after that day you spent with your father what actually happened on your visit to the East Wing, and as no one cared to discuss the matter, I took it upon myself to conduct my own research. Rodney told me nothing, just saying you both spent time alone discussing the situation, and he did remember you left the room with a notebook. So I was curious and thought that I had a right to see what the content of that notebook held."

"Mother, why couldn't you have asked?"

"Because I know your father had told you not to tell anyone, least of all me."

"I don't think it gave you the right to search through my things and just take it."

"I am your mother, your guardian, and I have every right to know what's going on. I don't want you to be distracted with all this nonsense when you have school and an important future in front of you." She felt it was her duty to know what her children were up to, even if it meant crossing the line of privacy. She knew Collin would never tell her, and in spite of the fact that she felt underhanded, she stood firmly by her decision.

"Can I have the book back? It's very important to me and the history behind those artifacts."

"Precisely, and that is why I have found potential buyers who I have allowed to review the book in order to make some sense of it."

James seethed. "Mother, what if they copy the book? That book is special. I can't believe you would allow anyone to take that book away from this house. Father would have been furious!"

"Don't you lecture me, young man! I am your mother, and I'm going to do what I feel is right. You have no right to talk to me this way."

"Mother, if that book is lost, I cannot tell you the damage that could be done. That book is an integral part of all those artifacts and clearly depicts the entire journey and collection."

"The book is in good hands, and I would never allow such a thing to happen. It's time you made your way to bed. We will discuss this matter further tomorrow morning." With that, she left the room, leaving Sir Thomas and James staring at each other.

"James, hold on a moment. Have another beer and let's talk further on the matter."

"Okay." James, knowing how his mother could be, decided to listen to what Sir Thomas had to say.

"First, I am fully aware of the notebook. I can also assure you that there is no way that I would allow your mother to give out this old document without good reason. Whether it had grounds for being valid or invalid, I have signatures, agreements, and all the necessary legal documentation. Registrations had to be made to ensure the true ownership of the notebook and its heritage."

"Well, that's a relief, but what's to stop them copying the book?"

"Technically, they could, but they could not publish it without legal action and grave consequences. I admit there is a risk, but this is a highly reputable firm, and they would not want to tarnish their image by doing anything that would be seen as devious and untrustworthy by the public. Frankly, the book is of little value without the artifacts to go with it. People would think it would be either a forgery or the ramblings of an eccentric old man. Anyone could make up the future after knowing the history we have now lived through. Believe me, a lot of thought has gone into this before allowing this outcome, and in addition, we have a third party involved because the notebook has to be validated for its age and authenticity. That being said, it's again of little use without the artifacts."

"That's good to know. I didn't realize that you were aware of my mother's actions, so this does place a different light on the matter. It only makes sense that she would involve you. I can at least respect her business and legal thoughts in the matter."

"James, what I would like to do tomorrow, if you would take the time, is to see the East Wing. Then I could have a better grasp of what your and your mother's perspectives are."

"Absolutely. I would be delighted to show you. I'll have Rodney called first thing in the morning, and after breakfast, we can take a look."

"Let's make an early start and try to be at the East Wing by nine, as I have to be back in London to see a client tomorrow afternoon." They both then got up to retire for the evening.

****

Rodney led the way down the long corridor to the East Wing, sounding like a jailor with his various keys. Sir Thomas was amazed at the intricacies needed to get into the room. "Whoever set this building up made sure no one without special authority would be allowed in here. I've never seen a vertical doorway of such magnitude on the opening to a ballroom." Once the vertical door had been opened, they entered the entryway to the second double-oak door with the enormous lock.

"Wow! I can't think of another museum room that could have such an impact on first impressions," said Sir Thomas, surprised at all he was seeing.

"This is truly a place for people to visit. The pottery and stone carvings with their detailed write-ups and the weapons used by various cultures in Africa and the Far East are truly collectors' items, not to speak of the clothing that has been preserved from different tribes. It gives an indication as to the climatic conditions and the necessities needed for their survival. It would take a lot more time than I've got today to fully process all the information here." It was clear that Sir Thomas had walked into a room way beyond anything he had imagined. James was excited by his reaction and the discerning way in which he observed every detail of the room.

"James, let's study the throne and fountain under the glass dome because that seems to be the highlight that the Earl had intended for people to appreciate. This throne has to have some significance. Do you have any idea of what that might be?"

"It is my belief that the throne signifies something divine and spiritual. The colored gemstones represent the seven chakras—"

Sir Thomas butted in, "Please explain that. I've read something about it but never really gave it much attention."

"The first chakra that you see at the base of the seat is red, and that is a ruby. From what I've read, this first chakra is associated with the body and the wellbeing of our body. The second chakra, which is orange to brown in color, is a garnet and centers itself around the belly button, as it is called. It is supposed to give us that gut feeling when we are faced with challenges or decisions. The third chakra is yellow, a topaz, and is centered just below the stomach. Its energy helps with the secretion of our digestive juices for digestion and also gives us that butterfly feeling when we are excited or nervous about something. The fourth chakra is located at the center where the heart is, and its color is green, an emerald. It gives us our feelings and the energy to balance the emotional issues of life. The fifth chakra is in the area of the throat. It's blue, a sapphire, and helps give us energy for the spoken word and our ability to communicate with our fellow man. The sixth chakra is in a place that many ancient tribes and monks of different religions believed to be where our third eye exists, and that is what science today refers to as the pineal gland. It's called the third eye, as its location is right between our two eyes above the nose. The stone here is the amethyst and is associated with our intuitions and the ability to develop a higher level of awareness that is present in all of us but not always used. It's a gland that gives us the ability to see beyond, but like all things, we must utilize what we have. It's like learning math; it takes time and effort to develop all these various feelings and understandings."

"And the last stone, James, what does it tell us?"

"Oh, yes, of course. It is the most important chakra of all and is located, as you can see, at the top of the head. Here you see a beautifully cut crystal ball within the crown, which symbolizes our connection with the spiritual power that is within us. This is used when we pray, when we try to connect to our angels for guidance and advice on our journey of life." James was extremely careful not to imply any information that would lead Sir Thomas to believe he was in the slightest way influenced by the writings of the Seventh Earl.

"Amazing that you know all this. I do believe I've had an education from a young man much advanced for his years."

"What actually resonates to my observation when I look at the way the angels hold the crown of jewels above the head is the positioning of the crown. In this placement, it combines all the energies of the stones into a final culmination of spiritual energy to the head, and therefore, is transmitted to the whole body. Of course, in the symbolic sense."

"I have never seen an ornament like this, let alone a throne. It's positioning beneath the glass dome is quite unique. This spectacular fountain has to speak to an intense belief the Seventh Earl must have had. What's your read on that?"

"Absolutely, and the fact that the crown is held by angels on each side and not connected to the throne sends a message for all generations. The very positioning of these artifacts in the physical sense somehow connects with the divine."

"I can see that. Well said, well said."

At that moment, Rodney returned and asked them if they were ready to leave. "I think so, don't you, James?" Sir Thomas replied.

As Rodney closed up the room, Sir Thomas had question after question, such as who cleaned the room, who took care of all the pieces, and so on. James told him Rodney had always been in charge, and he was the only person entrusted with all that lay within those walls.

"I could see that the room was a fine ballroom once, but in today's world, unless you're entertaining dignitaries from around the world, a room that size is hardly necessary. Selling these artifacts would just leave a vast empty room only good for conventions or weddings. The room, with some refurbishment to the interior, could make a spectacular museum, and with the right curator, people would come to see this display from far away. I think the potential is enormous." Sir Thomas was quite convinced yet completely dumbfounded. "Never thought I would ever see a room like that. Has your mother seen it?"

"She must have, but being a pragmatist about life, I don't feel she appreciated what Father saw in it."

"Well, when the people come to visit such an exposition, she will realize the validity. That room will more than pay the bills for this farm; I'm certain of it."

Sir Thomas was full of energy as he made his way back to the drawing room. James's mother was reading the morning paper, and Sir Thomas couldn't wait to give her his opinion.

"Thomas, my dear, did James take up too much of your time looking at all those relics?" she said as a foregone conclusion.

"Not in the least. That room is nothing short of spectacular!" he said with conviction.

"You're kidding. The place needs fumigating, if you want my opinion. It gives me the creeps."

"No, I believe with a good business plan, that room can make this farm some very good revenue. Of course, it will require the service of an experienced curator, and with a little imagination, James's heritage can be turned into something very special and be of great interest to the public at large." He sat down on the sofa beside her.

"That will cost money—money we don't have. How are we going to renovate those cottages and do all that as well? The time and effort this is all going to take—Claudia has enough on her plate trying to make ends meet here with the farm," she said candidly, a little disappointed that Sir Thomas would even entertain the possibility of reviving the room.

"That is why I would like to pass by the farm office on the way out, with your permission, of course, and catch this woman who seems to run everything and get her viewpoint."

"Run everything? I think not. Without my constant direction, she would have a hard time."

"I was joking, Phillipa. Of course she looks up to you and rightfully so, in spite of your differences, but I need to know a few things if the bank is going to take a serious look at this possibility."

"All that's behind us now, but please don't let's get off on a wild goose chase trying to resurrect Collin and James's dream."

"No, of course not. Let's just review the possibilities, okay?"

"I suppose so. No harm in it. If you're going to see her, you better rush. The farm office closes at noon on Saturdays."

"Then I must be off. I have a four o'clock appointment with a client in London. So, see you tomorrow night in the city?"

"Yes, and thank you, Thomas, for taking the time. Sorry about last night. The kids will come around. I think it was all a bit of a shock, don't you?"

"Yes, dear. See you tomorrow."

He jumped into his Bentley and hastily made his way down to the farm office. The building was located in the lower part of the estate, where the good grazing existed for the dairy farm. This was the center for most of the administrative work on the estate. He quickly jumped out of his car and rushed in the front door, finding that the staff had already left. Seeing the staircase, he assumed that there may be people working on the second floor. He climbed up, and there, to his amazement, was only one person working in the office at one end opposite another office, which he assumed must have been Collin's at one time.

"Hello. I hope I'm not imposing. You must be Claudia."

"Guilty as charged. And what can I do for you, kind sir?"

"I am Sir Thomas Ringstone. I wanted to pop by and take a little of your time to discuss the business of the farm. I realize this is late in the day, so if you would prefer I came back another time, I would be happy to do so." He was testing her out to see just how dedicated she was.

She immediately stood up from her chair and said, "So, I get to meet the famous Sir Thomas. I am here to help you with whatever you need, sir." She eyed him up and down very seriously, giving him a slightly flirtatious look. She liked the way this man presented himself with such polite consideration. She had become so used to dealing with matters of the farm that

THE RISE TO POWER

she'd almost forgotten what it was like to be in the company of such a good-looking and well-mannered person. Their eyes met for a brief moment, and anyone present could definitely feel a measure of energy passing between the two of them.

"Claudia, I know you have been faced with the financial burden of the estate, and I know you're looking at various options to turn things around."

"Yes, sir. It's not an easy task. We have forty-two cottages that need renovation for potential lease, but that's going to take investment. There was a time, I'm sure you would know, when farm hands lived in all these cottages, but with the advancement of machinery, the number of staff has dropped. The capital investment needed now well exceeds our cash flow. The marketplace is more competitive, and foreign imports are lowering prices."

"I totally understand, Claudia. I have today visited the East Wing with James, and frankly, I see potential there."

"How?" she asked curiously, fascinated by his apparent enthusiasm.

"Those artifacts are worth a fortune!"

"I know the Countess wants to sell them, but to me, that seems like a short-term solution to a longer-term problem."

"Precisely. But if we can renovate the room and open it up to the public, there's no telling how much revenue could be earned."

"But that takes money, which is something we don't have."

"Quite true. You have a background, or I believe more correctly, a degree in business administration, so let's work up a cash flow projection of what we believe we could earn on this venture. I in turn will try to convince the bank to loan money against the phenomenal value of those assets after an appraisal has been made of the room."

"Sir Thomas, I like your idea, but I don't have a clue what kind of revenue we could expect from this venture."

"I understand. So I will collect all the necessary people to help you with these estimates so you can do what you do best, and that's produce the numbers."

"You are the last person I would expect to see on a Saturday offering to solve all my worries." She was filled with appreciation and warmth. "Can I get you a cup of coffee? It's so impolite of me not to have asked you before."

He thought about it, knowing he needed to leave, and then said, "Do you know a good pub around here where we can have a quick drink? You see, I must be back in London by 4:00 p.m."

"Yes, follow me in your car, and then you can be on your way."

"First class. Let's go."

Claudia felt as though this intruder had swept her off her feet, and she wasn't going to miss a beat from this man of action. They walked through the threshold of the old pub she picked, which would put him in good stead to catch the right motorway to London.

"I shall have a pint of lager. What will you have, Claudia?"

"I'll have a glass of chardonnay."

"It's so much better having a little chat outside the office, don't you think? I've heard so many wonderful things about you, Claudia, and judging from His Lordship's will, he obviously held you in high esteem."

She blushed at the inference, then regained her composure to say, "His Lordship was a great inspiration to my life, and I must say, I enjoyed every day I worked alongside him."

"So what does your husband do? Does he work close by, or does he have to commute?"

"Oh, I'm not married, sir. My boyfriend met with a motorcycle accident four years ago. We were at Cambridge together, and we planned to get enough money saved so that we could get married. It wasn't to be. Soon after I applied for this job, His Lordship helped heal me from the devastating loss I felt for my partner. I can honestly say His Lordship is one of the finest men I've ever met. He was never improper or incorrect, but there were times when he gave me a little heartfelt affection, and it was so appreciated."

"That was Collin—always taking care of the damsel in distress. He had such a big heart."

She began talking again, and Sir Thomas took a serious look at her, becoming more and more enamored. She had a beautiful face, he thought, with soulful, kind eyes and a classy femininity that made her look so out of place on a country estate. He realized he was talking with a highly educated, beautiful woman who could get a job working anywhere. She must have been really in love with that boyfriend, and this job had helped to heal her.

They got to know each other better, and Claudia was excited at the prospect of working with a man like Sir Thomas, full of energy and good, logical conversation. She then began to wonder why he too wasn't married, which she knew from the Countess. Of course, she had no clue that the evening before, the Countess and Sir Thomas had announced to the children their plans to become engaged.

CHAPTER 8

THE ART OF SPORT

James, about to begin a new adventure, headed to the town of Banbury to meet up with Peter. He'd packed all his stuff quickly and couldn't wait to race in a go-kart at Peter's father's track. The drive from Lincoln was tolerable—about two and a half hours—and he arrived just after lunch. As Rodney drove up the long driveway to Peter's house, James noted that, by Penbroke standards, Peter's was a modest home, but it was a typical English country manor house that spoke of its Tudor heritage and looked warm and inviting in its natural surroundings. Particularly noticeable were the beautiful gardens that surrounded the courtyard on the entrance to the house.

Peter was eagerly watching from his front sitting room for James's arrival. As they pulled up, Peter ran out of the house to give James a warm welcome. James was surprised to see that Peter's sister was also there to meet and greet him. Peter gushed, "James, it's so good to see you. We've been looking forward to your arrival. We can't wait to get you out on the track to have fun with the karts. This is my elder sister, Kate, who, let me tell you, drives like a bat out of hell. It's all I can do to keep up with her."

James eyed her up and down. He thought, *A woman who likes to race karts? That's a first.* He continued to assess the lanky girl, whom he knew to be seventeen. *She's not bad-looking, but with that riding suit on, she looks like a real tomboy.* "Nice to meet you," he told Kate.

James and Peter got the luggage out of the car, and Rodney departed. Peter said, "Let me show you to the guest room." They climbed up the carved oak staircase and along the creaky floorboards to a large room that overlooked a beautifully manicured lawn and rose garden.

James thought that the house had character and warmth, and he felt immediately welcome. "Peter, many thanks for the invite. I'm really looking forward to this. As for your sister, if she's that good, we better set up a strategy to beat her, don't you think?"

"Sounds like the James I know; but first, let's see how you do behind the wheel. Don't worry about a suit and helmet and all that stuff. We'll set you up."

"Okay. Give me a minute to unpack, and I'll be down." James was a little apprehensive about the prospect of Kate making him look bad; with his competitive nature, he hated to lose.

James came downstairs a short time later, and the three of them walked outside and through the back garden to the track. "Wow, this is awesome!" James exclaimed as he looked at the track layout. The track wasn't like the kind of racetrack at a real racecourse but was a private road course about a mile and a half long. It had been made from an old, disused airport that Peter's father had bought when he moved his business from Birmingham. James remembered Peter telling him that his father had decided to buy the three hundred-acre farm, where he had sufficient buildings to house his machines and do the development work on car bodies for the up-and-coming world of Formula One. The track made a perfect testing site and created the opportunity for his children to enjoy the sport of motor racing; Peter's entire family was avid followers.

"Let's make our way over to the building on the other side where the karts are. There we can get suited up." Peter was looking forward to showing James something he felt he was good at. James had more than shown his prowess in enough activities at Sterling; Peter felt it was his turn. As they walked, Peter explained, "The karts are not your average go-karts. These karts are capable of speeds of over sixty miles per hour, and they are close to the ground, so you're going to feel everything. Do you know what the racing line is on a race track?"

"I don't have clue what you're talking about." James's heart started to beat a little faster as the reality of taking a hot rod on the track for the first time was starting to get through to him.

"Well, let's get suited up, and before we put our helmets on, I'll explain what we will do." They suited up, then Peter said, "Follow me for the first few laps, then I'll wave you on and will follow you. This way, you'll get the rhythm of the driving line and learn all the breaking points and the time to accelerate. I'll go slowly at first, and let's see how you do, okay?"

Peter then turned to his sister. "Kate, you go on ahead, but give James a chance, okay?" He knew his sister. Having grown up in a guy's world, she was fiercely competitive.

James could clearly see that eye-of-the-tiger look as she courteously smiled at him. She hadn't done much talking so far, and that had unnerved James a little.

Peter fired up the karts for the both of them. After they had their helmets on, Peter led off out of the garage onto the pit lane to the track entrance. By now, James's heart was beating so fast that he could hear it thumping in his eardrums. He followed Peter through the first lap and started to get the hang of the apexes and the point of accelerating on exit. The karts had so much pep that he found it easy to overshoot when a second corner came up quickly, and then he would lose his rhythm. He would slowly catch back up to Peter and try again. James found the direct steering of the kart very precise, and on the sharp corners, it was quite a workout to keep the kart on the track.

This is not as easy as it looks, he thought. At that moment, Kate went flying past him like he was standing still, which embarrassed him further. Slowly, lap after lap, James began to learn the track and pace himself. *Learn the track first,* he told himself, *and then get faster.* Peter now waved him on ahead, and for the first time, he was in front. This was quite different; he felt for a moment as if he had forgotten all he had learned. His pace slowed, but then, bit by bit, he started to get his confidence back. With every lap, he began to remember the track in its entirety, and his pace started to pick up. After a few more laps, they all pitted in. Stopping in the pit lane, they got out to share their experiences.

"You're doing great! You're learning the track, and that's the most important thing. Now I'm going to let you loose, so just do your own thing. You've got the basics; keep up the rhythm and your speed will increase. First, let me put some more petrol in the kart. I don't want you to get stuck out there," said Peter.

As Peter ran off to get the petrol, Kate came up to talk. "James, we all started just like you, so don't feel you have to be the best on the first day. Learn the track—that's number one—and after that, have fun." She smiled at him teasingly as she went back to her kart.

James was intrigued. He liked the challenge of a woman who had self-confidence.

James went out again on his own and overshot his first three corners. He thought, *Calm yourself. This is not a race. Forget about everyone else and concentrate on every corner.* After several more laps, James was getting maxed out, but he was getting faster and faster. Although he was still far from having Peter and Kate's abilities, both of whom kept passing him lap after lap, he knew he was beginning to improve, and in a few days, or perhaps by the end of the week, he could at least give them a run for their money.

Exhausted, the three of them headed back to the house to take a bath and prepare for supper. As they walked, James said, "That's a blast, Peter, but I'm sure I'm going to feel it tomorrow. My arms are aching like hell, and my ass feels like it's numb. So are the tops of my legs. Who would guess that sitting behind the wheel would be considered exercise?"

Peter joked, "Well, that's our strategy—wear you out on the first day, and after all the kind words of encouragement, we take off the gloves on the next day!"

"Better not. I'll get you in the end, and that's a promise. I just hope it's by the end of this week and not next year," retorted James sportingly.

"Let's meet down here in the lobby sitting room for a lemonade shandy or something around six thirty, and you can meet the rest of the family before supper."

"Sounds good," James replied as he headed to his room. As soon as he closed the bedroom door and jumped on the bed, he fell sound asleep.

A while later, James suddenly awoke and shot up from the bed, wondering where he was. Then he remembered he was at Peter's home. He panicked as he wondered what time it was. He grabbed his watch from the bedside table and saw it was six thirty-five. He was late. He took a quick bath, shaved, put on his best trousers and a clean shirt, combed his hair, and then ran down the hallway to meet the family downstairs. As he descended the staircase, he could hear them all laughing.

"Caught you napping! Just can't take all the excitement, huh?" Peter teased.

"My God, it's almost seven. I'm so sorry! You guys really knocked me out."

"You're here to relax and have fun, so think nothing of it. Here's a lemonade shandy to bring you back to the real world," said Peter, still laughing.

James looked around the room and noticed that Kate looked quite different. She was wearing a low-cut summer dress with high heels and had on more makeup and a waft of perfume. This made him feel more embarrassed.

"Well, James, you're usually in control, so it's good to see you off balance for a change." Peter was enjoying the half-dazed look on his friend's face. "Time for introductions. This is my father, Victor Lloyd."

"Pleased to meet you, sir. You have an amazing place here."

"And this is my mother, Sarah Lloyd. She's the one who keeps us all in order."

Peter's mother said, "We are so happy to have you with us and to get to know you better. We certainly enjoyed watching you play cricket. You're an up-and-coming talent, I do believe. Don't you, darling?" she asked, turning to her husband.

"No doubt about it! I certainly wouldn't want to be on the receiving end of one of your balls being thrown at that pace," replied Victor with marked enthusiasm.

Mrs. Lloyd asked, "So, James, how does it feel after your first experience with the kart?"

"It's quite a challenge. When you watch people from the sideline, you never appreciate the effort and skill needed to push that kart to the limit. Learning the track is one thing, but driving the kart to experience the amazing traction you can have through a corner is another."

"Quite true," replied Mrs. Lloyd. "Well, let's all go to the dining room and get something to eat. I'm sure you are all starving."

They filed into the dining room. Mr. Lloyd sat at the head of the table while Kate and Mrs. Lloyd sat on one side and Peter and James sat on the other. It was clear that Mrs. Lloyd had gone to a lot of trouble to prepare a first-class meal. Her staff was very attentive to all their needs during this special occasion.

Suddenly, Kate asked, "James, I want to know what it's like to be born a lord."

Modestly, James replied, "Well, for me, I'm the same as anyone else—not better, not worse."

"Yes, I know that, but all the heritage you have to live up to—is that not a stress? People knowing who you are wherever you go? With all the attention, can you ever be your real self?"

James had definitely underestimated Kate. She had a boldness and frankness that he wasn't used to from a young woman. He replied, "I believe being yourself and being natural is important. Yes, I do have the responsibility to live up to a heritage, but I'm just a human being like anyone else. My father was my mentor, and he taught me a lot. That's why he sent me to Sterling—so that I would be treated like everyone else. Eton or Harrow is normally where well-known people of position tend to go."

"I like that. From the first time I saw you today, I noticed how well you get along with Peter, and actually, how easy you are to talk to. My experience is that people from privileged backgrounds somehow expect more of others."

"I hope you always know me as such a person. And now, if it's okay, I have a question of my own." James turned to Mr. Lloyd. "Mr. Lloyd, sir, please enlighten me about your business. Peter said you are into precision machining sheet-metal bodies that are aerodynamically designed for race cars, and so on. How did you get started?"

"It's a long story. I was a race car driver, and having grown up in my father's small machine shop, I learned the practical skills for machining that I have today. In his shop, I learned to read blueprints and design sheet metal parts for the aerospace industry, and so, with my passion for motor racing, I started to develop designs that I believed would be very helpful to the sport. Between all those skills, I earned enough money to move our small shop ten years ago from Birmingham to where we are now, and the business has continued to grow ever since we came here. You may or may not know that the Silverstone Race Track is not far from here, and I do a lot of testing there, also. There are going to be some big changes in design. Next year, Formula One engines will start going to the rear of the car, as opposed to the front-end engines we've had during the fifties."

"Fascinating. Would you or one of your staff show me around your shop tomorrow?" asked James, intrigued. He had never seen a real manufacturing shop in action.

"I would be delighted to give you a tour and answer any questions you may have."

"Thank you, sir."

They were now well into the second course of roast lamb. James, with a curious interest in Peter's mother, turned to her and asked, "Mrs. Lloyd, I know nothing about you, but I somehow feel you do something very different, and I believe it's something you're good at." Peter rolled his eyes. James knew he had struck a chord and was now even more curious.

"Well, James, I am a writer. You may have seen my name on a book in a bookstore."

"A writer? No, I don't know a Sarah Lloyd who is a writer."

"My pen name is Sarah McKenzie. I go by my maiden name."

"Oh, yes! I absolutely know your name. You are a well-acclaimed psychic. Your work is fascinating, and I think that you have an amazing ability." James was stunned. He had no idea Peter had a famous mother.

"So you believe in those things and have an interest in our planet and that which lies beyond?"

"I absolutely do, and after your husband has shown me his business, I would humbly ask to have a moment of time with you, because I have some exciting things to discuss."

"I thought you had something to say. I will enjoy the visit. We have a date for tomorrow afternoon. That's when I'll be free."

Peter spoke up. "James, you are the last person I would ever have believed would have any interest in that stuff. You always amaze me."

Mr. Lloyd then said, "I can see we all have a lot in common, so let's finish up with supper and have a last drink on the patio with a good coffee, and I for one am going to smoke my cigar." He was delighted that James had received his wife with such openness and looked forward to the ongoing relationship. He too valued and admired his wife's abilities and the times that she had been helpful to him in his ideas and work.

****

James was up early the next morning. He knew that Peter and Kate would sleep in, but he also knew that Mr. Lloyd would be on the job early, and he wanted to learn all he could about manufacturing in what he thought to be a highly skilled area and an integral part of the future. He met Mr. Lloyd in the kitchen as he was busy making the coffee and toast for a quick breakfast.

"Up at seven? I'm impressed, James. You could have come over later."

"My father was an early riser, and when he had something to explain, he expected me to be available at the crack of dawn, so nothing better than starting the day ahead of the workforce."

"I always like this time of the morning because I can think and plan my day. The shop starts at eight, but I wander over around seven thirty, and then, some of my senior staff come in and it gives us a chance to get the day set off on the right foot. I used to do this at the end of the day, but now I do it earlier, because everyone is fresh. Also, while the family is home, it gives me more time to spend with them."

After coffee and toast, they strolled across the courtyard, got into Mr. Lloyd's Land Rover, and then drove over to the workshop buildings that were on the far side of the racetrack. The machine shop was about fifty thousand square feet.

James was interested in hearing about Mr. Lloyd's innovations that he was implementing to increase his output on aerospace components. Mr. Lloyd continued to explain all the intricate details carried out in his machine shop as he and James walked slowly around the building. James was amazed at the speed of the cutters on the router heads as they churned out chips of aluminum in massive amounts within seconds. They examined the overhead templates so that James could understand the process and the cutters, which were all made in-house in their own grinding shop.

"But if the cutters were unbalanced, there would be terrific vibration in the head. Would that not affect the quality of the machining?" asked James.

"Good observation. Every cutter is balanced just like a car wheel before leaving the cutter grinding shop, so when the cutter is put to use, it's able to cut the aluminum just like butter! And more important than that, we want all the heat of cutting that metal to go out in the chip and not be transmitted to the part, which would create distortion."

James and Mr. Lloyd spent at least two hours walking the shop floor talking to various operators and chatting about the newly implemented process for metal cutting. James saw this as the future, and having been well educated by his father to be always on the lookout for new businesses and methods of production, James could see the long-term potential Mr. Lloyd and his company had.

They returned to Mr. Lloyd's office, where they both enjoyed another cup of coffee, and Mr. Lloyd continued to answer James's questions. After a few minutes, Peter came in. "Good morning, Dad. So, James and you have done the royal tour?"

"Not quite. I've yet to show James the body shop where we do our sheet metal work. Perhaps you can do that?"

James, realizing that phone calls were piling up and Mr.

Lloyd needed to attend to business said, "Thank you, sir, I really enjoyed the tour. I think you're building a method of production that is going to really make a mark in the aviation industry."

Peter and James went over to the body shop on the other side of the concrete yard facing the machine shop. There were lines of cars on jacks being ground and polished with hand wheels for the paint shop. "The machine shop bores me," said Peter. "This is where the action is for me. Here we make prototype bodies for various manufacturers for Formula One and the Le Mans Series. These are very skilled people, and a lot of the work is done by hand."

James could see where the smallest parts were worked in pyramid rollers and then hand-worked, cut, and welded. It was like watching a bespoke tailor at work on a suit but with a much more resistant material. It was poetry to see how these artisans could produce such an incredible product. When Peter showed him the work the paint shop did at the finish, he could only drool at the end product. "Amazing! Truly amazing. It's so stimulating to see people in production producing such fantastic parts. I bet a shop like this takes some close management."

"You bet. It's taken Dad nearly twenty years to get to this size. It didn't happen overnight, that's for sure."

"What's so great is that you can get up in the morning, walk over here, and learn the business right under your nose. If you're not an expert by the time you're twenty-five, I'll be on your case."

Peter teased, "Big warning from His Lordship. I better behave myself."

They made their way back to the house, as lunch would be ready, and James knew that he would be meeting with Peter's mother after lunch. As they walked back, Peter said, "Last night, I thought you were going to think my mother was another one of those fruitcakes out there whom only the gullible believe in. I was shocked that you knew about her, and more than that, you believe some of this stuff. Is that true, or were you just being polite?"

"I truly believe in what your mother has to say. I can't wait to meet with her this afternoon. I have had some experiences of my own, and I am aware of something else. It's a long story; I'll fill you in some time, but only if you have an appreciation for this type of knowledge."

"I admit my mother has had some amazing insights. When Dad was starting out, if it wasn't for the money she made from her writing, I doubt that he could have afforded the equipment we have today. Building a business is risky, and a lot of good people go under, as I am sure you know. But to answer your question, I do, but I fear public opinion, especially being at a school like ours. It's the last thing I want to walk around talking about. Who wants to be thought of as a freak?"

"Yes, you've got a point, but believing and understanding something doesn't have to be shared. Use the insight to help others and they look upon it as wisdom, being wise, and so on. Just get the best out of it, and keep your personal feelings to yourself."

"I like that. Good advice."

Mrs. Lloyd had prepared a light lunch in the nook next to the kitchen. They all busily chatted about the events of the morning, and after having a delicious key lime pie for desert, Mrs. Lloyd asked James to follow her to her study.

Peter said, "Beware!" and then marched off laughing.

Mrs. Lloyd's private study was not at all intimidating. She sat down at a round table next to her desk and asked James to take a seat. She had incense burning on her desk, saying that it gave the environment more of a relaxed feeling. The study was at the far end of the house, where everything was very quiet. The room looked like a miniature library with all her books and awards lining the shelves along with many other books from authors she admired.

"So, James, are you ready to have a reading?" she asked calmly and soothingly. "Think of all the things that you have questions about, and meditate on those for the next few minutes. I will get you a nice cup of herbal tea which will help to relax you, and then you can get the most out of what I will be telling you." She left James there to think while she quietly went to fetch the tea.

When she returned with their tea, she sat down and asked to take his hands into hers. She held his hands for what seemed like an eternity to James but was actually only a few minutes. It was natural that he was slightly apprehensive when she started. "We see you back on Atlantis, the age before this age. Are you aware of Atlantis?"

"Yes, absolutely," he replied.

"You could have left, but you didn't. Do you know why?"

"I wanted to somehow avert disaster but couldn't."

"Yes, but there was a greater reason for staying. Yes, you wanted to stay behind because you loved your incarnations there, but there was an even stronger reason why you stayed. Your master chose not to tell you when you met him, but he's telling me now."

"Really? What?" he asked anxiously.

"There was a woman that you loved very deeply, and you had unfinished business that you wanted to resolve. She had already left you, but she didn't go to the mainland of Egypt; she went to her parents' home. You had promised her that, somehow, you could turn this thing around. She had waited and waited, not wanting to leave. She saw that your passion for your work excluded her; otherwise, she would have been happy to die with you. But because she thought you believed in your work more than her, she left. She hoped that you would follow her, but you did not. She had second thoughts and wanted to be with you again. She loved you so much she couldn't let go. You both died before she could see you again. You will meet her again because this is your twin flame. She is not alive right now, but I am not allowed to tell you anything else. The previous relationship you had with her was quite spirited. They tell me that you are meant to be together, but as you are both so independent, it's going to take a lot of work. You two want to become one, and you must, because this is your destiny. It's as though you are completely different, but it's by connecting that you will evolve to where you should have gone before this present age of man."

James's heart nearly broke. "If there ever was such a person, I have no memory of it."

"James, you must understand that a lot of the people who have reincarnated have come from the Atlantean age. They have waited for this time because they have regrets for the mistakes that were made previously. Those who did not have further need of an earthly existence advanced to a higher level of energy, like your master. That choice was there for you, but because you enjoyed your position and power, you didn't want to give it up. Your motives were not bad, as there were those who sought power for many of the wrong reasons. You have to learn that power comes from outside you; you are rewarded with that by your actions.

"Love is the most powerful force in the universe. It connects all that is good for the very creation we live in. The talents you have been able to master are yours already; you have many, and good fortune has been allowed to you. The purpose, they say, is so you will play a great part in this new age of unbelievable technological explosion. All those Atlanteans who were born near the end and soon after the Second World War are changing the very face of our planet right before our eyes. Success has come easily to them because they know the road and have had much practice. The value of all of this is only if it brings about a society that becomes more highly evolved and is more spiritually aware.

"The reason I am telling you all this is that you have been

brought up with love and are being trained for a position of responsibility. This is no accident, as you have a destiny to fulfill, which is to aid in the enlightenment of all that surrounds you and beyond. In this way, our Earth can move forward to an age never reached by any civilization before on this planet. You want to be a part of that legacy and finally reconnect with your true love on this journey."

"That's a lot to put on a person's shoulders," James said, feeling excited but slightly overwhelmed.

"Yes, it is, but you can do it. It's what you want. I don't say that it will be easy, and you will have to again go through many of the temptations that you advanced beyond before, but remember: angels can fall, so we can't do it alone. Reach out to your guides and meditate. You have a family on the other side waiting to take you there, but no one does it alone; it takes a team. Now, let's take a break, and then we can talk. I want to evolve the very essence of you!"

"I agree. You have given me a lot to think about, but I must first understand your ability to understand what you are seeing."

"Good point."

Mrs. Lloyd left the room, and James went to the restroom to splash water on his face and get ready for round two. After a few minutes, they returned to their respective seats, and Mrs. Lloyd asked James if he had any questions.

"Yes, naturally. You have told me a lot about the how and the why of my present-day situation, but I am concerned about my mother. How solid will her new relationship with a person who is also a guardian in my life turn out?"

"He's a lawyer. I can see him. He's tall and very attractive. He likes your mother and feels that it would be a good match, but he's confused. I believe there is someone else. He likes the ladies, this man, but as he knows, he's getting older; he's anxious to settle down. He's an excellent friend to you and will play a valuable role in your life." She then asked, "You find your mother difficult, don't you?"

"Yes. She's very pragmatic and doesn't believe in my efforts to preserve an important part of our heritage." James wanted her to understand more about him but was testing her to see how perceptive her psychic abilities were.

"Your mother is an important part of who you are. Her drive and force of personality are characteristics you need in order to accomplish your goals. Your father was kind and empathic, which gave you the example of humility. Understand that all the qualities we inherit are necessary for us to obtain our goals; it's in their misuse and negative application that they can bring our downfall. Your mother may sound cold and aloof at times, and you wish she showed more affection, but it is there within her. She started out her life in a very different way from that of your father."

"That's the best way I ever heard it said. You make me value and see personal qualities very differently. Thank you." He then shifted gears and asked, "So, this woman, or girl, that I knew on Atlantis, the person I am supposed to connect with, is she English or from some other culture?"

"I can only tell you that she has powerful eyes, is extremely competent, and is every bit her own person. She will be strong enough to one day stand up to you, as it is essential for you to learn this. I am told she is beautiful but in a very unusual way. She's like you but different, and the quality you'll love most about her is the warmth and heart she radiates. James, the one weakness that prevails through all your lifetimes is the desire for power. Don't misunderstand me; it takes ego and leadership to make things happen. You must realize that this power is given to us because we have earned it, and it will be taken from you if you abuse its force.

"It's in learning to love from the heart and having the empathy that your father well demonstrated that increases your force and influence around you. When we start to think we are doing it all by ourselves and become filled with delusions of grandeur, we fall. Throughout history, politicians and celebrities have fallen from grace through the misuse of power; the things that they have worked so hard to attain are lost and taken from them."

"Your words of advice are comforting. I am still a young man, but I can see it in daily life. How fortunate Peter is to have you for a mother," James said with admiration.

"You're not as young as you think. You have the mind of a twenty-five-year-old already, and by the time you are twenty-five, you will think like a forty-year-old. However, tested you will be, for experience is a great master. We just can't make too big a mess of our learning. The challenge is even greater when you are in the spotlight!" she said, laughing. "People will think that you are fortunate, which you are, but it's not many souls that would take on the challenges you're about to face. It takes courage and character, and that's why you have such a huge following from above. They know the good that's in you, and they also know the test of being human is, at times, overwhelming." She then asked, "Do you have any further questions before we close the session?"

"Well, there is one. We are in the process of restoring a room, a very large room known as the East Wing at our home. My mother would like to sell all the artifacts and use the money for the restoration of our disused cottages. I, on the other hand, would prefer to see this room restored and opened as a museum to the public. This was a collection created by the Seventh Earl, and I feel the artifacts will never lose their value. Do you think I am wrong?" he asked anxiously.

"I am told your decision to restore this room and open it to the public will bring much-needed revenue to the estate. More importantly, it will give the world the opportunity to see things that will give great experience to many thousands of people and open up minds to learn more about esoteric and spiritual matters. This room was lovingly created for just such a purpose by your grandfathers and was preserved for the very day you open it. You cannot count the good that will come from this; it is truly a special room."

With conviction, James asked, "Would you be interested in seeing this room for yourself and becoming a part of the advisory committee we are trying to set up?"

"I certainly would, and I would be happy to help write up any presentations or pamphlets and help with its promotion. This can only bring great good. This is a much-needed opportunity as we march into a new awakening, which you will experience in your lifetime on this planet." Mrs. Lloyd paused for a second, then said, "Just a minute. I am getting something else." She was in deep meditation for a few minutes, then added, "James, tell me about this throne you have. I see it in this room you're talking about. It's very powerful and has a distinct purpose. It was created with knowledge not known today; it's way ahead of its time."

"You can see that? Yes, I sat on that throne, which is a unique design. After taking my seat, I got transported through a vortex to a star system in the constellation of the Pleiades, and that's where I met my master."

"They want to tell you something. You know why you were able to do that?"

"Frankly, no, I don't."

"Not everyone can do that. Other people could sit on the throne and would get dizzy and feel strange, and they would know there was an energy field, but they would be unable to explain it."

"Funny. That's what my father said before he died."

"You know why they couldn't transport?"

"No, why?"

"They're not aligned. You are aligned, which means the seven chakras of your body are in balance. Very few people are aligned, so the entity that is you cannot leave the body so easily.

A person could sustain physical damage to their body as a result of the tremendous energy needed to travel the vortex."

"Really!"

"There's a purpose for this throne, which I am allowed to tell you. In order for people to travel the vortex, they have to be educated and learn how to become aligned. I have written many books on this subject but never with this possibility in mind. We have met for a very great reason."

"What's that?"

"A school must be started to instruct people how to advance and learn this balance of alignment, which is done by monks in the Himalayas and various esoteric groups throughout the world, but it's relatively unknown by almost all the people here on this planet. We will talk later. This is something major and very special."

"How is it that I can do this?"

"James, it's not because you are better than other people but because you have carried this ability from your Atlantean culture to this age. You know naturally how to do it. It's easy for you, while others have to learn the ability. It can be taught, as you have been taught. We don't lose the things we instinctively know. So my reason for telling you is that you can help others to learn. Also, know that having balanced and aligned chakras is one of the finest things for your health."

"Okay, you're on. Why don't you come and try for yourself?"

"I will. I would love the challenge."

"Excellent."

James recognized that Mrs. Lloyd was a wonderful person who truly believed in her abilities. She had and would stop at nothing to grow and develop herself. James had never really looked at her as he had other women. She was, after all, Peter's mother, but beneath her humble presence and soft smile was a person that had no need to stand out. She was already there. Her tall figure and intellectual beauty stood head and shoulders over other women. She wore a dainty summer dress that flowed with elegance, and her light-colored sandals and bare legs were similar to her daughter Kate's. She was attractive with so little makeup, and her eyes expressed everything. It was as if she could look through to your very soul. She had no need to be provocative because her heart vibrated from every inch of her being. She was a person who had a beauty beyond physical appearance. You could see all the way to her heart, and that was more beautiful than any outward appearance could display.

They looked at their watches and couldn't believe that it was almost six o'clock. Everyone would be wondering where they were.

James cleaned himself up and met everyone out on the veranda for a drink. It was apparent that the family had been talking about James, and after giving him his lemonade shandy, Mr. Lloyd started in. "So, James, when you graduate from Sterling, as I'm sure you will successfully, what are your plans for the future?"

"Well, sir, as you know, my family is in the banking business and—"

Mr. Lloyd butted in, "Really? I had no idea. What is the name of your bank?"

"Bannerman's. Bannerman's International on Threadneedle Street in the city."

"Your family owns Bannerman's?" Mr. Lloyd looked very puzzled.

"Yes, sir, my family started in the investment banking business just after the coronation of Queen Victoria in 1838."

"Fascinating. I would so love to hear about your family's history. I'm sure we all would. Do you mind sharing the story of how your family has become as prominent as it is today?"

"It would be a pleasure, sir." James continued to explain his family's history, as had been told by his father, and referenced the many books he had now read on the subject.

"In short, we were a competitor to the East India Company. The transportation of spices, silks, teas, herbs, diamonds, rubies, and other gemstones led them to even greater heights. They became traders of these commodities as well as buyers for other merchants. Eventually, the success of these enterprises led to the opening of the bank and the holdings we now have in the Far East and around the world. I think that's about as quickly as I can say all that without boring everyone to death!" He laughed, and everyone joined in.

"Truly amazing, James. So you will inherit the investment your family has in this bank, and of course, your estate in Lincolnshire. With a bank like Bannerman's and your estate, you won't have to work another day in your life, I bet."

James quickly responded, "On the contrary, sir. I plan to run my family's bank, and I won't rest a day until I do just that."

"Good for you! So many people of privilege sit back collecting rent from poor farmers and tenants. You can imagine that I, as a self-made man, to some extent have little respect for much of the aristocracy, who frankly have never done a day's work in their lives. It sounds to me like you intend to make good use of your position in life and that's to be respected and commended. Your father and mother have done a fine job raising you, and you show that drive within yourself. I noticed that by your prompt timing and alert attention on the tour around my shop and through the detailed and intelligent questions you asked." Mr. Lloyd was proud to have such a sound young man in his house. He was a man short on praise, as Peter would confirm, but his admiration could be clearly felt by all at the little family gathering. "It's been a pleasure getting to know you, James. I believe Peter has an excellent friend and example in you."

"Sir, I thank you for the compliment, and I would also like to mention that Mrs. Lloyd has been a great help in sharing her insight and abilities with me this afternoon. It will take me a while to reach her level of development, for sure."

Mrs. Lloyd thanked James, then Peter said, "Mom, you got another one reeled in!" He then added laughingly, "None of us know where she comes up with all this stuff, but we can all say that she's right most of the time."

Mr. Lloyd pointed his finger at his son and jokingly warned, "Watch yourself, Peter, or she'll get you later."

They all began to laugh and then headed out for supper, all busily exchanging stories. James had found a real chemistry with the Lloyd family and hoped that this would be the first encounter of many.

In the days to follow, James did improve his lap times, but he realized that getting up to speed with Peter and Kate would take a lot more practice. It was an exhilarating experience that took much more concentration and effort than he'd ever thought.

On the day James was scheduled to leave, Rodney arrived on time to pick him up. James exchanged hugs and goodbyes with the family feeling that it had been a very special week.

CHAPTER 9

A NEW VENTURE

Sir Thomas sat in his study at his London home, many thoughts running through his mind. He had all the figures he needed except a more detailed financial statement of the farm's current position. Claudia had worked hard on the numbers, and he could clearly see her competence. Phillipa had been very quiet recently, and they had not been seeing each other as much as before. Yes, he'd been busy, and he wanted to get all his facts in a row before meeting with the bank's board, but he could have been available if she'd wanted to see him. He had called on a number of occasions, but she had been busy. They were starting to lose touch, and in a way, he didn't mind. Phillipa was more flamboyant than he was and enjoyed meeting the rich and famous. She would think nothing of flying down to the south of France to meet some wealthy foreign aristocrat or to stay on a friend's yacht in Monaco. He was at an age where he wanted to be with a woman who would show more commitment, and he would like to have another child—a son. The bachelor life was lonely, but the truth was, he wasn't in love, and he couldn't see the reason for marrying anyone unless he was.

He pushed back from his large mahogany desk and stared at the painting of his father when he was a younger man. He knew his daughter may produce a son, but it wouldn't be the same as having his own son, an heir to carry on the Ringstone name after almost one hundred years in the city. They had prospered, and he was proud of what he and his family had accomplished.

He got up to pour himself a drink—his favorite, a good malt whisky—and to fetch a nice Cuban cigar. He sat back down on the sofa, took a big puff on his cigar, and started to think about Claudia. *There's a woman*, he thought, *who would be perfect for me. She's in her mid-thirties, young enough to have a child, and probably wants one by now. She's attractive, smart, has no baggage, and we seem to get along so well.* He knew he felt something for her, but he couldn't define it. They had met now on a number of occasions in order to get all the facts together for the East Wing project, and each time he went away thinking more and more about her.

"I'm falling in love, damn it. I really think I'm falling in love," he said out loud, laughing at himself. He hadn't said a word to her about his feelings or even been out with her on a date. They had the occasional lunch here and there to get the proposal together for the bank, but that was all. He wondered if she felt the same way about him. He thought, *I think she does. I will be making a damn fool of myself is she doesn't.*

He decided to call her and ask to see her over the weekend. They still had matters to discuss, and he knew Phillipa probably wouldn't be there.

For the first time, he was nervous making the call, as he knew the relationship was about to move in a different direction. He would be extremely careful in how he went about inviting her out for the evening and then proposing that she return with him to London to meet with the shareholders and board. This way, the bank would be able to connect with someone, besides himself, directly from the estate. *It's a great idea*, he thought.

He called her private line and anxiously waited to hear her voice.

"Hello?" said Claudia.

"Claudia, this is Thomas. I was planning to come up to the estate this weekend to go over the final numbers and pick up the latest financials you have on the farm, a year to date if you have one?" he said with a little less confidence and more humility than usual.

"Oh, that would be wonderful. How does the forecast look?"

"The forecast looks great. I'll just need to know what the farm can afford and the cash flow that will be needed to get this venture off the ground."

"I have everything you need, sir."

"I was also wondering if we could go out for a bite on Friday evening if you are not too busy and don't have any other arrangements."

"I would be delighted. It would be so nice to get away from the estate for an evening." She was cautious with her enthusiasm, not wanting to be overly optimistic.

"Excellent! Then we can discuss the next steps to getting this introduced to the bank."

"I look forward to seeing you. Drive carefully in that Friday night traffic."

"I will. Bye."

He jumped up in the air with excitement. Even over the phone, he could feel the same energy from her as he had felt. He knew this was going to be a great weekend, and he couldn't wait to look into those beautiful, electric, big brown eyes again.

Claudia put the phone down and started to think. She knew now that he wanted to go out with her, and she had been so flattered by his phone call, but she was nervous. She had heard rumors about his possible engagement to the Countess, although she was aware that they had not been seeing much of each other lately. The Countess had taken no interest in the plans being drawn up for the East Wing. In her opinion, Claudia thought they were totally unsuited for one another. The Countess was too dominant and selfish and would find someone more fun loving and less demanding. Sir Thomas was more of a career-orientated person with goals and a desire to accomplish. He needed a wife who was more understanding of him, someone who would be there for him, a partner that would listen to his daily troubles, and be there to enjoy his happier moments. The Countess wouldn't give that much of herself to any man, in fact, to the contrary; she needed the attention from her partner, which His Lordship had always given.

She poured herself a glass of wine and mentally prepared herself for tomorrow evening. She picked up the phone to book Sir Thomas at a well-known pub and hotel on the other side of Lincoln. She knew that meeting him at the estate would be trouble that could potentially start gossip, which assuredly would find its way back to the Countess. His arrival during normal working hours was appropriate, but after hours was another matter. She would meet him there and take her own car. The hotel was far enough away from the locals so no one could even be aware of their secret liaison.

After making the arrangements, she called Sir Thomas to let him know. "Sir Thomas?" she said politely, not wishing to disturb his evening in case he had guests.

"Yes? Oh, Claudia, it's you. Is everything okay?" he asked anxiously, hoping he hadn't overstepped his mark with her.

"I have booked you a room at the Armoury Hotel on the other side of Lincoln. I think this would be the best place for us to spend our evening together, unless you have a better place?"

"I know the place well. An excellent choice. I was actually thinking about that myself. I look forward to seeing you there around seven o'clock in the bar. Does that work for you?"

"Absolutely. I'll see you then. Good night."

Sir Thomas was impressed with her tact. She was making sure that their evening together would be a private affair. He hadn't been quite sure how to handle it, yet Claudia had, in her efficient way, organized the whole situation with ease.

Friday evening arrived, and Claudia fumbled through her wardrobe trying to find a suitable outfit to wear. She had worked hard to get together all the financial data that Sir Thomas had asked for. In case her expectations for the evening didn't turn out in the romantic way that she had imagined, at least there would be work to discuss.

She was nervous. She hadn't had a date since her boyfriend had been killed. She wanted to impress Sir Thomas and show him that she was a woman who knew how to dress for the occasion. It was late summer, and the evenings were getting a little cooler, so she decided her black skirt would be appropriate. It was a little above the knee to provide added allure. She decided to wear a very light pair of stockings, as she had long tanned legs, and she thought she would show them off with a fetching pair of black, high-heeled shoes. She was tall for a woman, about five eight, and in heels, she was at least five eleven. She chose a white silk blouse that had a frilled collar with a plunging neckline, allowing her to proudly show off her nicely proportioned front. She then went to work on her makeup. She piled on the mascara and used a pale pinkish-purple lipstick to accentuate her lips, not a color she would wear to the office but a color that would convey a more romantic intent. She was half-Italian and always had a light, natural tan. She decided to let her hair down to her shoulders to show off her normal length, rather than brush it back in a clasp, as she was known for doing. She wanted to make this an informal romantic evening, so looking more natural with a girlish look, she thought, might be more appealing. To top it off, she put on her favorite perfume, Bal a

Versailles.

Sir Thomas pulled into the hotel parking lot in his Aston Martin; he thought by bringing his sports car, Claudia would be impressed. It would convey a more youthful image to his intended girlfriend.

After checking in, he took a long, steamy bath and shaved his face as smoothly as he could. He put on his favorite checkered shirt with a cravat, and then donned his tweed suit that he always wore when he went to the country. He wanted to be in the bar before seven so that Claudia would not have to wait, and he could have a drink before she arrived.

At seven, Claudia, punctual as always, walked through the entrance lobby of the Armoury Hotel and into the bar, where Sir Thomas was already seated, reading the news.

He stood up to greet her. "Claudia, how wonderful to see you. You look stunning, might I say?" He was attracted to the way she looked with her hair down and the extra height from the sexy pair of high-heeled shoes.

"Sir Thomas, with a compliment like that, you could win any woman's heart," she said with a laugh. She sat down next to him. She could see in his eyes that he approved of the way she looked.

"A drink, my dear?"

"Oh, it's Friday night, so why not! I'll have a scotch and soda."

Sir Thomas yelled over to the barman, "Another scotch and soda, please."

"Coming right up, sir."

"Claudia, tell me all about yourself. I want to know everything."

"Well, Sir Thomas—"

He interrupted, "Stop right there. From now on, my name is Tom or Thomas, please."

"Okay, Tom it is. There's not a lot to say. My mother is Italian and my father is English. They met in Italy forty years ago. My mother was nineteen and my father was twenty-four. It was the end of the First World War. My father was in the British navy, and my mother was a nurse. He was visiting a friend who was wounded in the war, and there he met my mother, and they fell madly in love. I look a lot like my mother but have more the personality of my father." She didn't want to alarm him that she would be high-spirited and have a fiery temper, as Italians were thought to have.

"What does your father do now?"

"After leaving the navy as a captain, he was chosen to be an ambassador with the British government. He is now ambassador to Britain in Italy, so my mother is very happy, as she gets to see all her friends."

"So he speaks Italian?"

"Yes, fluently."

"And you speak Italian too?"

"A little, but I would pick it up quickly if I lived there. As a child, I spoke in Italian a lot with my mother, but since I moved out when I was eighteen, I don't practice much."

"So you moved around a lot growing up?"

"Yes, and it was difficult because I would make friends and then say goodbye. I learned a lot of different cultures, so in a way, it has made me more independent in life."

"So you worked and got jobs before going to Cambridge?"

"Yes, and I had to work hard to get through the entrance exam. Luckily, I won a scholarship."

"Now I'm getting to know the real Claudia. How impressive—a scholarship. So you're not just a pretty face. You have a very fine brain to go with it."

"I suppose so, but I always had a head for numbers. I wish I had taken the time to become a chartered accountant and served my tenure with a good firm to get my articles."

"You still can, if that's what you want, but I don't think that's necessary. Your credentials speak for themselves. You could get a high-level job in London anywhere. I would be happy to help you if that becomes a consideration." He was trying to impress her with his connections.

"I thank you for that. I will remember when the time comes." She was impressed that he saw her competency above her looks. "So, Tom, what about you? We've had two drinks already, and you haven't taken a moment to talk about yourself."

"I've booked a table, so let's go eat, and after I know all about you, I promise to bear my soul. Deal?"

"Deal." She laughed as he escorted her into the dining room for dinner.

He had reserved a small table for the two of them in a quiet corner of the restaurant so they could continue their intimate exchange. The two were so engulfed in each other's conversation that they were almost oblivious to anyone or anything around them.

"Now, tell me about the young man that you fell in love with who met with an unfortunate accident."

"His name was Paul. He was studying physics and wanted to become a teacher, and eventually a professor. He had an insatiable knowledge for trying to find other forms of energy that would replace our increasing need for fossil fuels. Sadly, he hit a bus while riding his motorcycle and was pronounced dead on arrival at the hospital in Cambridge. I had warned him about his appetite for speed, but he would never listen. In the end, I wouldn't ride with him. Frankly, I was scared."

"How awful."

"It was, and it's taken up until this last year to get over it. I had to finish my education at the university, of course, but I sank into a shell and just focused on my work. Lord Penbroke gave me the job as farm administrator and treated me like one of the family. I also liked to help with a lot of their social occasions. I never asked for extra money, but he so appreciated my dedication that he left me a sum of money I could never hope to save in a lifetime."

"What a fine man he was, and he saw you had the makings of a person who could lead and become successful. He knew that one day the farm or the estate would not be enough for you." Sir Thomas then shifted back to the topic he was most interested in. "All right, this is my last question. You were in love with Paul, obviously, but do you really think he would have been your life partner?"

"You don't know how many times I've asked myself that same question. Was it just physical attraction or because he was a risk taker and a fine boat racer and a good conversationalist? I don't know. I can say that I see things very differently today than I did then. For instance, I can see what a great job you do as a lawyer. You really empathize with people and show such a depth of interest that it's almost therapeutic." She laughed.

"By God, I'll sell my practice and take up being a therapist," he said, appreciating the compliment. "Okay, it's your turn. Ask me anything you like."

"Be careful. Anything?"

"Yes, I can take it."

"Okay, here goes. Why is a handsome man like you not married to an equally eligible woman?"

"Wow, you know how to get to the point. I'm impressed. Well, I was once married to a girl I met when I was at school, and we swore to be sweethearts forever. We had a daughter between us who is currently working in the medical field; she wants to become a doctor, and I am very proud of her. Her mother and I now have a decent relationship. The experience for me was much like what you've been through. At that time, I had to work very hard to earn my law degree. The great times we shared disintegrated, and we woke up one day and realized that we were two very different people, with different goals and interests. To put it bluntly, we had nothing in common. She didn't want the type of life I wanted; in fact, she felt uncomfortable around people who were successful and educated. She remarried and now has a life with a man who has a very modest income, and she's quite happy to live in that manner.

"I was your age when we divorced, and since that time, I have obviously met a number of women, but none I would choose to marry. The difficulty I have had is that when you are successful and have something, it's hard to know whether a person truly loves you or not. Plus, not every woman wants a man who works as hard as I have had to. It isn't because I need the money; the clientele I have demand my attention and services. So, in a nutshell, that's it."

"Thank you for sharing that with me." She looked deeply into his eyes and with a flirtatious smirk asked, "It wasn't so bad after all, was it?" She then grew serious and said, "I believe you've told me part of the reason why you're not married, but I still suspect there's another reason that is more private. I understand if you don't want to tell me."

Sir Thomas wasn't used to having a woman probe into his personal life, but he was very enamored with Claudia. He decided it was time he shared himself with someone. "You're right, and I was careful not to say everything because I didn't know how you would take this, but since it's truth-serum time, here goes. When a person gets older and meets other potential partners for his or her life, that other person can have so much that comes with them. In my case, I have the one daughter who is an adult, and both my parents are deceased, so my situation is fairly simple. Nearly all the women I've met have had dogs, teenagers, aunts, uncles, grandparents, and ex-husbands who have visitation rights. Then there is the issue of their friends and whether they would blend with my friends. Claudia, it's more complicated than you could possibly imagine. Believe me, I have tried. In most cases, I have preferred to just know the lady I'm with and leave it at that. If the relationship doesn't develop from there, the interest starts to drop. I know there are cases where it has worked out, but unfortunately, because I'm so committed to my work, it has not worked out for me, so there you have it." He felt relief at sharing his real feelings.

"It makes complete sense to me." Claudia didn't think any less of him for his rational explanation. She would have had the same doubts herself—with him or any other future prospect—or the same reasons. "Now that we've made it through the tough stuff, tell me what Thomas likes to do outside work." She made eye contact and moved her body a little closer, with a slight tilt of her head. This man fascinated her, and she wanted to be sure that they had things in common.

"I like to just get out of the city, like now, to get away from people and the intense type of work I do. I know many well-to-do people, so over the years I've learned to hunt, shoot, and fish. Now I would like to concentrate more on golf and be a much better player than I am." He then suggested, with some apprehension, "Claudia, would you like to come upstairs and have a last little chat and a night cap? Please don't think that I want to impose anything improper by this invitation."

"I would love to," she replied, then teased, "What makes you think that you could do anything that was improper without my consent?" She enjoyed watching him blush bright red.

Their hearts were pounding as they climbed the staircase to the second floor. He nervously put the key in the door, and as soon as they walked through the entrance, they turned toward each other with so much force to embrace that they lost their balance and fell right onto the bed. Their passion was intense, and they shared a kiss that seemed to last an eternity. He thought, *You are the one that I've been waiting for all my life.*

"Tom, take off that jacket, undo that cravat, unlatch those cuff links, and give me a real hug." She felt completely at ease with him after their first embrace. She knew he needed a woman in his life to lighten him up.

"You're right. I do so want to hold you in my arms, and it's hard with all this stuff!" he said, laughing. "I suppose I'm a bit old-fashioned."

"A bit? I'll knock that out of you. A man of your means needs to enjoy life a little, and I've spent too many years being down in the dumps myself, so it's good for the both of us, don't you think?"

"Claudia," he said, embracing her again and looking into her eyes, "I can only say that tonight is one of the greatest moments in my life. I couldn't bear the thought of never seeing you again." They embraced with intensity and kissed again. "Now, before I lose my head completely, we do have a couple of things to discuss." He tried to regain his composure.

"I know. We have the numbers to go over."

"No, that can wait. I want to take you to London tomorrow so that the bank can meet you. I would like you, with my assistance, to make the presentation for the East Wing." He knew that she would be an absolute hit with the shareholders. This would also give them an opportunity to ask questions about the current position of the estate.

"Go to London? Tomorrow?"

"Yes."

"I must go back to the estate then and pack a bag. How long will we be there?"

"I thought that in order not to alarm anyone at the estate, it would be better if you met me back here for breakfast and left your car here. Then we can go together in mine. We will be there until Monday afternoon, and then I can drive you back here to your car."

"Yes, I best be going then. I need to pack and leave early tomorrow morning before anyone arrives at the office. They will wonder where I have gone, so I will leave a note for Arthur, the farm manager, and say that I had some business to take care of and will be back in the office on Monday. They won't be surprised; they've been telling me to take a break for ages."

"Claudia, it's been an evening I can never forget. I look forward to seeing you tomorrow."

The two of them hugged and kissed, and then Claudia hurriedly collected her handbag and left.

CHAPTER 10

EXCITING OPPORTUNITIES

When Claudia arrived back at her cottage, she found a note pinned on the front door. It was 11:30 p.m., and she wondered what could be so important that it couldn't wait until the morning. She had experienced a beautiful evening with Sir Thomas and was floating on air, so she decided to leave opening the note until the morning.

Her alarm clock went off at seven, as usual. She jumped out of bed and then remembered the note. She sat down at her little kitchen table and opened the letter.

> *Claudia,*
> *I don't know where you are, but I would like you to call me when you get back, and if you have time, come over to the house so that we can discuss how the project is proceeding for the East Wing in respect to the bank.*
> *Countess Phillipa*

Claudia was furious. She ranted, "She's in London all week with her social life. The one time I go out, she has to have my complete attention after hours. That woman is becoming too much. I bet she heard that I went out for the evening and wanted to use the situation as an excuse to show her authority."

She knew this request presented a problem and would prevent her from going with Sir Thomas. Her mind went in circles as she sipped her first cup of coffee. She couldn't be deceptive; it would ruin her integrity. How could she keep the Countess happy and meet Sir Thomas by 9:30 a.m.? She knew she must call Sir Thomas first to let him know and then make a plan.

She waited until 7:45 a.m., then called. "Thomas, sorry to bother you so early."

"No, not at all. Is everything all right?" he asked, noting that she sounded a little concerned.

"When I arrived home last night, I found a note on my door from the Countess, and she wants to see me immediately. I don't want to say the wrong thing or in any way compromise the situation between you two."

"Well, she does have a way of showing up and demanding immediate attention, I can attest to that. Go into work, and then around nine, go over and see her. After that, you can give me a call, and we can make plans from there. Let's not assume anything. Let her speak with you and tell you what's on her mind, and then we can put the pieces of the puzzle together and go from there." He remained calm, knowing Phillipa well.

"Thanks, Tom. I'm so sorry I won't be there sooner. I so want to see you."

"It's just another hurdle we will have to clear. I'm sure there will be a few more to come, so be patient, my dear. We'll find a way." He wanted to give her reassurance.

"I feel so good when I talk to you," said Claudia.

Claudia arrived at the house at nine. Knowing the Countess would be up, she made her presence known to the butler, and he escorted her into the small breakfast area where Phillipa was sitting. "Claudia, had a late night, I do suppose? Well, good for you. I hope the man you're seeing is worth the time of day. A smart woman like you needs an intelligent, well-bred man of means. Anyway, what's happening on the East Wing project?" Claudia breathed a sigh of relief, feeling that the Countess had been left out.

"Well, ma'am, I have prepared all the cash flow numbers for the bank. Sir Thomas has been very helpful in providing the appropriate staff to help in estimating what expectations we might have. I have also prepared the current financials on a year to date for the bank on the present situation of the farm." Claudia did not like the uneasy feelings she was having. It was not her way to be deceptive, and now, with the feelings that she had for Sir Thomas, she disliked the possibility of being compromised.

"It appears I'm going to have to make an appearance at the bank. After all, I want to see how everyone else sees the matter," Phillipa said with an air of confidence that the situation needed someone of her stature to see it through.

"Yes, My Lady, of course."

"However, I would like you to be present. I value your opinion, and as you have worked so hard on the numbers, it's only right you should be there. They need a contact at the farm that they can call upon, if I'm not present, for updates and details. I can see that. I'll call Sir Thomas, as we will need him to be there too." She felt in complete control of the situation and now looked forward to getting all the attention.

"Yes, your Ladyship."

"And Claudia, we'll go down together and you can stay with me at the London house. It'll do you good to get out of here for a change." She believed that she was doing Claudia a favor. The Countess was not mean-spirited; she just liked to have center stage.

Claudia replied, "I'll call Sir Thomas, if you like, and make all the necessary arrangements." She was quickly thinking of a new plan.

"Please do, and let me know. Thank you, Claudia. You're always a model of efficiency."

Claudia quickly drove back to her cottage to call Sir Thomas, who had taken breakfast in his room to await her call.

Sir Thomas answered on the first ring. "Claudia, what's the game plan? Have you met with the Countess?" He was anxious to hear about her meeting.

"Yes, and I think she's happy with the progress on the project, but she wants to be present at the meeting with the bank. She's invited me to stay with her in London, as she believes that I should be there. She's asked me to call you so you will be present too."

"Oh, Phillipa, she has to be front and center when it comes to the deal. Okay, I understand. Now listen, this is what we'll do, and this is only if you agree. You have some friends in London?" he asked hopefully.

"Yes, I do."

"Excellent. So here's the plan. Tell her you would like to take this opportunity to visit your friends in London. Take the train from Peterborough to King's Cross Station, and I will pick you up this evening. How does that sound? Tell her I am out of town but will be back Monday morning for the meeting with the bank. This way we can have some time together to discuss our plans for the future, if this is what you want."

"Brilliant. She would prefer to be alone anyway, I'm sure. I know she's just being considerate, offering me a place to stay, because she will be doing her social activities as usual. She's only here to keep an eye on the kids and make sure everyone is behaving themselves."

"We have a plan, so I won't leave here before midday. Call me back to confirm."

Claudia hurried back to talk with the Countess and confirm

the plans for Monday morning. The Countess said she understood that she would like to take the opportunity to see her friends and even offered to reimburse her for her train and other expenses for the trip.

Claudia was now excited and couldn't wait to call Sir Thomas. "Everything has been arranged," she told him, sounding relieved.

"Claudia, I have another idea. I'll drive down to the station at Peterborough. You can leave your car there, and then we can drive in my car to London. How about that?"

"That would be even better. We can meet in the car park. What car do you have?"

"I brought my Aston Martin, so when you park your car, stand by the front entrance to the station, and I'll pick you up there. So when will you be leaving? It's ten thirty now."

"By eleven, so let's say twelve thirty at Peterborough."

"I'll check out right away and will see you there."

Claudia hurried to pack everything she would need for the weekend and headed out. She parked at the station and went to the entrance to wait. Sir Thomas pulled up on time, and the excited couple shared a kiss and embrace before driving away.

They talked the entire time, so when Sir Thomas turned into his neighborhood, Claudia was surprised to see that nearly two hours had gone by. Claudia noticed that they were in a very prestigious part of North London. As they pulled up to the front gates of Sir Thomas's home, Claudia said, "Thomas, this is an entrance to a mansion, not at all what I expected for a home in London."

"My grandfather, believe it or not, lived in this house, and I remember visiting him as a young boy. London has grown since that time, and now, this would be considered a large property for this part of London. I have about three acres, and with the high hedgerows, my garden is completely private." He felt great pride as he drove through the front gates into a large courtyard where he had a six-car garage shaped in an open square at the side of the house. He parked the car in the courtyard so that his chauffeur/butler could take care of the luggage.

The red-brick house had tall white columns surrounding the front entrance. The black double doors and large brass handles looked imposing behind the columns. His longtime manservant, George, welcomed them both into the house and eyed Claudia with a smile of approval. Claudia was impressed with the front entrance. The staircase to the upper balcony was on both sides and hosted wrought iron and brass railings on each side. The ceiling had a glass atrium that poured a large amount of light onto the black-and-white marble floor. It was an impressive sight. Penbroke Court had a large entry lobby, but the tasteful beauty of this house was definitely among the more baronial high-end homes one would expect to see in London. Sir Thomas explained to Claudia that Highland House, as it was called, got its name from its position overlooking the well-known Hampstead golf course.

Claudia couldn't wait to explore the house, and Sir Thomas delighted in showing her around. His pride and joy was his lower-level swimming pool inside the house, which opened out onto a terraced patio that extended toward a well-kept manicured lawn and garden.

"Thomas, this place is beautiful. You must be very proud. What a wonderful place to have to retreat from your hectic life in the city. And you have your golf course right behind you. You must be one of the luckiest men in the world."

"Yes," he replied, "but even luckier since I met you. As much as I love this place and my memories here, I have never lived here with a woman. This place needs life and soul, and you seem to bring it all alive again. This has been such a happy house, but I have only lived here for the last five years since my father died." He was pleased that she loved the house. "Let's go for a walk on the heath. It's a beautiful afternoon, and we can take old

Red Bones for a walk as well. It's time he got out and had some exercise."

"Red Bones? That's a funny name for a dog."

"Yes. It's a name we gave him because when he was a puppy, he was always burying bones, and his paws got covered in red clay. Let's go unpack, put on some casual clothes, and get some fresh air."

They hugged each other again and kissed, and then they ran upstairs to the bedroom to change. "Ah ha! So I'm sleeping in your room tonight?" She grinned.

"Claudia, I do apologize. I believe George has made a mistake. He should have put your clothes in the guest room."

"Sounds like a planned mistake to me," she said, laughing again. She had just taken off her skirt and heels and dropped them to the floor when he came over to her side of the bed and pulled her directly into his arms. They kissed passionately and fell on the bed. Minutes later, clothes were flying in all directions, and then they lay naked and embraced. The physical passion was so intense that neither one was able to let go of the other. Neither could wait any longer to release the pent-up emotion that they felt for one another. The lovemaking lasted for nearly an hour, and then, in silent bliss, they fell asleep in each other's arms.

A while later, a bird hit one of the bedroom windows, and Claudia immediately awoke. She had slept so soundly and never felt so at peace. She jogged Sir Thomas awake, and he looked up at her and said, "You know how to wear a man out. That's the best nap I've had in months!"

"You don't do such a bad job either, Sir Tom!" She was looking like she wanted to start all over again.

"By God, it's six o'clock. I am famished. I know a great little restaurant where we can get a bite," he said with marked enthusiasm. They took a shower and got dressed.

That evening, Sir Thomas wanted to have a conversation

about Claudia's future. He realized that what had happened between them was serious now, and there would be no going back. He wanted her to be a part of his life, but he wanted to do it right this time and really get to know her. Whatever situation the future held, it had to be the right decision for both of them.

They strolled over to the little bistro that was not far from the house. He had eaten there many times before, and it was next door to a great old pub. It was a relaxing way to spend an evening after a hectic week of action.

"Claudia, I've been doing some thinking, and if you believe there can be an 'us,' I would like for you to come and live with me so that we can get to know each other better. How do you feel about that?" He put his arm across her shoulders.

"I would love that, but as we are not officially engaged, how would people here view that?" She was actually more concerned for his reputation than her own.

They sat down at the table, and Sir Thomas ordered a bottle of wine. He then said, "You have a point. As much as I want to be with you, I agree we mustn't rush it. There are too many people who, if things are not done in an intelligent way, would frown upon our relationship."

"I completely agree."

"When we get back to the house, I'm going to call my good friend Nigel Thompson, who is the managing director at Bannerman's. He has a job opening that I think you would be ideally suited for. The woman who has done this job for the last twenty years is retiring, and she would be delighted to train you."

"Just a minute. I have a job already. Lady Phillipa is going to going to have a fit if I up and leave her just like that. I would appreciate knowing what this job opening is all about." She worried that Sir Thomas was being too hasty.

"I understand. The opening is for the head of the accounting department. The woman there now, Rita, will teach you all you need to know, and with the knowledge you have already, you would be the perfect candidate." He was excited at the prospect.

"Working in the city? That would be quite a change. I love my job, and I would miss the children, but then again, if we are to be together, then a change must take place. Life is full of challenges, but I do know that when I am not with you, I'm going to miss you every moment, and I'm sure I will be daydreaming about you! Now don't get a big head," she said, nudging him with a laugh.

"Oh, Claudia, I feel the same. I wish we could be with each other every day from now on, but we have to do this carefully and slowly. The next thing I suggest is that you call Phillipa tomorrow and tell her you have seen your friends. Ask if it would be possible to stay with her and go to the meeting on Monday rather than turn up independently or with me. This will give you the opportunity to tell her your plans in a thoughtful way. You can then train someone for your position before you leave."

"Excellent idea. Then, if she returns to Penbroke, I can get a ride back to Peterborough to collect my car. Also, I could take the time, a day or two, after I have found the right replacement to come to London, learn the new job, and most importantly, see you!" She slowly started to see a picture emerging that made sense.

"Good thoughts, Claudia. We have a plan, and I think it's important that we take things slowly. In addition, I have a small flat that's not too far away that I rent out. I lived there when I was a single man. My daughter was grown up, so it was just me, and I was close to my work. It's actually having some renovations done, and it would be a perfect place for you to stay when you're here and when you start your new job with Bannerman's Bank."

"Oh, Thomas, you think of everything. But what if Mr. Thompson doesn't think I'm up to the task?"

"Don't worry. He trusts me. He's also a client of mine, and besides, I think when Phillipa knows you're still with the family in a way, she's going to like having someone like you as a contact at the bank. You see, things may work out better than you think."

"Very good. I am beginning to like the whole idea much better."

They finished their pasta and wine and popped over to the pub where Sir Thomas could smoke his cigar and have a glass of his favorite malt whisky. As soon as they opened the door and walked in, some of his old buddies yelled out to him. "Thomas, you bring a beautiful woman like that into this pub, the least we can do is buy you a drink." They laughed as he and Claudia found a seat.

"Behave yourselves, you lot. This is Claudia, and you better treat her well." Each one came up and introduced himself, and then they asked her what she would like to drink. They passed the rest of the evening with good banter and plenty of jokes.

When they arrived back home, Sir Thomas immediately made a call to Nigel Thompson about Claudia. "Nigel, I think I have the perfect candidate to replace Rita. Her name is Claudia, and she works for Countess Phillipa Bannerman. She will have to give her notice and will need about a month to make the transition."

"How will the Countess take that?"

"It won't be what the Countess likes, but Claudia wants to make the change for many reasons. She'll see you on Monday morning because we have to discuss the loan project for the estate. She has prepared all the figures for the project. She has her CV with her, and from what I can determine, she is just what you are looking for. Anyway, just thought I'd give you a heads up. I hope you have time to meet with her one on one."

"Please give her my number and ask her to call me so I can at least get a feel for who she is. Tell her she can call me anytime tomorrow."

"I certainly will. I think you'll like her."

Sir Thomas hung up the phone and turned to Claudia. "You're all set. He wants you to give him a call tomorrow morning so he can learn a little bit about you."

"Seems like tomorrow is going to be a busy day."

The couple joined hands and went up to bed. They shared a night of lovemaking and then slept late. It wasn't until George politely hit the gong at nine thirty that the couple stirred.

"Oh, better get up. I know George has prepared one of his great Sunday morning breakfasts, so we mustn't disappoint him!" Sir Thomas nudged Claudia, who was still content to hold onto his arm and just moan at his insistence. It had been years since she had felt this kind of bliss, protection, and love, and she wanted to savor every moment.

George had gone all out, preparing a feast. The newspapers were suitably placed at one end of the table for selection. Red Bones, after parading around the room several times, was retired by George to his quarters.

"Coffee or tea, my dear?" asked Sir Thomas.

"Coffee sounds good. I need a good shot of caffeine to wake me up from this spell you've put me under."

"I hope you never awaken. I'm equally as spellbound." He looked at her adoringly, thinking that even in her pajamas, she looked beautiful. He knew he was lucky to be with a woman that surpassed his wildest dreams.

While looking through the morning papers, Sir Thomas turned to the social columns and noticed that there was a picture of Countess Phillipa with a very good-looking man he knew from the city. Nicholas Blythe was from the North of England and had inherited a huge ladies' clothing factory from his family. He had become noticeably high profile since he had been involved with many of the fashion shows exhibited all over the world. Nicholas was, in his own right, a great designer of women's clothes, and on top of that, he was a board member at the bank. Sir Thomas, knowing that Nicholas was a single man and a notorious playboy, wondered if he would even be present at the meeting on Monday. Since he knew Phillipa would be there, he would bet money he would be present, and in addition, he felt concerned because he knew Phillipa was an absolute target. Nicholas was educated at Eton and knew many of the jet set. He sensed trouble and would watch the situation carefully. He said nothing of his observation to Claudia and moved onto other news.

"It's about time I called Mr. Thompson and got to know him a little better, I think," said Claudia, starting to plan her morning.

"Good idea." He gave the number to Claudia, and told her she could use the phone in his study.

Claudia walked to the study and made the call. "Good morning, Mr. Thompson. I do hope I'm not disturbing you too early for a Sunday."

"Not at all. Thank you for giving me a call. As I told Sir Thomas, I just wanted to have a brief chat before our meeting on Monday. I understand you've put a lot of work into this project for the Countess, so I'm anxious to see your plan. My concern is that you work for the Countess; I don't want to do anything to jeopardize our relationship, so I need to be sure of your intentions."

"I quite understand. I worked for Lord Penbroke for three years and the Countess for almost two years now, but as you can appreciate, after having spent time in Lincolnshire, which I have enjoyed, I feel it's time for me to find something that would be a little more challenging. I have not had much of a personal life in the last five years, which I will explain to you completely in my interview, and London poses a better future for my life and also my skills." She wanted to sound committed but not too full of herself.

"I completely understand. Tomorrow will be an interesting day. I know Sir Thomas thinks highly of your work on the project, and as I have the deepest respect for his advice, I very much look forward to meeting with you. This job is a challenging one but would pay significantly more than you are earning now. We require the best, and a lot of my opinion will be based on what Rita Holmesly, a steadfast employee of the bank for the past twenty years, has to say. She's retiring, and if you are the right candidate, she will give you all the help you need. Many thanks for the call, and I look forward to meeting with you tomorrow."

"Thank you, sir. I look forward to it as well."

Claudia was happy to have made the introduction and decided to make a call to the Countess in order to plan the next day. "Countess, this is Claudia. I hope I'm not bothering you too early in the morning."

"Goodness gracious, no. Where are you? Are we going to meet at the bank tomorrow, or what's the plan?"

"I was wondering, with your approval, if I could come and stay tonight at your home, and then we could both go to the meeting at the bank tomorrow at ten?"

"Of course. I look forward to you coming. I don't have anything planned this evening. I had a late night last night, so we could get a bite and make an early night of it." She was pleased that Claudia had called.

"I look forward to seeing you, say around five?"

"Excellent. I'll see you then."

Sir Thomas walked into the study to hear the end of the conversation. As Claudia hung up, he said, "Well, my dear, it seems you have got your day well planned. What I will do is drop you off close to where she lives, and she'll think you arrived by taxi, which would be appropriate."

Sir Thomas and Claudia spent the rest of the morning and early afternoon walking Red Bones and enjoying some of the sights around London. Later in the day, she packed her things and put on a nice summer dress so that she would look presentable to the Countess. Sir Thomas then dropped her near the home in Mayfair. They had discussed the conversation she was going to have, and she was now fully prepared for any outcome.

Claudia knocked on the door and was greeted by the Countess. "Come in, Claudia. Now tell me what you've been up to. It's been a long time since you visited London; in fact, I can't even remember when."

"Yes, it was time I saw my aunt and uncle, who live in North London, not far from the A1 motorway near North Finchley, and bring them up to date on my life. When my parents were away doing their ambassadorial duties in different parts of the world, they were a big force in helping me with my education. For the holidays, I used to see a lot of them, and they always came to visit me when I was at Ste. Anne's." She hated telling lies to the Countess, but the things she said about her aunt and uncle were true, at least; they had been her godparents and always taken care of her on behalf of her parents. Even though she hadn't seen them in a good while, she had always written and stayed in touch with them.

"They must miss you, of course. That was a nice thing to do. I thought after Friday night, you were out painting the city and having some fun," she said with a laugh. "Let's go out to a little place I know and have a quick bite and a chat about tomorrow."

The Countess had Rodney order a taxi. She knew just about everywhere to go, and only being four years older than Claudia, she enjoyed her company and actually wanted to know her better. They arrived at a well-known cafe she liked on King's Road, and as always, she was greeted by all the staff. It was a nice evening, so they sat outside and enjoyed a glass of wine before ordering dinner.

"Now, tell me about tomorrow," the Countess said impatiently. "Bring me up to date. I don't want to go into a meeting not knowing what I'm talking about."

"Sir Thomas has a firm idea on what we want to present, and he has any number of experts in the field of museums and so on who have advised me what to expect in terms of people and what to charge for visitation and parking. We show that the cost of renovation to the East Wing and the preparation for both the asphalt and grass parking areas to be around seventy-five thousand pounds. This figure is enough money to sustain us for the first year as we build up to the number of visitors we might expect. In our first year, we project around five thousand, doubling year by year, and then tailing off after three to four years. The promotion and pamphlets needed will be the greatest cost outside the renovation at first, and then, the employment of staff comes next."

"How long will it take until we can start doing renovations to the cottages for rental?"

"We believe a good two to three years." She was being conservative.

"Really? It's going to take that long?"

"I have all the details, and I will give a full explanation tomorrow at the board meeting."

"I understand. We'll just see what kind of support we get, won't we?"

"I think it will be positive, but it's hard to know these things for sure." Claudia knew deep down the Countess was not in favor of the project, but she would see her true colors in the meeting.

As they started their second glass of wine and began to eat their meal, Claudia began to discuss her situation with the Countess.

"Your Ladyship—"

The Countess interrupted, "Oh, Claudia, we're not on ceremony now. Call me Phillipa."

"Phillipa, I have thought long and hard about my future with you, and I believe it's time for me to move on," she said nervously.

"Move on? What does that mean? You want to leave?"

"You know I love my job and being with the family, but I'm going to be thirty-five. I must find a life for myself, and I don't believe it's going to be in Lincolnshire."

"So, what's your plan?" the Countess asked in a guarded voice.

"I have some job opportunities in London, and I also believe it would give me the opportunity of meeting someone."

"Well, I can't blame you for that, but I have a feeling this project has put a lot of fancy ideas into your head. Is Sir Thomas part of this?"

She seemed to have an uncanny sense of intuition. She was a woman who knew life and didn't get where she was by being stupid. She also knew that Claudia was someone more innocent and that men of education could be an influencing force. Claudia was attractive, and some local man from Lincoln wouldn't hold her good looks and intelligence for long. She needed someone who could match her abilities. The more the Countess thought about it, the more she understood.

Without giving Claudia a chance to respond, the Countess said, "Claudia, I understand, but I need your help to find a replacement. You've had a big hand in this project, and I hope I can count on your support even if it's only part-time." The Countess was smart. She didn't want to fall out with Claudia. She may need her help one day, and she knew she had been an extremely good employee.

They finished their meal, and when they returned to the house in Mayfair, the Countess did something that was quite unconventional for her. She turned around and gave Claudia a huge hug. She had tears in her eyes. Claudia was quite moved by her impromptu actions and burst into tears herself. They both knew it was the end of a chapter in their lives, and they hoped to be friends in a completely different way in the future.

CHAPTER 11

THE BOARDROOM

The next morning, Rodney drove the Countess and Claudia to the Bannerman International Bank on Threadneedle Street. The building had expanded several times over the years since its beginning in 1838. The Bank of England, which was established in 1734, was across the street. This was the heart of London and the financial capital for not only England but for many parts of the world, particularly in the Victorian era when the British Empire extended itself to almost half the world. The Bannerman Bank building was not as impressive and imposing as some of the other bank buildings, but it was in a critical location, and after being in business for more than one hundred years, carried great prestige amongst investors and the banking community. The eight floors of the building were spread out, and walking through the entrance lobby with its high ceilings, prominent paintings, front desk, and marble floors gave the impression that one was entering a place of refined distinction.

"Good morning, Countess," said numerous lobby staff and porters as she passed by. "Wonderful to see you again." It had been some time since the Countess had visited the bank, but she noticed that all the old staff members were still there.

They were greeted by a porter who had been instructed to escort them to the eighth floor. As they walked to the elevator, he told them, "I believe you will find everyone has arrived for the board meeting." The big brass doors opened, and the porter set the lift for the eighth floor.

Claudia was taking everything in with the expectation of one day walking through these doors to her new job. She couldn't help wondering just where she would be working and if her interview would be positive.

The elevator came to a stop. The porter rolled back the door, saying, "Here we are, madam." Rose, the secretary, was waiting to escort them to the boardroom.

This top floor was comprised of a front desk for the secretary, offices for Nigel Thompson and the chief accountant, and an office where Lord Penbroke had once worked when he was in the city. There were also two conference rooms. The meeting would take place in the large conference room, as a number of the shareholders and senior bank staff would be on hand for the meeting.

The Countess paused for a moment and asked if she could take a look at her husband's old office with Claudia. As she walked in, she couldn't believe that everything had been left exactly the way she had seen it the last time she was there. The room was impressive, with a full-sized partner's desk with a rich, deep inlaid burgundy leather top, Lord Penbroke's favorite high-back dark-brown leather chair, and all the paintings he had loved as well as pictures of the family placed strategically about the room on shelves and credenzas.

The office had to be at least twenty by twenty and had a small round table at the side of the desk where four or more people could sit and discuss the bank's affairs. The Countess could still smell the aroma of his pipe tobacco, which together with seeing the room, brought back many old memories that momentarily saddened her.

Rose, understanding the Countess's sadness, asked, "Can I bring you a cup of tea or coffee, and you can take a few minutes before going into the boardroom for your meeting?"

"What a lovely idea. I would love a cup of tea. How about you, Claudia?"

"Oh, yes, the same for me."

Claudia was impressed with the room and thought about how this older style of architecture, with the high ceilings and the wood floors, was just the sort of taste His Lordship would have.

"Claudia, I'm surprised that no one has cleared this office out. I will talk with Sir Thomas. These things need to be sent back to Penbroke."

"Phillipa, I believe leaving some paintings might be a good thing. After all, James will be taking this office one day, I imagine, and I'm sure he would appreciate some of his father's things as a memory."

"Yes, you're right. James would love some of these pictures too. I'll just have a few of the personal things taken. Well, I do believe we must get to the meeting and not keep everyone waiting. Let's take our tea. We can walk in and wake them all up. Men love to see good-looking women." They both laughed. The Countess was wearing all her finest jewelry and looked every part of the very beautiful woman she was; however, Claudia, in her skirt and jacket, would not go unnoticed.

As they entered the boardroom, everyone went silent and waited to be introduced to the Countess and Claudia. "See what I mean," the Countess whispered to Claudia. "All men are the same."

Sir Thomas, as the acting chairman, said, "Countess, we are

all delighted to have you here. It's been too long. What I would like for everyone to do is to introduce themselves one at a time. We'll go around the table, and when it's your turn, please tell us a little bit about yourself so that the Countess and Claudia will know whom they are addressing, and I can have a chance to remember what you all do." Everyone laughed. Sir Thomas was in his element in this type of environment and knew exactly how to get everyone warmed up and working together.

Claudia and the Countess sat at the far end of the conference table, opposite Sir Thomas. Then the introductions began.

The gentleman on Sir Thomas's left began. "My name is John Klondike, and I have served as a shareholder and board member of this bank for the past fifteen years. I represent investment groups and some charities which are well known to many of you here."

The next person stated, "My name is Peter Hawthorne, and I am managing director of Lloyds Bank Investment Group. We have had great success working with Bannerman's over the years. Not only are we actual investors with Bannerman's, but we appreciate their loyalty in passing on customers that do their day-to-day banking at our main branch."

"My name is Nicholas Blythe," began the next man. "Our family business goes back a few years. We started our business in the cotton and wool industry as far back as the Industrial Revolution of 1760—almost as far back as the Penbrokes."

He hoped to give the Countess the feeling that he was equally as important as she was. He was also looking at Claudia with interest. He continued, "Over the years, we have developed factories here in the North of England and export a lot of our products to Europe. We are about to market our products to America very shortly. My father has served on this board for many years and was a close friend of His Lordship during that time. In his later years, he asked me to take up the position on his behalf."

Claudia now looked at the man with interest. He was slightly outrageous in his dress for the meeting, wearing his old Etonian blazer and cravat, a casual pair of slacks, and penny loafers. He was strikingly good-looking, with curly blonde hair and blue eyes that focused directly on her. He looked to be around thirty-eight years old. She didn't like his untraditional blazer in a meeting where everyone else had worn a suit out of respect for all who were present. He had to think a lot of himself to dress like that, she thought.

The next person jumped in. "My name is Roger Handley, and I have my own investment business which in turn invests with Bannerman's. I have also been a board member for more than ten years."

Claudia paid close attention as the next gentleman introduced himself. "My name is Nigel Thompson, and I have been the managing director of this bank for the past fourteen years. The Countess knows me, but I will be a new face for you, Claudia." Claudia smiled, liking him immediately. He looked sincere and kind, and she could see him being good friends with Sir Thomas.

"My name is Sir John Pearson," began the next man at the table. "I'm a stockbroker in the city, and I have worked with Bannerman's on their investments. I have also been a strong investor with this bank for many years."

Finally, it was Rita's turn, and Claudia again listened with great interest. "My name is Rita Holmesly, and I have been in charge of the bank's accounting for the last twenty years." Claudia instantly liked her as well. She looked to be in her late fifties and was immaculately dressed. She had a presence that exuded complete confidence. Her dark brown hair was cut short but stylishly, and her petite features were appealing.

Sir Thomas stepped in and stated that all the shareholders were present and that Rose would be taking the minutes of the meeting. He then turned to Claudia and said, "I believe it's your turn Claudia, so take it away."

Claudia had made copies of all her notes, projections, and accounting figures, so she stood up and walked around the table distributing the materials. Having made a number of speeches before in class and at Cambridge, she knew how to take charge in a meeting like this. She thought a little introduction might be helpful. She began, "Ladies and gentlemen, thank you all for being here today. To let you know a little about myself, I obtained entrance to Cambridge University, where I gained honors for my studies in finance, business, and accounting. I worked for His Lordship for three years, and at present, I work for the Countess as the estate's financial administrator. As such, I have composed these figures for you today."

"So, you would say you're in the hot seat, would you, Claudia?" Sir Thomas was trying to cut the silence and tension by getting a good laugh. It worked.

Chuckling, Claudia answered, "Definitely. A lot of thought has gone into this project, and I am here to represent what the Countess has been advised would be the best course of action. Penbroke Estate faces a challenge, as farming has become a less profitable industry with the amount of foreign imports we are now experiencing. With our need for more capital equipment to compete and the employment of less staff, one would normally think that farming would be a more profitable business. However, the fact is the margins are actually less. There are many ways to solve this situation. The farm holds good cash reserves; His Lordship, being the responsible man that he was, saw to that. The implementation of newer equipment will certainly help but not in the immediate future. We have to make plans for the long term, so we have a number of projects in mind, this being the first. We believe this project will bring in the most income to support the development of the farm for the future."

Sir John Pearson, who had been reading the notes Claudia distributed about the East Wing and opening the estate to the public, jumped ahead of Claudia and asked, "Would you please explain exactly what the East Wing is about and why there's so much interest in opening up this beautiful estate to the public?"

"Certainly," Claudia replied politely, fully prepared to describe the project in detail. "The East Wing holds what we believe to be, outside of the crown jewels, some of the most valuable jewelry, gemstones, and artifacts presently known. The values of the estimates we have received are well in excess of a million pounds. In some cases, it's hard to even price an item, as if it were sold, it would probably get broken up between various jewelry suppliers. It's the feeling of James, to whom Sir Thomas is the guardian, that when it comes to such a valuable collection that took the Seventh Earl so many years to bring together, this special room and its artifacts should be appreciated by the public at large. In this way, the items will be held for posterity in a manner the Seventh Earl would have envisaged. It's not just a matter of cashing out on the situation; it's about a heritage that could be viewed as a national treasure, if you see what I mean."

Sir Thomas then picked up the conversation to express what he knew about the project.

"I have spoken many times to James on the matter, and after seeing the room myself, I have to agree with his thoughts. What's the worst case scenario? If it doesn't work and we decide to sell the artifacts, there's enough collateral to support ten times the amount being requested."

"I don't agree at all," said Nicholas Blythe, who had secretly discussed the matter with the Countess the previous Saturday night and wanted to support her position. "If James wants to convert this room into what sounds like a museum and create some kind of history to be associated with it, it's a project he should fund himself and not impose it upon the bank."

Claudia started to speak, but Sir Thomas interrupted. "Let me take this, Claudia. I act as the guardian to James, and outside of his allowance, he does not have access to any funds until he is twenty-one. He is more than happy to repay the loan if the farm hasn't done so before that date. It's his firm conviction that we must do everything possible to protect the heritage that has been passed down to him. If this project can work, it will provide valuable income for the estate and keep the artifacts at Penbroke Estate. James has his inheritance in trust as well as Lord Penbroke's investments. The funds will become James's property but not until he reaches the age of twenty-one. The Countess has stated clearly that she does not want to fund the project, so I am advising the bank that as we have the funds available through James's inheritance, we make a loan that is completely covered by the money we have already."

Nicholas replied, "Look, I understand all this heritage stuff, but if James wants to start a museum, then ship the artifacts away from Penbroke. Seek out a group of investors, which I'm sure would be available, and a museum curator. Then, nobody is out any money. Who knows—you'll probably find a better location for the public and do much better, and then the Countess won't have to put up with swarming crowds of people at her estate."

Sir Thomas, realizing that Nicholas clearly did not understand the project at all, stated, "I suggest that Nicholas, and anyone else who may have doubts make a trip to the estate. You will see that to move these priceless possessions to another location would be a crime. After taking a good look at the East Wing, you will have the same feelings I had after James took the time to show me. Does anyone else have something to say on the matter? I realize that you all need a little time to go over the numbers, so maybe we can take a short recess here and then answer any fiscal questions you may have."

Rose quickly replenished the coffee and biscuits in the boardroom during the break while Claudia and the Countess went off to powder their noses.

Frustrated, the Countess, who believed the whole thing was

a waste of time, said, "I can't understand how Sir Thomas has changed his mind on this fantasy James has. The selling of these treasures will bring an adequate amount of money to the estate, and the cottages will get renovated, as they should. Renovating the East Wing delays the whole matter for another two to three years."

"Phillipa, you have a point, but as Sir Thomas believes, you can always sell the artifacts and more than pay off the loan. Besides, James is, I am sure, making good earnings on his investment of 61 percent with the bank, and as he can't touch that until he's twenty-one, the bank is actually in a very good position to make the advance."

"I get all that, but the thought of all those people wandering around the estate bothers me."

"I understand. I guess we'd better get back."

"Yes, absolutely."

Once everyone was seated, Sir Thomas opened the meeting again. "So, any questions?"

Sir John spoke up. "I have to agree with Nicholas on this matter. It's going to take two to three years, judging by these cash flow figures. Regardless of whether James or the bank has the money, I can't see why you would turn a beautiful estate into a museum if you didn't have to. People of the aristocracy who open up their homes for public viewing don't do it because they want to—they do it because they have to in order to pay for the cost of upkeep."

Peter Hawthorne jumped in next. "I agree with the proposal. If this treasure is as you say it is, then it should be held for posterity, and people should be allowed to view history. Selling these priceless objects at what would be bargain-basement prices would be a great shame after having held them in the family for over a century. This is not a cut-and-dried situation; this is a very different request, and I see no harm in everyone being a little patient, as Sir Thomas says. If the project doesn't work, you can always sell the assets. I knew your husband, Countess, and I'm sure that he did not hold those artifacts in that room for no good reason. I also know the East Wing, and as it is separate from the main house, I believe you wouldn't be bothered in the least. I'm sure all measures will be taken to have a separate entrance and parking away from the house, as I see here in the notes, and in no way should this impair your privacy." Peter was a sharp financier who knew a good investment when he saw it. He also knew that the Countess spent very little time there anyway.

"Okay, any more questions?" asked Sir Thomas. "If not, I propose we put the matter to a vote."

Everyone agreed. Sir Thomas instructed, "Those in favor, say aye." Three hands went up. John Klondike, Peter Hawthorne, and Roger Handley were in favor. Sir Thomas then said, "The nays, show of hands please." The Countess, Nicholas Blythe, and Sir John Pearson voted against the proposal.

"Well, I suppose it's up to me to make the casting vote, and as acting chairman for James and His Lordship, I vote in favor of the project," said Sir Thomas.

The Countess didn't look at all pleased. The moment the meeting broke up, Sir Thomas went over to talk with Phillipa and offer to take her to lunch. He wanted Nigel Thompson to spend some time with Claudia. He also knew that by voting against her, he would probably end their relationship, as it had been, but he didn't care. He knew now that Claudia was the woman for him. However, he was wise enough to know that they all had a future together, so there was no sense in not staying good friends.

Nicholas was very curious to meet Claudia, and as Sir Thomas left the room with Phillipa, he quickly went over to ask Claudia a few questions. "Claudia, excellent presentation, and a very impressive background, I might add."

Claudia could tell he was a smart talker, but he was a shareholder in the bank, and he had a family history that was more than impressive, so she knew she must take the time to be polite and talk to him. "Thank you, but not impressive enough to have your vote, obviously."

"Oh, it's nothing personal. I just couldn't see how the Countess would want all that around her house. I know I wouldn't. Aside from that, though, how is it that such a beautiful woman as yourself is stuck away in the countryside of Lincolnshire?"

"It's a long story, Mr. Nicholas."

"Phillipa tells me you're single. How have you managed to pull that off?"

"Again, it's a long story, sir." She was becoming impatient with this personal and direct line of conversation. "Sir, I apologize, but I do have another appointment I must go to." Nigel Thompson was motioning for her to follow him.

"Perhaps I can give you a call sometime and come over to see this room for myself."

"Please do, sir. I will be happy to have someone show you around."

"I really don't live that far from you, even though I spend a lot of time at my London home."

"I really must go. It was a pleasure to meet you." She began walking away.

"And you, too. Not what I expected at all." He smiled confidently.

Claudia hurried down the hallway behind Mr. Thompson to his office. He closed the door behind her. "Have a seat, my dear. Very impressive presentation. Not an easy sell, but you had Sir Thomas on your side, and that always helps. I've read your CV. A scholarship to Cambridge? Not something that is achieved easily. Watching you handle yourself during the meeting gave me great confidence in your abilities. You know how to stand up for yourself, and in a job like Rita has, knowing the job is one thing, but dealing with people is another. She has told me she already approves of you, and in a moment, I'll ask her to come and visit with us. I have just a few standard questions to ask. First of all, how is the Countess going to handle this?" He looked apprehensive.

"We had a long conversation at dinner last night, and she totally understands that I need to have a job in a city like London where I can earn more and have the hope of a new life. My boyfriend met with an untimely motorcycle accident, and the job working for His Lordship gave me the time to get past those days. Now I'm ready to move on and have a new future."

"Excellent. I'm so glad that the Countess is behind you, but does she know you'll be working here?"

"No, not yet. I thought I would wait until we met to be sure, and on my return trip with her, I will discuss the matter. I know she'll be happy for me. We've recently become very close. In fact, last night she asked me to call her Phillipa, which showed me the appreciation she has for my time with her, and she said that she wanted to always stay in touch. I think she will like the idea of me working here. I will still be working with the family in a way, and she'll have someone to at least talk with her at the bank. I also have a very close relationship with James, rather like a mother/son relationship. He listens to my advice, and I am very proud of him and his progress at Sterling." She hoped that sharing such private information would make Mr. Thompson feel that there would be a comfortable connection for the future wellbeing of the bank.

"I would much rather you deal with the Countess than I. I have always advised her to talk with Sir Thomas. I didn't want to compromise my relationship with His Lordship. She's a very direct woman and likes to get straight down to the facts, and that's not always possible. It's important that you have a good relationship with her."

He picked up his phone and asked Rose to send Rita in for a meeting. Rita was excited to meet her, but Claudia also knew that the Countess would be returning from lunch and that they needed to have a hasty discussion. Nigel asked them to go to Rita's office so she could show Claudia some of her tasks. As they left, Claudia thanked him for the opportunity.

Before long, Phillipa returned and was ready to leave. Claudia politely excused herself from Rita and said that she would call and spend at least two days the next week going over the work. Sir Thomas told her that a taxi had been called for, and the Countess was waiting in the lobby. They stared at each other for a moment, and he told her he would call.

Sir Thomas then went to see Nigel. He knocked on the door and heard, "Come in, old boy. Lovely to see you. I'll get a coffee, and we can smoke a good cigar."

"Well, what do you think of her? Claudia, I mean. Is she not right for the job?"

"Absolutely! A scholarship to Cambridge, her presentation—all top notch, I thought." Nigel sank back into his chair, enjoying his coffee and a moment to relax with his old friend and a cigar. The meeting had been a little stressful for Nigel. He found dealing with people like the Countess and Nicholas Blythe a little intimidating. Professional people and businessmen were okay, but socialites were not his field of expertise. He continued, "Rita likes her very much and is delighted to work with her. I think she'll be a spark of new energy around here, and we need a little of that."

"I found her easy to work with on this project. She's polite, hardworking, and strong when she believes she is right. I knew she would be the person for you."

"Damn fine woman to look at, too; don't you think?"

"Now behave yourself with her. I know she won't put up with any nonsense. Anyway, with that beautiful wife and family of yours, I have always been envious, Nigel."

"I know. We've been together over twenty years now, and I would have to look far and wide to replace her. Anyway, where's

Claudia going to stay when she comes to work here?"

"Don't worry about that. I'm helping her find a place."

"Ah ha! You have an easy eye for her too, I can see. But a single man like you and a nice young woman like that—time you settled down, old boy. You've had your days of gallivanting around. In fact, I could see you two working very well together. An ideal match, I would say. Make my life easier at the bank too."

"Who knows, Nigel. You know I have a few girlfriends, but there's nothing too serious at the moment. Time will tell." He wasn't ready to tell his friend the truth about the situation just yet.

"Don't wait any longer, my friend. It would be nice to have you over to dinner as a married man for once! All joking aside, you're too good a man to be on your own, and there's nothing like family life. I always enjoyed coming to your home when your father was alive. What a sense of humor! Those were good days, and I miss them."

"We'll have them again. I promise." Sir Thomas put out his cigar and gave Nigel the signal that he too must get back to work.

On Claudia's drive back to Lincolnshire with the Countess, she had full opportunity to discuss everything that was going on. "Phillipa, Nicholas Blythe—who is he? Do you know him well?"

"Somewhat. We've had a few social occasions together. Strapping young man, but he's too much of a womanizer, I fear. His family is extremely wealthy, and he has quite a business behind him. He's a little eccentric. Being a designer for women's clothing, he likes to look different and stand out. He's in all the magazines. Don't you read them?"

"I don't. I hadn't a clue who he was, other than he's obviously intelligent and good-looking, but a little too full of himself for my liking."

"Really, you have sized him up. You obviously find him attractive, but I warn you to keep clear unless you want a man to break your heart. He's a man I would keep on a leash." Phillipa suspected that he had hit on her, and she didn't know how to deal with it.

"Well, he was rather pushy and said he wanted to come and visit the East Wing and that he would give me a call." Claudia knew that if he arrived unannounced, Phillipa would suspect something between them. "I told him I would have someone show him around, but as he voted no, I really can't see the purpose in his seeing the room without seeing you first, Phillipa."

"Quite right. You did the right thing. He did back me up, but he should be talking to me directly about such matters."

"So, if he calls, I shall put him in your direction, Your Ladyship," she said with a grin, knowing it would make the Countess happy.

"Oh, I'm going to miss you, and the sad thing is, I'm just getting to know you. You've been very reticent and shy, but I'm learning to like you more and more."

Claudia knew it was time to bring up the subject of working at the bank. Cautiously, she said, "Phillipa, I have something to pass by you."

"Whatever might that be?"

"Nigel Thompson has offered me a position at the bank, and if it doesn't offend you, I would like to take him up on that offer."

"Has he? And what position has he offered you?"

"It's the manager of accounting for the bank. Rita Holmesly is retiring, and she is going to train me for her job if I accept."

"Well, congratulations! You deserve the job. You would make a perfect director of the business accounts. I can't think of a better job for you—and a good salary, I suspect! Plus, it means that we will keep in touch. I will come to see you, and we can have lunch together. Don't worry—I'll take care of you. An attractive woman like yourself needs a good friend, and I want to be that person, Claudia." She grasped Claudia's hand with warm affection.

"I'm so happy, Phillipa, that you support my opportunity, and you know I'll always stay faithful to your needs should you require help with the estate."

The two of them were blissfully happy at the outcome and evolvement of their relationship. They couldn't stop talking all the way back to Peterborough Station, where Claudia had left her car.

CHAPTER 12

LIFE IN THE CITY

Claudia wasted no time trying to find her replacement. As soon as she arrived back at Penbroke, she placed an advertisement in the Lincoln newspaper, and she began clearing out all the things in her desk and taking care of unfinished business. She had only a few personal possessions, as the cottage had been equipped with all the necessary furniture and kitchenware. She had spent very little on ornaments and extra furniture. She had focused on her work to take her mind off Paul. Now her life was starting to change, and she felt like she was coming alive again. She was regaining her confidence and looking forward to the new challenges that lay ahead as well as her growing feelings for Sir Thomas.

That evening, she began packing her things. As she was doing so, the phone rang, and she ran like a schoolgirl to answer it. "Hello?"

"Is this the lady that ran off and deserted me?" asked Sir

Thomas, laughing.

"Absolutely not! I've been thinking about you all day and miss you."

"I feel the same. I miss you terribly."

"I'm going to be in London on Monday and Tuesday next week to work with Rita, so I was wondering if I may take a room at your splendid mansion?" she teased.

"My dear girl, my home is yours. So that means we have another weekend together? Splendid!"

"I thought you would approve. I must be back by Tuesday evening, though, so I can carry out the interviews for my position." Changing topics, she said, "I noticed you had a meeting with Nigel Thompson. Did he have anything to say that I should know about?"

"No. You obviously bowled him over like you did me."

"Thomas, seriously, he must have said something."

"Yes, he thinks you're a great choice. He was impressed with the way you handled yourself at the meeting and is looking forward to working with you. He's also happy that Rita likes you, as it helps make the transition so much easier."

"I'm so happy. Thanks for all the support you gave me in the meeting. Nicholas Blythe strikes me as a tricky character."

Cautiously, Sir Thomas asked, "In what way?"

"Well, he came over to talk with me and wanted to know if he could come and visit the East Wing. Obviously, I couldn't just brush him off, so I was polite and said that I would have someone show him around. I told the Countess about it, and she said if he called to have him call her directly."

"Smart girl. You did the right thing. He does have a reputation, but he's a very successful ladies' clothing designer, and besides coming from an extremely wealthy family that supplies all his materials, he's smart and likes to wear clothes in a way that shows his flair for style. It's his way of marketing himself. I doubt you've heard the last of him. He's persistent, but I think you've got his number already." His words carried a hint of jealousy, as he knew someone like Claudia, who had looks and brains, would be just the kind of challenge Nicholas would like.

"Now, Thomas, no need to get protective. I can handle myself, but it does tell me you care about me, and that's important."

"My dear, you are very important to me, and anyone who imposes himself on you, I will take care of. Mind you, only at your request." He quickly added the last part, not wanting to sound too possessive.

"Have no fear. You're the man for me," she said flirtatiously.

"And you're the woman for me." Shifting gears, he said, "Now, if you're coming down for the weekend, I want to show you my flat, where I think you will enjoy staying, and also show you where to take the tube to your work."

"That would be marvelous! I'll look forward to that. It's always nice to have a picture in your mind of where you're going to be."

"Give me a call when you leave on Friday, and I shall be waiting for you." The two of them blew kisses like teenagers and then hung up.

The next morning, Claudia called the house looking for James. She knew she had a hectic week of planning, so she wanted to see him first thing. Rodney answered. She requested that James come and see her if he was available. Rodney went to check and then came back on the phone and told her James would be straight over.

He arrived in the old Land Rover, and after they exchanged hugs, she suggested that they go across to her cottage so that they could have a private chat. She had already prepared tea and chocolate biscuits for them.

As they sat down in her cottage, James said, "I can't believe it—you're like our second mom, and you're going to leave us to our mother."

"Don't worry; she'll have someone equally competent to

oversee you guys during the holidays. Besides, you're almost a grown man. Look at you; you'll be well over six feet. You've caught up with me already. I wish I could be one of those lucky young girls you're going to meet someday."

"Well, if I meet a lady like you one day, then all my prayers will have been answered."

"James, I won't be so far away. I am going to be working for Nigel Thompson, the bank's managing director, so I will be working for the family as I am now, just a little farther away. I will be managing the accounts there, so when you come to the bank, we'll meet up again, and hopefully, work together. Now, what do you say to that?"

His eyes lit up. "You're kidding? You're going to be working at Bannerman's?"

"Yes, sir," she said as she reached out to hold his hand.

"That's terrific! You and I will make a great team, I just know it, and we'll make things happen in a way that will make people take notice. Once you get settled, may I visit you, and can you educate me a little on how the place operates?"

"You can be sure of that. There won't be a thing I won't teach you or tell you about." She felt like James was one of her own children. Though he'd been a bit of a daydreamer when he was younger, she had grown to admire his qualities. He was so much like his father but with more drive and force about him somehow.

"So, I see you got approval from the bank for the development of the East Wing."

"You can thank Sir Thomas for that. You sold him on the idea that day you took him around to show him the artifacts. He was a big force in getting the loan for this development."

"That's good to know. I like Sir Thomas. I feel he is a good man, and I look forward to working with him after I get through university. I think Father chose the right man to watch over the bank until I become of age. Let's be frank: I'm going to need a lot of help before I can be of use, but I'll work hard and show everyone that I mean business."

"I know you will."

"I want to tell you about someone I met. Her name is Sarah McKenzie."

"*The* Sarah McKenzie?" she asked with interest.

"Yes, the writer and psychic. She is amazing, and she wants to help the company we contract to do the marketing for the East Wing."

"That's fantastic, but how do you know her?"

"She's my friend Peter's mom. She goes by her maiden name as a writer. Do you read her books?"

"All of them. I agree she's amazing, and I would love to meet her sometime. To have a reading with such an accomplished woman wouldn't be cheap. You're a lucky young man to know her; she's very popular." Claudia was thinking about the burning questions she had about Paul, who died and left her so abruptly.

"I'll organize that for you." He liked the fact that there was something spiritual about Claudia. *That's why she resonated so well with his father and the reason he liked her,* he thought.

"I must get back to work now. I have a lot to organize, but I so appreciate having this time to talk with you."

"The same for me, and please let me know whom you choose for your replacement so I can follow up on the progress of the East Wing."

"I will let you know before you return to school."

They gave each other a big hug and a kiss, and then they parted.

Friday night, Claudia headed out to Sir Thomas's for the weekend. Her Mini Cooper was packed to the top, but she was excited to see where she was going to live and to start her new life. She'd been shut away in an isolation of her own choosing, but it was time to come out of her shell. Her new job in London would be the beginning of a new life for her, and her relationship with Sir Thomas only made the change more appealing. She couldn't wait to be in his arms again. She had never felt so protected, loved, and at peace. She was also glad that she had developed a new relationship with Phillipa, as it made the transition easier.

She parked her car in the courtyard, and George opened one of the garage doors to let her in. Sir Thomas was there to greet her. The next morning they transferred all her belongings from the Mini to his Bentley in order to make room for both of them, and then they set out to view the flat he had in mind for her stay.

Since it was Saturday morning, it didn't take long to get from Hampstead Heath to Knightsbridge. Sir Thomas's townhome was located in Pont Street Mews, just behind Harrods' department store.

"Thomas, this seems like a very nice part of London." Claudia was growing excited at the possibility of her new home.

As they drove up to the entrance, Sir Thomas put his card in the machine to open the gate. He stopped outside what looked like garage doors to the adjoining townhome. Claudia laughed and said, "Thomas, you are leading me on once again, I know it." She gave him a shove with her elbow and a big look of amazement, to which he just chuckled.

"Come on, let's go explore." He got out of the car with confidence. He then unlocked the door, and they stepped inside.

To Claudia's amazement, there was a staircase that divided the dining room from the kitchen. "This is certainly no ordinary London flat." She looked at the beautiful kitchen with all the latest appliances and a dining room that would easily seat eight people.

"So, let's see. The second floor—you might like that a little better." He had a big smirk on his face. He was clearly having fun sharing his place with a person he loved so much.

"What are you talking about? There's more room on the ground floor than I had in my little cottage at Penbroke!" She followed him up the staircase to the second floor. On the left, the door opened to a large living room, and on the right, the door opened to a master bedroom and bathroom, again with all the latest furnishings and amenities. She could see that Sir Thomas had modified the bedroom to be more spacious, as it appeared that there were once two bedrooms with a bathroom in between. She explored the second floor and came upon another little staircase. She curiously wound her way up, as it twisted back on itself, and at the top, she found a smaller bedroom and bathroom for a guest.

"Thomas, this place is amazing! You old devil, telling me of your lonely days living in your little flat. Anyone would be delighted to have such a beautiful place in one of the most prestigious areas of London." She ran down the staircase and into his arms. "You're so good to me."

"Well, my dearest one, it's all yours to do with as you wish. There's only one condition," he added slyly.

"And what's that?"

With a twinkle in his eye, he replied, "That you allow me to come and visit you."

She laughed. "Of course! As much as you want. I would be so lonely without you." She gave him another big kiss and a hug.

"Let's go unpack your things, and then we will toast the moment with an excellent bottle of champagne."

"Tom, you think of everything."

"That's my job—to keep my clients happy."

"I'm not your client, I'm . . . " She paused for a moment, not knowing how to say the words, and then she said what she had wanted to say from the first day she met him. She looked deep into his eyes and said, "I'm madly in love with you." She looked at him anxiously, wondering if she had said too much.

He smiled. "If it's any help, I'm madly in love with you too, and I can't bear a moment of being without you."

They quickly unloaded the car. Sir Thomas let her take care

of her smaller items and went to the kitchen to open the bottle of champagne. As she descended the staircase, he pushed a glass toward her. They clicked their glasses and gazed into one another's eyes until they couldn't stand it any longer.

"Let's go test that bed out." He grabbed her hand, and they ran up the stairs to the bedroom to release their pent-up passion.

****

Working with Rita on Monday and Tuesday was a rewarding experience for Claudia. She spent every moment taking in all the hard-learned experience Rita had at the bank dealing with investors, the staff, international affairs, and the businesses in which Bannerman's had investments. Understanding the financials for the many types of businesses and the currencies they had was a study unto itself. Bannerman's held investments in 138 different companies that spanned the globe. The bank had offices and operations in Hong Kong as well as its wholly owned subsidiary, Trans Global Shipping Lines. Knowing how to alert the appropriate staff in the event of investments not performing and watching those companies that were in danger of going under took the perceptive eyes of an experienced accountant. This was not a business one could learn quickly, and Claudia's lunches and time with Rita were invaluable. She had the comfort of knowing that Rita would be available to give her advice even after she left.

Now, Tuesday evening, Claudia was thinking about the many things she needed to take care of as she made her way up the A1 motorway to Penbroke. She thought about the replacement she needed to find; she knew she had to find someone the Countess would like. He had to be smart and have some good looks, and the Countess had to take a liking to him. It was important that the new person keep the interest level needed to make the place profitable. She worried a lot about that. Phillipa really had left the heart and soul of the estate's finances to her, and she needed to find someone who would take the same amount of consideration as she had for the estate's wellbeing. Plus, the East Wing was going to be a completely new project. Someone would have to manage it as a standalone operation if it were going to have any chance of success.

As she arrived at the estate and walked into her cottage, she felt strange since she had moved most of her belongings to Pont Street Mews. She had left only the necessary items for the last month of her stay. She was tired after working with Rita and decided to get to bed early so she would be well rested for the next day's interviews.

The next morning, as soon as she arrived to work, Claudia scanned through all the CVs that were on her desk, but none of them seemed right. She decided to call the Countess to discuss things with her.

When the Countess got on the phone, she greeted Claudia warmly. "Claudia, wonderful to hear from you. How did things go with the training for your new job?"

"Great, but there's a lot to learn. I had no idea how many investments Bannerman's has. It's going to take me a while to get up to speed, but I love the work and the diversity."

"How are we doing with the interviews?"

"That's what I wanted to talk to you about."

"Okay. What's on your mind?"

"I don't think we have the right plan for the estate now that we are going ahead with the plans for the East Wing and eventually the cottage renovations. If we have the revenue for the estate that I have projected, then we need much more than an accountant. In fact, even if I were still here, we would need someone else, as the job requires skills I don't have. Since the passing of His Lordship, we have lacked that person with estate management experience and an adequate bookkeeper."

"You're absolutely right, Claudia. Since Collin was managing the estate overall, we are missing that knowledge and experience. I can see that. So what do you suggest?"

"In my opinion, the estate needs a general manager who can run all these activities, someone with a background in estate management, farming, and accounting. Those people don't grow on trees and won't come cheap. My thoughts are, we need to put an advert in the Lincoln paper, but more importantly in the *Farmer's Weekly* and possibly, *Country Life* magazines. If someone has the ability to meet the requirements, he will need a house if he has a family."

"You're right. We'll have to step up to the plate and get the best. With the investment we have here and in our discussions with the bank, it's going to take a person of some measure to handle everything that's about to take place here."

"I can be helpful in working with this person from the bank, and in a sense, keep an eye on things for you and advise you if I think anything is not quite right."

"Claudia, I'm so happy you say that. For me, this whole situation is a bit overwhelming, and I'm going to need help. You know I will reward you for that extra effort. You have a big job now in the city, and I know how hard you work, so you minding the store is worthy of compensation."

"Phillipa, that's very kind and considerate, but you know how much I care about this place, and I would do it anyway."

"Time is money; I understand that. Anyway, we will have some times together in London, so we will stay in touch."

"Great. I will go to work on this right away. I appreciate your blessing, and I know time is of the essence." Claudia was relieved that the Countess understood the situation and that matters were now headed in the right direction.

As soon as Claudia hung up the phone, she received a call from Nicholas Blythe. Despite her irritation, she remained professional. "Yes, sir, what can I do for you?"

"Good morning, Claudia. How wonderful to talk with you, especially after having met you at the board meeting, which you handled with ease and eloquence."

"I thank you for the compliment, but I'm sure you had a reason to call other than to compliment my presentation."

"Absolutely. I was planning to make a visit to see this room, or East Wing as you call it. I want to understand why anyone would go to all this trouble, and more importantly, take the time to understand your viewpoint."

His smooth words were not impressing Claudia. "Mr. Blythe, I am only the administrator here. If you want more of an explanation, I think you should call the Countess, as she has advised me that anyone who wants to visit the East Wing must have her approval."

"I plan on coming tomorrow morning and will be at Penbroke around eleven. Let the Countess know, and if she has a problem, she can call me." He was politely stern, not wanting anyone to dictate what procedure he should take when an offer to see the room had been made at the board meeting already.

Claudia curtly replied, "As you wish."

"See you then. I'm looking forward to our next encounter." He hung up before she could respond.

I hope he's not going to be a problem, she thought. She didn't have time to dwell on it any longer as she heard a voice shout from the office that there was a Sarah Lloyd waiting to speak with her on line two.

Curious, Claudia answered. "Hello?"

"Claudia, James gave me your name to contact in reference to the East Wing. I was wondering if I could come tomorrow and take a look."

"Mrs. Lloyd, please kindly refresh my memory. I'm not sure who you are."

"I am Peter Lloyd's mother, and James came to stay with us this summer. He mentioned this project you're doing and asked if I would be of help."

"Yes, yes, of course. You are Sarah McKenzie, the author. I've read all your books, and I think you're amazing. Tomorrow morning around eleven would be great, as we have another person who is visiting us for the same reason."

"I look forward to meeting you then, and perhaps we can discuss a potential plan."

"I look forward to it as well. See you then." Claudia was overjoyed. Sarah was just the deflection she needed to stop an imposing Nicholas Blythe. She laughed to herself, thinking maybe Sarah could give her the lowdown on him. She laughed again as she poured herself another cup of tea.

Claudia called to fill Phillipa in on the visits scheduled for the next day. Once she was done, she added, "Since Ms. McKenzie will be here, I don't mind giving the tour by myself if you have other things to take care of; I won't have to be alone with Mr. Blythe."

The Countess, intrigued by the whole thing, replied, "I'm not going to miss this for the world. James and the girls are getting ready for the school term, but I'm sure James will want to be a part of this gathering as well. We'll see you in the morning."

CHAPTER 13

THE THRONE ROOM

Claudia started work early so that she could clear her desk before the visitors arrived. She told her secretary to escort the visitors to the East Wing at eleven. At ten thirty, she headed over to meet Rodney, who had become known as the keeper of the keys.

James and the Countess were already there waiting, but James had informed Rodney not to open the doors until everyone was present. The opening of the room was an event in itself, and he didn't want anyone to miss that impact.

Nicholas and Sarah both arrived on time. They introduced themselves to each other and then followed the secretary to the East Wing.

As Rodney opened the huge portcullis and the two large oak doors to the room, all who were present uttered murmurings of amazement. Even the Countess had forgotten the beauty of this room. Nicholas walked the perimeter, interested in the different clothing and artifacts that had been collected. Sarah made her way directly to the throne, with James close behind. Claudia had no idea what was within these walls and was stunned at the collection.

"So, James, this is the throne you spoke of. It's so beautiful that it would be almost impossible to describe. And this is where you sat? May I?"

"Be my guest."

Sarah couldn't wait to experience this moment. As she sat on the throne, James could see an aura of shimmering light all about her, and he could tell that she was swirling her way through the vortex. Everyone watched, but only James knew what she was experiencing. She was back within an instant, her eyes wide open. James suspected she had gone to the same place he had been. She stood up and looked over at James with a huge smile.

"So?" James asked.

"You and I must have a little discussion. That is the most powerful experience I've ever had." Her already blue eyes were shimmering from the experience; the joy she exuded gave James the answer he was expecting. She had traversed the galaxy, as he had done, and she couldn't wait to share their stories.

Everyone looked at her, puzzled, wondering what it was all about. Nicholas wanted to sit there as well, so he could experience what she had. He proudly marched toward the great chair and sat down. The others could see him becoming dizzy, and then his head fell forward. He jumped off almost as quickly as he had sat down. "I don't know what that chair does, but I've never felt so strange in all my life. That chair is different. What's its origin, James?"

"The throne was found in the foothills of the Himalayas. It belonged to a monastery, and as the Seventh Earl tells us in his notes, its history dates all the way back to Atlantis." James figured Nicholas wouldn't even begin to understand.

"Atlantis? The lost continent of Atlantis? That's a load of bunk; no one has ever proved the validity of that civilization. I remember chaps in school fantasizing about the islands. However, there is something very strange about that throne. I can at least attest to that."

"Would you like to learn?" asked Sarah politely.

"Learn what? Not about Atlantis. But I would like to learn about that throne, yes." He looked at her curiously.

"The Atlanteans had the ability to transport themselves through time and space. The throne creates a vortex, but if your chakra points aren't aligned, you don't have balance. Your fear will stop you from having the experience you should have had."

"If you don't mind me asking, who exactly are you?"

"As I told you when we first met earlier, I am the mother of Peter Lloyd, who attends the same school as James. However, my pen name is Sarah McKenzie. You may have heard of me or read some of my books."

"You are well known, to be sure, but I must tell you that I don't believe in that sort of thing, and frankly, I look down on anyone who does. We have our religion and our Bible, and if anyone wants knowledge of the afterlife, they need to follow that." He was far from a religious person himself, but he knew that what he'd experienced was real. Whether the throne was good or evil, he couldn't quite understand.

"The throne is not evil; it is something you could learn from."

"So now you can tell what I'm thinking?"

"It's in your aura. You're afraid, and that's quite normal. Most people would be, so don't feel for a moment that yours is not a normal reaction."

Nicholas turned to James. "James, you've sat on that throne before. What did you experience?"

"I hope I'm correct in saying exactly what Sarah felt; however, I'm sure our experiences are different, but they are there for each one of us."

"So you intend to put people through this teleportation experience and make a buck at it?"

"Nicholas, you too can learn those skills. We want to set up a school so people who want to become more spiritually aware can learn what we call *divinessence.*"

"I don't know where all this is going to lead, but you're obviously into this stuff, so tell me how you're going to run a bank one day. I'm not sure that my confidence wouldn't be clearly shaken with a chairman that has his head filled with this kind of activity. Thank God for Nigel Thompson. All I can say is, I hope Sir Thomas has enough sense to see this as a commercial operation and not some mumbo-jumbo idea for a bunch of quacks."

"Look, it's for each person to choose his or her own way. I can assure you no one is going to be sitting on that throne unless they have had a lot of instruction from Sarah and her staff. You were allowed only because you didn't ask before sitting down, so I can only apologize if this was not a positive experience. That being said, you have to open your mind to the possibility that others will have a different point of view."

James could see Nicholas was the type of person who could be a bully and liked getting his own way. Anything he saw that threatened his belief or control was unnerving to him. He liked his power and position. He saw this venture as an infraction on all that he believed.

Claudia was quietly watching the situation unfold. The Countess was a little perturbed with Nicholas's statements, but being a pragmatic person and similar in nature, she saw some validity to his comments.

Nicholas didn't want to stay any longer; he bid his goodbyes and wandered back to his car, with the Countess accompanying him.

James asked if Claudia and Sarah would like to go to a pub and have lunch so that they could talk further on the subject. "Let's leave my mother with Nicholas; she knows how to talk to him."

As James opened the door to the little pub in Penbroke village, he asked, "So, Sarah, what did you experience?"

"It was awesome. I was able to talk to my master, who is a woman, and she told me so much. It was so rewarding to feel totally there in the Pleiades star system. As you know, I channel a lot of information to help others, but to have someone talk to me about my family and so on was beautiful. I will share the experience with you sometime, James, but most of it was about my life for a change. I did learn how this room and the school will fulfill a tremendous need worldwide. You have no idea what goodwill come from this project. Books will be written about it and films will be made. It will take time, but slowly, people will come. By the turn of this century, it will be a destination for many people throughout the world. We are all playing a small part in the evolvement of our race so we can move onto other much-needed work in our universe."

"Mrs. Lloyd, I have read your books, and I must say what a privilege it is to be here with you. Would it be possible to sit with you before you leave?" asked Claudia politely.

"Of course, my dear, but you don't have to sit with me. You have the ability to find out for yourself."

"How do you know that?" Claudia was confused.

"You are a very beautiful person, inside and out. I can see it from your aura. You can sit on that throne, and your own master will tell you all that you need to know."

"Really? Can I, James?"

"Of course."

"I know the answer you are looking for, and you will find it," added Sarah with confidence.

After lunch, the three went back to the East Wing. Rodney had left the portcullis open and the doors unlocked, so they walked straight to the throne. Claudia nervously approached the throne, not wanting an experience like Nicholas had had.

She sat down slowly, and then, within a flash, both Sarah and James could see she was gone. Within almost the same instant, she returned, but both James and Sarah knew she had been away much longer. She had the same starry-eyed look Sarah had had.

Claudia slowly got up from the throne feeling as if she were floating on air. "That was truly an experience. Was I away long?"

"No, it was only an instant from the time you sat down," replied James.

"Really? It seemed like I was gone for ages. So, time is different on other planets?"

Sarah answered, "Yes, we are a denser three-dimensional planet, so time and space are more distorted. Did you get the answers you were looking for?"

"You were right. I got all the answers I needed. It was an experience I will never forget. It clarifies so many things that I believed incorrectly. I can't understand why Nicholas had such an unfortunate experience."

"My dear, we are not all ready for these types of things. The biggest barriers are fear and lack of trust, but you have that spiritual alignment and trust, so the vortex is able to take you to your destination."

"What a great team we're going to make," said James, excited that Claudia could experience what he and Sarah had.

"James, I had no idea you had done this. Does your mother know?"

"No, and I don't plan to tell her. She would experience exactly what Nicholas did, and we don't want any more negativity. In time, she may come around, but let's just leave it at that."

"Now I see how you have progressed so greatly since your father died. This was a wonderful legacy he left you. You have shown great maturity in sharing this with no one except Sarah."

Sarah said, "I must be getting along. I have a plan in mind, and when you get nearer to starting the project, Claudia, perhaps you could give me a call?"

"I will. It was a delight to meet you finally."

The meeting broke up, and Rodney was summoned to close up the room. Rodney showed James and Claudia back to the house, where the Countess was waiting to have a final conversation.

"By God, we shook up Nicholas. I don't think he's ever had an experience like that before," laughed the Countess.

"Yes, that was unfortunate, but he should have taken a little more time to get to know Sarah. I think she could have helped him a lot," James said, disappointed with Nicholas's gutless response.

The Countess replied, "No good talking to someone like that. He wouldn't understand if you tried. But don't worry; I'm going to see him in London soon, and I'm far too good a customer of his for him to not support the bank. He knows I know all the people he does business with. In time, he'll talk about it, but I think he just wants to go away and try to understand what really happened. Good will eventually come of it, I'm sure."

"More importantly, Mother, what do you think about it?"

"Well, darling, to be honest, I had forgotten what was in that room. It always gave me the shivers. But to see Sarah McKenzie's eyes glow like that after being on that throne tells me there's something to it. If Nicholas would have gotten up and said nothing, I would have had my doubts, but his negative experience also indicates there's something there. I believe Sarah will be an asset. I know her name, and she's not where she is for nothing. You know I'm not a great believer in all those things, and it's probably because I, like Nicholas, would be a little nervous. I think with time, I will want to have some answers to many questions in my life, but I'm just not ready yet. I now believe what you're doing is right, and who knows? I might even take a course myself."

"Mother, I'm so glad you see what I have felt all along. I can't tell you what this means to me." James hugged his mother for the first time in a long time.

"Oh, James, that was nice. My son loves me, and that's the most important thing of all."

The three parted ways, content with the day's happenings. James went upstairs to finish packing. He thought about everything that had happened and the experience with Nicholas. He knew that there would be others like him—naysayers. He must get used to that and stand his ground and continue to believe. In time, more and more people would come to understand the wonderful gift the Seventh Earl had given to them all.

Claudia headed back to her cottage, lost in thought. She was happy to learn the real reason for Paul's early departure and was anxious to tell Sir Thomas about it and the true feeling of release she felt from this experience. She had learned so much about her family and the amazing connection that she and James had shared in many lifetimes together. They had reincarnated for a reason, and the purpose was now clear.

Phillipa headed to her room, reflecting on the day and how proud she was with the way James had stood up to Nicholas. He had taken the high road, she thought, and Nicholas could certainly learn a thing or two from her son. James had shown the understanding that Collin had shown to her—a quality she so missed.

CHAPTER 14

THE WORLD OF FASHION

It didn't take long for Claudia to find the right person for the job, as she had advertised extensively. By the end of her last month, she had been successful in finding the right candidate. His name was Keith Pruett, and he would move his family from Scotland to Penbroke. Having attended the Agricultural College at Cirencester, he had experience in estate management and farming. His professional experience had been with two large estates, the most recent of which was an estate in Scotland that had to open to the public—offering sporting activities, such as hunting, shooting, fishing, riding, and sailing—in order to pay for the upkeep of the twenty thousand-acre property. The grounds were not blessed with rich soil, so sheep farming and beef cattle contributed to the bottom line. His education also included accounting, an absolute necessity for a good business manager at Penbroke. Keith had a good nature and consistent work ethic, according to his references. He was leaving his job in Scotland after ten years because his wife was finding life in the Scottish Highlands a little too remote.

Keith had daughters who attended a boarding school in Hertfordshire, so his family needed a sensibly sized home to spend their holiday time together. The Penbroke Estate cottage had been divided into two, so Claudia had given instructions to the maintenance staff to return the cottage to its original configuration to better meet the family's needs. The family was used to country life, and Keith's wife had even been brought up on a dairy farm in Devonshire.

Keith had met the Countess, and she thoroughly approved of his energetic hands-on ideas for implementing the East Wing project. She also liked his ideas for renovating the cottages. The farm was holding its own at the moment, but the extra income would help to make them more competitive with new investments in capital equipment. Keith was living at Claudia's old cottage temporarily until the whole place was ready. He was traveling every other weekend down to Devonshire, where his wife was now staying with her family.

This was a relief for Claudia, as she was now expected to be full-time at the bank. All the children were back in school, so the Countess was free to spend more time in London.

Over the next few months, Claudia became quite proficient at her new job. She had dinner with the Countess on occasion and kept her up-to-date on all that was going on, but she felt very comfortable with the work Keith was doing at the estate.

Claudia and Sir Thomas were seeing a lot of one another. She stayed at the flat in Knightsbridge during the week and then went to the house in Hampstead on the weekends. Sir Thomas was dreaming up the perfect engagement scenario, but he thought he would wait until closer to Christmas to propose. Phillipa had seen him from time to time, but she was now seeing another socialite and was spending a number of weekends in the south of France, where she enjoyed going this time of year. The weather wasn't perfect, but anything beat the cold and dampness of an impending English winter.

One morning, as Claudia was working in her office, Nicholas Blythe stopped by. "I was talking over some of my investments with Nigel, and I couldn't help but notice that you were here now. So, had enough of the estate and dusty old thrones? Come to live with us in the big city?"

"Well, well, it's been a while. If I remember correctly, you barely said goodbye on your last visit to the estate. So, what do I owe the privilege of seeing you this time?"

He ignored her question. "Where do you live? Or do you commute?" He sat down in front of her desk.

"Nicholas, that's a personal question. I don't pry into your personal activities, and I would appreciate you doing the same."

"Claudia, look, I've done nothing but have admiration for you since your presentation in the boardroom. Please don't act so defensively. All I want to do is show you around London. It's the least I can do for a new girl who's come to live among us."

"I am busy at the moment, but maybe in time, we could have lunch. And I would be happy, as you are a shareholder of this bank, to get to know you better. But please allow me my personal life for now. A job like this is very demanding. It's taking all my efforts to give the bank and people like yourself all the relevant information you need so that you feel comfortable with your investments." She tried to sound all business.

"Now, Claudia, I may look stupid, but a woman like you doesn't go unnoticed. If you think for one moment that I believe you go home every night without seeing someone, a boyfriend or someone, you're kidding yourself."

Claudia was becoming frustrated. She took a big breath and blew it out, without saying a word.

He continued, though he sounded more humbled than she had ever heard him sound. "Look, I like you, and I'm coming by tomorrow to take you out for lunch. I have told Nigel so he won't think I'm being improper, and we can take it from there. After lunch, you can tell me to get lost, and I won't impose upon you again, or you'll see the charming person I really am."

"Okay, but remember, I like my job, so I'm back here by two o'clock, or I will be in serious trouble." She hoped this would get rid of him.

"Thanks, Claudia. You won't regret this, I promise."

When he finally left, she got up and went to Mr. Thompson's office and knocked on his door. He answered, "Come in, Claudia. What's up?"

"It's this Nicholas Blythe; do I have to go out to lunch with him?"

"You don't have to, but it would be advisable. He is a shareholder and is considering further investment in the bank. In a sense, he's a client, and as you are single, I think it would be a nice treat, especially for all the hard work you've done. Claudia, give it a shot. What have you got to lose? The man won't eat you, for God's sake." He laughed.

"I wish I could be sure of that. I will keep you informed, as it is my responsibility." Claudia preferred to treat the whole matter as an official duty, as her father would have done as an ambassador.

That evening, she couldn't stop thinking about Nicholas. She didn't trust him; she knew he was up to no good. She hadn't told Mr. Thompson about her relationship with Sir Thomas, so it was still a secret. Even the Countess didn't know yet. She was concerned that if she told Sir Thomas about the lunch, he might overreact and get jealous. It was a business luncheon, and she would treat it as such. She was resigned to the thought and decided she wasn't going to lose any sleep over it.

The next morning, she dressed a little more formally than usual in a new business suit and blouse. She also wore a little more makeup than usual. She was going to look the part, even though her heart wasn't in it. She knew that Nicholas was trying to make it look like business, when what he was really trying to do was take her out on a date.

The morning passed quickly, and as expected, Nicholas arrived early for the appointment. She made a point of waving to Mr. Thompson before her departure as a way of saying it was his idea, not hers.

She was impressed, however, with Nicholas's white Rolls Royce. She also liked that he was dressed appropriately for a change, in a pin-striped suit and shoes to match, and she approved of his burgundy-red and blue tie. He was making an effort to conform, Claudia noticed.

They chatted politely about the weather and London politics on the way to the restaurant; it wasn't until they were seated for lunch that Nicholas started to get more personal. "Claudia, I know you haven't had the best impression of me since our first meeting. I would like today to be the first, and hopefully, one of many more meetings where you get to know the real me, and in exchange, I want to better understand you."

"Nicholas, I know you are trying very hard to impress me, but you really don't have to. I am not that special, and with a reputation like yours, why would you even bother?"

"That's where you are wrong. In all my years as a bachelor, I've never met a woman who is as beautiful as you are and who has the brains to go with it. Looks and brains are not a common combination, but for a woman to have both at the highest level is enough to blow any man away. The funny thing is, you don't even identify yourself with that image, and that makes you all the more appealing."

"I know you are not trying to flatter me. I truly believe you are being sincere, but I am looking for a man whom is a little older than you are and who has had his days of taking out younger women." She told the truth and hoped it would stick.

"Yes, I can understand your point of view, but when a man finds a jewel of a person like you, why would he look any further?"

"When I am ten years older and you are also, you can get a woman younger than I am now. I want to be with someone for the long term. I have spent far too much time alone. Can you understand that?"

"Completely. So let's work on being friends, and as time progresses, we'll see what the future holds." He knew it was a good time to back off.

"Amen to that. So tell me about your business. I see you in all these magazines, so I feel quite special sitting with you today at lunch." She noticed people looking over at their table.

"When I got out of school, my father put me to work in our factories. I learned the trade, so to speak. In the past, we sold our merchandise to wholesalers, who in turn sold to the garment industry. In my early thirties, I decided to make a go of it alone, but obviously with the goodwill of my father. I realized I had a flare for design and women's clothing. Our shop here in London has brought me a lot of attention. Many of England's top families wear my products and like my designs."

"I admire your courage to step out and make something of your life. From what I read, your clothing is popular in all of Europe and the States. You are an exciting man for any woman to be with, and you're not bad looking, to boot!" She thought it was only polite to make a compliment, as he done nothing but praise her from the start.

"Thank you. That's the first nice thing you've said to me since we met. I'm going to savor that while we choose lunch and a good bottle of wine. Roast beef on the trolley for you? It's what I normally have when I come here."

"Yes, a great idea. Looks very tasty." She hadn't eaten much the night before, and now, feeling a little more relaxed, she realized she was starving. A good slice of roast sirloin was just what she wanted.

"So tell me a little about yourself. Your CV, by the way, is very impressive. You should be very proud. To be the best takes hard work, and when we become successful, people forget what it took to get there." He was hoping to make her feel there was more substance to him than she previously recognized.

"When I left school, I worked several jobs to gain experience and to help pay for college. Even though I had a scholarship, I still had to eat and pay my bills. It was there that I met Paul, who was studying to be an engineer, and we were so in love that it seemed a perfect match." Claudia continued to tell the story of her first love and the tragic loss she had experienced.

"I can understand. Losing a loved one can be a heartbreaking experience. I too had a similar situation with a girlfriend. After leaving school, she died of leukemia, and I haven't met anyone like her until you came along."

"I never realized that. So you and I share similar circumstances. The only difference is you go out with a lot more women than I do men."

"Yes, but it's the business I'm in. Women are always fascinated when a man knows how they should be dressed. I'm like you; I've been just as lonely." He hoped this would get to her. He was telling the truth, and not many people knew this about him.

"How many people really know about you, and how many women know if you are sincere?" She was looking at him in a different way.

"No one."

"Why?"

"Because you are the first person outside my family I would ever wish to share that with."

"You are a very different person than what I thought. You certainly don't wear your heart on your sleeve."

"It's what pushed me to do the design work I do now. I just wanted to plunge my whole life into my work. Go out with women, yes, as part of my work, but no one has ever compared to my Mary. She was the person for me. We shared the same interests and hobbies."

They finished lunch, he paid the bill, and they got in his car. As they drove along, she noticed that he wasn't taking her back to the bank. Concerned, she asked, "Nicholas, where are we going?"

"My business. I want to show you where I work and what I do. Don't worry; Nigel knows all about it and approves."

She laughed. "Oh, you schemer. You got me out to lunch as a trick, and you know it." After an excellent bottle of wine, she felt very happy to be in his company, something she could never have predicted.

They parked on the lower floor of his four-story shop at a very carefully chosen location on Vigo Street. This street was at the intersection of the famous Savile Row. Savile Row had been known for being the finest place to buy a suit for men since the mid-1700s. Nicholas thought the location was perfect because the men who had the money were just around the corner and would be able to treat their women with the same consideration. His maintenance man/caretaker for the building was on hand and ran to open the door for Claudia.

They climbed into the lift, and Nicholas pressed the number four to go to the top floor where all his offices and administration staff were. The doors opened, and Nicholas proudly walked by all his well-dressed staff to his office with Claudia, who was sizing up his business very quickly. Nicholas's office was not what she had imagined. Everything was glass and chrome, including his desk, his small conference table, and his private bathroom. The pictures he had on the wall were of beautiful women wearing a variety of fashionable clothes, obviously designed and made by him.

"Impressive, Nicholas. Definitely a woman's taste, I would say." She gave a nod of approval.

"Well, that's the business I'm in. N'est-ce pas?"

"It's appropriate, I agree."

Nicholas called to his secretary, "Jane, could you ask Jackie to come up to my office for a moment?" He had a plan he was going to put into action.

Moments later, Jackie, Nicholas's assistant, walked in. "Yes, sir, is your client ready?" Jackie had a great gift for fitting a woman into the right clothes. She knew that what looked great on the hanger didn't always look good on a person, and she knew exactly how to carefully adapt her client to what she really needed.

Nicholas turned to Claudia. "Ms. Langley, my assistant Jackie is here to accommodate your every need. Try on anything you like, and then we can discuss the details later." He made the necessary introductions, winked at Claudia, and then motioned Jackie to leave. He could tell that Claudia was anxious, so he thought it best to take her down to the showroom himself.

"Now, Nicholas, I'm not here to buy a bunch of clothes from you. I had a wonderful lunch, but your clothes are way out of my league. I'm used to buying clothes at much more modest shops than this."

"Please, I want to indulge you. You can go down to the showroom and pick out any number of dresses you want, and it won't cost you a penny."

"And what do you want from me in return?"

"Nothing. Relax, will you? If I want to spoil you, that's my business. Can you not indulge me?"

"You promise that you expect nothing from me in return? Because I can't do something like that. I would never take advantage of you, and I would expect the same from you."

"Claudia, I promise that after you have chosen whatever you want, I will not ask a thing from you."

"Then I must be the luckiest woman on the planet. Let's go! I can't wait."

They descended the stairs to the third floor where Jackie was waiting to show Claudia the winter collection. Nicholas went back to his office to take care of business. He summoned his photographer to his office and told him to take pictures of Ms. Langley and tell her that they were for her so she would have a special memory of the day. However, Nicholas had another idea in mind. He knew she was exactly the kind of woman that could sell clothing. Her long legs, her sculptured face, and her classic deportment with a hint of Latin, would appeal to his clientele, which ranged in age from the late twenties to around fifty. With one phone call to the editor of *Fashion World*, Claudia, he knew, would be front-page material.

About an hour later, Nicholas went down to see how things were going. Claudia looked magnificent in her tweed skirt and topcoat. He thought, *With the right pair of short fur-trimmed boots and a fur hat, she would look magnificent on the page of a magazine.* She was beaming from ear to ear; she'd never had so much attention, and she was enjoying it thoroughly.

"Nicholas, you know how to get a woman hooked. I love your designs, and I have found four outfits with Jackie's help. They will need a little adjustment, as I suppose my legs are a little longer than normal, and the jackets and dresses need adjustments in the front. I am told that's not a tall order, so I can come back after the alterations are done."

"Now, what I want you to do after you have finished here is for Jackie to take you down to the ground floor, where we have our cosmetics department. A trained consultant will work with you to advise you on how you would look best and give you a few tips." He was cautious in his wording; he didn't want her to think she had no idea how to make herself up.

"Oh, that will be so much fun. I want to experiment with some blushes and shades. I know I am still not totally knowledgeable in the ways of makeup, especially when it comes to a place like London."

Good, he thought, *she took that well.* He returned to his office to let the girls do their thing.

When it got close to closing time, Nicholas went down to the ground floor to see how Claudia was doing. As he turned from the elevator, he couldn't believe the job his staff had done on her makeup. "Claudia, you look stunning." All his staff agreed.

"Nicholas, I've never been able to get my makeup to look like this. What I've learned today is priceless!" She got up from her stool and gave him a big hug.

"It's my way of saying thank you for coming today."

Nicholas was not one to show this kind of emotion easily, but Claudia could see from the water in his eyes that he was ecstatic with her response.

He whispered to her quietly, "Go upstairs, and I'll help you pick out any evening dress you want. Grab an evening coat because we are going to go dancing to celebrate the day."

Claudia was on cloud nine, wondering what other tricks he had up his sleeve. He had been so kind and generous, and she was in it now for whatever was ahead. She was going to make the best of it because she had never before had a day like this.

Nicholas walked up the stairs with her and picked the very dress he thought she would look fabulous in. It was low cut and came to just above her knees. The white satin looked amazing against her skin. The back had a crisscross pattern with a see-through shade of lace, and the strapless front slightly revealed the very best features of her beautiful body. He grabbed a pair of thinly strapped charcoal-black high heels, and he took a black evening coat, long and classical in design, with a large collar that lay across the shoulders. The first center button of the coat was just below the bustline so it would not detract from her graceful form, and the large collar could be unlatched to hide any hint of her cleavage. This was what he did best; he knew exactly how to make a woman look fabulous.

The pair headed out again, but this time, Nicholas had his caretaker drive them to their destination.

"So, where are you taking me tonight, kind sir?" asked Claudia, who was feeling like a princess going to a ball.

"We are going to the Fantasy Bar on King's Road. I think you'll like it. It's a fun place with plenty of good music."

"Sounds intriguing. I can't wait to dance. I know how to do all the rock 'n' roll steps, so I warn you to get ready!"

Claudia remembered King's Road from the evening she had spent with Phillipa. She never dreamed she would be going out to a place like that again so soon. The place was new and had all the latest gadgets, from strobe lights, to crystal balls that showered the dance floor with different-colored speckles, to very powerful speakers. There was a long bar, tiered seating, and a fabulous dance floor. The place was busy and alive. Nicholas certainly knew where to go to have fun. The owner gave them the best table in the house so that they could chat intimately in between dancing.

Nicholas ordered a bottle of crystal champagne on ice. The two looked radiant as they clicked their glasses to the sound of Jan and Dean's "Fun, Fun, Fun."

"Claudia, I want to thank you again for coming, and I also wanted to apologize for my behavior at Penbroke when we were in the room of the East Wing." He had wanted to say this for some time.

"Really? Why now?"

"Because I didn't tell you or anyone, for that matter, that when I sat on the throne, I could feel Mary reaching out to me, and I was just too afraid to go there. I've been so angry at God for taking her away from me that I was confused and became rude and cryptic in my conversation with James. I have regretted what I said ever since."

"You did act strangely, and I didn't understand why you became so defensive all of a sudden. You're not the first person that's felt that way, nor will you be the last. All of us have issues. Sarah McKenzie knew how you felt but had far too much class to say anything. James did handle the situation well for a young man. He will make a fine chairman when his day comes. I believe you'll be very proud to know him, as I am."

"Tell me something. Did you travel through that vortex?" he asked apprehensively.

"Yes, I did, and I got a lot of answers to why Paul died, and that has helped me completely release him, as he wished. I also learned a lot of other things, but they were private matters about my family."

"Well, that's enough for me. If you experienced what James and Sarah did, then I'm sold. It's real. There really is something there, and it's truly amazing. I can't think of another place anywhere that has a treasure like that. I want to attend classes with Sarah McKenzie. I want to grow and see a new way of life and believe that there is truly something more. With my strict Roman Catholic upbringing, I was taught that dabbling in experiments of this nature was wrong. It's not that I don't think that throne is a force for good. I was taught that we should listen well to our teaching and be true to our faith."

"That is the blind ignorance that we were all taught to believe, but with this throne, there lies an opportunity to help many people seek what they should do with their lives."

"Well, let's dance before we get smashed on all this champagne."

"Good idea!"

The two of them danced until they were completely out of breath and needed a break. They staggered back to their table, eyes lit up with the magic of the moment. Their ears were hissing with the sound of the music.

"Let's order some snacks before we drink too much more." Nicholas motioned to the staff to bring them both some sandwiches and mixed vegetables. "Claudia, this is fun. I haven't danced like this in a while, and like you said, you certainly know the moves."

"With all these new groups coming out, it's hard to keep up

with all the talent. I particularly like the Beach Boys, but I think we need to do a slow one next, don't you?"

They ate their snacks while slowly sipping on their champagne and some sparkling water.

As the evening rolled on, some slow songs started to play. As Claudia had suggested, they got up to dance again. It was the first time they had held one another in an intimate way, and it became clear that there was a strong attraction between them. He could smell the beautiful fragrance from her Bal a Versailles perfume. Her soft cheek rested against his face, and he knew this woman was the one for him. He knew nothing about her relationship with Sir Thomas, and like Sir Thomas, he too felt he was the luckiest man in the world.

After a few more dances, he noticed it was getting close to midnight. For the last dance of the evening, the DJ played Elvis Presley's "Can't Help Falling in Love (with You)." The couple pulled each other close and danced in romantic bliss to the soulful sounds of Elvis's suave voice.

Nicholas's driver picked them up as planned, at midnight. In the distance, Claudia could hear the sound of Big Ben chiming. She couldn't help thinking that she was like Cinderella. She asked to be dropped off at Harrods with some of the bags she had already. Nicholas thought that she was staying with the Countess but thought it inappropriate to pry. He did get a beautiful, passionate kiss from her before she left the back seat of his Rolls. He was overjoyed.

Claudia slowly walked to the flat. She hoped that Sir Thomas wouldn't be there to interrogate her. This had been one of the finest days she had ever experienced. Fortunately, there was not a sound in the flat, and she couldn't wait to drop into bed and fall fast asleep.

CHAPTER 15

CHOICES

Claudia awoke to the sound of her telephone ringing. It was Sir Thomas. "Claudia, are you all right? I was worried sick about you. I wish you had given me a call. If I hadn't been out with a client, I would have come over." He knew she went to see Nicholas Blythe because he had called Nigel Thompson the night before. He assumed that she spent more time with him than planned and probably went out with him that evening. However, he was going to see what she had to say before making any comments or accusations.

Still groggy, she said, "Oh, Thomas, let me get up and get some coffee, and then I'll call you back."

"Call me at my office, and then we can talk." She noticed a slight undertone of irritation.

"I will. I promise."

She slowly got up. She hadn't drunk that much in a while, and she had quite a hangover. She went downstairs to put on the kettle. As she sat drinking a strong cup of coffee, she decided to call Nigel Thompson. It was nearly ten o'clock, and he would be wondering where she was. "Nigel, I've had a hectic week, and I wondered if you wouldn't mind me taking a day off? I will make it up to you."

"Absolutely, my dear. You deserve it. Nicholas Blythe has just invested a quarter of a million with the bank, and he has bought out Sir John Pearson's shares for a good price. He is now a 10 percent shareholder of the bank; outside James, he is the largest shareholder we have. I don't know what spell you put him under, but you certainly have done something we've all been trying to do for years." He sounded exhilarated.

"Well, congratulations! That is some positive news. I was glad to be of assistance."

"Take the day off, and we'll see you bright and early tomorrow."

Claudia was flabbergasted. She wondered, *What is he planning to do? He did have an agenda, and he wanted me to have all the praise for his making this investment.* The more she thought about it, the more confused she became. *Now I don't know whether I'm in love with the man or just infatuated!*

She got up and paced the room. "What must I do?" she asked herself aloud. "Make a decision between Thomas and Nicholas? Oh, this whole situation is a powder keg. I must call Thomas and tell him the truth. I don't know what else to do. He must already be suspicious if Nicholas has made that kind of investment this quickly."

This is ridiculous, she thought. *After five years of being on my own, now I'm stuck with choosing between two of the most eligible bachelors any woman could hope to meet.* She wasn't typically a smoker, but she kept a pack in the kitchen drawer for stress relief and was now burning her way through it.

Frustrated, she picked up the phone to call Sir Thomas. "Thomas, I do hope I'm not disturbing you."

"No, not at all. I'm so glad you called."

"I had an unusual day yesterday, and I think we need to meet so we can talk about it. I believe it's going to take some time to explain all the details. It would be better if you could come over, as I have taken the day off. I'm exhausted."

"I was afraid of that. Nicholas is quite the charmer, and I suspect he's worked his magic on you. I will be over later this afternoon, so rest up, and we can go and get a bite somewhere, okay?" As a man of the world, he knew that hustler had compromised her, but he would stay calm.

"Okay, see you later, then." ·

Claudia was relieved and decided to let matters unfold as they should, but there was only one problem—she felt distant from Sir Thomas and had a deep need to see Nicholas right at that moment. She would ask for some space from Sir Thomas if need be, and she would find somewhere else to live until she could sort out her thoughts. She had no one to turn to who would possibly understand her dilemma. She poured another cup of coffee and thought about the whole saga.

Then an idea popped into her head. She could call the Countess. She was the one person who could give her advice. The only risk was that she might be jealous of Sir Thomas and Nicholas vying for her attention at the same time. However, she'd had the opportunity to have either one of them and hadn't taken it. It was a risk Claudia was prepared to take. This would be a good test of their relationship.

She got up the nerve to call Phillipa. "Hello, Phillipa. I do hope I'm not disturbing you."

"Claudia, how are you, my dear? I was just thinking about you the other day and wondering how you were doing." She sounded like she missed her company.

"If it's possible, I would like to see you and get your advice on something."

"Really? About men, I'm sure. Welcome to London. I wondered how long it would take before someone recognized the catch you are," she laughed.

"How did you know?"

"Let me guess—it's a toss-up between Sir Thomas and Nicholas Blythe, and there may be a third I don't know about." She was teasing, which both surprised and relieved Claudia. "Of course you can see me. How about tonight?"

"That would be splendid. Around seven thirty at your place?"

"Yes. We can go for dinner at the bistro on King's Road. I look forward to seeing you, my dear."

As expected, Sir Thomas arrived around three thirty. Claudia had made herself look respectable for his visit. She opened the door and gave him a big hug and a kiss. Then they went to the kitchen where she had opened a bottle of wine in preparation of the much-needed talk.

"Well, my dear, it seems you've made old Nigel happy at the bank. Nicholas Blythe wasted no time in buying up Sir John's shares and putting a hefty amount of money into the bank. So what is it you have on your mind?"

"Thomas, I'm confused. Yesterday, I had a day that I thought I was going to hate. I went to lunch with Nicholas solely for the bank at the insistence, in a way, of Nigel Thompson, who of course, knows nothing about us. The day turned out to be so different than anything I could have imagined. I got to know Nicholas a lot better; he's a much nicer person than I gave him credit for. His intentions are so forceful that I'm completely confused."

Sir Thomas took a long sip on his glass of wine and then proceeded to open up one of his cigars. Claudia grabbed a cigarette to calm her nerves.

"You've taken up smoking?" asked Sir Thomas.

"Not really. It's just been a challenging day, and I needed something to calm my nerves."

"Claudia, you know my feelings, of course, and I would be

terribly sad to lose you, but I don't want to be with someone who wants to be with someone else."

"Thomas, I know what I feel for you is sincere, but I never thought I could feel this way about anyone else, and it's confusing me terribly."

"He's quite the charmer; I'm sure you know that. There are plenty of women who can tell you their own story, but I know we can only experience these things personally. As much as I love you and want you in my life, I would never want to go further unless you want me. You have to be 100 percent sure that you are with the right man. That being said, you can't imagine how I'm feeling at his moment; the very thought of you not being a part of my life would be devastating."

"Do you want me to move out? I will if you want me to." She looked pathetically humble, feeling as if she'd jilted the most honorable man she'd ever known.

"Claudia, I didn't get into this relationship with you for you to be unhappy or unsure of the choice you're making. Nothing has to change for now. Give yourself a week to think about things. After all, you've only been out with this person one time, and for all you know, it could be infatuation. It's understandable; you've been shut away so long in Lincolnshire, and then, all of a sudden, men are pursuing you. You are a very attractive woman, and Nicholas won't be the last, I can assure you. So there's no need to rush things. Take your time, and be sure of your direction." He spoke wisely, as only a man of his age and experience could. He thought, *If she doesn't see the value in me, then I'm not right for her, as much as it would deeply hurt me.*

"Thomas, you are a brick of a person, and right now, I'm a basket case. I'm so inexperienced at this sort of thing, and I'm sure you're right. I want you to know that I intend to not see either one of you until I can make up my own mind because feeling like this is terrible. I want to do my job well and be of value to all who have put their trust in me."

"If you weren't that type of woman, I wouldn't be sitting here with you now. I know you will sort things out in your own way, and that's your right. I hope it's in my favor. I'll just have to wait and see."

"I promised Phillipa that I would see her tonight, so if you don't mind, can I take a rain check on getting a bite with you? I promise I will make my mind up soon. I hate hurting people; it's just not who I am. But there's no need to rush off; we have plenty of time to finish the wine."

"Talk to the Countess. It's time she knew the way things are. She's a practical woman, and she'll give you some good advice, I'm sure."

Sir Thomas and Claudia finished off the bottle. She knew that she wouldn't find another man like him. She doubted that Nicholas would treat the situation with such calmness and maturity. They talked about many things, and the air between them slowly began to clear.

He appreciated her honesty, and he realized how challenging a new life in London could be for a woman as attractive as she. Her innocence was appealing and was what made her so endearing to many people. Finally, he put out his cigar and finished his last glass of wine. He then got up, gave her a hug and a kiss, and said, "I know you'll find your way. You're too intelligent not to. Even if it's neither of us, you will be with the right person, I know that for sure."

After he left, she got ready to meet the Countess. This was becoming a more hectic day than she had imagined, but at least matters were finding a direction.

Once she arrived at Phillipa's, they caught the taxi to the bistro. Claudia looked across the street, thinking about the night before when she was listening to the strikes of Big Ben. She didn't feel much like Cinderella right now.

They sat at Phillipa's usual table and placed their orders. The Countess began the difficult conversation. "So, what's bothering you, my dear? I'm your girlfriend now, and you can tell me anything you want." She was enjoying the moment.

"You were right earlier. I've being seeing Sir Thomas, and I believe he has quite an affection for me." Claudia went on to tell the Countess the whole story from beginning to end.

"You've been a very busy girl, but I know Nigel Thompson is very pleased with you. In spite of the situation, you are improving the bank's position, and he's very happy about that. If you are going to survive in London, my dear, you're going to have to get a lot tougher. There are many eligible younger and older men out there who would snap you up in a second. I know you're not a flirt, and even though I blamed Sir Thomas for a while for bringing you here, I now believe it's turned out to be the best thing in the world for you." She took a drink of her chardonnay and then continued. "Nicholas is a younger man, around our age; in fact, I believe he's the same age as I am. Anyway, he's had a wife already; were you aware of that?"

"I had no idea!"

"It's his work. A man like Nicholas has been brought up with privilege. He's the product of a very tough and strict family. He broke away several years ago to get into the fashion trade, and as you have seen, he's done very well, to the point that when his father died, he left everything to him. Men like Nicholas have a need to prove themselves because of the suppression of their early years. Mind you, it's done Nicholas no harm; quite the contrary. A weaker man would have buckled under the stern man I knew his father to be. He did exactly what his father wanted, which was to go out into the world and prove that he was worthy enough to run the empire he's inherited. He is incredibly wealthy, but his primary goal is to make the business he already has grow into an international business. What does that mean for you?

"This man needs a wife that looks beautiful, can entertain and add sparkle to his social life, and frankly, have his kids and make a home for him. He is eligible enough to have any woman from twenty-five to thirty. They are more able to have the kids he'll want to continue on what his family has done for a very long time. As much as you have enchanted him, he will only look around for a younger woman if he does indeed marry you. It may take time, but say ten years from now, when you are not old but not as beautiful as you are now, he'll think he missed an opportunity. He's actually only waking up to the fact now as he has been playing around too long. A younger woman is better, because she won't be as knowledgeable about life as you and I are, and he will have her happily at home being showered with gifts and taking care of his children. Do you get the picture?" Phillipa didn't want to crush her expectations but also didn't want her to make a wrong decision that she may spend a life-time regretting.

"You explain it with a clarity that is so easy to understand and that makes perfect sense."

"I know you think Nicholas is a lot of fun, and he is. He's everything a woman would want. He's good-looking, he knows how to dress a woman, he has money, and he's a great dancer as well."

"So you've been out with him?" Claudia asked innocently.

"Of course. Many times. I doubt he gave me the romantic time he gave you. I'm sure he truly meant everything he told you. He is a man of his word, I can vouch for that, but you have to see the reality of the situation."

"Now, as for Sir Thomas, he's also good-looking, as men tend to get better with age, but he is more stable. He's in need of a wife, and I had thought seriously about him myself. In my case, I found that he's too tied to his work and clientele, and as a re-sult, we drifted apart. He needs a professional woman like you. You can speak all that boring jargon about legal matters, money, and so on."

Claudia listened closely to her friend's advice. She had underestimated Phillipa's experience and had no idea that she thought things through with such depth. She was quietly admiring her and realized how His Lordship must have valued her down-to-earth perspective of life.

Suddenly, Phillipa's countenance changed to a deep sadness. "The truth is that when Sir Thomas first brought up the idea of marriage, I was flattered, but I soon realized that I'm in no hurry to get married again. Collin was the love of my life and will be impossible to replace. I have come to realize how selfish I've been and what a valuable role he played as the father to my children. You, Claudia, have also played a valuable role in taking care of my children. They all love you very much, and I want to thank you for all that you've done. I've learned an important lesson, and that's why I'm making a greater effort to parent and take the time Collin did to really know and understand my children." She took out her handkerchief and started to weep. "Oh, I've been so selfish, and I do miss him so. I never realized how lonely I could be. It was such a shame that he died so early. God certainly teaches us all the lessons we must learn, and the things I've learned since Collin died have changed my whole outlook on life. I never realized the jewel of the man I had while he was alive. No woman could have a finer husband. Maybe someday I'll be ready to marry again, but I'm in no hurry."

Claudia was amazed to realize that Phillipa had held back many of her feelings over the years and was even more surprised that she had now opened up. She came across as such a direct, intimidating person, but deep down, she was very sincere. Wanting to console her, Claudia said, "I love your children immensely and have appreciated your letting me be a big part of their lives. It has helped alleviate some of the pain of losing Paul and not having children of my own. I don't know why, but I've always felt a special connection to James in particular. He has come such a long way since His Lordship passed. I believe it has made James much more mature and responsible. I also know

His Lordship loved you greatly. He told me so many times."

"Thank you for those kind words, Claudia. They mean a lot to me." Phillipa took a deep breath, gathered her composure, and shifted back to the topic at hand. "Going back to Sir Thomas. He's more predictable, and he can be a lot of fun, but he's more of an intellectual like Collin. Those are the best men, from my own experience of men, in the long run. The others can be more entertaining, but they can also give you a lot of heartache."

They finished their dinner, and Claudia thanked Phillipa for her invaluable advice as they parted. She was so glad to have her as a friend; with every visit, it seemed they were becoming closer and closer.

As she headed home, Claudia decided that she would go ahead and take the week, like she said she would, to think everything through.

The next day, Claudia went to work feeling rejuvenated. It was Friday, and she was looking forward to having some time alone over the weekend.

Nigel Thompson popped into her office to congratulate her again on her day with Nicholas. He told her that from now on, they were partners, and she should call him Nigel except when he had company.

As soon as he left her office, Nicholas called. "Claudia, my God! You took the day off and I didn't know how to get in touch with you. Shame on me for not getting your number." He was laughing.

"Well, it's just as well; you were too busy buying up the bank to notice," she teased.

"Well, that's the spell you put on me. I still can't stop thinking about you. How about you?"

"Nicholas, that was the most fabulous day I think I've ever had. You had me seeing stars, but Cinderella has to come back home sometime."

"Cinderella, I've got news for you. The editor of *Fashion*

World magazine wants you to do a photo shoot," he said with unmistakable excitement.

"Now pull my other leg. You're kidding?" Her heart started to beat fast.

"Come to my office tomorrow morning at nine o'clock, and we'll get the ball rolling."

"Nicholas, tomorrow is Saturday. It's the weekend."

"Precisely. There will be less traffic, so you can drive over to Vigo Street, and we can discuss the photo shoot with Darlene Jenson. She can't wait to meet you."

"Give me a minute to take this in. A photo shoot for *Fashion World*?"

"You got it. This is the big time. I'm telling you, this is an opportunity in a million. Most women would die for this kind of opportunity."

"I don't know what to say. What should I wear?"

"Come in slacks, blue jeans, whatever. We'll dress you here."

"Okay, I'll be there. You promise this not a joke to get me to come to your place?"

"I swear it's not, but it's a good idea for another time." He laughed again.

"You're amazing. I'll be there."

"It's what I do. Bye."

The next morning, Claudia made sure she was on time. She hadn't told anyone, as she wanted to make sure that Nicholas wasn't pulling some kind of hoax to get her to his shop. She went in the front door and ascended the staircase to the second floor. Jackie was there, and she took her directly to Nicholas's office.

"Good. You're on time. I would like you to meet Darlene Jenson, who is not only a great friend but the editor of *Fashion World* magazine." He then turned to Darlene and asked, "Doesn't she look beautiful?" He was proud of his new model.

"She's perfect! Just the right features and lovely, long legs.

We'll have to hide the front porch a bit, but we can be creative with that. Our models tend to not be as blessed as you are, Claudia."

"Well, it's a pleasure to meet you." Claudia was a little stunned and didn't know what to say.

"Jackie will take you down to our makeup room, and we already have the fall designs we want you to put on. Then we'll do the photo shoot. Darlene wants to do an interview with you after that so they can do a write-up on you for the magazine and introduce you to the world."

"I will follow your lead; it's all new to me."

In addition to Nicholas's normal staff, Claudia found herself surrounded by people from *Fashion World* who knew exactly the look they wanted. They advised the makeup artists as to exactly what coloring, hues, and tints they required. It was a fall shoot, so they wanted colors that radiated warmth against the snowy background. They liked her hair color, and they wanted her to have a classy, outdoorsy, country-life look. The hairdresser brushed out her hair to give it a more natural look. They didn't want her face to be covered because of her excellent jaw line and the natural features she possessed, so they decided to pull her hair back into a small ponytail at the base of her head. They used a fan-shaped clasp to secure her ponytail. The end result was a slightly sophisticated look that showed the real beauty of her face.

"To the fitting room," announced Darlene, and the entourage followed. They had set up a room featuring a snowy winter background with a tree in the foreground. Claudia wore a tweed jacket and skirt with heavy hose and small winter boots with fur trim. They argued about the hat and eventually settled on a small mink hat that gave her a sportier look.

It took them over three hours, but after many clothing adjustments and scenery changes, they got the look they wanted. Apart from a cup of coffee and a quick sandwich, these people didn't stop for a moment. Claudia was amazed by the whole experience. She realized that being a model takes patience and long hours. Models may make good money, but they earn it. It was a long day, but she was excited to see what the results would look like in the magazine.

Around five o'clock, Nicholas appeared. She realized then the dedication people in the fashion industry give to their work. It was a labor of passion, and all those that shared that passion were a part of achieving the best. It was an exhilarating experience, and she could see how it could be addicting.

"Well, my dear, had enough of everyone pampering and adoring you all day?" said Nicholas, preening over all the work his team had worked so hard to accomplish.

Darlene spoke up. "She's been great, and we have thoroughly enjoyed working with her. Not all our models are as intelligent as you are, Claudia. They don't always understand or synchronize to our way of thinking. You do it perfectly, and as a result, this is one of the shortest shoots we have had in a long time." Darlene really liked Claudia and her whole demeanor.

"Well, I consider myself fortunate to be surrounded by such a great team of people." The people around her began to applaud and cheer. They had all worked hard, and a model didn't always appreciate that, so they appreciated her comment.

"Claudia, as everyone is now through, Darlene wants to take a moment to interview you, so get cleaned up, and come up to our offices."

"I wish I could go home just like this, but there's no snow!" Everyone laughed.

A few minutes later, Claudia sat down with Darlene in a vacant office, and they spent the next hour talking. Darlene was impressed with her modesty and outstanding scholastic record. She was really looking forward to publishing her story as well as seeing her on the front page of their winter issue.

After the interview, Nicholas invited both Darlene and Claudia to dinner. Claudia thought about it and accepted, but Darlene made it clear it couldn't be a late night. She was already behind with the winter issue, and she would be working Sunday to get the magazine off to the press by midweek.

As they were casually dressed, they went to a small café just around the corner from the store, and after a few glasses of wine, Claudia got to know Darlene very well. She could see that they could be close friends and loved hearing the story of how she got to be the editor of *Fashion World* at such a young age.

After they ate, Darlene departed, giving Claudia a chance to talk with Nicholas. She began by thanking him. "That was quite a day. I never dreamed I would experience something like that in my whole life. That's every girl's dream. Thank you, Nicholas. I'm excited for your clothing line, but also for you."

"Claudia, you were amazing. You still are amazing. You gave up your whole day to do this and never complained once. Plus, you've never asked me how much you get paid for doing a gig like this? You're one of a kind." He looked longingly at her, obviously still infatuated after their last encounter.

"Nicholas, I have some confessions to make."

Intrigued, he said, "I'm listening."

"I have to tell you that I have been in a relationship with Sir Thomas for a while now, and I do care about him very deeply, to the point where we are considering engagement in the near future."

Nicholas looked shocked. "My God, that man's old enough to be your father. Good-looking, old-school type, I admit, and he has certainly done his rounds with the ladies, I can assure you. But to see a beautiful woman like you hitching your wagon to a star like that, I don't know."

"You can think what you like, but he's whom I'm attracted to, and his counsel and advice have been invaluable to me. He has been nothing but a complete gentleman."

"Well, if that's all you need, then I'm obviously wasting my time. I took you for a more intelligent person than that. Here you sit with a career that could potentially make you a million, an heiress, and you have time for him. Please don't get me wrong; you don't have to choose me, but why him?" Nicholas didn't understand her choice.

"I've given myself this week to think things over, so I would sincerely appreciate it if you would respect that. You've come into my life like a tornado, and yes, it's good, but I have to be sure of my feelings. It's okay for you men to go out with whomever you choose, but you don't know how easily a woman's standing can be damaged if she jumps around from man to man."

"You can take all the time you want, but get this through your head—I want to be your friend, no matter what. You and I click, and I don't find that every day of the week. I will call you about the magazine and keep you abreast of today. You'll be paid a hefty sum of money for what's about to launch your modeling career, so think it all through. It's a lot, I know, and you must do it for all the right reasons." He took her hand and gently held it, hoping she understood his sincerity.

It was late, so they said their goodbyes and then drove home, where she went straight to bed and fell immediately asleep.

CHAPTER 16

IN THE LIMELIGHT

It was the end of October, and the magazine would be out by the first week of November, before the Christmas rush. Nicholas was quietly waiting for the issue to hit the stands. Claudia had no idea what was about to happen, but she knew it could be something that would change her life forever.

On her way to work one morning, she stopped by the newspaper stand to pick up the news, and there was her picture on the front of *Fashion World*. She wondered how many people were going to recognize her. She immediately took out her sunglasses and proceeded to catch her train. By the time she reached her office, everyone at the bank was talking about her.

Nigel was the first person to pop his head around the corner and talk to her. "My God, woman, you never sit still. There are not many women I know that can take care of an important job like you do, help the bank get investments, go out on the weekend, get a photo shoot, and end up on the cover of a magazine.

When you have time, please tell me your secret; as a lesser mortal, I'm blown away!" he joked.

"Nigel, if you don't think I'm firmly rooted in taking care of business, then you haven't met the real Claudia yet."

"I know. You're just a complete enigma to me. I hope you stay with us because I, for one, would miss a person like you who is so responsible and dedicated." He was a little shocked that she wasn't taking a moment to share the joy. Any other person would be basking in the sunlight of such an occasion.

"It's just probably a flash in the pan, and no one needs to get overexcited. Time will tell if it's something that will appeal to the public. But as I've worked so hard over the last few months, maybe I can negotiate a raise?" She grinned.

"Name your price, my dear lady, and I'll get it approved."

"Nigel, I love what I'm doing, and I'm not going anywhere."

"That's a relief, but I wouldn't blame you if you did."

The phone rang, and Sir Thomas greeted her as she answered. "Claudia, you've been busy! Congratulations are in order, I do believe. I know you're busy, but I want to hear all about it." She noticed that he sounded distant, as though she were slowly moving off his radar screen.

"Thomas, thank you for the compliment, but I'm just doing my job. We have to see how it all works out. We can't get too excited yet."

"I know, but it isn't everyone that gets on the front cover of a magazine." He didn't understand why she wasn't more elated.

"I know, and I am overjoyed that the shoot turned out to be a success, but it's early yet, so let's wait and see what kind of reaction we get from the media and the public."

"I have to go, but please let's meet up soon; I want to hear all about it."

"Of course. I'll give you a call."

Throughout the week, Claudia had been flooded with calls and conversations. She was now looking forward to the weekend. She wanted to really analyze what had taken place because so many things had happened so quickly. The one call she was expecting from Nicholas hadn't come.

However, as she was talking with Rose at the front desk Friday afternoon, his call came. Claudia went into her office to take the call. "Nicholas, what's up? I'm surprised it took you so long to call."

"And for a very good reason. You can't imagine how busy I've been, thanks to you."

"Really? In what way?" She was anxious to hear his news.

"I have a lot of other journalists wanting to know all about you, for starters. Of course, I have kept your contact information private, but be aware, the press is interested, so dress a little incognito when you go out. The public and other fashion editors are showing an intense interest in who you are, and of course, it's bringing a lot of people to the shop. What I want to do is propose that a little further down the road, we do an invite to the shop and have a public introduction to Claudia Langley. That way I can get the press—television, maybe—and turn what is a major event for both of us into an opportunity for people to know who you are. I think this is a fantastic opportunity for your career, if you are interested. By the way, I have a life-size image of you on my showroom floor; that way I can remind myself how beautiful you are every day when I come to work."

"Nicholas, you don't have to do that. You've only got to come and see me in person, and I think you've got enough photographs of me to remind you of that."

"You're wrong. Nothing beats life-size," he said jokingly.

"I want to see that. Anyway, are you thinking around the first week of December for the publicity?"

"Yes, something like that. When you get a moment, we'll get together and plan something with my marketing group, who wants to maximize your introduction and that of my shop to the national and international markets. It's been a crazy week, and I'm sure for you too, but a lot of people are getting to know who you are, and that's going to make you a very well-known person. Your life will change dramatically. I can't thank you enough, Claudia. You've brought me the best Christmas present I could dream of. Things won't be the same for you, trust me; you're going to get a lot of business out of this, so take advantage of it! I've got to go, but what's your number at home? I'll call you over the weekend if that's okay."

"Sure." She gave him her Knightsbridge number, and then she packed up to head home.

It was a quiet trip home. She had decided to take a taxi, take in the week's developments, and give Phillipa a call to get a woman's perspective.

"Hello, Phillipa."

"Claudia, look at you! Who would have dreamed this would happen? I'm so excited for you, my dear, but I didn't know you were keeping this under wraps!"

"Nicholas called me at the last moment on a Friday afternoon and asked me to come to his shop for a photo shoot. He had mentioned it before, but I thought the whole thing was a joke, and even when he called to ask me over on a Saturday, I still didn't believe him. So I'm just as shocked as you are."

"Well, that Nicholas doesn't mess around. When he sees an opportunity, he goes after it, and because he's so connected, things like this can happen. You must be over the moon. What a wonderful surprise, and I might say, even though I'm a little jealous, you look beautiful. The only thing is that it will probably make your life more complicated personally."

"If you're going to be in London, can we catch a bite of lunch tomorrow?" asked Claudia. She was missing her company.

"My dear, I would be delighted. You better wear some sunglasses now that you're a celebrity."

"I'll come to your place around eleven thirty to pick you up, if that's okay."

"Perfect."

The next morning, she arrived at the Countess's Mayfair home and rang the doorbell. The Countess was ready because she had some shopping to do. She thought they would have lunch at Harrods, and then she could do her shopping afterwards.

"Well, my dear, it seems there's never a dull moment for you these days."

"I know. You wouldn't believe how shocked I was. On my way to work on Wednesday, I stopped at a newspaper stand to get the latest news, and there was my picture on the front page of *Fashion World*! I immediately put on my sunglasses and proceeded unnoticed."

"Oh, you're just at the beginning. These things take time, but once it gains momentum, you'll be taking a cab every day to work. That's the way it works. If you become well known, people will never stop asking you for autographs, and the press will be following you to know all about your personal life. Welcome to the bright lights of celebrity. It has its moments, but it can be a curse sometimes."

"I'm sure you lived through similar circumstances."

"Absolutely. When I married Collin, I think everyone wanted to know everything about me, down to my blood type. It's become less now, but if I get caught with some high-flying person, then the press is all over it. That's the road if you have that way of life, I'm afraid. It doesn't go away. You just get used to it and get better at handling situations that could be compromising if not handled wisely."

They took a seat at the bar and both enjoyed a smoked salmon sandwich and a glass of champagne. The Countess wasted no time in asking the question she was dying to ask. "Have you made your mind up about Nicholas and Thomas?"

"I love Nicholas. He's such an exciting person to be with, and his drive and ambition are certainly to be admired. After a lot of thought, though, I believe Thomas is the best choice for me. I'm thirty-three now, and it's time I settled down. I want to have a child before it's too late."

"I think you're headed in the right direction, my dear. Let's be realistic. Unless you want to be in the fashion industry, and you could be, your modeling days are not going to be much more than five years, so you can participate in the business, of course; but is it what you really want long term?"

"No, you're right. I was trained for what I'm doing now at Bannerman's, and I like my work. If the odd modeling opportunity comes up, I'll take the time out to do it, but it's not what I want for the long term."

"Then you know what your next move is. Have the life you deserve. As much as I love London, my life wouldn't be the same without my children. It makes for a fuller life. We all need family life and the dimension that goes along with it. Being successful can be very lonely, so you must choose wisely. You may be the best whatever, but if you don't have that special person to go home to, it all lacks purpose. Eventually, the drive you have seems without a reason. I'm sure Nicholas is seeing that, and for that matter, Thomas is too.

"Well, I must get my shopping done, and then I'm headed back to Penbroke, so let's get together in a week or two, okay?"

The Countess, as usual, had given Claudia valuable advice, and Claudia appreciated every word. "Thank you, Phillipa. You've always had time for me, and I can't put into words how much your advice has meant to me." Claudia gave her a big hug.

As soon as she arrived back at her apartment, she called Sir Thomas. She was anxious to tell him of her decision.

He was happy to hear from her. "Claudia, how are you, my dear? Quite a week, I suspect."

"Can I come over to see you?" she asked warmly.

"Well, I was going to come down your way, but if you would prefer, by all means. I'll be waiting."

"I want a break from the city and would like to spend a moment with you if you have time to talk. I know it's not been easy for you, but I have had to deal with some of the same issues too. I think it's time we reconnected and got matters cleared up between us."

"I'll be waiting, and George will open a garage door for you." He was hoping that she was coming to stay the night.

Claudia quickly changed, threw some casual clothes and a nightdress into a bag, and headed to North London. Since it was a Saturday afternoon, the traffic wasn't too bad, and she knew she would be there in around half an hour.

When she arrived, Sir Thomas greeted her with an enormous hug and kiss. He was beaming from ear to ear, pleased that his true love was in his arms again. She changed, and they went for a long walk across the heath.

Sir Thomas began the conversation. "Well, my dear, quite a week, I think. Don't you?"

"Oh, Thomas, it was an exhausting one, filled with trying to decide on my career, thinking of how you were feeling and the intensity of Nicholas and his needs, and doing an important job for the bank. Yes, I would say for a little old country girl like me, it was a lot."

"Country girl, my foot! Your photograph is halfway across the planet as we speak. I must admit, Nicholas knew exactly how to dress you in a countrywoman's outfit. You looked absolutely radiant and stunning. That magazine is going to fly off the stands; there's no doubt about that. I'm so very proud of you. That took a leap of faith, and to Nicholas's credit, he did come through for you. Good for him."

"So, you liked the way I looked?" she asked, hungry for his approval.

"Claudia, I think you're beautiful first thing in the morning with no makeup and in the simplest outfit. You are so beautiful in the photo. Of course, now I have to compete with thousands of other admirers. You haven't heard the last of this, and by Christmas, my bet is you're going to be a household celebrity in more places than merry old England. If I didn't feel like I were the best man in the world for you, I would be feeling very intimidated."

She stopped walking and turned to him. "Rubbish. I'm still the same person that I was a week ago, and I'm going nowhere without you."

"You really mean that? You mean I'm the person for you?"

"The one and only. It's you and no one else." She leaned over to kiss him, and it turned into a long, romantic affair.

"By God, you had me worried there for a moment. I thought I was going to be sidelined, not necessarily for Nicholas, but you're going to get many offers, and I wouldn't blame you if you did take a moment to make the very best decision for yourself."

"I told you I would take the week to think about it, and I did. I can't say that I wasn't infatuated with Nicholas. It's not often a man takes you out to a store and lets you walk out with everything you like, teaches you how to make yourself up, then pulls out a complete evening outfit to wear. Then he takes you to a place where you dance your heart out. What woman in the world wouldn't be blown away by a man that could provide such privileges? But the simple fact is, there's that little thing called reality. It's about being with the people you love and where your heart and future lies. You and I have a lot in common, and I love what I'm doing at the bank, and that's the highest priority on my list. You see, I'm just a boring, practical woman deep down."

"Practical? Yes, I can believe that, but boring? Not for a bloody moment. I don't think you know how entertaining you can be, and that's because you have a brain to go with those looks of yours. That makes a big difference." He kissed her while lifting her off her feet.

She laughed. "Thomas, I don't think I would be happy with anyone but you. Yes, Nicholas is good-looking and a lot of fun, and I'm sure we would get along in business, but I want a personal life. I'm also committed to James, Phillipa, and so many others. I couldn't give that up. They are my family in a sense, and I would miss them terribly."

"You're a wise woman. Well, I have a little surprise. I have invited the Countess for dinner tonight, and she and her boyfriend are coming. George is preparing a fine meal for all of us," Sir Thomas said, hoping for her approval.

"Oh, thank goodness I have the evening dress I wore the other night, and the shoes, too. I was going to take them back to the store, but what the heck. He hasn't said anything, so one more night won't hurt."

"Wonderful! Let's go back and get cleaned up."

Claudia was excited about her decision and at last felt some peace. The stress of the past ten days had been too much to take in at times, but so many good things had resulted that it all seemed somehow necessary.

A few hours later, the front doorbell rang, and Sir Thomas and Claudia descended the staircase together. Claudia looked as exceptional as she had the night she had gone out with Nicholas.

George opened the door for the dinner guests, and the Countess, Nicholas, and Darlene Jenson from *Fashion World* entered. Claudia looked dumbfounded and was embarrassed to be wearing the evening dress that Nicholas had hand-chosen for her.

"Thomas, you planned all this and you didn't tell me a thing. I'm going to get you back for this," Claudia muttered as she gave him a small punch to the ribs.

Everyone yelled, "Surprise!"

Red Bones, awakened by the yelling, went careening through the house. Everyone laughed, and then George dragged him off to the kitchen.

Nicholas smiled and said, "I love that dress you've got on. It's so you."

"You ought to know. You're the one that chose it," she said wittingly. "I'm so sorry. I had it in the car to return to you, but since I arrived with only casual clothes, this was all I had to wear tonight, so forgive me."

"That's what they all say. Sorry, but you're guilty," he joked.

The Countess interjected, "Nicholas, you have excellent taste. She looks fabulous." She leaned in to give Claudia a hug.

Darlene was introduced to Sir Thomas, and he took Nicholas and Darlene on a tour of the house. Phillipa and Claudia went into the room with the bar, and George handed them each a glass of champagne.

"I didn't think I would be seeing you again so soon, Phillipa," said Claudia, acting surprised.

"I have to admit, after I thought you were going to call Thomas, I gave him a hint, and when you arrived, he let me know, and so, here we all are. I think it's good for everyone to get together and break the ice, don't you?" said Phillipa, happy with the choice Claudia had made.

"Yes, and I'm so glad to see you again."

"Don't you love this house? Now this is what I would be perfectly happy to have. No huge estates and no Mayfair: just this."

"I know. I hope it all works out for the best. I gave Thomas such a hard time. I realize now he's the best man for me, and I don't want to go back to the dating scene again. I'm happy to be the wife of a man like Thomas and do my work at Bannerman's," said a relieved Claudia after a stressful week of indecision.

"Don't forget a little modeling here and there certainly won't hurt the bank balance," said Phillipa, winking. "Stay on good terms with Nicholas. He understands your situation."

Darlene, Thomas, and Nicholas rejoined them moments later, and they all shared stories of the past week.

Claudia said, "Darlene, thank you so much for coming tonight. I enjoyed meeting you last Saturday."

"The pleasure was all mine. You are going to have a few more such days, if that peaks your interest. I know you are very committed with your work at the bank, but we'll work around that. You're such a delight to work with; all my staff enjoyed working with you so much. You can't believe some of the models we have to put up with just because they've made a name for themselves and they have a contract. I feel our relationship will last for many years, as you are the perfect age for the type of clothing Nicholas wants to market to his clients. We have some very interesting avant-garde products coming up in the future, so we'll make a fashion queen out of you again, hopefully before too long."

George summoned everyone to dinner. Darlene sat next to Nicholas, and Claudia sat opposite Darlene in order to get to know her better. Sir Thomas sat between Darlene and the Countess.

Nicholas leaned toward Claudia and said, "I think the man you have chosen is extremely suited to you, Claudia, and I'm sorry for any impropriety that I may have imposed upon you. You have to know I wasn't aware how close you two were. Anyway, if I have helped conclude your direction, then I have been a good force in your journey. That being said, if you have any doubts, I'm happy to be second best and pick up with you again. Seriously, though, I truly value our relationship. I believe we can have a great future together in fashion, which will benefit us both."

"Nicholas, I had a wonderful evening, and you were an absolute gentleman at all times. I look forward to working with you and helping you in any way I can."

"Good. Now that we've got that out of the way, we can enjoy the party." Nicholas raised his glass and said, "I believe we all need to toast the woman of the year for Darlene, Sir Thomas, and me, and hopefully, for the Countess too."

"Cheers, and well done, Claudia," they chanted as they

clicked their glasses.

George had prepared a magnificent beef Wellington and carefully chosen three bottles of Margaux claret from the cellar for the occasion. After a delicious dessert of apple strudel and Sir Thomas's favorite ice cream, coffee, cheese, and after-dinner drinks were served.

Sir Thomas decided this was an appropriate time to do what he had wanted to do for many months. He walked over to the other side of the table and asked Claudia to stand up, and then he got down on one knee and said, "Being the love of my life and the steadfast woman I know you to be, will you accept my humble request to become my wife for now and forever?"

Claudia was speechless; she looked at everyone around the room and then straight into his eyes and said, "Sir Thomas, to the man I love, I am humbled by your request and absolutely accept your offer to be your wife."

Sir Thomas opened the box and revealed a five-carat baguette diamond ring surrounded by smaller sapphires. He placed the ring on Claudia's finger. All three women were in tears, touched by the moment. Everyone then raised their glasses to the newly engaged couple.

Later that evening, after everyone had left, Sir Thomas and Claudia sat on the large sofa sipping their drinks and talking over the evening. They were happy that everyone got along so well. Claudia said, "I had no idea you were going to propose. You took me by surprise. The ring is exceptional. I've never worn a ring that size in my whole life."

"Only the best for the very best, and that's you. A surprise? I can't leave you on the marketplace any longer. You're too hot a commodity. I know a good deal when I see one, so I've got to lock you up for good," he joked.

"You old devil. I'm just glad you think I'm that hot. Will you always think so?"

"Always."

CHAPTER 17

RELEASING THE PAST

Following Collin Bannerman's death during the winter of 1958, it took a full five years for the family to reconstruct their lives. James was doing well at Sterling, the girls were thriving at their school, and the Countess was stronger. The family was beginning to focus on the future.

Claudia was making more money than she could have ever believed possible. Her marriage to Sir Thomas had taken place off the island of Majorca on the yacht of Sir Thomas's good friend Alan Weinstock, who had been the owner of Bannerman's accounting firm for nearly half a century. They married in the spring of 1963, and by the end of that year, they decided to have a child. Claudia hoped it would be a son and heir for Sir Thomas. She loved her life at Hampstead Heath, and she had been elevated to acting chairman at the bank with the full consideration of the board, the Countess, and Nigel Thompson. She was a valuable asset for the bank.

Nicholas Blythe had made the Queen's honors list for his innovation and contribution to British exports and job employment in the North of England. He was awarded a medal of honor and was now referred to as Sir Nicholas Blythe O.B.E. He continued to build on his relationship with Claudia, and the two worked well in the development of his business in the fashion industry. Claudia was an asset to him in terms of investing his money with Bannerman's.

The estate had moved forward under the excellent leadership of Keith Pruett. The East Wing, parking lots, tearooms, souvenir shop, outside patio, and school were built as quality temporary buildings and strategically placed all together. They were open by the beginning of 1963. The marketing plan had been completed with Claudia's help. Her relationship with Darlene had helped them secure great interest from many editors of tourism magazines. A great deal had been written about the Seventh Earl's collection. All his notes had been printed out in large script and posted on the walls of the Throne Room. In addition, copies of the Earl's paintings had been made, each with its own historical write-up. They were distributed around the walls of the room for visitors to see. The Throne Room, as it was now referred to, looked magnificent. All the artifacts had been thoroughly polished and cleaned. The floors had been sanded and stained. A walkway of carpet had been strategically placed around the room. Visitors could pass through and view each piece as they made their way to the throne and the fountain, which were the main features of the room. They'd then move on to the souvenir shop. The whole room had been repainted, and all the gold leaves had been touched up on the fountain and the throne. The original notebook was now kept locked away at the main house. Sir Thomas had taken care to retrieve all the necessary documents from the various companies. Each one had different areas of expertise and had been paid to evaluate all the treasures in their entirety.

The parking lots were able to handle up to five hundred cars, and there was adequate parking for coaches and busses. The manner in which Keith Pruett had managed the implementation meant that the privacy of the main house was not affected in any way.

Sarah McKenzie had started her school, and it was becoming almost a full-time job. She had moved to Penbroke during the week to train staff who could teach in her absence. The school was slowly starting to stir interest from many places outside the United Kingdom. Sarah had taken over the marketing, as she saw no need to spend unnecessary money on a marketing firm after the school's initial opening. The future looked very promising.

James was attending his last term at Sterling. He had added Carl Longford, the number one scoring batsman, to his close circle of friends. Peter, Carl, and James spent many hours practicing in the nets getting ready for what would be their last season together. James had also become very close to a young man named Kent Harkins, who was from Texas, in the United States. Kent was six foot five inches and weighed nearly 265 pounds. In rugby, he played at the number eight position in the scrum. On one occasion, they kept the ball in the scrum for over twenty yards as Kent pushed the whole scrum unit of the other team completely off their feet and then picked up the ball and crossed the line for a try. He was a character to be reckoned with, not only for his size, but for his incredible sense of humor and popularity with everyone at the school. He represented what everyone epitomized a Texan to be—simply larger than life. His father was in the oil business in Texas, and he had sent him to the school in Scotland hoping to make him tougher than he already was. The harsh discipline of English boarding-school life was something parents of well-to-do families liked their sons to experience. It was a school well known for preparing a student who was going into the family business or a demanding profes-

DAVID FRANCIS

sion of some kind. Cricket was foreign to Kent, but he always enjoyed hanging out with James and the gang.

Becky and Flick were now at Benenden and were fast learning that boys existed on the planet. Phillipa had her hands full keeping an eye on them. She was paying more attention to them than James, as it was actually easier for her to visit the girls from London since they were near Cranbrook, in Kent. Becky was seventeen, was making good progress, and was about to become a prefect, while Flick was fifteen and a half and was becoming quite a handful.

Phillipa, whose life had been fairly uneventful personally, was still feeling lonely. As fate would have it, she met a very special person while she was visiting some wealthy friends on their yacht in Monaco.

It was a quiet evening in May, and she was sitting on the back of the yacht visiting with her friends, John and Jennifer Melroney, who were in the shipping business and had connections to Bannerman's Trans Global Shipping Lines. While they were talking, they told Phillipa that an old friend of theirs, who was Italian but spoke great English, was going to join them for drinks before heading back to Tuscany. They thought that Phillipa might find him entertaining.

A short time later, the gentleman made his way onto the yacht. John greeted him and asked, "What's your poison, old boy?"

"I think I would like a martini for a change."

John went to the bar to pour his drink, and Jennifer made introductions. "Antonio, I would like to introduce you to Countess Phillipa, who is our house guest for a few days."

Phillipa got up to shake his hand, and she couldn't help thinking that she knew him.

"Phillipa? Not Phillipa, the dancer? I don't believe it!"

"Antonio? The classical guitarist who never left me alone for a moment?" she said, shocked at the realization.

"That's me. Your Italian Tony. You really remember me?"

"How could I have forgotten you? I can't believe you're here."

"I want more than a handshake, my dear. I want a hug." The two embraced as the Melroneys looked on in amazement.

"Antonio, here's your drink. So you two know each other?"

"Yes. It's a long story. If Phillipa doesn't mind, I'll tell you," Antonio offered.

"Of course not, but I need another drink if I'm going to listen to this one," Phillipa said.

"When I was a young man, I had a dream of playing in a band. I had always played the guitar with my father. I then graduated to a classical guitar, which I also love very much. Then it was time for me to go to England and learn English. It was there that I met a beautiful woman, who could dance, sing, and act, and I have to say, I fell in love, as young people do. Well, it's a long story, as I said. Phillipa found this very good-looking English aristocrat, and I suppose that was the end for me. But I tell you, my dear, I never, ever forgot you, and to see you here tonight is like a dream come true. Now your husband can come and kill me for saying all that."

"My husband passed away almost five years ago, so I am footloose and fancy free, as the saying goes," said Phillipa. Normally, she would never be a person to offer herself so easily, so the Melroneys knew there must be a lot more to the story than they were being told. "How did you meet the Melroneys?" she asked.

"They were on vacation in Tuscany about four years ago, I believe, and they came to visit my vineyard. They liked my wine, and we have been great friends ever since."

"You have a vineyard in Tuscany? You never told me that when you were in London. I thought you were as poor as a church mouse."

"You see, I wanted you to love me for Antonio and not my money. Plus, my father thought I was a crazy young man with a dream, and he wouldn't send me a penny." Everyone laughed.

"How did you do with music?"

"I did well, and I could have made a living doing what I loved, but I always had plans to return to my father because the vineyard is a family tradition. I was trained in it as a young boy, and as the only son, I loved my father and would never let him down." He chuckled and then added, "I was also idealistic then, and I wanted to be loved for me."

"Did you get loved for you?" asked Phillipa in her usual direct manner.

"No. I was just another poor Italian boy, but I had a lot of fun with a lot of very pretty women."

"Oh, you were incorrigible, as I remember, but extremely handsome and loveable too."

"So, you still like me?"

"Antonio, who in the world couldn't like you? You're an entire entertainment package built into one person, and you know you're still very handsome."

"I thank you for those kind words. Now, please tell me about yourself."

"Well, I'm taking a break from my family at the moment. I have three children who are all teenagers. You can imagine what that's like. We do have a lovely place in Lincolnshire, but I prefer living in London. When the children are in boarding school, I go to the city, where most of my social life has always been."

It turned out to be a joyful evening. The Melroneys enjoyed watching their friends, who obviously had an interesting history together, interact. At the end of the evening, as Antonio got up to leave, he asked Phillipa, "Since you are a free woman, would you like to come visit me in Tuscany? I'll show you how we crazy Italians really live."

"When are you free?" She was curious to see his place.

"Right now." Everyone laughed.

"Are you going to be here tomorrow morning?" Phillipa

asked anxiously.

"Yes, until midday, and then I will drive back. It takes around four hours, but it's a beautiful drive."

"I might join you, if you have room."

"I will call you tomorrow, and if you want, I will come by in my Ferrari and pick you up." He was trying to impress her. He hadn't forgotten that Phillipa did appreciate the nice things in life. He was now a man in a position to offer her such things.

When he had left, she said, "I can't believe I just did that!"

Jennifer replied, "Oh, it'll do you a world of good. It's about time you had a little romance in your life. You've been through a lot, and this is just the tonic you need."

John interjected, "Isn't he a character? We've always loved his company. He sends us his wine, and I have to twist his arm to send me a bill. And he can really play that guitar! I'm sure you'll get serenaded; that's his style."

"Let's call it a night and see what tomorrow brings," suggested Jennifer, and the three of them headed off to bed.

The next morning, Phillipa decided to go to Antonio's home in Tuscany, which was located southeast of Florence in the beautiful wine country. As they drove, they talked about old times, and Phillipa couldn't wait to see his home and meet his children. It was a beautiful day, and with top down on his two-seater, she could see for miles over the deep blue Mediterranean Sea as Antonio drove the coast road toward Genoa. They stopped at an old café he knew for a bite of lunch and a bottle of Chianti before continuing their journey. As they neared Tuscany, Phillipa noticed a pleasant increase in temperature. It wasn't full summer yet, but the beauty of spring and the tree blossoms made the journey all the more scenic. Tall cypress trees lined many of the roads south of Florence.

Around mid-afternoon, Antonio turned into his driveway. The large impressive gates gave the vineyard a historic character as they drove up the long driveway to his villa. She could see row upon row of beautiful vines that were beginning to show a fullness of the grapes that would be harvested at the end of summer. The villa was large and had all the character one would expect, including big stone courtyards with overhanging plants that gave such a richness of color and warmth to the estate.

"How big is your vineyard?"

"It's around 150 or so hectares; in acres, it's close to 400," he said proudly.

"That sounds like a pretty good-sized vineyard to me," she said, impressed.

"My dear, it's a good size. There are bigger vineyards, of course, and there are a lot smaller ones. However, size isn't everything. It's the quality you produce and the reputation you earn that is important."

"When I get my luggage in the house, I want to explore everywhere with you. The scenery is so beautiful and so different than what I'm used to at Penbroke."

Antonio motioned to one of his staff, who immediately came to unload the car and take all their belongings into the house. The inside was like nothing she had ever seen before. It wasn't like a Spanish home or hacienda. It had a large entryway with a pretty fountain in the center, marble floors throughout, and a large, beautifully carved oak staircase leading to the second floor. The sound of the fountain gave the home a natural feeling. It was elegant for what would be termed an Italian country house.

Antonio showed her to her room. She admired the floors and the rugs. She couldn't help but notice the spectacular view of the surrounding hills and vegetation. As she looked out from the back of the house, she could see a huge open veranda on the ground floor that surrounded the whole exterior of the villa. After unpacking, she made her way downstairs. She then walked through a large drawing room appointed with family paintings and a huge fireplace. She could imagine the families gathered around the fire in the winter months. She then walked out onto the veranda, where Antonio had chilled a bottle of his best chardonnay for them to enjoy. She sank back into a large, comfortable wicker chair and felt completely at home.

"You like my little house on the prairie?" asked Antonio, smiling.

"It's beautiful. I love the scenery and the style of life that you have. I'm sure you have worked hard and still do to maintain your vineyard and reputation, but what a wonderful way of life. I don't think I've been anywhere quite like this. I'm so happy you brought me here. What a coincidence meeting you on the Melroney's yacht, and what a lovely surprise. You are even more handsome than that crazy, fun-loving young man I knew in London. To think you grew up around all this; you must have missed it terribly."

"Oh, I had my fun in London. I loved my music, and I loved you. My beautiful Phillipa, I can't believe you're here in my home. It's like a dream come true. I look at you, and I have to keep pinching myself that you are here."

"Tell me what happened to your wife. She was obviously the mother of your son and daughter." She wanted to hear his story before his children arrived home, which would be soon.

Antonio sighed. "Carina was a beautiful, tall Swedish woman with lovely blue eyes. My daughter, Sabrina, looks a lot like her mother. Childbirth was not easy for her. Having Piero was difficult for her, and when she gave birth to Sabrina, I wanted her to have a caesarean section. However, it was not the way for traditional Catholics. Giving birth was a very sacred duty. She could not stop bleeding after she gave birth, and she died shortly after. I was so sad and angry for many years, so I just poured my heart into my two children and my work. I have met other women, but none could replace my Carina. It's been seventeen years now, and I have always felt that Carina was with me, watching over us. When I walk through the vines, she talks to me. When I have a problem, we discuss it and she helps me find an answer."

Phillipa was silent for a long moment, then said quietly, "All those years, such a good-looking man like you should have had someone in his life."

"It's not so easy when you have kids. It would have been easier if I had found someone quickly, but as my children got older, they resented another person who was not family. Now they are old enough that they want me to find someone. Until you, I haven't found anyone who I felt could be a part of this family, though."

At that moment, Phillipa heard the sounds of two teenagers rushing through the house.

They ran to give their father a big hug, and then they saw he had company. Antonio said, "Children, I would like for you to meet someone I knew a long time ago and is very special to your Papa. This is Phillipa. Be polite, as she is a countess."

Piero was very warm and welcoming. Phillipa looked at him, thinking how handsome he was and that Rebecca would definitely like him. Sabrina then bent over to give her a hug, showing the warmth that Italian people so freely give. Phillipa was struck by her beauty and a disposition that was more sophisticated than her years. She would be a catch for James, she thought. Their English was very good, and Phillipa could see that they had been well educated and brought up to have excellent manners.

"Papa, we have good news. As it is now the end of term, I can tell you I was first in math," said Piero, pleased with his progress.

"That is wonderful! You have your mother's brain. She could calculate anything," he said as he beamed with pride.

"I came in first in languages, French and English, so now you can send me on holiday to France and England like you promised," added Sabrina.

"Well, that's a discussion we will have later, my dear."

"Papa, I will make us all supper. Do you like pasta, Countess?" Sabrina asked.

"My dear Sabrina, it's my favorite. That, with a nice bottle of wine, is the best." Phillipa thought about how mature and advanced Sabrina was. Not having a mother had made her stronger, she suspected, and in a way, she was like a little mother to the two men. She noticed how close and loving the family appeared to be, talking to one another as equals, but with respect.

The children ran off to prepare supper while Antonio went to open one of his favorite Chiantis for the evening meal.

Piero was setting the table on the veranda when Phillipa started to question him.

"So, Piero, you are going to be like your father and help him with the vineyard?"

"Yes, but I want to do some other things first. I hope all my grades are good so I can travel to America and England. I have a reason. I think one day we can sell a lot of wine to both countries. I would like to improve my English and learn the way of life so I understand the people better."

"That's very good. My son, James, is eighteen also, and it's his last term. He will be finished in the next three weeks. You must come and visit us, and he can take you horseback riding. If you haven't had any experience, he can take you out on the beach, where it's a very good place to learn."

"I would love that. I can ride, but not very well."

Sabrina started to bring in the supper, and the family gathered for the evening meal. Unlike many places in the world, the Italians had no problem with their children drinking wine at the evening meal. "Let's all make a toast to the end of term, the summer, and the arrival of the Countess to our home," said Antonio, raising his glass.

Phillipa enjoyed the conversation and learning all about their lives, Italy, and their expectations for the future. After the meal, the children left the couple to have time together. Antonio poured himself a large glass of brandy and opened a box of Cuban cigars.

Phillipa had taken a moment to clean herself up in her room and put on a summer dress and sandals to feel more relaxed. She returned to have her favorite after-dinner liqueur, Strega, which was Italian and was a very smooth drink after a meal.

Antonio said, "Tomorrow, I will take you around the vineyard and you can see how we do things here—how we store the barrels and age the wine." He got up and took Phillipa by the hand. "Let's take a little walk before the sun sets and feel the night air coming on."

As they strolled around the house and along the driveway, Phillipa felt a strong attraction for Antonio. His warm and polite manner was starting to stir feelings in her that she hadn't had in a long time. She remembered how much she had been in love with him when they were young and in London. Here they were again, and that same attraction was still there. It was a case of opposites attracting; she had a Scandinavian look to her skin, with brilliant blue eyes and fair hair, whereas Antonio was handsome, taller than the average Italian, and had dark brown eyes. At forty-seven, his hair was graying slightly, which gave him a more distinguished look. He had taken care of himself; he carried a little more weight now, but it was appealing. As a count himself, he had a lot of prestige, which he had not disclosed to Phillipa. As they walked between the vines holding hands, she couldn't imagine a more romantic place.

"I talk to my vines. They are like family because we take care of them. We love them, and they give back to us."

"You talk to your vines?" This was foreign to Phillipa, but she loved the idea. She felt so comfortable being with him that she thought she could tell him anything.

"Of course. Don't you talk to your flowers in the garden?" he said with a whimsical smile.

"Maybe, but not enough. That's probably the reason I don't connect with being in the countryside of England. I can see you feel this whole place; you are connected to it and somehow you can feel that energy. Your home is warm, inviting, and loving. Who wouldn't feel welcome at such a lovely place?" She had never realized how much she was missing in life. All those beautiful trees and flowers they had on the estate. She should get out of the house more and connect with all the beauty the estate had to offer. That's what Collin did, and she saw something now that she had never understood before.

"I know we Italians are romantics, unlike you British, but there are so many things to love other than people. It can make your life so much richer." He was proud of his little world. She could see how the Melroneys had loved his company and coming to his home.

As they walked slowly back to the house, and the sky was starting to darken, he put his arm around her and drew her toward him. Phillipa felt helpless and wanted him to draw her in to his body. He gave her a warm hug that made her feel so at ease and comfortable. Her passion was starting to rise as he whispered in her ear, "I'm so happy to have you in my arms again, my bella Phillipa." He then gently looked into her eyes, and in the gentlest manner possible, proceeded to kiss her. He looked at her again, and the couple couldn't resist a more passionate embrace and kiss. They were now reconnected. Time had made no difference. Their love was real, and they were together again.

The two walked back to the house and onto the veranda to finish their drinks and Antonio's cigar. They knew that this night was going to be a very special one. Antonio brought his guitar out and played several romantic Italian serenades. His voice was just as she remembered. They whiled away the night hours, and then arm in arm, they retreated to his room.

The next morning, Phillipa awoke and found that Antonio

had gone to check on his vineyard. For the first time in a long while, she took a long, hot bath and sang to herself. The importance of finding love again had lifted her spirits. She knew Antonio was the man for her. She had spent a great deal of time in the company of so many would-be suitors, but none of them came close to evoking the feelings she had now.

Phillipa got dressed and made her way down to the veranda, where the maid was busy cleaning up after their night. Sabrina was reading the morning paper and sipping her coffee.

"Buongiorno," said Sabrina.

"Good morning! So, what are you going to do for the summer holidays?" She was admiring Sabrina's pretty summer dress and the small flower placed neatly in her hair.

Instead of answering her question right away, Sabrina said, "My Papa likes you a lot, and I'm so happy for him, and you too. You look right together. It's time he had someone to love; he's been so devoted to raising us, but he must take more time for himself. He has a good staff, and he needs to travel and see the world. He works too hard, and having you here just this short time, I can see the change in him. This morning, he was singing wherever he went. We know he's happy when he does that. Now, you asked me where I want to go for the summer. I would love to go to England. By mid-summer, it gets very hot here, and England sounds like the perfect place to visit."

"Then you must come and stay with us and meet my children. They need to learn some Italian, and you can work on your English, although you speak it very well already."

"That's because of Papa. He says that whatever I do in life, I must know English because it is the language of travel. He often speaks in English to us when we're alone."

"He is a person that is very comfortable with other cultures. I knew that when we spent time together when we were young. However, his English has greatly improved over time." She remembered Antonio speaking with a broken accent, but she always liked that about him.

Antonio walked in, gave Phillipa a kiss, and asked, "Are you ready to take a tour?"

"I'm just finishing my coffee, and then I would love to see everything. You can educate me on wines." She was showing an interest that she had rarely shown about anything at Penbroke.

The two made their way in his old jeep to the main buildings, where all his administrative staff worked. They stored all the different years and blends from the vineyard in those buildings. As they walked through the door of a huge, high-ceilinged barn, she could see all the barrels with their various markings. It seemed like a lot of wine to her.

"Now, my dear, you can see the wines that we keep for aging, which you would call shelf wines. They can be stored for many years. Then there are those wines that we keep for only a few years, then release to market. The older wines come from our oldest vines. They have roots that have penetrated deep into the soil, and from them, we get our richest bouquets. Then we have other barrels that we store port in, and some are for sherry, which is mainly just for local and our own use. The barrels are of different woods, and again, different ages. They too help in creating the flavor that people like and what we are known for. You follow me so far?"

"It's quite a business. You must be very knowledgeable to produce such choice."

"Our vineyard has been in operation for over 130 years, but it was a lot smaller when we started. When my ancestors started, we had only ten hectares, or around thirty acres. Over the years, we have expanded slowly and developed the business that you see today."

They passed through the workshops where the wine presses were and where the fermentation process took place, and then they went into the administration building. The buildings were very old, and as Antonio explained, the house where the offices were now was once the home of his grandfather. It wasn't until the 1930s that they built the villa they lived in today. The hallways were lined with photographs that dated back to the turn of the century showing many of his ancestors and the celebrations that took place each year after the harvest. Like the history of the earls of Penbroke, the vineyard carried its own fascinating story. He introduced her to all his main management, who had offices on the second floor of the house, and to his manager, Ferdinande D'Alesio. He explained that he had started as a small boy with his father and had learned everything about how the vineyard worked. Ferdinande had been instrumental in finding other varieties of grapes in order to create the unique flavors their vineyard had become famous for. He proudly showed their awards in the tasting room, where visitors from all over the world had come and signed their names in volumes of books, dating back at least forty years.

As they were walking around the tasting room, a woman entered with a check she needed to be signed. She was well dressed and extremely pretty, and Phillipa couldn't help but notice her. She looked educated and very smart, and Antonio took the opportunity to make the introduction. "This is the woman who makes this place run and watches every penny, aren't you, Sophia?"

She responded in perfect English, eyeing the Countess very closely. "Indeed, I do."

Phillipa could feel a hint of jealousy coming from Sophia. She would bring the matter up later, as she was curious about their relationship.

Antonio then drove her through the vineyard, showing her all the different vines, explaining their ages and when they were planted. After they were done, he asked, "So now you are an expert, yes?"

"Hardly. I couldn't possibly come close to being an expert yet. However, I will slowly learn all about your fascinating business because I have such a wonderful teacher."

"Many people don't understand what we go through to bring about the very best wines and our never-ceasing effort to create new and more exciting flavors."

They drove back to the villa for lunch. As they ate, Phillipa mentioned how fascinated she was with his business and what a wonderful future his children would have. Then she brought up Sophia. "That's a nice-looking woman you have taking care of your accounts."

"Sophia has been with us since she left the university in Milan. She comes from a very nice family and has a good knowledge of what we do here. We've all taught her. At first, it was a lot, but she is now my best negotiator, and you know men—they like someone attractive to deal with."

"She's married?"

"No, not yet. She's tough, and most men would find her very dominant to live with. She has a boyfriend, but he runs around after her like a schoolboy. I guess she's happy with that." Antonio knew where Phillipa was headed.

"You could have fooled me. She definitely has an eye for you. If you don't want to lead her on, you should be careful." The two children sitting at the table agreed with Phillipa.

"I hope you are wrong, but I suppose that could be a problem. A pretty woman in the workplace could present a situation, but she knows I would never do something like that. Look at my two pairs of eyes over there. They watch their Papa very closely, and I don't think they would approve of me having a relationship with her." They agreed and then laughed.

In truth, he did fancy her. In fact, she had been his mistress for several years. The staff knew about it, but the kids knew nothing. Antonio had been alone for a very long time. He could hardly be blamed for falling for such an attractive woman, but as she came from a very different background, it would not be acceptable in social circles for him to have a woman like Sophia.

He would lose his credibility very quickly. He was walking a tightrope, and he knew Phillipa was far too street-smart to miss it.

"I think I must talk with her. I would hate to lose her because she knows so much about my business, but maybe a man would be better in that position. I'll take your advice. It's time she moved on, found a man, settled down, and had a family. Phillipa, I have you now, and I want to keep you. I've waited too long to be a happy man again."

Phillipa stayed a few more days, and Antonio showed her around their local town of Florentino. She was able to buy some souvenirs and items to take back home. He enjoyed showing her his favorite restaurant and some of the history of the area.

Phillipa was excited to have reunited with Antonio and meet his lovely family. On the way to the airport in Florence, she kept thanking him and said she couldn't wait to see him again in England with his kids.

As Antonio returned home, he knew he had a difficult task ahead of him. He had to replace Sophia, and it would come as a tremendous shock to her. As much as he would miss her, she needed to find a younger man. At thirty-one, she would never be accepted by his kids, and she was too strict and lacked the personality for them to like her. She had never taken the time to get to know them and do things with them. All she wanted was Antonio. He was a very eligible bachelor, and most women would do anything to get his attention and have the way of life that he could provide.

He arrived back at the house and went over to the business. It was late in the day, and he knew Sophia would work later than the rest of his staff, as she always waited behind to see him before leaving. He found her in her office. As he entered, he had a terrible feeling in his stomach, but he knew he must bring their affair to an end.

"Sophia, my dear, we must talk," he began.

She got up from her desk and walked around the other side to sit on his lap. "So, you miss me already? I knew she couldn't make you as happy as I could. I've been dreaming of making love to you all week." She put her arms around him, but he resisted. "What's the matter? No one is here. We can make love all night if you want."

"Sophia, we have to stop this. It's going nowhere. You know we can never be together. I am at fault for loving you and giving you hope that when my children are grown, we can be together."

"I've been happy to wait."

"I know you have, but it's not fair, and it's not right. You need a man to have children with to have a full life. You know that you're not going to find that out here. You need to be in a large city where the opportunities for a very pretty woman like you are available." He was feeling a tremendous temptation to make love to her again, but he knew that it would lead nowhere.

"You actually like that snobby English woman? She'll never make love to you like I do." She began taking off her small jacket and opening the buttons on her blouse to make herself irresistible to him.

"Sophia, I don't want to have an argument, but this has to end." He pushed her off his lap and then pushed her away. "Sit down, and let's discuss your leaving."

"It's simple. I won't. I love you too much, and you'll never find another woman who will love you like I do."

"We can discuss the matter, or I will have you taken off the premises. Which do you want?"

"You want to get rid of me? How can you do that after all I've given you? I love you, and you know that no one takes care of your financial affairs or gets contracts like I do."

"I know all of this, and I'm happy to reward you for all of that, but if you don't do as I ask, it will end badly, and I don't want that. You are a beautiful young woman, and there will be plenty of very well-to-do men who will want to give you the life you deserve. It's not here, and as difficult as it is for me to do this, we must do this for both of us. I am a lot older, and what you have is an infatuation. You need a man closer to your own age and a life where you go out at night instead of being tucked away here in the countryside."

"What are you prepared to give me if I go?"

"I will give you one year's salary so that you can find another job, and this will help you get on your feet. I know you have saved money in your time with us, as the cost of living here is less, and there are fewer things to do."

She began to cry. "When do you want me to go?"

Antonio hated to see her cry, but he knew her leaving was necessary. "Leave at the end of the week. Tell everyone that you want to move back to the city so that you can meet someone and have the life that you deserve. It's been a great experience, but you're not getting any younger, and it's time you found someone to love. They will all understand; you know they will."

"Can we spend one more night together?"

"Only when you have moved out and found another place. I promise then that I will take you out, but only then. I want to see you happy, Sophia. I know it's hard, but it's for the best."

"Okay, I'll be gone by the end of the week, but you keep your promise." She looked at him accusingly.

"You have my word on it."

CHAPTER 18

THE LAST SCHOOLDAYS BEFORE SUMMER

James was having his best season ever. Now at eighteen, he stood six foot three. His imposing stature and ability to accelerate to the wicket meant that he could bowl the ball faster than ever before. His team was unbeaten, not because of the great batting season, but mainly because of James's ability to get wickets. His statistics for getting people out over the three years he had been in the first X1 would be almost impossible for someone else to reach, let alone beat. He had become known as the Flying Scotsman, and teams from other schools hated facing his ferocious deliveries. He had offers to play county cricket, but that wasn't what he wanted. He would, however, play a few matches with the old-boys' team, named the Sterling Scots, during the summer holidays down in Cornwall, but for James, that was about it. He was focused on the future and choosing which university he would attend.

During his last year, he had struck up a relationship with his house matron. It all happened one evening after a cricket match when James was taking a bath. He was soaking his tired body when, much to his amazement, the house matron walked in. She was checking the bathrooms and replenishing them with soap. She thought the boys normally took a quick bath in the morning and usually used the showers in the locker rooms in the basement after a match. She was surprised to see James.

"James, the warrior, resting his tired body. How many did you get out today?" She seemed to enjoy catching him.

"Matron, I had no idea that you would be checking the bathrooms at this time of day. I apologize for my present state."

"James, I'm your matron, which also includes being a registered nurse. Have you any idea how many naked men and boys I have seen over the years since I've been here?" she teased.

"I don't have a clue. It's a first for me, and I wouldn't want to shock you."

"James, relax." She slowly walked toward him, and without batting an eyelid, she firmly sat down on the edge of his bathtub. She peered over the bathtub and could see that he was well endowed. "Well, God certainly blessed you. Have you had a chance to demonstrate your skills with a young lady yet?" She spoke with such confidence that James was speechless. "When you've finished your bath, come over to my quarters, and I will check you out to see if you're still in good shape for the rest of the season." She got up and walked off with the same confidence she'd shown when she'd helped him with his difficult beginning with his housemaster, Mr. Caldwell.

"Yes, Matron, I'll be there immediately." He felt a little embarrassed at the encounter.

After he got dressed, he walked to the infirmary, which was next to her quarters, and knocked. She invited him in, told him to strip down to his underpants, and then slowly worked her way over his body. "Apart from a few bruises and a little water on the hip, you're in pretty good shape. Continue to exercise, but bowl as little as you can and save this for the matches and a little practice where possible. Now, come and sit over here. I want to talk with you. James, I have watched you ever since that first day when you were in trouble with Mr. Caldwell. Look at you now, almost a grown man. You have done so well, and here we are in your last term. I too will be leaving, as I now have a job in London. The person I was going to marry has immigrated to Australia, and I didn't want to go. So I, like you, will be choosing a different way for my future. I'm going to be a nurse at a London hospital. I believe you have another hour before lights are out in the dormitories, so come back to my quarters, and there, we can speak more privately."

She locked the door to the infirmary, and they walked into her room. She turned out the light as they entered, and then she shut the door and proceeded to take off her white coat and hang it in her closet. He saw that she had on a very sexy tennis outfit. Her tight sweater showed the distinct outline of her body. She had on white sandals with a small heel that showed her well-shaped, tanned legs. Her dark blue eyes were aglow. She wasn't beautiful, but she was pretty. Her long hair and sharp, alert appearance had sex appeal. James thought it was her self-confidence. He had felt the same way toward her since the very first day they'd met.

She sat down on the side of her bed and motioned him to sit beside her. "James, you're a very good-looking young man. I want the truth. What experiences have you had with a woman?" she said speaking in a softer tone, looking at him with a warmth and allure he hadn't seen before.

"None. I have often thought about such an encounter, but to be honest, the opportunity hasn't presented itself yet."

"What would you say about my being your first? Do you find me attractive?" She crossed her legs and leaned toward him in a way that was hard to resist.

"Matron, everyone in this school thinks you're the best-looking matron we have. In my opinion, apart from that, you're a very good-looking woman in your own right."

"From now on, call me Vivian," she gently whispered in his ear, and then she kissed him softly on the lips. They smiled at one another, and then James took her firmly in his arms and gave her that passionate kiss he'd fantasized about for years. After a few minutes of kissing, she pushed him back and said, "Now I'm going to teach you how to make love to a woman."

In the old days, fathers of well-to-do families had taken their sons to bordellos to learn the mysteries of making love to a woman. Vivian knew James's circumstances, and she decided she was going to fulfill that role. She took off his clothes and then motioned for him to pull off her sweater. To his delight, she exposed two beautiful, plump breasts with beautifully appointed nipples. She could see how ready he was. She dropped her short tennis skirt to the floor and skillfully pulled him forward by his extremely erect equipment. She slowly guided him in the right direction. He was so excited that he came almost immediately. Being a nurse, she wasn't surprised. In fact, she was flattered that he found her that desirable. She patiently awaited his recuperation as they lay arm in arm. He recuperated quickly, and as they began again, she whispered in his ear, "Hold back, slowly, slowly. There's no hurry. Relax and experience this beautiful time we're sharing together."

James was in heaven. This was his first encounter, and Vivian wanted it to be a special experience he would always remember. As he held her more tightly, he could smell her intoxicating fragrance and feel the softness of her skin. James was experiencing something beautiful. He knew he was in the arms of a woman who was an experienced lover, and that gave him comfort and ease. He slowly got the hang of things as she started to become more intense with his every action. After a good half hour of releasing all his feelings, they both lay back and savored the moment.

"That was incredible. I'm so sorry that I came so quickly at first, but the situation was so overwhelming, I just didn't know how to contain myself."

"James, that's completely normal and to be expected. In time, you'll learn to control those muscles, and you made a great deal of progress today. I can say that you satisfied me. I don't want to sound flippant, but I am a little older than you, and very few men have satisfied me sexually in my life so far. It's a problem, and a subject that's taboo. You'll never know how important it is for a man to be a good lover. You probably know a woman can come many times. If you can learn to be slower at first and hold yourself back, develop those muscles and self-control, you'll please any woman you have the good fortune to know. She can then feel the true measure of your heart and love."

James had had a very special encounter. They were happy to have shared a moment that both of them had wanted for a very long time.

****

James's friends had made his last year a lot of fun. His girl-friend at Saint Andrew's girls' school, Sandra, had also added some flame to his spirit. He was anxious to see her after the school term ended. The Sunday before they were to go home, James, Carl, Peter, and Kent decided to go into Saint Andrews to a pub that was out of bounds to them. They were all eighteen, so they could sneak in the back, have a pint of beer, and meet up with the girls. They peddled as fast as they could after school lunch to get there before closing time at two o'clock. Sandra had promised to meet James there.

As they walked in, they greeted the bartender, whom they knew, and James placed his order. "Pint of Best Bitter, Ralph. The first round is on me, Ralph, so run us a tab."

"Yes, sir, Mr. James."

At that moment, Sandra arrived. James was glad to see her one more time before the holidays. She lived in Surrey, which wasn't exactly next door, but James knew he would take the time to drive down to see her. She gave him a hug and asked him to get her a small shandy.

The whole gang sat outside, lit up their cigarettes, and discussed their last days.

Kent said, "Well, I've had enough of all your Brit education. If that English master asks me once again to properly pronounce my name, I'm going to deck him."

"You've just got to learn to speak like a Brit, and then it'll all work out," replied Carl.

"I'm a Texan and proud of it, and if y'all can't understand me, then to hell with it!"

"Y'all!" everyone yelled, then laughed.

"Just wait until you get to my side of the ocean. Don't forget who won the War of Independence."

Peter teased, "Now look here, old chap, all those people who wrote your constitution were Brits. They spoke with English accents—Washington, even Jefferson, although he loved the frogs. Don't you see it was a civil war between Brits that wanted a way of life away from George III? America is just another British country that's a republic. With all those immigrants, the language just got screwed up a little, that's all. Don't feel too bad about it, old boy."

"By God, I need to get home to some sanity before I kill the lot of you," Kent fumed.

Moments later, a car pulled into the parking lot outside the pub. The car was well known to all the lads, and they just hoped the man inside was not whom they thought it might be. To their dismay, Mr. Caldwell got out and was heading straight for them. Peter groaned, "Oh my God, this is it. We're all going to get expelled!"

Mr. Caldwell reached their table and asked, "Do you know

what the punishment is for what you're doing?"

"Yes, sir."

"Then don't just sit there; go and buy me a pint of Worthington E. If you're going to be expelled, you might as well enjoy the moment, don't you think?"

James ordered, "Get a pint of beer, quick."

"I knew you would be here, so I came along just so you don't forget who's the smartest when you come back as old boys," he said, laughing.

The old buzzard was just yanking their chain. He knew the lads went out for a pint sometimes, and since they were of legal age, he didn't have a problem with it. Sometimes it was allowed if a master accompanied the group, so his being there would let them off the hook if they got caught, and he would get a couple of pints of beer out of the deal.

James put his head in his hands. "My God, sir. We thought we were in for it."

"I would never do that to a bunch of good lads like you've been, especially just before the end of term. After all, in a few days, you won't give a hang about what I think, or the school for that matter. I would be doing exactly what you're doing. You just should have invited me is all."

"We didn't know that you like to go out, sir," Carl added apologetically.

"Well, now you do, so when you come back to visit, take me for a pint."

James was reminded that Caldwell wasn't such bad man after all. Strict, yes, but human.

"We'll certainly remember you for today's visit, that's for sure. We'll be talking about this for many years to come."

"I'll miss the lot of you. You've all contributed greatly to the school. As a master, one never knows how boys are going to turn out. You, James, were quite a testy little character when you arrived, but you've matured, and your exam results have been good. I'm sure you will go to the university of your choice. Your contribution to our cricket matches will be hard to repeat. I think your father would have been very proud of you. I know I am. You deserve your title and family name. I know you will do well in life and help others on their journey too."

"Thank you, sir. Coming from you, that means a lot."

Peter asked, "What will you be doing during the summer holidays, sir?"

"I'm going to Greece with my daughter and son-in-law. I want to explore the ruins. Even though I am a math teacher, my hobby has always been archeology, and studying ancient ruins teaches us a lot about our ancestors."

A lot of banter and laughing amongst the group was exchanged, and then they realized they should get back to school. James, however, wanted to spend a little time with Sandra alone. He told his friends, "I'll catch up with you later."

After the others had left, Sandra held James's hand and said, "I'm going to miss you so much. It's going to be hard not knowing when I'll see you again."

"I know, but I hope to get a car if I can twist my mother's arm, or I'll just drive the old Land Rover down to see you. Then I can bring you back to my place, and we can spend time together."

"I don't know that my family will approve of me leaving home with a young man. Perhaps when they've had time to visit with you, they will change their mind."

They hugged and kissed each other, knowing that it would be the last time for a while. They had spent so many hours together, taking packed lunches into the countryside and getting to know each other. They had helped each other prepare for upcoming exams. Theirs was more than just a love affair—it was a friendship.

"I've got to get back," James said, giving her one last kiss and embrace. "I'll come to see you. I promise," he told her as he mounted his bike.

When he arrived back, he took Kent to one side to talk with him. "So, where will you go to university?" James was curious about American universities.

"My father will send me to Harvard so I can get a good grounding in finance before I enter his business. I must do some practical work in the field first."

"Harvard. That's one of those Ivy League universities, right? Is a degree in business from that school of any value?"

"I'd think so. It's just about the best business degree you can get in North America. The problem is getting in there. There's a waiting list, and if you've had family there, it helps. Being a good student is obviously important too."

"So you have family that's been there?"

"Yes, but I had to get my grades up in math and English, which is why my father sent me to this boot camp of a place. For all its sins, this place knows how to bang an education into a man's head. I was a terrible student who fooled around too much. My father got tough and sent me here. Even though we all gave each other a hard time, I can truly say that I wouldn't have missed coming here and meeting guys like you. Our education in regular schools is very weak, and if you're not a natural student, which I'm not, you're not going to make it to Harvard. Whether you've got money or not, it doesn't matter."

"I'm down to go to Cambridge, but I want to learn about America. I think going to university there would be a tremendous opportunity. Besides, you guys are smart business people, and as my family is in the banking business, I want to get a head start on how others do business."

"I think you've got the right idea. The fact that you are a lord always impresses the faculty. If you have the grades to go to Cambridge, you'll certainly make it to Harvard."

"Will you help me? Can I come to visit you in Texas? I want to learn about the oil and gas business and how you guys live." James knew his family wouldn't approve, but he felt he would get his own way if Sir Thomas were behind him.

"Of course. I'll be happy to help you. I'll talk with my dad when I get back home. But I won't be going to Harvard right away. I've got to get some practical experience first, and then you can come visit. We can both go to Harvard to register and see if our applications get approved. It would be great to be with you at Harvard. We can find an apartment nearby."

"They don't have dormitories?"

"They do, but believe me, having an apartment is a lot better, and it's within walking distance to the university."

"That sounds great. Count me in. You have all my coordinates. I need all your information so I can give you a call. Then we can plan my coming to see you if your dad will approve."

"Sure. I know he'll just love having an Englishman in his house, especially after we dumped all that tea in the harbor and told you lot to get lost. However, you did help the South with the Civil War, so he'll think it over." Kent had a devious look on his face.

"Your dad hates the Brits?"

"Of course. Why do you think I'm at school in Scotland? He has some Scottish ancestry. You know they have never loved you Brits either."

"Maybe I can talk him around. I certainly don't feel that way about Americans!" James sounded concerned.

"We're not Americans. We're Texans. We were a country like England once, so we like to feel our independence, if you know what I mean."

"I'll just have to get to know Texans, then, won't I?"

Kent burst out laughing. "James, I'm just giving you a hard time. You should know me better than that by now."

James started laughing. "You really led me on for a moment. I was beginning to wonder about the whole thing. You can see why we give you such a hard time now. You know how to dish it out, that's for sure. No wonder your dad sent you to boot camp!"

That night, James went to sleep with one thing on his mind. He knew Sandra would be taking the train back to London, so why couldn't she take the train with him to Peterborough and stay over the weekend? She could meet Rebecca, who was almost the same age, and then he could drive her back to her home in Surrey. Her parents surely wouldn't mind that, he thought.

James had some free time on Tuesday afternoon after three o'clock, so he jumped on his bike and cycled over to Sandra's school. The staff at the school was surprised at the audacity of this young man entering the administration offices and requesting that he speak with Sandra Cole.

The head mistress came to talk to him. "What are you doing here, young man?"

"Madam, I have a message for Sandra that I would like to personally deliver to her, as it will affect her trip back to her home in Surrey." He was being as polite as possible.

"How is it a young man like you has this information? Surely her own parents would have called the school or talked to her personally if there had been a change." The head mistress was very suspicious of his motives.

"I understand your concern, but my parents wish her to stay with us so that she can meet my sister Rebecca on her way back home. We live in Lincolnshire, and I know her train goes through Peterborough on her return," he said, trying to make the situation sound very formal and planned.

"Young man, you wouldn't be trying to see her yourself by any chance?" Clearly this educated woman was not going to be fooled by any plans he might have up his sleeve. "You have to understand that any student at this school has a very planned return, either by car, bus, or train, to their parents' home. Any change in that has to come directly from her parents or guardian."

"I certainly wouldn't be here if I were wanting to make arrangements that would not respect the protocol of your school.

I would just like the opportunity to talk with her, and then she can make the decision with her parents accordingly."

"You certainly have some nerve coming over here. That being said, you look like a person who has character, so I will allow you to talk with her, but rest assured, no plans will change without the permission of her parents."

He was asked to wait in the front hall and was told Sandra would meet him there. It seemed like ages before Sandra finally arrived, but the head mistress wanted to test his patience and validity.

"James, how did you get here?" She was excited to see him.

"On my bike."

"You cycled all this way to tell me what?"

"Can you talk with your parents and get their permission to stop over for the weekend at my home? I will be getting off at Peterborough, and my chauffeur will take us both to my home. You can tell your parents that you're meeting my sister Rebecca, or something like that. Look, you're eighteen; we are adults. They have to understand that we will be in the company of my mother. I can tell you she won't allow anything out of the ordinary to happen."

"I'm so flattered that you would go to all this trouble, and yes, I do want to come if it's okay with your mother. I've just got to talk my parents into letting me travel back with you, and I know they won't allow me without talking directly to your mother. It's only normal; they don't know who you are or what your intentions might be." She was excited at the possibility but fearful of her parents' response.

"We'll give it a shot. If we don't try, it won't happen. Tell them what a fantastic person I am and all that stuff. Do it for us." He wished he could take her outside and kiss her at that very moment. The head mistress was watching the couple from the upstairs balcony. She thought of how beautiful young love was. If any man had ridden his bike all that way, he had to be sincere, and she had to acknowledge that, whatever the outcome.

"Okay, I'll do it."

"Here are my mother's numbers in London and at our home in Penbroke." Then he whispered, "I love you," and gave her a quick kiss on the cheek before anyone could see—or so he thought.

After he left, the head mistress descended the staircase into the front lobby. "Sandra, who is that young man? He's very determined."

"I'm so sorry this happened," she said politely.

"Not at all. That young man is in love with you. If he could take the time to ride all that way to see you, I am a good enough judge of character to know he's sincere. How lucky you are to know such a strong and ambitious young man. Who is he?"

"He comes from a very fine background and is very respected at his school, Sterling Heights, for his achievements. His name is James Bannerman, and he is the Tenth Earl of Penbroke."

"A lord indeed, and he was so modest. I could tell he had been brought up properly. Keep an eye on him, my dear. That man is going places. Make sure you have your parents call me before any changes are made." She walked away, chuckling to herself at the whole episode.

The next morning during break, James went to the school pay phone to call his mother and make her aware of his plan. He knew he needed to speak with her before Sandra's parents called.

"James, why at the last minute do you want this girl to visit? And don't give me some made-up story; tell me the truth."

"Mother, over the last year, I have been seeing Sandra. Yes, she is my girlfriend, and she has helped me immensely with my homework and in preparing for tests. I would so appreciate it if you would allow her to stay with us for just a few days. Who knows—I may never see her again, and she's helped me so much. Her parents live in Surrey, so Peterborough is a stop on the way home for her." James hoped that by presenting a picture like this, he would get more understanding from his mother.

"I suppose so."

"Her mother will call you to see if you agree and to obviously be sure her daughter isn't going somewhere she shouldn't."

"Fair enough. I don't see why not. You've worked hard, and you're now eighteen. It would be a nice treat for you after your final year. Remember, I trust you, James. You are a man now, and although this girl is probably the most important person in your life right now, you have a long way to go. If it's what you want, I will tell her mother that it's okay for her to stay over."

"I can't thank you enough."

"I look forward to seeing you soon and hearing all your news. Lots of love."

"Thanks, Mom, and I love you too."

James was ecstatic and wasted no time informing the head mistress at Sandra's school.

"James, I've heard a lot about you from Sandra. I will pass the message on, but as I told you, I must hear from her mother first. If we don't speak again, it was a pleasure meeting you. You certainly follow through with matters, and I like that; it shows you to be a responsible person. Good luck for your future."

Late Thursday afternoon, James was called to the phone. "James, you did it!" cried Sandra on the other end. "I think my mother was so impressed to talk to a countess that she completely agreed, so I'll meet you at the train station in Edinburgh at ten o'clock so that we can catch the train together."

"This is great! We're going to have so much fun."

"I can't wait to see you. Until tomorrow . . ."

James enjoyed bragging to his friends about how he managed to arrange for Sandra to go home with him.

Peter asked, "What did you have to do to pull that off?"

"Connections, old boy, connections."

"The virtues of being a lord, I suppose; you're just more

believable than the rest of us commoners," Carl said. They all laughed.

Before James left the next morning, he dropped by to see Vivian at the infirmary.

"James, I hear you have a girlfriend," she said, smiling.

"Yes, I do. Our time together was so special, Vivian, and I'll never forget it or you."

He was a little sad that they weren't able to get to know each other better.

"James, I'll miss you. I wish I could be that lucky woman you'll find. But I'll be watching you from a distance; you can be sure of that. Here is my address and contact information in London, so let's keep in touch. Should you ever need a nurse, remember me." When the last boys rushed out the dormitories and the room became quiet, he grabbed hold of her and gave her a hug and a kiss.

"I'll miss you too." Then he left.

It was a day of mixed emotions for James as he took the bus to the station in Edinburgh. He had spent the last five years with these people and created a bond. He knew he would miss them. While he was having those thoughts, someone came up to sit behind him.

"His Lordship gets to go home with his girlfriend. How very pleasant. The rest of us commoners have to go home in the traditional way. Just remember, James, you're in the real world now. My brother and I have not forgotten that afternoon you humiliated us at the Coffee Pot; we shall get even, and maybe slightly ahead, when the appropriate time comes."

"Gordon, you don't intimidate me for one second. I'll just deal with you like I did before. All bullies are cowards, so you belong on a long list, unfortunately. One would think after all these years, you could find it within yourself to have more re-spect for yourself and others. This place has taught you noth-ing," said James, not wanting to have anything to do with such a twisted mentality.

"Be warned, I intend to get even. My brother and I are not without means, and we'll see that you face what's coming to you. All you spoiled upper-class brats need to learn you can't throw your weight around just because you have a title." His voice and tone were malicious, and James took it as an idle threat that he would never back up.

When they reached the train station, James said his final goodbyes and ran to the front of the station. He asked the ticket master which platform was for Peterborough, and then he ran over the bridge to the right platform. As he descended the stairs, he saw Sandra. They embraced one another as the train pulled in, and then they opened the door of the carriage and quickly hunted for a quiet spot where they could be alone.

CHAPTER 19

FREEDOM AND INDEPENDENCE

James and Sandra were happy to be alone. They could talk freely after constantly being under supervision and having only a few hours of being together at a time. They felt a tremendous feeling of independence. James had never seen Sandra dressed up the way she was now. As she had put up her light raincoat in the rack above their seats, he noticed how nice she looked. She wore a summer dress with stockings and high heels, her nails had been polished, and her face was beautifully made up. Her blonde hair was pulled back behind her small ears into a ponytail. Her light blue eyes and full lips added to her beauty. He was in the company of a very pretty woman. Sandra wasn't a tall woman, but in high heels, she was about five foot six, which for James, was the perfect size. She laid her head on his shoulder, and he started to feel overcome with desire.

"Sandra, I know I'm wrong to think about you in this way, but seeing you look like this for the first time, I just want to hold you in my arms for the whole journey."

"I could say the same thing about you. In your school uniform and tie, all neatly dressed, you look so handsome, but you look even more so now. However, if I kiss you now, your face is going to be covered in lipstick." They both laughed.

"Let's go down to the dining car and get something to munch on. We can have a cup of coffee or tea. Otherwise, I don't think I'll be responsible for what happens next."

"Good idea. We don't want to look like a wreck when we arrive."

They walked through the other carriages until they arrived at the dining car. They sat down, and a waiter brought them a menu.

As they ate, they traded stories about their families and growing up. They had always been limited to such short periods of time spent together, so they enjoyed having the extended time to get to know each other better.

After they had finished eating and were exhausted from talking and laughing, Sandra suggested, "Let's go back to our seats and relax before the train arrives." She wanted to sit next to him and just be close together. The pair fell asleep holding onto to one another.

When they awoke, James saw that the train was about fifteen minutes from Peterborough. Rodney was on time, and they got into the back of the Rolls and headed for Penbroke. Sandra was feeling a little anxious, as she was about to meet his family, and although she had seen the Countess and Sir Thomas briefly, she had no idea what his home or family was like.

As they entered the tall, impressive wrought-iron gates and slowly drove up the driveway, Sandra noticed that on both sides were large fields where the horses grazed and a few scattered trees. It was quite unlike the heavier vegetation she was used to in Surrey. They eventually arrived at a second set of gates that opened into a large courtyard and central fountain. This made the house seem extremely private. "This place is enormous, James. I feel like our home would fit into this courtyard at least three times." She was feeling a little overwhelmed.

"Don't worry. It's just a house, and once you're inside, it will feel more inviting."

It was around three o'clock when they arrived, and Rodney brought their small bags into the house. Their main luggage would be sent by a truck from their schools and arrive at their respective homes a few days later. James led the way to where he knew his mother would be waiting.

"So, you are Sandra? How pretty you are, and how lovely to have you come stay with us for a few days," said the Countess, who was an expert at making people feel at home.

"Countess, I can't thank you enough for allowing James to arrange this. We've been wondering when we would see each other again, and this sounded like the perfect opportunity, so I thank you again for your understanding."

Rebecca walked into the room and introduced herself. "Hello, I'm Rebecca. And your name is?" she asked confidently. James noticed that she was developing a refined and dignified manner. She had been a little on the gawky side when she was young. She had taken after her father and was taller than average for her age. She was now filling out, however, and James was proud to see how feminine she looked. He figured she probably had a few boyfriends. "Would you like to come and see around the house, and then I can show you your room?"

"Yes, I would like that very much."

After the two girls left, the Countess said, "You devil. She's very pretty and seems intelligent too. I like your choice. I want to get to know her. We'll have dinner here tonight, and then we can discuss all these matters." She motioned to Rodney to bring some afternoon tea. "Now, sit down. I want to talk with you."

"Mother, first of all, thank you for allowing Sandra to come. I can't tell you how much I appreciate it."

"You young people. It's only natural and healthy at your age to want friends, fall in love, and so on. My only advice to you is to be sensible. I can see you like this girl very much, but it's so easy to make decisions that lock you up for the rest of your life. Take it one day at a time, and be careful when it becomes too intimate. The temptations are enormous, and you have to be careful about having children. The whole thing can get messy. I want you to have fun, and I won't say this again. Every parent has to forewarn their children of the potential consequences to their best interests, and after that, it's up to the person." The Countess was fairly broad-minded about such matters and only wanted the best for her children.

"Mother, rest assured, I have thought of all those concerns, and I'm in no hurry to rush into a situation that's going to slow me down."

"So, have you made any decisions yet on a university?"

"I thought I would wait to see what my exam results are, and then we could make decisions from there."

"I agree. You have the whole summer to make the right choice. I'm sure Sir Thomas will give you some valuable advice and help you make the best possible decision."

They finished their conversation, and James decided to go see how the Throne Room was doing and talk with Keith Pruett. He opened the side gate from the courtyard and walked toward the East Wing. He could see coaches and a parking lot that had a fair number of cars off in the distance. He slowly made his way toward the room, forgetting it was now surrounded by a staff that were checking tickets and didn't know who he was. He decided he better go back to the farm administration building to find Keith. He found Keith in Claudia's old office and told him that he wanted to see the room.

"Yes, My Lord, of course. Let's go take a look. But first, I will get you a small staff badge so that you can get in anytime you want and people don't have to know who you are unless you introduce yourself." He was used to dealing with dignitaries and understood how they might not want to be singled out, especially in public.

"Good idea. I like that." James looked around the office and saw that quite a few changes had been made, and all for the better. His father's office was still there, and Keith had respectfully not touched it in case James might want to use it.

The estate staff came up to congratulate him on finishing school. They looked up to him as the next heir, the young blood so needed after his father's death that would give purpose and reason for the Penbroke legacy to continue. He was tall, and the women were taking particular notice of him.

Keith and James got in the Land Rover and drove to the new buildings. The staff they passed all knew Keith and tipped their hats as he made his way through the various inspection points to a small parking area at the back of the temporary buildings.

They walked over to Sarah McKenzie's school. Sarah had just finished a class and was happy to see James. "James, I can't stay long, but I do want to show you what we've done. I know Peter will be home, just like you, and I haven't seen him in a while, so I'm anxious to get home."

Keith interrupted, "Sir, I'll leave you with Mrs. McKenzie, and then you can make your own way back."

"Many thanks, Keith. We'll get together soon." James wanted to get a handle on how the farm was doing.

"James, let's take a quick walk around, and then you can see the finished product." Sarah started at the beginning, and they followed a few groups. The staff members that had been trained in all the writings of the Seventh Earl were lecturing each group. They had been educated to speak with authority on all the artifacts. Sarah had done an amazing job, and she'd done a lot of it on her own time, without any pay, simply for the love and experience of the work. She knew the benefit to her was her school. Training people to go to that next level of understanding would sell books, souvenirs, and the history of Penbroke. There was a growing curiosity about the room, which James witnessed as he followed Sarah. Obviously, the throne was the main attraction. With all the refurbishments made, it stood out as the glowing attraction.

"I can't believe such a wonderful job has been done. The room always looked great to me, but now the whole place has life, and seeing people so anxious to know all about it is re-deeming. It is a great tribute to all those years that my family waited to open this magnificent legacy to the world."

"I think what we have is amazing. More importantly, it is an educational process which is creating enormous interest. You won't believe how many skeptics there are, but they can't deny what stands in front of them. The biggest barrier I have to face is fear. People, although curious, are afraid of things they don't understand, but we have seen them come back with others to try and probe further because they have to agree that the throne is an anomaly." She spoke with a passion for what she was do-ing. Sarah was perfect for the job, and how lucky he was to meet her. It was her abilities and her enthusiasm that made the whole thing work. She was absolutely the very best choice he could have made.

"I want to come back when it's quiet and look at everything again. It's hard to really critique all the things we have when the public is here; however, it does make one see the place in a very different way."

As they walked back to the school, Sarah asked him what his plans for the future were.

"I don't know. I just think going to university right now is not the right direction for me. It's what all my ancestors have done, but I have a farm that needs to be run and a bank that I need to learn about. I think I'm going to get my articles with a good accounting firm; that would be the best direction for me right now. This will leave me free to both learn and keep an eye on the businesses we already have. There's a lot of social life that goes with being at university, and it takes a number of years to get those degrees. I don't have a father or mother running the show, so I need to get in there and do the best I can. After all, I'm not going to need to get a job; I already have one. For those that want to become lawyers, accountants, and so on, I can see the need. I feel I can learn more from the experience in the day-to-day and take some courses that help me better understand what we already have. What do you think?" James was still partially undecided and valued Sarah's opinion.

"I completely agree. What you have is a huge career in front of you, and as you rightly mention, your father's passed on, so you need to get involved with what you already have. What you will learn in the day-to-day, a university can't teach. When you need further education, get it. Then it will have a practical meaning so that you can apply your knowledge more specifically."

He gave her a big hug and asked that she bring Peter over so that they could go riding on her next visit. She agreed, and they parted.

James walked back to the house and cleaned up after a long day. He wanted to look nice for Sandra, so he put on a sports coat and cravat, and then he splashed on plenty of aftershave lotion. He made his way to the front drawing room, where the others were having a drink. James poured himself a beer and then walked over to Sandra. She was wearing a cocktail dress and looked even more beautiful than she had on the train. Becky was also dressed up, as was Flick. James noticed that Flick certainly had changed. She was starting to look exactly like his mother. As a young girl, she had always been a bit of a tomboy and prankster, but she was certainly becoming an attractive young woman at sixteen and a half.

The Countess asked, "James, what have you been up to?"

"I went to visit Keith Pruett, Sarah, and the Throne Room."

"What do you think of the progress?"

"I think that Keith has done a splendid job of getting the farm up to date, although I have yet to sit with him and get into detail. Then I went with him because I needed a pass to get into the East Wing with Sarah. She is doing a fantastic job; it looks like it's on the road to becoming a successful enterprise."

"What's the Throne Room, James?" asked Sandra curiously.

"Tomorrow I'll show you around. Every place like this has its deep, dark secrets, and the East Wing has a story all of its own, which I will share with you." He was trying to create an atmosphere of intrigue.

"Oh, this is something you definitely haven't shared with me." She imagined all sorts of ghostly apparitions that must exist in a home like this.

"He'll keep you suspended in all sorts of stories for hours," said Flick.

"Don't let him lead you on. It's all hocus-pocus. But if it brings people here, then it's a good thing," said the Countess, smiling at James.

"Sandra, don't listen to them. James has a fine project, and I think you'll be very excited to see what he'll show you," Becky said dismissively.

Sandra shook her head. "James, you're full of surprises. Just when I think I know all about you, I'm told something new."

"Dinner is ready," said Rodney, and they all piled into the dining room. As they were fresh back from school, Phillipa had arranged for all their favorite dishes to be prepared. They sat down, and James said grace. He also thanked his mother for having everything prepared for the evening.

James began teasing his sisters. "How are you two getting on at Benenden? Any boyfriends we should know about?"

"Of course, but we had that conversation before you arrived," replied Flick.

"Now I can see why James is so understanding of women. He

doesn't have one mother; he's got three," Sandra laughed.

"He's got three mothers all right, but we don't think he understands the first thing about a woman. We should know, growing up with him." Flick was quite the provoker, so she felt like giving him a hard time in front of his girlfriend.

"See what I have to put up with! It's a wonder I'm functional with women at all!"

The girls hooted with laughter, and then his mother stepped in. "Now, be nice to your brother. He is a little outnumbered. However, it's good for him, and he'll get even, I'm sure."

"Oh, don't we know that," Rebecca said, then added, "All I know is he's the only brother I ever want."

"Becky, you are a sister to keep," James said, happy to have some reaffirmation.

The Countess said, "Sandra, tell us all about you. We want to hear about what you think of school in Scotland. I'm especially curious as to why a family would send their daughter all that way."

"My father, who has had to make it from the ground up, so to speak, isn't a believer in boarding schools. He prefers day schools and family upbringing as a more responsible way of raising his children. However, my mother, who had a boarding school education, convinced him otherwise. So he agreed, but only if I went to a school that was strict and taught women the art of cooking and seamstress work—a school that catered to the things that he believed a woman should be capable of doing and a school that wasn't too close to boys' schools. He was brought up in a very different way. Scotland is remote, and although I was very homesick at first, I can say I had a better education than I could have ever imagined."

"Your father sounds like a disciplinarian. Nothing wrong with that. We need more people like that in this country."

"He's very much a disciplinarian, but he has a great sense of humor, and although his methods are unorthodox, he's been very successful, so I guess it works."

"So your father and mother live in Surrey, close to London and his work, I imagine?" The Countess was now even more curious about her father and who he was.

"Not exactly. We have what you would call an estate, much smaller than this one, but it has a dairy herd and is set in a very scenic area between the borders of Surrey and Sussex."

"He has a dairy farm and a manufacturing business? When does he ever rest?" asked the Countess.

"During the week, he stays at his flat in London, and then he goes to the farm on the weekend."

"And your mother goes too?"

"Sometimes."

"This man sounds all work and no play, but that's what it takes to make it happen. I well know that, and I admire it." The Countess turned to James. "Well, James, that sounds like a man you should meet. People who start with very little and build something great don't do so by luck alone." The Countess was happy that Sandra was there; she thought she might be a good influence on James.

"If you allow me to take Sandra back to her home, I hope to have the opportunity to meet her father," James said, sensing the perfect opportunity to make his pitch.

"I completely agree. I just bought a little Mini. You can drive her home in that. I think that would be a good experience for you."

They continued talking and getting to know one other for a while longer. Then the Countess announced that she was tired and was retiring for the evening. Becky and Flick went to watch television, and James and Sandra went into a small side room to enjoy some port, coffee, and a cigarette. The room had a door that led out onto a patio at the side of the house, and it was quiet and secluded. They sat down on a two-seated patio chair, set their drinks down, and embraced, happy to be alone.

CHAPTER 20

GETTING TO KNOW SANDRA

After breakfast the next morning, James took Sandra on a tour of the estate. He wanted to go to the Throne Room first, before it opened to the public, so Rodney opened the doors for them at nine.

"James, this is the most unbelievable room I've ever seen in my life. You've never once mentioned anything about this place to me, and I thought I knew all your secrets."

"It's not easy to tell someone about a place like this because, first of all, they'd think you were talking a lot of hot air, and then they would never understand what I'm about to show you."

"I can see that no one would believe that a place like this would exist. Let me read the writings on the wall first, and then you can explain what I don't understand." Being a detailed person, she went around the room reading all the explanations given by the Seventh Earl, and then she arrived at the throne. She read about the throne coming from Atlantis and its special energies. Then she turned to James and asked, "So what if I sit on that throne right now? What will happen?"

"You'll have one of two experiences. You'll either go somewhere, or you may see something that frightens you, and you'll feel dizzy and get off the throne . . ."

"First of all, what do all these beautiful stones represent?"

"They are the seven chakras of your body, from the base of your spine to the diamond on the top. If you are what is called an aligned person, you will have an experience that will be very beautiful. If you don't, then it doesn't mean you won't be aligned one day; it just means you're not ready. Are you still sure you want to try?"

"Have you experienced this?"

"Yes, I have. It's something you won't forget, but not everyone is ready for it, and it's important that you know that," he cautioned her again.

"If you did it, I will too."

She sat on the throne, and James watched nervously, hoping she would not have an experience like Nicholas Blythe. Then, he could see the energy rising and the brilliance that was shining in her eyes and around her head. He knew she was gone and would be back.

Seconds later, she got up from the chair in a slight daze and said, "James, I've never experienced anything like that. It seems as if I've been gone for at least an hour. That's the most incredible experience a person could ever have. I need to take a moment and think it all through. I know it was only momentary for you. It's strange how time is so different there."

"So tell me all about it," James said.

"Well, I've known you many times before. I was on Atlantis too, and we knew each other then. It's no accident that we've met up again. My master told me all about my father and why I had chosen this life. It's unreal. If someone doesn't believe in the afterlife after meeting a person of such profound knowledge, nothing would make them. It's as though we are all here to usher in a new age of enlightenment, something that's only just beginning and will be in full progress by the year 2030. We are at the beginning of the Age of Aquarius, on the cusp, so to speak. If we do the things we should do as a human race, we will discover amazing technologies. More than that, we will lift the dimension of human thinking to a new level, a more spiritual level. It's as though this is the real religion and what we've all been striving to attain for centuries. I also learned that we only teleport our spirit, not our body. In the days of Atlantis, they could teleport whole spaceships with astronauts. I learned how they had to take different spacesuits for their protection based on the different atmospheres they would encounter on other planets. It's all so fascinating."

James was pleased to have someone his own age with whom he could share this experience. "Let's go have a cup of coffee while you process your experience. I knew you made it because I could see the light that surrounded you. You looked almost angelic. It was unbelievable to watch you."

They went over to the tearoom outside, which was opening up for the day. They sat down at a table on the patio. "That room is special. Do you know how many people would see things in a different way for the rest of their lives if they could experience what I just did?"

"I know, but you are one of only a few that has experienced what you did. That's why we have a school for people to align their chakras. We teach them balance, to go of their fears, and how to do exactly what you just did."

"So, all this time you have known about things like this and you have never discussed this with a soul at school?" She didn't understand.

"Sandra, if I spoke to a bunch of lads in a tough school like Sterling about an experience like that, how far do you think I would get? I would be put on the crazy list."

"I suppose so. I know I couldn't explain something like that to my parents."

"Exactly. But with time and patience, more and more people will become spiritually evolved, and then a better understanding of this incredible universe we live in can be gained."

"I've never felt such a calling in my whole life. That experience is more real than you and I talking right now." She felt as though she had been awakened from a long dream.

"It's very special, yes, but we must face the fact that we are here for the now. We must respect our duty and do what we were meant to do here on this earth."

"You're right. I mustn't get carried away, but it's hard not to. If our lives could be like that, why do we tarry so long in this dimension?"

"Some people like it here and they don't want to give up this reality, even though they die and live again. It's an enormous subject, and we have the rest of our lives to discuss it."

James figured it was time to start seeing other parts of the estate, as the public was beginning to arrive. He took her to the farm buildings, the dairy farm, and then to the stables. She loved the horses, and they decided to go for a ride after lunch. James got the keys to the Mini, and they drove to the little pub in Penbroke to have a drink and a snack.

As they drove, they continued their conversation. "James, you have such a vast world to oversee—a huge farm, a bank that has interests all over the world. How will you do it all?"

"You fail to recognize that I was brought up to do this, as my forefathers have done for centuries. Obviously, we can't do it all ourselves, so we need good people, and they have to be managed and watched. People think that just because you and people like us have been born to wealth that we are greedy and selfish, but they don't recognize the immense responsibility that goes with it. It's one thing to have all this, but it's another to run it and run it well," said James, thinking deeply about the subject.

"We have an example to set and must inspire others to achieve great goals for themselves. Let's face it—not everything we will do will turn out the way we want, but we have to stay in there and have the faith to make it happen."

"James, my master told me that you and I are a lot older than our actual age. It's not that we remember everything from our past lives, but we carry over with us the things that we have worked hard to learn, and so, intuitively, we know how to do certain things. There are other things we've yet to master, but even in the dimensions above us, we are always learning and developing. Thank you so much for allowing me to have this experience."

After lunch, they returned to the estate. Flick loaned Sandra her riding britches and hat, and James and Sandra headed to the stables to ride.

Joe greeted them saying, "Good afternoon, Mr. James. I've got your horses ready. You can ride Foxy, and Miss Sandra can ride Day Dream. She was a polo pony, so don't stand up in the saddle; otherwise, she'll slow down."

"I have longed to get on horseback. I have a horse at home named Prancer, and he can fly like the wind. Let's see what you're made of, James."

The two of them had fun riding along the beach in front of Penbroke. Sandra's skills far outweighed James's, and it wasn't hard to show him up with her experienced abilities.

"A horse knows who can ride them and who can't. I have a lot more practice than you think," she said, smiling flirtatiously.

"So you're saying I'm not much good?" James asked, feeling a little humiliated.

"Not at all. You know how to ride, but you've got to know how to win. Have you got a field where I can jump a few fences?" She wanted more of a challenge than just galloping down the beach.

"We do, but you'll need a horse that jumps. We have a point

to pointer, a steeplechaser, that you can ride if you want." He was testing her nerve.

"Now, that's more like it. Let's go and do that." She smiled at him, clearly enjoying seeing him feel sorry for himself.

As they trotted up the beach back to the small pathway, Joe met them. "That lady can ride, sir."

"Shut up, Joe. I know when I've been outclassed."

"James, you can't be the best at everything. You've got to leave room for others," said Sandra.

"Okay, that's enough. Joe, Sandra wants to ride one of our steeplechasers in the paddock with the fences."

"Really? Now I *know* she can ride." He leaned toward James and quietly whispered, "She's had a lot of experience. You can see that. She's a natural on a horse, and those horses know it."

"We'll see how she does with Bullet. That'll be a good test."

"Yes, sir. I'll saddle him up right away," Joe said as he went to get Bullet ready.

"How did you learn to ride like that?"

"That was nothing. I have a show jumper that I compete with all around the country. I was the number one tennis player at my school, and I shoot and fish for salmon. Anything else you would like to know, Your Lordship?"

"I suppose you're one hell of a good student on top of that, right?"

"I got four A levels. I missed history by a hair."

"I've known you for nearly a year, and you've never once told me any of this."

"Well, you never asked."

"I knew that was coming. I apologize for not taking a greater interest in you than I have."

"That's okay. It's far more fun this way."

Joe had Bullet ready to ride. The horse had done several "point to point" races with Joe riding him. He had placed and won one event, so Joe was anxious to see how well she could handle him. Joe helped her mount, as Bullet was a big horse at seventeen and a half hands. He was also in shape and had been out racing only two weeks before.

"Aren't you going to ride with me, James?"

"I would, but we would be changing the height of the jumps all the time, and that would take too much time, so I'll just watch my princess show me how it's done."

Joe led her out to the field behind the stable and then let her go. She cantered around the perimeter and slowly warmed the horse up. There were some higher fences for show jumping, and then there was a straight line where there were some brush fences, the type you would see in a steeplechase race. The run with four fences was about a half mile, so she carefully jumped him over some of the higher show-jumping fences first, which were closer to the paddock, and then she turned Bullet into the straight to take the racing fences.

"Just look at the control she has over that horse. It took me a good month to be able to ride Bullet like that," said Joe, watching in awe. Then she was off flat out. She took all four fences, and Joe had his stopwatch out to time her. "I'm not sure, but I think she is a lot quicker than I am. She's coming back to try again, so I'll double-check." Off she went again. "She's definitely quicker than I am, sir. If she could ride him, she would win races on that horse. She's a natural. That young lady's got talent. Forgive me if I'm imposing, sir, but she's got a lot going for her besides her obvious good looks."

"You're right about that, Joe. She's quite a surprise, to say the least." James realized how thoughtless he had been to not know she had such ability after all this time.

Sandra brought the horse back to the stables after a few more runs. "That horse is a dream to ride. He's smart and well trained. I would love to ride the races with him. He's got fight in him, and he's good at correcting himself."

James and Sandra walked back to the house. "You're a dark

horse, to use the pun. I think you know exactly how they think, and I'm going to be very careful before I open my big mouth again. God, you had me fooled, but in a nice way. If Becky and Flick could see how you ride, they would be amazed."

"We must all go out together, and then I can help them with anything they don't know already."

"That's a splendid idea. In fact, Peter and his mother are coming over on Monday, so we can all go out together."

The weekend went fast, and Sandra went out with his sisters on the Sunday. James took some time off to walk around the estate so that he could have a meaningful discussion with Keith on Monday morning about the farm and its financial position. He also wanted to think about his future and whether to delay going to university in order to get some hands-on experience in accounting. He had just received his exam results, so he could now make his final choice.

James and Sandra spent Sunday night at a nice restaurant in a larger village called Horncastle. They took the opportunity to talk about all they had done that weekend.

"On another subject, when do you plan on taking me home?" Sandra realized that her parents may want to hear from her.

"I thought Wednesday morning we would head out and be at your place around tea time, if that works for you. If you want to call, we can do that when we get back to the house."

James put away the car while Sandra went to call her mother to let her know that they would be arriving Wednesday and that James would be driving her home.

"Sandra, I know you have had a wonderful time, but your father wants you to leave tomorrow," her mother said on the line. "He feels you've had enough time with James, and it's time you got back here after being at school. He feels that as much as he respects James's kindness in bringing you back home, it would be better if you caught the train at Peterborough, and he'll pick you up in London. He has some ideas that he wants to discuss with you about your future." Sandra was silent and felt disappointed that James wouldn't be taking her home, but she had to agree.

"I understand, Mom; you've allowed me to be with James, and it's time I returned." Sandra was sad in a way, but she was also anxious to see her family again. She quickly told James the change in plans, and James understood. They had had a wonderful time together, and they now wanted to make the best of their last evening together.

They were quiet for a few minutes, and then he said, "Sandra, maybe a break will do us good so we can really know our true feelings. We'll see each other and date, and if it's meant to be, it will happen. We must trust in that."

"You're right. We are going to meet other people that we may find attractive, but if I'm meant for you and you are meant for me, then we'll be together."

It was getting late, and James, knowing it was their last night together, took her by the hand and said he'd meet up with her in the guest room after he'd taken a bath.

As he came out of the bathroom with a towel around his waist, he found Sandra standing in his room, dressed in a very revealing short lace nightdress. She had craftily walked down the long corridor to his room, which was further away from his mother's. She had thought it all out. Her long blonde hair fell naturally around her shoulders. As she approached James, he could smell her perfume, and he became aroused. She released the tiny silk straps on her shoulders to let the nightdress fall to the ground.

"My God, you look incredible. Am I dreaming, or what?"

"You talk too much." She walked forward and tugged away his towel. She put one hand over his mouth so he couldn't say another word. It was obvious the way James was feeling, as his equipment was now doing all the talking.

She whispered, "Don't worry. It's safe, I promise. Trust me."

They fell onto his bed. James remembered his encounter with Vivian and how attentive she had been to him. He slowed down to caress Sandra's beautiful, petite body against his large and tall build. He felt the warmth of her full lips and slowly worked his way across her whole body. He was working overtime not to become overwhelmed by his intense desire. It was the first time after being with Vivian that he had the chance to explore the sensual beauty of a woman, and it was so different from his first encounter. The two spent a good part of the night showing each other how much they cared.

After their energy was spent, they held each other close and talked. Sandra wiped tears from her eyes and said, "James, I wanted to be your first love, and I know you wanted that for me. So whatever happens in our lives, we can always remember this night and this moment when we gave ourselves completely to one another."

"It's hard not to love you. You say the most beautiful things."

Neither had ever felt such a beautiful completeness, and they cherished the experience.

The next morning the couple, tired from their intense night-time escapade, jumped into James's car after Sandra had said all her goodbyes. James made sure she caught the right train and escorted her to the platform for the eleven o'clock to London. The sad couple kissed and waved their goodbyes as the train pulled out of the station.

CHAPTER 21

THE ESTATE AND
ITS FUTURE

James arrived back at the estate and met up with Sarah and her family and Peter's girlfriend. It was only midmorning, and Sarah told James that she wanted to take them around the Throne Room. Then they would meet up with James again to plan the rest of their day. After the tour, they met at Sarah's school. James began to organize the group. "Sarah, I know you have a class. Who wants to sit in on the class, and who wants to go riding?"

James continued, "I know Peter's girlfriend, Hilary, and Kate want to go to the class. Perhaps it would be better if everyone goes riding this afternoon."

"Okay. Peter can come with me this morning," James agreed, "as I need to go around the farm and check on a few things. We'll meet up at one o'clock for lunch and then go from there."

"Sounds like a plan."

James and Peter left in the old Land Rover to see the farm. As they drove, Peter was impressed. "James, this place is amazing! I can't believe the size of it—quite a property to take over. And that Throne Room! The things you have in there—the jewelry, the throne, and those artifacts—must be worth a fortune. I can see why you have wanted to keep this legacy and open it to the public. No one would ever believe something like that could exist."

"Yes, it's very special. It's taken some time to get it to look the way it does now, but I think it's been worth it."

"Tell me, can you actually experience something sitting on that throne?" asked Peter, thinking it might all be a hoax.

"Yes, you can, but it's not something you want to do without someone giving you some education like your mother's doing."

"I would never believe that something like that would be possible."

"Well, you have the best person to talk to, and that's your mom."

"My dad and I go along with her, and we know she's got some special insights, that's for sure, but we don't fully believe all the stuff she explains. How is it you do?"

"I can't explain it, and that's why I never told anyone about it when we were at school; I knew it would all sound too far-fetched."

"So you mean to tell me that you've sat in that chair and met your master on another side of the galaxy?"

"I have experienced just that, but it's not for everyone—and you have to be ready. Realize one thing: this life is what you make of it; the other is a great help, but we have to live our lives, take all the advice we can get, and then do something about it."

"That's what I like about you, James. My dad feels the same way after meeting you. You obviously understand the spiritual world, but in your own way, you're very practical about it. I can see why life has blessed you with a lot. You have the temperament to see it all in its right place."

"Well, here are the farm offices. Come on in, and one of the staff will get you a cup of tea or whatever you like. I've got to spend a moment with our farm manager."

James was anxious to hear exactly what Keith thought about how things were going. As they walked in the office, Keith greeted them. "Your Lordship, please come in and take a chair. I've kept your father's office just as it was in case you may want to use it."

"Keith, first of all, we can do away with the formalities. Please call me James. You are the boss here, and we must work closely together if we are going to make this place a success."

"I appreciate that, sir."

James continued, "I'm sure you know as well as I do that the world is changing, and having a close working relationship is the key to any successful venture." Keith had always dealt with owners who were quite aloof and acted in a manner that was superior. He welcomed James's down-to-earth introduction.

Getting straight to the point, James asked, "So where are we with this project? Do we have cash, and are we making progress?"

"It's not been easy, and I must say Claudia has been of immense help. Without her, I couldn't have learned all that was needed so quickly. In answer to your question, the Throne Room is at least paying for the interest on the loan, and although this is our first year, we will be able to break even from what I can see. It has taken quite a bite out of the loan, but fortunately, we were able to do the entire project for just under sixty thousand pounds. This has left us a cushion to pay everyone and get through the year with at least a few thousand to the good. I believe by next year, we will start to see income accumulate to where we can start the renovation of the forty-two cottages. This will slowly bring in more revenue. In short, a lot has been accomplished. There's no doubt in my mind that this will be the key to transforming the entire farm and the business."

James nodded his approval, and Keith continued with his analysis. "The arable farm has been good, and the market garden products have all brought in good revenues. The herd needs enlargement, but that's only if we expand and update our milking parlor. We can be more profitable on the farm with better equipment, larger fields, and fewer employees. The farm, however, does pay its way; it can absorb the cost of the gardening, the stables, and necessary upkeep at the main house. So we've got a long way to go, but I've cut everywhere I can, such as in buying unnecessary feed and storing grain and produce for too long a period, even though we may take a hit on price. I believe cash flow is everything. The day will come when we can have the luxury of better buildings and storage facilities, but it's not now. I have also engaged a small firm that is very reliable and takes a 10 percent commission on all the grants that we can get. Eventually, we can do this ourselves in-house."

"I appreciate your oversight. I am obviously taking a break right now after my last term at school, and I hope to spend time with you and go around the farm and get into more specific details. I want to understand the directions you have planned as well as the budgets and cash flow forecasts you have prepared. When I go to the bank in London, I want to be in a position to speak with authority on all our progress. You sound like you've got your finger on the pulse, and Claudia speaks very highly of your implementation of the East Wing project on time and under budget. It was a risk, but what you've just told me makes me happy. I think Mrs. McKenzie is a big factor in helping us. I would like to think about giving her some consideration eventually."

"I completely agree. Since we released the marketing firm after the opening of the Throne Room, she's saved us a lot of money, and I'm sure she'll be a big factor in our future revenues. Because of her efforts, we haven't needed a museum curator— only professional advice and part-time staff. The one thing we are learning in our first year is just how seasonal this venture will be."

"Many thanks, Keith, for meeting with me. I must get going, but I will be in touch soon. Good to have you aboard!"

Peter and James left the office and began to tour the farm, the stables, and the estate. "You've got a job right here without going to London," Peter said, shaking his head.

"I know, but the bank is the engine that pays the bills."

After they finished the tour, they went back to the house. Everyone was ready for lunch, so James suggested they go to the pub for a bite. Once at the pub, they sat outside and discussed the Throne Room. Katrina and Kate were interested in hearing more about the history and how James became so involved.

James told them, "I know it's not your average situation, and you know, I've never discussed our plans at Penbroke. For me, it was a personal journey to acknowledge the works of the Seventh Earl. This is something that is real, and if you want to experience what has been given to me and to all of us, you now have a chance. Will it change your life? For some of you, yes; for others, it's just realizing that there is something more for you to understand. Something more does exist, and maybe through your religious faith, you know that already. The Throne Room is just living proof of what is out there and beyond. It is for each one of you to learn in your own way the beauty of the universe we live in. I am not the author of this place; I have been a person that believes in the works of the Seventh Earl. I have, as any good grandson would, made sure that those dreams came true, for the one thing that he wanted was for everyone to experience what he worked so hard to bring back here to England."

The group was quiet for a moment, absorbing all that he had said.

Finally Kate added, "Though I haven't spoken with a master, I do know that the collection by itself is spectacular. The fact that you have gone to all this trouble makes me believe in it."

James knew Kate was not someone to play games. He felt the same attraction to her that he'd felt at Peter's house.

James continued to answer all their questions. After they finished lunch, they headed to the stables.

Joe saddled up the horses and said that he would come along to help anyone who was not comfortable riding. Katrina and Peter were new to the sport while Kate said she had some experience. James and Kate rode out in front, and the others followed Joe.

Kate followed James down to the waterfront, and then they started to canter. "So are you going to be my teacher, Your Lordship?" Kate teased.

James started laughing, sensing that something was up. "I don't know the answer to that, but I soon will, won't I?" James was riding Bullet, who at James's prompting, took off like his name. Kate, who was riding Foxy, took off as well. The pair ran for at least a mile. At first, Kate was right on his heels, but Foxy wasn't as fit as Bullet, and in the last hundred yards, Bullet pulled away with tremendous force. James then slowed him down so Kate could catch up.

Kate said, "That horse you're on can go. I did my best to keep up with you, but I guess she ran out of steam. I don't think she's as fit as your horse, but she's got power!"

"Let's walk for a bit and cool them off. Then we can have a run back."

"James, this is a fabulous place for people to learn to ride. Someone like Joe could run a little business for you, teaching people how to ride. I'm sure the people who will one day rent your cottages would love to go riding."

"What a great idea! I was wondering what we should do about the cost of keeping up our stables. I like your idea; it's a very good way to keep the horses that we race and improve our earnings."

"I would love to have a job like that. I know my father would prefer I work at his business. However, as mother is over here quite a lot, I could help out with the horses. What do you think?"

"You would be interested in making the stables a profitable venture?" James was intrigued at the thought of it.

"Not forever. I could get things started, and then you could hire someone later to run it, or Joe may be your man." She wanted a break from her dad and taking care of his accounts. This was something she would prefer to do and would give her time away from her family.

Bullet was getting fidgety, so James suggested they go back. They cantered back, and as they rode together, James realized that he liked Kate a lot. She wasn't as pretty as Sandra, but she had something else he couldn't explain.

They caught up with the others, and Peter confessed that he fell off. Thankfully, nothing serious happened. They all had a good laugh at his expense. Then Kate rode up beside James and asked, "Do you have a paddock where I could do some jumping?"

"Yes, but the best jumper is the horse I'm on. This horse is a racehorse, a steeplechaser. Do you think you can handle him?"

"No problem. If he's a handful, I'll soon learn how to manage him," she said confidently.

James smiled. "Joe, Kate wants to take Bullet into the jumping paddock, so let's get everyone back, and she can show us how it's done."

Kate mounted Bullet and made her way to the paddock while everyone followed to watch.

"You found another rider, I see," said Joe, who outside his own racing, hadn't seen this much action at the stables in months.

Bullet was excited, and Kate ran him around the perimeter just like Sandra had done. He was fairly warmed up from the gallop they'd had. She took the fences with the poles on them before going to the brush fences with the half-mile straight.

"She looks like she knows what she's doing. She's not as elegant as Sandra was, but let's see what she does in the straightaway," said Joe.

She started to turn Bullet toward the straight, and then she took off.

"She's going too fast at that first fence, sir. The horse won't be smooth—he'll jerk her before jumping." Joe was right; Bullet did jerk her, but she managed to get him over, nearly losing her seat in the process. At the second fence, she had him more settled down, and she flew over with perfection. Then she started to loosen the reigns and give the horse a little more head as she negotiated the last two jumps.

"Not bad for her first time riding Bullet. I can honestly say I didn't get over those fences as quickly as she did," admitted Joe.

James replied, "In fairness though, Joe, the horse knows his way over the course now. That must help. You're pretty good yourself, and it's thanks to you that they can have the fun they're having."

"Here she goes again, sir."

This time Kate had Bullet under her full control; her competitive spirit wasn't going to be satisfied until she had it down.

"She looks like she's going a lot faster now, and she's got a good rhythm. She races go-karts, and I can tell you, she's extremely quick, so speed doesn't scare her," bragged James, who admired her guts and persistence.

She arrived back at the stables, and everyone clapped as she dismounted. "Was that to your liking, Your Lordship?" she again teased.

"Kate, you've got guts, and yes, you know what you're doing out there, without a doubt."

"I thought I had lost him and myself at the first fence. He's so strong that it took me a minute to get his head back, but what a thrill he is to ride. If you ever need a rider to run a race with him, please put me on the list."

"We'll keep that in mind, won't we, Joe?"

"Absolutely," replied Joe. "Well ridden, Kate. He's quite a beast to contain when he wants to get going. You showed him who was boss, all right."

Everyone thanked Joe and then headed back to meet up with Sarah. She was sitting outside on the patio in front of the Throne Room, chatting. Sarah asked, "Well, how did it go?"

Peter said, "Kate showed us all how to ride a horse. It's not enough for her to race karts; she has to race everything she can get her hands on."

As he approached, Sarah took James to one side. "I had time to talk with your mother. I like her. She's direct and to the point, and she has a bigger heart than you think. She's just so different from the man she married. Don't be surprised if she hasn't met someone you're going to like."

"Really? Whom?"

"You'll know in good time."

"I have to tell you; I really like Kate. She's got guts, and she not only knows how to drive karts, she can ride the hell out of a horse too."

"She was so proud to let you see her ride. She knows she's pretty good. She's not someone to blow her own horn, though."

"I'm learning a lot from all you women. I think you are the chosen race, and we men just walk about thinking we are."

Sarah and her family soon said their goodbyes and headed home. It was nearly evening, and as it was getting cooler, the Countess motioned for James to come inside. Supper would be ready soon.

CHAPTER 22

GETTING DOWN TO BUSINESS

James asked Claudia to set up an appointment with Alan Weinstock on Friday to pursue the chance of becoming an auditor. That could lead to him getting his professional articles in chartered accounting. He'd thought about it after Sandra had gone. He was now convinced that this was the type of hands-on experience he wanted to get before entering the bank for his future career. He also thought, as Minyard and Weinstock had been the company auditors for the past fifty years, that this was the obvious place to start to get his experience. Claudia, in her efficient way, had set up the appointment for two o'clock that afternoon in order to give James time to catch the train and get to the bank on time. She had also invited him to stay over until Sunday so they could go to the bank on Saturday for James to understand more about the business.

As he walked in, Claudia was overjoyed to see him and rushed to give him a hug. "James, it's wonderful to see you again. You just get taller and taller!"

"It's great to see you too, Claudia."

As they exchanged small talk, Alan Weinstock arrived. He greeted James. "Pleased to meet you, Your Lordship. So you're ready for life in the big city?" James towered above the man, who was only five and a half feet tall. His slick black hair was combed straight back, and his double-breasted suit and expensive watch made him look the part of a high-end city man dealing in the world of finance. He wasn't attractive, but he had piercing dark brown eyes that lacked soulfulness, which was typical of a man who scrutinized everything before making a decision.

Claudia asked, "Rose, could you take Mr. Weinstock and His Lordship to the small conference room and get them some coffee?"

"Please call me James. My title is a formality. It's 1963; we can talk as equals when it comes to business."

"James, I've put a lot of thought into your request. I'm hard-pressed to know why an earl would be interested in doing the grind work of an auditor, working long hours, when you could get a business degree at any one of our universities with your marks."

"Mr. Weinstock—" James began.

"Please, call me Alan."

"Alan, sir, I want to learn the basic ground rules of auditing, as it is necessary for a person like me to know the nuts and bolts of what our business is made up of. Having a business degree from university is only as good as the person who uses it. I want to be involved in the day-to-day and have work experience; in this way I can, if I want to, go to Harvard and get an MBA. My time at university would be better served with some practical hands-on knowledge to back it up."

"I can see that your mind is made up. How do you think a man in your position is going to like being told what to do by people whom you can, quite frankly, buy and sell for breakfast?"

"Well, sir, I went to one of the toughest schools known, and I had no problem taking orders and being treated like the rest. In time, if I'm good at what I do, I'll have earned my stripes. No one has to know who I am. I'm just another auditor doing his job." James didn't like that this man had more reasons for not making it work than solutions. He expected more from a man that Bannerman's had been loyal to for almost half a century.

"James, I frankly don't see it working. My business has worked for this bank for a long time, as you know. The fact that you would be an auditor at my firm, I believe, would compromise the integrity of our company's ability to have what we call a complete arms-length relationship for the future."

"It seems no matter what I present you with, you see a problem. You haven't offered me one solution to my modest request. Am I to believe just because I'm a lord that I'm not fit for employment?" James asked sharply.

"Not at all, James. There are many firms I can recommend that I'm sure would be happy to have your services. I just believe that for us to hire you would compromise our integrity and relationship for the future."

"Please, sir, don't bother yourself with that thought. I will find my way accordingly. I will remember this, and I can assure you that it doesn't help our relationship for the future, I'm afraid." James's instinct was that this man had something to hide.

"James, I know you're upset, but you can understand it's not easy for me, either. Bannerman's is a very prominent bank. I am under serious scrutiny from the Bank of England and other government auditors."

"I do appreciate you taking the time to visit with me on such short notice. I guess I'll just have to get my finger out and find a good accounting firm."

Weinstock was a little unnerved by his response, thinking that if he did have a good relationship with another accounting firm, he could one day lose an account that had, over the years, made him a very rich man.

They shook hands, and Weinstock departed. James sat in the small conference room for a moment and thought about what had just taken place. He felt that Weinstock was not straight, and the fact that collusion could exist between his accounting firm and the bank was rubbish. He could have that relationship with any member of the staff at Bannerman's, and they could be paying him an exorbitant sum of money without anyone knowing it. The fact was that James would know his business inside out and would know exactly how much he'd been taking advantage of Bannerman's for years. He took a deep breath and walked down to Claudia's office.

"How did it go?"

"Not well. I don't like that man. He's clever, but he's not straight."

"If he feels that hiring you would compromise his position, you can't take offense, James."

"That's baloney. He just doesn't want me to know what he's charging Bannerman's. I bet we pay him a small fortune every year, and I wonder how tough we are with someone who appears to be so supportive of everyone here."

Claudia had never seen this look in his eyes before. "James, are you insinuating that we are all in one happy conspiracy to screw the bank?" She was feeling attacked and a little hurt.

"Claudia, you wouldn't do a wrong thing to anyone, I know that."

"Well, then, what is it that you're saying?"

"Look, I know this man takes very good care of everyone here, and why wouldn't he? It's in his very best interest. But how tough are we when he presents his quarterly bill?"

"That gets approved by Nigel. I just pay it if he tells me to. I have, however, questioned the amount from time to time, and I agree that his charges seem extremely high." Claudia knew that Nigel and Alan had many meetings that didn't involve her, and she began to suspect that there could be some validity to what James was saying.

"Claudia, I didn't come here to spend the rest of the day talking about this. Perhaps it's for the best. I'm sure Sir Thomas will have another suggestion before the day is over."

"I get your point. There are a lot of things you need to know. I won't tell Thomas because he's got a lot of things on his mind, running his own affairs. However, there are things that I don't like and you should start to learn about." She got up from her desk and gave him a hug. "I've been so looking forward to seeing you again. It's been a long day. Let's get out of here. I'm anxious for you to see my new home."

After taking the train to Finchley, they arrived in her car at Hampstead Heath. James teased, "This is impressive for a London home. No wonder you love it here."

"I do love the man I'm with, but the house does help," she joked.

George greeted them as they entered the house. James looked around and said, "This is definitely a home to talk about. I absolutely love this front entrance."

Sir Thomas walked into the room and put his arms around James. "Hello, my boy! How's my grown-up lad?"

"It's great to see you again, Sir Thomas. Thank you for having me over."

"My home is always here for you, James. You're like a son to me." They walked to the bar, and Sir Thomas said, "Name your poison, my boy."

"I see you're drinking some wine. A glass of the red stuff will do just fine, thanks."

The three of them moved outside to the patio. It was a lovely summer evening, and Sir Thomas wanted to hear all of James's news. "So, James, you're probably sick of this question, but have you made up your mind as to what direction you want to go now?"

"I have, sir, and my mind is definitely made up. I want to go with a good accounting firm and get my CA before entering the bank."

"And the meeting with Alan? How did that go?"

"Not well. He thinks he would be compromising his arms-length relationship with the bank if I joined his firm."

"Yes, I could see that, but how many of his auditors go and work for companies he does the accounting for?" Sir Thomas sat thinking for a moment. He was too wise to implicate his friend, but he had his thoughts as to why he wouldn't want James knowing too much about his personal business.

"Do you think he's overcharging Bannerman's?" asked Claudia.

"I hate to say that he may be. I've thought that for some time."

"So James's suspicions are well founded?"

"Claudia, you see those quarterly invoices. What do you think?"

"I have often thought they were high, but Nigel signs off on all of them and says he's gone over it with Alan. As he's my boss, I pay the bill."

"James, as you know, we've all been in the city a long time. I send him business, and he in turn sends me business. For me to be aware is good. I have suspected that Nigel was in league with him. His bill is one of the largest we pay annually. In his favor, he has kept us squeaky clean with all the various auditing authorities. I cannot get involved, but Claudia, there must be a way we can find out if we are getting value for our money, surely?"

"As Nigel takes pride in overseeing this bill because of its cost, he has access to far more information with our junior accountants than I do. If I go poking around, people are going to talk unless Nigel is a part of that evaluation."

"When is Nigel going on holiday?" asked James.

"Brilliant!" said Claudia. "He goes in another week. Two

weeks after that is all the time I need to find out the truth, and I will be acting on his behalf while he's gone. I don't like to be devious, but if we are paying over the top, I need to know."

"So now we have a solution, and hopefully it's not as bad as we think; otherwise, we'll be looking for another managing director," said Sir Thomas.

"Claudia could do that job and hire someone else for her position," suggested James.

Sir Thomas laughed. "James, I think we're going to need you at the bank a lot sooner than predicted. Where do you get those instincts?"

"I just think in all companies, there's a lot of fat. My thoughts are pay the right people well and run a lean, mean operation."

George brought out some snacks and sandwiches. Sir Thomas opened another bottle of wine, and they refilled their glasses. He then said, "Now we must get Lord James in the right company. I'm going to call Ron Smith at Smith and Barlow's and get you an appointment. You'll like them, James. They don't do the big high-end companies like Minyard and Weinstock do; they do more manufacturing, media, and service companies. I think you would prefer the diversity, and that will prove helpful to you when you analyze the portfolio we have at the bank. They're a family business, and they have sons who work for them. I think you will find the environment friendlier, and you could have good exchanges with them and learn a lot."

"I always love meeting with you, Sir Thomas. You're all about seeing the big picture. I would definitely be at a disadvantage without your experience and counsel."

"James, that's what your father entrusted to me. I will not miss a moment to advise you and lead you as best I can on the journey you want for yourself. Your road is extremely unorthodox compared to what we all experienced, but we are moving into a new era, and I can't fault your decision to learn from the ground up. Knowing your business is essential, and the world is becoming a tougher, more competitive place, I believe your choices are good ones. You're not afraid of hard work, and that's an essential ingredient to success."

Sir Thomas poured himself a glass of malt whisky and lit a cigar. Switching topics, he said, "James, Claudia has a little secret to tell you." He smiled at her.

Excited, Claudia said, "James, I'm pregnant. I'm about two months along, so I have to take it easy and watch my eating and drinking. I've had a few sick spells, but it hasn't affected my work so far."

"Congratulations! I know how important this is to both of you. I don't have to ask what you want, but if it is a girl, I'm sure you'll both be happy."

"Of course we want a boy, but for me, I'm happy to have a little girl as well," Claudia beamed.

"So what's the name for a boy, Sir Thomas?"

"Alexander, of course. I've always being a fan of military warfare, and I've always admired Alexander the Great."

"And a girl?" asked James.

"I suppose it'll have to be Alexandria," answered Claudia.

The next morning after breakfast, James and Claudia went to the bank. No one would be in the offices, and Claudia could go over some things with James without anyone knowing. James couldn't help but sneak a look at his father's old office. He loved sitting in his big chair, and he looked forward to the day when he would be there full-time.

"James, you know when you get busy with your audit work, you can always come here and work. It's quiet, and I'll give you all the combinations and keys."

"Thanks, Claudia, I appreciate that."

"Let's make some coffee, and then we can sit in the conference room, where there is more space, and I will give you my best read on where I think the bank is at the moment." Claudia walked out but returned shortly with the coffee and a big pile of papers. "I think you're going to find this very interesting."

"I can't wait to know the real position of the bank," James said.

"I'll tell you what each business is doing, and then we can have our discussion afterward. Our biggest moneymaker is Trans Global Shipping, which nets 10 percent of revenues of around one hundred million pounds before taxes. Second is our bank in Hong Kong, which nets 9 percent of our investments of around twenty-five million pounds after taxes. The rest of our investments net 2 percent of investments of over one hundred million pounds before taxes. The bank has cash reserves of around fifty-eight million pounds; about 50 percent is invested with Lloyds Investments, which nets around 5 percent before taxes. The remainder of our cash is in long-term bonds and risk-free placements, which net around 3.5 percent before taxes. We keep a reserve here at the bank for special appropriation and investment of about ten million pounds. So, if I take all the cash we receive annually after all costs and taxes have been paid, we are making seventeen million pounds after taxes per year. You can see this bank is a very profitable enterprise."

"That's a huge amount of money after everything is paid. I had no idea we made that amount."

"Yes, but here's the rub. If we take a closer look at the balance sheet, we can see that Trans Global is cash flowing around twenty million pounds, and the bank in Hong Kong provides two and a half million, so if we stand back and look at the total picture, we are receiving two-thirds of our profit from two entities. I believe the bank in Hong Kong is making double that, which means over 70 percent of our investments comes from two sources. The money we have invested with Lloyds and in bonds doesn't require much management. If we look at all the people we employ to keep track of all those companies and small investments, we would be better off to divest. We don't need the headache of administrating the finances we have in all those businesses. Even if we take a loss on our investments, we'll make it back with Lloyds or whomever. We will reduce a lot of the staff at this bank and increase our cash supply to make investments that we can control. Look at all the money we've invested in these other businesses, which were profits taken from mainly Trans Global Shipping."

"We have to rethink this whole business. For example, where does Trans Global operate from?"

"From here. We keep quite a tight rein on that business. It is our main moneymaker, but it will need new ships. In the past ten years, very little capital reinvestment has been made, and if any business deserves it, it's Trans Global. Also, we need to move more toward containerization, as that's the way all freight is going to be transported in the future. So that will mean we need to have an office at Felixstowe. This business needs a lot of our attention if we are going to maintain our position and increase our market share."

James paced and lit up a cigarette. He thought about the whole business and where to go for the future. His father had taught him a lot when he was young, but now it all seemed to fit into place. He realized the world was changing, and things were going to be quite different in the future.

"I think we need to change our business model within the next two years," James said. "Like you say, we should divest ourselves of all these businesses that don't make us much money. That will increase our capital position and allow us to reinvest into Trans Global. I also believe that someone needs to go out to China and take a hard look at the business there. If this one person we've got running that operation is siphoning off money for his own purposes, we need to know. Then I believe we need to get down to maybe less than ten serious investments, for example, more wholly owned subsidiaries, like Trans Global, that we can run all the finance from our business in London. In a sense, we already have a lot of capital that's earning money, but some of it should be invested in businesses that have potential for the future such as construction, from commercial buildings to apartment complexes, like they have in America. It's good to be cash rich, which we are, but with inflation, our money buys less each year."

James continued, "I believe investing in commercial properties could be a very good place to put our excess capital. This building could be a great income producer and a start to a new business for us. Also, I would like us to buy out John Klondike and Roger Handly. If they think we're going to change our business model and take a loss from divesting out of these smaller businesses, they might be encouraged to take a decent price for their shares and leave. Finally, I don't know what we gain by being a bank. We're not a bank in the true sense of the word. We were once a merchant bank that made loans to foreign governments and the Crown, we participated with other banks to capitalize business growth, but those days are long gone. I'm sure there was a prestige to being a bank, but frankly, Lloyds can be our bank, and we don't have to have all those auditors breathing down our neck. We are really a conglomerate, a multinational, that has investments in different companies. So I believe we represent something quite different to what we may have once been."

"James, what you're suggesting is a huge change, but I will compose a proposal for our next board meeting, and I believe that this could be an opportunity for you or Sir Thomas to express your views. I agree with much of what you say. Times have changed. We have a good cash position, and we need to look at new options. It won't be done overnight, but by the time you become chairman of the board, a lot could be changed already. You, of course, would be kept up to date."

"Are these small- and medium-size businesses that we've invested in mostly through the London Stock Exchange?"

"Yes, we have about fifteen brokers who do nothing but concentrate on investing in everything from airlines and mining to haulage, manufacturing, and oil and gas exploration. It's all over the map. Apparently, ten years ago, in the early fifties, your father and Sir Thomas made the decision that with the bank being extremely cash rich, it should use money to invest in the stock market to turn an investment of around one hundred million into probably double that. I believe the bank has invested about seventy-five million of that. The rest is the present book-market value that we would be lucky to get back if we took our money out. Our brokers have injected in the region of five to ten million a year into companies that have high-growth potential but more risk. So there will be winners and losers. I see the whole thing as a huge amount of money that could be used in a more controlled way. If we sell, we are going to have to sell off strategically and slowly. We should let those brokers go. Keep one very competent person to slowly divest us out, claiming that we have a new business model. It won't be liked, but that's the way it goes, and we could be in for a big loss," said Claudia, wanting James to understand the potential consequences of such a decision.

"Even if we take a loss and walk away with fifty million, we made twenty-five million over the years, so we could get the money back. We hit the balance sheet with a big loss, and that way we won't be paying taxes on our other performing businesses."

It was late afternoon, and they decided to go back to Hampstead Heath and talk with Sir Thomas about the plans for the future. When they arrived, Sir Thomas was outside practicing on the putting green he had set up for Claudia and himself. "James, you've got to get into this golfing racket. It's good for business and a lot of fun."

"Claudia, you like this sport?" asked James.

"I do. It takes my mind off everything, and it's good exercise as well. We are members at the golf club here, and we have a pro that gives us lessons, so we're starting to improve."

"I'll have to think about that, but not right now. Now, I've got to get a job and get my life moving on the right track." James and Claudia sat down to watch Sir Thomas, and George brought them some tea and biscuits.

"James, tell me about this young lady your mother says you like so much."

"We knew each other at school in Scotland. She is a lovely person, and yes, we've become very close, but we are still young, and as much as I hate to say it, we'll see in time if we're meant to be together. I will be here in London soon, and so will Sandra, so we can at least see each other occasionally."

"So you're still a good boy, in the way a young man should be?"

"Of course, with caution." James had a big smile and was blushing slightly.

"James, remember what we discussed at my little cottage," said Claudia. "I know someone like you has to sow his wild oats. That's normal. But I also think you should be wise about those things." She kicked his leg playfully.

"Oh, Claudia, you'll always be the one and only for me. I was just born at the wrong time."

"You're so cute when you blush, but you don't fool me with your feigned innocence."

Sir Thomas noticed their playful behavior and teased, "Now behave, you two, or I'll have to come over there and sort you out." He headed in their direction to join the conversation. "James, you just have to realize that these women run the planet, and we have to do as we're told." He winked as he sat down with them.

"Only because we allow it," said James, laughing.

"You'd better watch yourself, young man," admonished Claudia. "Thomas, on a more serious note, James and I have been going over the books, or more correctly, the figures. I'll let James have a chat with you about it while I change into something a little more comfortable."

"Sir Thomas—" began James.

Sir Thomas interrupted, "James, please call me Thomas. We know each other well enough by now, and besides, you're a man now."

James began to repeat the discussion he and Claudia had shared at the bank earlier. Sir Thomas listened carefully, taking in every word.

"I agree, but you'll lose money, maybe a lot."

"Yes, I understand that. Let's replace the fifteen brokers we have, because we're obviously not going to be making any more of these investments, and put one sharp man in charge of strategically divesting the money we have invested over the period of one year. Then we can take the hit if we have one and apply the tax loss to the more profitable parts of our business."

"You're becoming a businessman already, I can see. Please continue."

James continued to fill Sir Thomas in on the rest of their discussion.

"James, for you, that would work. I believe it's your intention to be there full-time, so I believe you can really take this bank, or more correctly, this conglomerate, to a place it should go. Your father was happy with the status quo, but times are changing, and there are many opportunities out there. I believe you're going to be the man to take advantage of those opportunities. It's a start, but first I want you to meet Ron Smith. Then we can go from there."

James left around ten o'clock to catch his train from North London Sunday morning to head home. He thanked Claudia and Sir Thomas for the time they spent with him and for dropping him at the train station. It was good to know the financial position of the bank and how wise some of his predecessors had been in accumulating the wealth they had over the last 250 years. He knew he would be as careful as he could be, but he wanted to make his family proud by taking the business to a new level. But before jumping into business matters, he looked forward to taking some holiday time at Penbroke.

CHAPTER 23

A SURPRISE ENCOUNTER

He pulled into the driveway just after lunch. As he entered the front hallway, he overheard a lot of noise coming from the back patio and garden, so he went to see what it was about.

His mother greeted him. "James, darling, you're back. Come and meet some dear friends of mine from Italy. This is Antonio and his children, Piero and Sabrina; they are staying with us until Thursday of next week. This is the family I visited when I was in Tuscany."

Antonio got up to shake James's hand, telling Phillipa, "What a fine young man your son is. I'm sure all the young ladies are after him." He smiled warmly at James. "Come meet my two children, who are around the same age as you."

Piero walked over to meet James. James noticed that although he was smaller, he was also good-looking. James shook Piero's hand and then turned toward Sabrina, who had remained seated. He was speechless when he saw her, stunned by her beauty.

She too seemed stunned by him, frozen in place.

James gathered his senses and asked Antonio, "Is everyone in Italy as good-looking as your family? If so, I must take a trip there soon."

James excused himself to clean up after his trip, saying that he would be back shortly. As he went to his room, he was puzzled by the strong attraction he was feeling. He had missed Sandra since she left, but now, upon meeting Sabrina, he was starting to have second thoughts. He felt rejuvenated and was anxious to know her better.

After his bath, he went back downstairs and joined Flick and Sabrina, who were talking. Becky had taken off somewhere with Piero, and his mother and Antonio were sitting by themselves on the sofa outside the drawing room.

"How is it you speak such good English, Sabrina?" asked James politely.

"I love to learn languages. I want to travel before I work, and of course, you must know English if you want to travel. Besides, Papa promised me we would go to England and France if I had good exam results, so here I am." She mesmerized him with her beautiful blue eyes, which, as he looked closer, had a slight hint of green interlaced within. Her eyes gave her a most unusual look; they seemed to shimmer in the afternoon sun. James found he could hardly take his own eyes off their magnetic presence. He had become clearly captivated by the presence of a young woman that he couldn't recall seeing the likes of anywhere. Her hair was light brown with blonde highlights; it was long and fell well over her shoulders and down her back. She was taller than most women, which he found becoming, especially with her accent and very feminine mannerisms.

"So what things do you like to do, Sabrina?"

"I play tennis, and I like to cook. Since my mother died when I was born, I have been the one who kept my brother and father happy with plenty of food. It's become a hobby. I know you have horses, and if you would be very gentle with me, I would like to learn, but I'm not very good." She exuded confidence and maturity as she spoke. James imagined that because she'd likely taken the place of her mother, she was more advanced than other girls her age.

"Do you have a boyfriend? Someone as pretty as you must have a lot of choices."

"I have boyfriends, yes, but nothing serious. I find most boys my age too immature and not ready to be with a girl yet. I like someone who knows his own mind—someone who is a man, not a boy—so I find older men more appealing."

He took her comment as a challenge and replied, "English boys are more mature, so hopefully, you'll find us more appealing."

"You look like a young man who has confidence. I bet you have many young ladies who like you."

"In a way, I'm like you. I lost my father when I was only fourteen. Losing a parent has made us grow up quicker." James felt an intense connection with her that he couldn't explain.

"I think you're right. I have never thought about it in that way." She had the urge to touch him, but she thought better of it, worried that he might think her too forward.

"I'm going to pour myself a glass of wine. Will you join me?"

"I'd love to join you. Do you have vino rosso?" she asked, smiling.

"Vino rosso? Italian for red wine, si?"

He poured them both a glass of wine, and they began to walk around the grounds. Sabrina was impressed with what she saw. "You have a magnificent home. I'm sure you would find our little vineyard far too small."

As she walked in front of James, he couldn't help but notice her form. She had on a light summer dress with a wide belt that neatly hugged her waist and gave form to her long legs and summer sandals. When she turned her head back, James still had to pinch himself; it all seemed like a dream. She was a mixture of Italian and Scandinavian—the unusual combination had created a unique beauty. Yet, she was totally unaware. She was soft and gentle. The tone of her voice was deeper than Sandra's, but not so deep that she didn't sound feminine.

As they continued to walk, he had an idea. "Sabrina, let's walk over to the Throne Room before it closes for the day."

As they arrived, Rodney was beginning to close the doors. James motioned that he wanted to show Sabrina around. He wanted to see her reaction to something that was very close to his heart.

"James, what is this place? Your sister mentioned something about this room, but we haven't had time to visit." She was enthralled at the beauty of the room as they entered.

"This is a collection that is a heritage from my forefathers."

"May I start at the beginning and walk around?" James walked silently with her, watching her every move and reaction. She began reading the writings of the Seventh Earl. "These things are amazing. No wonder people come so far to see all that has been collected. So is all of this true? He knew all these things?"

"Why don't you see for yourself?" His heart was beating fast knowing that he was taking a big risk, and yet he felt that she was a very spiritual person.

They walked over to the throne. "So this is the throne that he sat on? May I sit?" she asked politely.

"Only if you believe you are ready to have an experience. Only a few have sat on that chair. We have a school that trains people in meditation and alignment if you would prefer to wait and get some instruction, but if you feel like you're ready, it's okay by me."

"What's the worst thing that can happen to me?" She was curious, but not afraid.

"If you have a bad experience, you may see something that

upsets you, and you'll feel dizzy; but if you are aligned with your god and trust in your faith, you'll have a surprising experience."

"It's so beautiful. How could something so beautiful harm anyone? I want to try."

She gently sat down with her back perfectly straight and her hands folded, as if she were in a state of prayer. Within seconds, the crown around her head started to light up. James could see by the tremendous energy and light that was starting to surround her that she was on her journey. Then, she returned. She just sat there for a moment, taking in all that she had experienced, and then looked up at him as tears began falling from her eyes.

"Sabrina, is everything all right?" James asked, nervously reaching out to help her up.

"That was the most beautiful thing I've ever experienced in my whole life. Since childhood, I've regretted not meeting my mother. I have always felt guilt that she died so that I could live. Finally, I was able to meet and know her." She grabbed hold of James and hugged him. He could feel her tears against his cheek. James lightly embraced her, and then took her by the hand and sat her down outside.

"I was gone for at least an hour, I'm sure. Was it long for you?"

"No, only moments."

"So time is different; I didn't think about that." Sabrina looked perplexed at trying to understand what James had said, but thought it would be a conversation for another time.

"James, I learned so much, and I'm trying to remember it all. My master is a woman, and my mother is a guide. My mother has been with me my whole life, and she says she will not leave until I return. She wanted to have me, and she has no regrets. She would've loved to spend her life with me as I grew up, but she has, in her own way, because I've always felt her presence. She knows that it made me stronger, a little like with you and your father. Also, you and I have known each other many times. I too was on Atlantis, and that's why we feel a connection now."

"How did I know you?"

"You're not going to believe this, but I was your wife. You had other women then, because things were different. I know I've just met you and this all sounds crazy, but it's what I was told. It's no accident that you and I are here today. It's meant to be. It's amazing, as we've only been together for an hour, but I feel like I know you completely."

"Sabrina, I felt that way the first moment I laid eyes on you, so much so that I went to change because I didn't feel that I looked good enough for someone so beautiful."

"We can't discuss this with anyone," said Sabrina. "They won't understand. You do, which is why you've gone to all this trouble to preserve this beautiful legacy." She still had tears of joy in her eyes and was holding onto him. "James, please, I hope you don't feel I'm being too familiar, as we've just met. I apologize if I'm a little too emotional, but your throne has answered many of the questions that I've prayed about. You'll never know the good you've done for me."

"Sabrina, you can hug me any time. I don't know any man that wouldn't want to hold a beautiful person like you. If you have feelings for me, I'm flattered."

"I know we will spend more time together, but before I leave, there is still so much I want to share with you . . . if you'll let me."

"I'm still amazed that a beautiful Italian like you feels the way you do about me. And I'm very moved by your experience. We'll go into this deeper before you go."

They walked back and rejoined the others who were motioning to James that dinner was ready. It was a little buffet that they had set up outside.

"So, James, what do you think of my daughter?" asked Antonio.

"I think she's beautiful and that you'd better keep a close

watch on her!" James joked. Then he added, "However, I think she's smart enough to watch out for herself; she seems very mature for her age."

"I can see from the look in her eyes that she likes you. I'm very happy for her to meet a young man like you."

"Antonio, sir, how does my mother know you?"

Antonio explained how they met, and James was fascinated by the story. It was a different side of his mother that he'd never seen or even suspected was there. Under all that straight talk was a romantic who obviously had been attached to this man. Looking at them together was like seeing a couple who were genuinely in love. Everyone present could feel the connection. It was easy for James's family to accept Antonio and his family; they all seemed to fit together so well.

As Sabrina and James circled the buffet table, she whispered, "James, I think my father is going to propose to your mom. He's very much in love. You should have seen him when she came to our villa in Italy. They were like school kids walking hand in hand through the vineyards."

"My mother has been lonely. Even though she has many friends, she needs someone in her life who she trusts. She has many men who would want to marry her, but I can see that she truly loves your father." He was happy at the thought of them being together, especially since it meant he would see more of Sabrina.

The next morning, Sir Thomas called. "James, I've got you an appointment with Ron Smith at Smith and Barlow. He would like to see you at two o'clock on Tuesday if that's possible for you."

"Yes, absolutely. I'll be there. Thank you so much."

"Their offices are at the end of Kings Road, just before you turn left to go to Putney Bridge. Why don't you come to the house afterward and spend the night?"

"I would love to. See you Tuesday evening."

DAVID FRANCIS

"Good luck, old boy. I know you'll like these people. They're good friends, and I think you'll like the diversity."

James went to tell his mother and Antonio the news, and they were excited for him. He'd planned to go riding, so James was now anxious to escort Sabrina and make the most of his time with her.

Phillipa advised, "James, go easy out there with Sabrina. She is not an accomplished rider yet, and I know you like to go tearing off!"

"Yes, James, we don't want you upsetting our horses either," added Becky.

"I promise to take it easy. Why don't Sabrina and I go first, and then we won't be in your way. Becky, will you lend Sabrina some riding gear?"

Becky and Sabrina went off to get riding gear, and James got changed. He was excited to spend more time with Sabrina. Once they were both ready, the couple walked down to the stables, and James introduced her to Joe. Joe saddled up Day Dream and helped her mount. Then James mounted Foxy, and he and Sabrina slowly rode toward the beach. He could see that she was a little nervous, and he was careful to make sure she didn't have a bad experience.

"Come alongside me, and then we can talk," suggested James.

"James, I'm so glad to spend this time with you. I thought about the Throne Room all night, I so enjoyed the experience. Tell me about the time when you visited your master."

James then took the time to tell her all about his first experience and how fascinated he was to learn about another star system, Atlantis, good and evil, and the last time he spent with his father. He then continued to tell her everything that Czaur had taught him.

"That's so beautiful. At least you know the truth, and that's why you have been given a lot—to set an example for those who are less fortunate. The danger is that we can get trapped into dramas that pull us away from our path."

"Are you feeling more comfortable now on Day Dream?" He was watching her closely and realizing that she had at least some knowledge about riding. "If so, let's start to canter."

Foxy took off, and he had to keep a tight rein on her so as not to leave Sabrina behind. However, he saw that she was keeping up, so he increased his speed gradually and then let Foxy go. She slowly caught up to James. She smiled and said, "That's the fastest I've ever gone. It's such a thrill, and these horses are so powerful, you can feel that they love it."

They started to walk by the edge of the sea, letting it lap at the horses' feet. James said, "This is the best place to learn because all you do if the horse is going too fast is just turn him toward the water. That will slow him down in a hurry. You may get a little wet, but it's a small price to pay."

They walked for a few more minutes in silence, and then Sabrina said, "I was there with you on Atlantis, and that's why we're here again. My father is Roman Catholic, and I have always been a very devout Christian. I do know there is more. The church teaches us faith, but I believe we can understand beyond that. However, it's only possible when a person is ready, so those of us that have the gift of intuition must help those who are learning to understand. We are not perfect as humans, but the very soul that's in us is. We must develop that part of us and grow away from our bodies which die and go back to the earth."

James looked at her as she spoke. She had a beautiful, calm energy about her, which was a huge part of her beauty.

She noticed he had become silent. "James you're staring at me. Is something wrong?" asked Sabrina, thinking she might be talking too much and that her excitement might be more than he could handle so quickly.

"No, nothing is wrong. I was just taking a moment to appreciate how beautiful you are. You are tall for a woman. You have long legs, a beautiful face, and all that God could present a young lady with in the front."

"You think I'm that beautiful?" She was flattered that James thought of her that way.

"I think you're drop-dead gorgeous. I could see you on a magazine cover." As he spoke, he remembered Sarah had given him a description of such a woman when she described as his wife on Atlantis. He thought, *Could this be the one I am truly meant to meet?*

"I don't really care about that, but I'm glad to hear you think I'm beautiful. May I pay you a compliment?" She was being flirtatious for the first time.

"Bring it on!" he answered anxiously.

"I've never met anyone in my whole life that I feel so comfortable with, and you're nice to look at as well. I'm sure you have many ladies tell you that. Still, looks are nice, but they're not everything. It's what's inside that counts, and I like what's inside you," she said with a smile.

James was pleased by her words. He smiled back at her, and then, with a gleam in his eye, he asked, "Are you prepared to give me a race back now?"

"Only if you give me a head start," she said, laughing.

"Go ahead and raise your hand when you want me to catch you."

She leapt ahead, but she missed him being beside her, so she raised her hand. He quickly caught up, and as he came up beside her, he leaned over to give her a kiss. They both lost their balance and fell off their horses onto the beach. Their hats came off, but they didn't care. They held each other and kissed, completely oblivious to the world around them.

When they looked up, the two horses were nowhere to be seen. James knew they would make their way back to the stables. The horses knew the journey in their sleep, and they also knew that after a ride, they usually got fed. James and Sabrina got up and walked back slowly, stopping at intervals to kiss.

She teased, "So, Englishmen do have passion? I've always thought they were cold and shy, but I'm learning that you are certainly different."

"I'm so sorry if you've found me a little too forward," he said, "but I would do it again."

She laughed. Their hearts were pounding with excitement. They separated as they saw James's sisters and Piero coming up the lane to the beach.

Becky joked, "Lost your horses, yet the two of you are not hurt? Looks very suspicious to me." She knew exactly what was going on. She herself was wishing she could kiss Piero, but with Flick tagging along, it was a little complicated.

James rolled his eyes at his sister, and he and Sabrina continued back to the stables. As they approached, Joe winked and said, "Well, sir, it was very peculiar, but I had to put away two riderless horses." Then he leaned toward James and whispered, "The women you bring here just get more and more beautiful, but I think it would be hard to top this one, sir."

James smiled at Joe and winked, and then he led Sabrina back to the house. His mother and Antonio had gone out to do some shopping in Lincoln, so he knew that apart from the staff, the two of them were alone in the house. He wouldn't go too far, though he longed to do so. He had experienced intense passion and release already this week, and he had to deal with that in his own way, but he was going to enjoy every moment he could spend with Sabrina.

That afternoon, they took a long walk near the beach and found a spot to put down a blanket that James had brought. They spent hours talking, kissing, and embracing. James was crazy about Sabrina and knew she was yet another person he was going to miss greatly when they parted.

"James, I know this sounds forward, and I don't want you to be upset when I say this, but we are meant to be together, and I believe we will be. I know it's not now, and I know you have another woman that loves you too. But I want you to know that I shall never love another man like I love you. We were together on Atlantis, and I came back for you. I want us to go to the place that both of us should go together." Tears began to well in her eyes.

"Sabrina, I never dreamed of meeting someone like you. You have to know I am very focused on my career. Still, we met only yesterday, and I have to say I feel the same. I need to get my head around this whole thing." He was feeling very confused.

"Go with your heart, James. You think too much. Your heart won't lie to you, and in time, you will come to know this. Yes, you will meet many women, as I will meet many men, but there's always that one special person. That person for me is you, and that will never change."

Her commitment took his breath away. "So you truly believe we are meant for each other?"

"There's not a doubt in my mind, but I do know now is not the time for us to be together."

"I do feel that you're the one for me, but I've got to get my career firmly in place, first."

As it was getting late, they headed back to the house. They walked in silence, each considering the future and what it would bring.

That evening the two families got together.

They spent the evening enjoying each other's company with plenty of good wine and food served on the outside patio. Later, they listened to Antonio play his guitar while Piero and Sabrina sang along. *They were clearly a loving, tight-knit family,* James thought. Everyone tried to join in, but not everyone had the beautiful voices they had. Then, Antonio wanted to see the girls dance, so he motioned to Piero and James to dance with the girls while he played his guitar. James held Sabrina lightly and formally at first, but the intoxicating smell of her perfume caused him to pull her closer and closer. He was doing

THE RISE TO POWER

all that he could to control his urges, and he felt she was doing the same. As Antonio finished playing, he said, "James, I know you like my daughter, so stop being so British and give her a big hug." James blushed, and everyone laughed.

As James had to be up early to make the trip to London, the group called it a night. James winked at Sabrina and headed off to bed.

The next morning, James dressed in his dark suit and went downstairs around seven thirty to have some toast and tea. As he was fixing his toast, he heard somebody slip up behind him. It was Sabrina.

"Sabrina, my beautiful surprise, you look fantastic. I was just thinking about you. Want some tea or coffee?"

"Coffee, please, but I'll fix it. You eat your toast. I could have fixed breakfast for you if you'd asked," she said sweetly.

After breakfast, he loaded his overnight bag, hopped into the car, and headed to London.

James found Ron Smith to be an extremely warm-hearted man in his late fifties who was very happy to have James join his firm.

"James, you have excellent exam results," started Mr. Smith, "and the report from your school at Sterling is first-class. We would be honored to have you join our team. I understand from Sir Thomas that you don't want anyone to know, except for a few people here, that you are a titled person. I respect that, and I think that's very wise. People will treat you as the person you really are, and in that way, you'll learn quicker. It can be quite a grueling couple of years, as you'll find out." As he spoke, his son entered his office. "James, I'd like you to meet my son, Dennis, who will take you under his wing and help you cram for those many exams you'll have to take. If you have the right work ethic, you'll sail through, I'm sure." Mr. Smith got up and shook his hand, and James then went off with Dennis to learn his first assignment.

Dennis was easy to get along with and liked the fact that he would be teaching a lord the trade. "More people should do what you're doing, James. These two years will be hard at times, but you'll remember them for the rest of your life. I'm going to put you with Sally, who is working at a company in Isleworth that's in the manufacturing business of electronics. She will teach you the basic work of collecting invoices that clients don't have always readily available and validating entries that are not clear. This is how we can produce an accurate income statement and balance sheet. Get here around nine next Monday morning, and then you can get started. Any questions?"

"What's the best means of transportation?"

"Bus or train. If you have a car, we do have some parking at the rear, although it's always tight. When you have a job to go out on, you can bring your car. We'll pay your mileage and out-of-pocket expenses related to the trip; you just turn in your expenses once a week."

"I guess that's it. I'll be here bright and early next Monday."

"You'll like the way we do things around here. No one is hard to get along with."

They shook hands, and James headed back to his car. It took him close to an hour to arrive at Sir Thomas and Claudia's home in Hampstead Heath because of the traffic. Claudia had just arrived home, and as Sir Thomas was going to be later, the two of them went out to the back of the house to have a drink and relax.

"I have a job, thanks to Thomas."

"That's great," said Claudia as they toasted the occasion.

"Where are you going to stay in London?"

"I haven't asked Mom yet, but until I get organized, I'm sure she won't mind me staying at her London home for now."

"Thomas may have a place for you if that doesn't work; it's behind Harrods' and a little closer to your work. He'll talk to you when he gets back. On another subject, James, I've thought a lot about what we discussed last weekend, and it makes complete sense to divest ourselves from the stock market. We are so reliant on those brokers, and I don't know how well Nigel controls their buying and selling. I think we can do just as well by placing the funds in a solid, safe investment and letting those brokers go. Then we can make more money without any overhead costs. There are a lot of things I'm going to check on while Nigel is on holiday."

"That's right, he's leaving on Friday. You can do a lot in two weeks."

"I know we do well overall, but it's our job to save where we can and stop waste and improve profitability."

Sir Thomas arrived, gave Claudia a kiss, and poured himself a glass of wine.

"I like Ron Smith and his son, and I start next Monday," said James. "I will be working with someone on an audit of an electronics company in Isleworth."

"I thought you'd like those guys. They're not flashy, but Ron Smith has done well for himself and runs a tight ship. I think the work they do will give you a greater experience, and you will have the opportunity to see inside different work places that you wouldn't normally see. In addition, I think you'll find the work more interesting. You'll meet people who come from all walks of life. A young man like you should experience just how tough life can be for some people who get by on so little."

Claudia turned to Sir Thomas and said, "I was talking about your place at Pont Street to James, unless you had other plans?"

"Of course you'll need a place and soon. James, if you don't want to be with your mother, you are welcome to stay there. I know on weekends you might want your own space, and knowing Phillipa, she probably would too."

"I don't want to be an imposition. I would of course pay you rent."

"You'll be back down this weekend. We'll go over there, and

if you like the place, stay there for a month and check out the area. Then, after that, we can look at a possible long-term proposition."

The next morning before leaving, Sir Thomas asked James, "We'll see you on Saturday, then?"

"Yes. I'll call ahead and let you know what time. Again, thanks for everything."

After his drive up from North London, he went to his room and changed his suit to more casual attire. On his way downstairs, he saw Sabrina, who motioned him to come with her. She had anxiously awaited his return, and they couldn't wait to see one another again.

That evening, everyone was summoned to the drawing room for a big announcement. The whole family was present, each holding a glass of champagne, as Antonio got down on one knee and proposed to Phillipa.

"My dear Phillipa, your Italian Tony, who has adored you since he first met you in London many years ago, requests your hand in marriage and pledges his love and companionship from this day forth."

Phillipa was so overwhelmed by his proposal that she could hardly get any words out. Everyone knew that the Countess was not given to great displays of emotion, but the love and humility she had received from Antonio had her wiping tears from her face. Her voice quivered as she spoke. "My dear Antonio, may this be the first of many happy days we spend—both together and with our families. I give you the same love in return and accept your proposal."

Antonio opened a box to give to Phillipa. She stood in awe of the beautiful gem that had been passed down to him from his mother, a magnificent seven-carat ruby surrounded by diamonds. Everyone gathered to view the special gift, and Sabrina was the first to hug her papa, while the rest followed in succession.

Then James proposed a toast to honor the announcement and the couple. "I believe two people could not be better suited, and the fact that they have known each other a long time makes the engagement very special. I, for one, am very happy to know Piero and Sabrina as well and welcome them into our family."

Before retiring that evening, Sabrina and James took a walk. Sabrina, saddened at the thought of leaving the next day, wanted to leave something for James to remember her by. She handed him a taped envelope and said, "James, this is for you, but please don't open it until I have gone. Promise?"

"Sabrina, I don't have anything for you, but I do promise to write and stay in touch."

They kissed passionately, and then she pulled away and said, "I must go pack and then turn in, but I will see you tomorrow before we leave."

During an emotional departure the next morning, James slipped a photograph of himself in an envelope to Sabrina. Antonio and his family then piled into the Rolls, and Rodney drove them to the London airport to catch the plane back to Florence.

After they were gone, James went back to his room to open the package from Sabrina. He had waited, as promised, but he was anxious to see what was inside. He took his pocketknife and opened the envelope, and out dropped a locket and chain and a letter, beautifully written. The letter read:

James,

You are my one and only love forever, no matter where I go or whom I shall meet. You will be the love of my life for eternity. You are my other half, the person with whom I have traveled so many lifetimes. I have again searched to find you so that we can pass our lives together. I have thought about you and have always known you were out there somewhere. God has answered my prayers. When I visited my master and met my mother, she told me I was once again with the man I have always loved. I know you have much to do in your life, so I will be patient, but always know I shall be thinking of you no matter where I go or where I am. One day I hope to be that one and only person you want to spend the rest of your life with. Then we can return to the stars and the divine universe that created us.

Il mio amore bellissimo, xxx/ooo Sabrina

James, like his mother, was not easily given to emotion, but he fell back on his bed and wept. The last time he had cried like that was when his father died.

Sabrina had opened up a place in his heart that he didn't know existed. He had never experienced feelings like he had for her, and the ache in his heart of not being with her was so painful. Then he remembered the locket. He rolled over to open the beautiful golden locket with its fine chain, and there inside was a picture of Sabrina with those electric eyes staring right through his soul with her beauty.

CHAPTER 24

STARTING A CAREER

James packed all his books, records, gramophone, and sound system together with all his suitcases into the Mini. He then said his goodbyes to the family and headed for London.

On his drive, James reflected on all the events that he'd experienced since leaving Sterling Heights. He knew he still had an affection for Sandra, but meeting Sabrina was so powerful that it had taken his breath away. He'd thought that Sandra was the one for him. He wondered how a man could love two women at the same time. Both were spiritual and had passed the throne test, and he had known both in a previous incarnation. Was it the force of Sabrina's commitment to him that was so powerful, or was it the real thing? Perhaps it was because she was the last woman that he'd met. Sabrina filled the vacuum he had felt after Sandra had left. He thoughtfully analyzed both experiences. He knew he would be close to Sandra in London, and he would see her and let time be the judge. He also was beginning to realize that having the position he had made him a desirable bachelor. He could one day give the woman of his choice a privileged way of life. His innocence was starting to diminish, and his awareness of whom and what he was—and what he had—started to take hold. He decided it would be best to throw himself into his work and let time decide. In the end, it would come down to the life he was going to lead and the woman most suited to his everyday life, as opposed to the romantic fury of the moment. Deep down he knew he could never deny the explosive attraction and connection he and Sabrina felt toward one another.

He met Sir Thomas at two o'clock on Saturday. He loved the little house and thought it was more than adequate for just him and maybe a friend. The fact that he could park the Mini made it all the more practical. Parking space in London was at a premium, especially in this high-end neighborhood.

On Monday morning James arrived early to work and parked his car in the tight little area behind the offices. He reported to Dennis's office to see what work he was expected to do. Dennis greeted him and said, "I'm going to send you out with Sally. She is our number-one auditor and has trained a lot of accountants. When you've learned the basics with her, we'll start to shoot you out on your own a little, and then we'll see how that works. There is procedure that we follow, and you must learn that. It covers every area of accounting. It's our job to audit, correct, validate, and finalize the accounts of any organization. You'll learn to conduct an audit where we give our professional opinion on the extent of our work as well as do clients' taxes. Obviously, we try to have the strictest codes for tax returns, but we can provide less detail if a client doesn't require us to do a full breakdown and cost analysis."

They walked together to Sally's office, and Dennis introduced them. "Sally, I'd like to introduce you to James Bannerman, who is starting out with us. He has proved himself to be an above-average student, so I believe with your skills, he'll pick up our procedures quickly."

Sally, a Londoner who spoke with a cockney accent, joked, "I didn't know I was going to be training a movie star. All those office girls will go nuts when they see him coming."

James immediately liked her; he knew that learning the job and about London was going to be fun with her.

"That's probably a good thing, especially when we're trying to track down entries we don't have invoices for!" joked Dennis as he left them to their training.

"James, love, we've got to go to this company in Isleworth, so today you can come in my old banger with me, and then you'll know the route for tomorrow. No sense in wasting good petrol." James followed her to her car, and as she got in, she said, "Now it doesn't start every time, so you may have to get out and give me a push."

The car was an old Vauxhall Wyvern and had seen better years. James waited as she tried to start it, and when it wouldn't crank, he gave her a push. She managed to get the engine cranked as she rolled down the road, and she yelled, "Hurry up and get in before it dies again." As he got settled in the car, she said, "Don't tell me you're fresh out of school and we're going to have to start at the very beginning."

"Sorry, but I don't know the first thing. I can count take orders; I'm a fast learner and a hard worker. I hope that will do?"

"It'll have to, love, but if I get you to chase down copy invoices, watch out for all those girls they got working there. They'll want to chat you up, and then we won't get any work done."

"I get the picture."

Sally parked the car, and they entered through the reception and into the office. A room had been made available for them to conduct their audit. "James, here's a list of what I want copies of, and be a darling and get me a cup of tea on the way back, please. Go to the bookkeeper's office, and she'll oblige."

James walked down the corridor and saw the office marked

"Accounting." He opened the door to a large office of young girls and a smaller office at one end that looked like the head book-keeper's office. He politely knocked on the door and introduced himself.

"Yes, what can I do for you?" asked a nice middle-aged woman.

He explained what he needed, and she yelled out to one of the girls to come to her office, then gave her the list. She then turned back to James and said, "Marsha will take care of you."

Marsha looked at him approvingly and said, "I'll bring these copies down to you in the next fifteen minutes. If you need anything else, just let me know."

"Could you please tell me where I can get a cup of tea?"

"If you go down the corridor, you'll see the the cleaning room and the office break room on the left. You can get what you want there."

"Thanks, Marsha. See you soon."

He went down to the break room and found everything he needed. He was greeted by a man in a very expensive suit. "Good morning, young man. You must be one of our auditors. My name is Lawrence Benton. I am the owner of this company, and if you have any questions, you're always welcome to come to my office and discuss matters."

James introduced himself and thanked Mr. Benton, and then he got Sally's tea and hurried back.

"Thanks, love. Getting to know your way around?"

"Yes. I met the man who owns the place, Lawrence Benton."

"He runs a good business and is good friends with Ron Smith. While we're waiting for the invoices, I'll give you a quick rundown on bookkeeping. First, you have the income statement, which is profit and loss. I'm sure you know that already." Sally continued to explain all the details of what made up an income statement. James listened attentively making notes as she spoke.

Marsha came in with the invoices and said that there were two she was still hunting down. Then Sally continued. "You see these little bits of paper? This is where it gets tricky. I see from looking at them that some are what we call capital items, or what would become assets, and the rest are recorded properly as costs in what I've just explained. The capital items or assets that we must list are equipment, such as machines. Assets have a value, and over time they are written off through depreciation. They are not costs to the income statement; they have to be dealt with differently, and as they've been included here, that will reduce profitability. That's what we're here for—to properly appropriate all the money that's been spent. Small business owners who are doing well often like to write off assets as a cost on the income statement and reduce profit; that way they pay less corporate tax. We can allow some stuff but not all. So we work to make the boss happy, but we've got to keep the taxman happy too."

He had a lot to learn, but day by day, James took it all in and made copious notes. He knew there would be exams almost every sixty days, and he must pay attention. He was having the best education at the hands-on level, and he was being paid.

James and Sally worked together for the next three months and built a great working relationship. One morning, Sally told him, "I want you to come meet my family at the Jolly Rodger this coming Saturday. You can show us how good at darts you are. It's about time you got out, away from these books, and had a good old time. I think you'll enjoy having some fun for a change. Be there at about seven, and then we can get a bite to eat as well. All right, love?"

"I'd love to. Thanks for thinking of me. You're right—it's time I got out and had a beer or two, and besides, I want to see how good at darts you are!"

On Saturday, he arrived at the Jolly Rodger on time and saw Sally sitting at the bar. As he approached, Sally said, "Let's grab

---

DAVID FRANCIS

a table before this place fills up."

Once they were seated, Sally introduced James to her family. He noticed immediately that her daughter, Lisa, was very nice-looking. Lisa said, "James, my mom talks about you all the time, so we just couldn't resist meeting you."

"Your mom is the best teacher I could ever have. I know I've been frustrating with all my questions, but she always takes the time to listen and teach me."

Sally said, "I wish all the young people had your abilities to learn as quickly as you do. Teaching you is easy, and you don't make mistakes."

James turned to Sally's husband, Bertie. "So, Bertie, what do you do, sir?"

"I work at a company in Hounslow; I'm a toolmaker and general machinist."

"I bet I know the name of that place. Aviation Manufacturing Corporation?"

"Yep. I've been there fifteen years, and although we have a very tough boss, he's a good man and takes care of his people. How do you know the company? Have you done audit work there?"

"I know his daughter."

"Sandra? She's working there now. Nice young lass, and pretty, too! So you know her?"

"Yes, we went to school near each other in Scotland. We see each other occasionally now, but since I've been on this job, I've shut myself away and dedicated myself to learning."

"Got your head screwed on right; a man's got to get his trade down first before he can get too serious about other things."

Giving James a flirtatious wink, Lisa said, "Judging from what mom says, it's time you had some fun."

"It is, and I bet you have a boyfriend or two."

She smiled at James. She had on a charcoal skirt with a leather black band around the base and a black blouse. Like her moth-

344

er, she was well endowed. She was tall like her father and wore a sexy pair of knit black stockings, which had a diamond pattern in light and dark black, and very high heels. Her face was well made up, and her pretty blue eyes stood out from her naturally fair hair. She reminded him of a prettier version of Kate.

"So, Lisa, what do you do?" James asked.

"I work as a beautician in London on Sloane Street. I cater to all those rich ladies that come to our salon to make themselves beautiful for their partner."

"That explains how pretty you look tonight."

"Mom, can I take him home tonight?" she teased.

Her mother laughed, "Now, behave yourself."

At that moment, their son Bob and his wife came in to join them. Bob was a tall no-nonsense man, as underscored by his leather jacket and jeans. His wife, Janet, was also pretty, but she wasn't as sophisticated in appearance as Lisa.

James said, "So now I've met the whole clan. What a great family you have, Sally."

Bob suggested, "Let's play a round of darts. Come on, James, we'll put a fiver down for the winner, agreed?"

"Round the clock?" asked James.

"You're on, mate," said Bob.

They were mid-game when two unsavory-looking characters tapped Bob on the shoulder and said, "Mate, it's our turn to play darts, so we'd like you to move over and let us have our game."

"I'm not going to stop a game that we're in the middle of. Let us finish, and you can have the board all to yourself."

"That's not good enough. We've waited, and now it's our turn."

"Look, mate, wait your turn," said Bob, more emphatically.

"You don't listen very well, do you? It looks as though we're going to have to remove you ourselves."

The two men started to drag Bob away from the board, and then James jumped in and said, "You let us finish our game, or you're going to regret it."

"Got ourselves a snobby little ponce, have we?"

James slammed his left fist into the biggest guy's gut and then blasted him right under the chin with a right hook; the man fell backwards onto the floor and then came flying back to take a shot at James. Bob and James beat the hell out of the two guys, and after a serious punch fest, they dragged them by their feet through the barroom and tossed them out into the street.

Then James turned to Bob and said, "I think we need to finish our game."

"Bloody hell, where did you learn to fight like that, mate?"

"We gave them a chance, and they got what they deserved."

"I bet you'll beat me at darts too," Bob said, laughing.

"Well, I need that fiver," James joked.

James did win, and he got his fiver, with which he bought another round of drinks.

"James, where did you learn to fight like that?" asked Lisa, astonished.

"I went to a very tough school."

"You're not just a lover boy now; you're a fighter too. If I need a bodyguard, I'm calling you," joked Sally.

"I would be pleased."

James enjoyed the rest of his evening and woke up with a severe hangover. He thought about Lisa, and he wondered whether they would have similar interests. He thought she was a nice-looking woman but seriously doubted that they would have anything in common. He was now thinking more and more about Sabrina, and that's where he knew his true heart lay.

****

The next few months passed quickly. James and Sabrina had exchanged several letters, and he always wore her locket. He felt bad that he hadn't made an effort to see her in Milan. He and

Sandra had also been out several times and talked on the phone, but he remained committed to his work. On the weekends he would go to the bank and spend endless hours going through deals and past accounting records. He wanted to understand the current position of the business and to thoroughly analyze the future direction he was committed to taking.

He also hadn't seen much of his family. He had received the birth announcement for Sir Thomas and Claudia's son, and he felt compelled to call them.

He called Claudia first. "Claudia, how are you all?"

"James, it's great to hear from you. We're all doing fine. You must come and meet Alex soon!"

"I promise I will. Tell me when and I'll be over. I'm anxious to see all of you and to catch up."

"Come over next weekend and you can see my little guy," she said, excited to see him again.

"Sure, but I'd also like to meet your son," James joked. "I'll be there on Saturday afternoon."

They talked for a while longer, and then he apologized for his lack of communication and promised again to visit soon. He then hung up and called his mother.

She was delighted to hear from him. "I'm so glad you called, James. I have something very important to tell you. Antonio and I have set a wedding date for May of next year. I'll tell you all about it when you come home for Christmas. We plan to have the marriage in Italy, and of course, I want the family to be there."

"Mother, that's fantastic. Congratulations! Of course I'll be there. I can't wait to see his vineyard and meet up with the family again. I so enjoyed their company." And mentally he added, *Especially Sabrina*, but he didn't say this out loud.

But as though she had read his mind, Phillipa said, "I thought you'd be happy, and I know Sabrina will be excited to see you again."

They chatted a while longer and then said they'd see each other at Christmas, which was only a few weeks away.

James arrived as promised and Sir Thomas was at the front door to greet him.

"So take me to Alexander. I'm so looking forward to seeing him." James followed him into the living room, and there in his little cot, quietly sleeping, was Claudia's pride and joy.

"Well, you've got your "General" Thomas, and he looks like a healthy boy with all that hair already," said James, who knew Claudia was happy that he took the time to come and visit. James walked over to Claudia, who was relaxing as she'd only been home a week, and gave her a big hug.

"James I think you're still growing. I bet you're taller than Thomas now!" she said, thinking how well he looked. She continued, "I can see that life in London agrees with you, and with all that hard work you talk about, I'm sure there's some lucky lady who's having a little of your company somewhere," she said, putting him on the spot.

"Actually last weekend was the first time I went out on a real bender and woke up with a terrible hangover. Sally, the woman I work with, had me meet up with her family and I have to say I enjoyed the evening immensely," he said, trying to fill in the gaps.

"What about Sandra, don't you see her?" Claudia asked.

"We've been out a few times but I'm sorry to say, I've been derelict in my duties. I know she's seeing someone else, and in fairness, I understand. She was my first heartthrob and we did have a lot in common, but since meeting Sabrina, she's the only woman I really think about. Mother plans to get married next May in Italy to Antonio, so I can't wait to get my finals out of the way, and then I can take more time to see her," he said, trying to explain his long absence.

"Well my boy, you're here now! So let me get you a glass of red, and let's all celebrate little Alex and Claudia for doing such a magnificent job," said Sir Thomas, who was running around trying to make everyone happy like an excited school kid.

"James, there's a lot to bring you up to date on. We went out on a bid for the accounting, and we were all shocked at how much we were paying to Alan Weinstock. Even when we made the proposal for him to reduce his costs, he couldn't meet the quotes we had. We all thought he was too embarrassed to reduce his price and just stated that we wouldn't get the same service he'd provided. In all reality, the firm we have now is doing as good if not better, for nearly half the price," said Claudia, who always had a mind for getting to the facts without a long drawn-out discussion.

"Well done, Claudia. I thought you'd get to the bottom of it. That's a huge savings for the bank. Anyway, I would like to propose a toast to you, Alex, and Thomas for every good fortune for Alex's future and I look forward to playing a role in his future, if and when it's needed. To the closest friends I have next to my family." The group all clicked their glasses in celebration of their newest member.

Sir Thomas then started, "James I have taken time to talk with the board about all the ideas you had when we last spoke at length. To my amazement, they all agreed. Bill Klondike and Roger Handley understood your new direction, and they happily took a handsome return on their investment and departed. As Claudia will tell you in greater detail, we have almost divested all our shares in the stock exchange, and to date, we have increased our cash surplus by seventy-five million. This is at present held in Lloyds with our other savings. So now you are an eighty-one percent shareholder. I think you are in a pretty good position to do what you like with the business when you come aboard," said Sir Thomas, proud of the direction they were headed.

"Well, since it's nearly Christmas, I think that's the best Christmas present you could ever give me. I don't know what

I'd do without all of you," said James, excited at what had been done. He had in mind to buy out Sir Nicholas but would wait until he was at the bank and then explain to him where his thinking was going and what his plans would be for the future. He knew Nicholas was a businessman, and provided he made a good return on his investment, he didn't think he would really mind either way. He also had in mind to appropriate a 5 percent holding for Claudia, which could accumulate over time with bonuses and performance, but he still had other plans before reaching his goal of completely reorganizing the business.

James enjoyed a delightful weekend with both of them and had the opportunity of holding a newborn baby for the first time in his life. It made him think about his own future and how long it would be before he would have the same exciting feeling that he knew Sir Thomas and Claudia were now experiencing.

Winter was starting to abate, and he'd made plans to meet up the next weekend with Lisa, so he picked her up from the shop as promised. Lisa had brought another set of clothes to change into, and James had already stopped at his mews for a change of clothes for the occasion. He had booked an evening at the Fantasy Bar, as Claudia had told him all about her experience there and how much fun she'd had. So James had kept that in his back pocket for a special night out. He walked over to Sloane Street to meet Lisa. It was a Friday night and he was hungry. He wanted to have a decent meal for a change and decided to eat at the Rib Room at the Carlton Towers. He also thought Sandra probably would've gone back home and this would make a special evening for Lisa before going out to dance. Lisa looked amazing and was dressed to the teeth in the latest fashions. She had on a tight leather black dress and her usual taste for wearing very high heels. She was borderline provocative, but something about her forward personality made it all seem right. She was a very good-looking woman and people stared at her as they were ushered to the their table.

"So James, have you been a naughty boy, or as mum would say, have you had your nose on the job?" Lisa didn't mince her words; she loved to tease and James thought, looking at her attire, of all the people to ask that question, she'd be the last.

"Now why would I tell you all my secrets when you surely have plenty of your own?" he asked as he ordered them both a glass of champagne to kick off the evening.

"I know you have this classy, goody-boy image, but deep down I think you could be a bit of a lad when it comes to women," she said, looking at him with a riveting stare and a little smirk. She was going to give him a real testing, because apart from being very attracted to him, she liked a man to have an adventurous personality and a little naughty was nice. She was no stranger to the opposite sex. Making women look beautiful for their man was what she did for a living. This gave her tremendous insight into the thoughts and gossip other women gave her on a daily basis.

"You don't pull any punches. I like that about you; you have personality and you're funny," he said, trying to throw her off the scent.

"Is that all? Don't I have anything else that appeals to my handsome prince charming?" She loved teasing him as he turned bright red; she knew nothing about his background, but it was obvious where she was headed.

"You're obviously an attractive woman, but I must behave myself, as your mother and father will be jumping down my throat. I don't think you need any encouragement from me.

"Tell me about yourself, I find you a bit of a mystery. You're educated, good-looking, you obviously come from a family that has more than the average bloke, so what's up with all the dedicated work ethic? Mum says you never stop. She's never had a student like you. What drives you so hard?" she said, getting down to brass tacks.

"My father died when I was fourteen and we were very close

and he taught me a lot of good values. He was in banking and he wanted me to be the best son I could be for my mother and the family. As the eldest, it's my responsibility to see that my mother and sisters are well cared for. So I want to be the best I can be at my profession. Then I can find the right woman and one day settle down, but my work comes first. That doesn't mean we can't all have some fun; otherwise Jack is a very dull boy!" He thought that would throw her off the scent again, and then he could start in on her.

"That's what I love about you. Inside all that upper-class image is a person with a real heart, and that's what mum and dad love about you too."

She started to change her tune and James looked into her eyes and thought she was street-smart, yes, but she would never settle for anything less than a man who had real character and substance. She could be a little brash at times, but she would one day develop a style that would work for her. He could also feel her curiosity and ambition to have something in life.

"I bet you've known a few lads, Lisa. You're nobody's fool, so tell me about yourself," he said, trying to get the conversation off him.

"I have, and I may look like and act like I know a lot, but I'm really more guarded than you think. I know I'm above average in the looks department, and I have men wanting to take me out all the time. I am in the habit of saying I'm busy because they only want one thing. Making love, to me, is something special, and although we don't come from a lot, my mum and dad have good values. I want something better for my life and I want to know people like you to better myself," she said.

James couldn't believe she had such a realistic and unpretentious viewpoint. "That's what I love about you," he said following her earlier comment, "you just speak your mind. You're a pretty woman, you know exactly how to dress and look to please a man or inspire a woman, but you want to make something of your life. That's what I'm all about. It's not where you start, it's where you end up!"

They finished their meal, and as he got up to leave the table, he got the shock of his life: Over in the far corner was Sandra with a very good-looking, well-dressed man. He looked a little older, probably in his late twenties. Sandra was busy talking away, but her partner certainly noticed Lisa. James said nothing and looked the other way and exited the room as quickly as possible. He thought that he was seeing other women, so it was to be expected. Nevertheless, it hurt to see someone he cared for so much with another person.

They arrived at the Fantasy Bar, and Lisa was excited at the layout and the great music.

"James this place is fancy, and I bet a drink here costs a bomb, but if you're in for it, I'm with you," she said, holding his hand and watching the look on his face.

The couple was escorted to a very nice booth overlooking the dance floor with all its colored lights and paraphernalia.

"James, I'm so excited to be with you. There's no halfway with you. When you take a girl out, it's first class, and you look so comfortable in these surroundings," she said, still trying to weigh him up but thinking that she was going to have to have a few close dances before she got inside his head.

At that moment, who would be tapping him on his shoulder after ordering another bottle of champagne but none other than Sir Nicholas Blythe? An equally illustrious-looking woman accompanied him.

"My Lord, how are you this evening?" he asked as James got up to shake his hand and introduce Lisa to Sir Nicholas, who was taking in every detail of the woman he was with.

"Nicholas, what a surprise! It's been a while." James remembered the strained circumstances they had met under at the Throne Room.

"Stacy," he said to the woman who was with him, "sit here

and get to know Lisa while James and I have a little discussion, if that's okay with you, sir?" Sir Nicholas was using the utmost tact. He'd wanted this moment to revisit with James for quite a while and this posed the perfect opportunity.

James and Nicholas sat at another table, taking their glasses with them. Nicholas offered him a cigar and the two started their conversation.

"James I've always wanted to apologize for my outlandish behavior when we last met. I had indeed conveyed that to Claudia. Hopefully she took a moment to explain the matter to you?" he asked in a conciliatory manner.

"She has. Think nothing of it. You had an unpleasant experience and that's quite understandable," said James, wishing to console one of his most important shareholders.

"You will be happy to know that I have been taking some lessons with Sarah McKenzie. She has opened my eyes enormously to things that I could never have imagined. She is an amazing woman. At the boardroom that day, I can only say with deep regret that I opposed the motion to develop the East Wing because I didn't have a clue what I was talking about. It's becoming a tremendous success and you were right to uphold your forefather's dreams and aspirations. That's what I do in my world of manufacturing and fashion," said Nicholas, feeling happy to have the right moment to explain his feelings.

"That's all in the past and you have more than shown your good faith in Bannerman's, for which we all respect. Also, being on the Queen's honor list is no small accomplishment, either. I respect what you do and how hard you work," said James, who liked his entrepreneurial pioneering spirit.

"So James, what are you up to these days?" he asked inquisitively.

"I didn't want to do the traditional family university thing, so I chose to get a job with a good accounting firm and become an articled chartered accountant," he said with pride at his journey so far.

"Splendid, that's exactly what my father made me do, work in the factory first. Then I proved to him I was a worthy son by starting the fashion side of the business, and now we are in Europe and the States. If only he could have been alive to see how our company has progressed. It would be so worthwhile to hear his words, but he did praise my work before he died and that meant everything to me."

"I know the feeling. My father died when I was thirteen. I wish he could have been here to see the changes we'll make. As you're older, I'll join the club," James said as the two hit their glasses and poured another.

"James, that's a damn good-looking woman you've got with you. What does she do?" asked Nicholas, who always had an eye for a model who could promote his line or help some other friend in the industry.

"She works at the beauty shop on Sloane Street. She's just a regular, ordinary young woman whose mother and I work together during the week. Lisa and I met at a pub and we promised that we would meet up and go out for an evening, so here we are," he said, wondering what Nicholas had in mind.

"James, you know the industry I'm in. I think she's a smasher for looks, but even at worst, I'm sure I could pay her more than she's making now at my place on Vigo Street. Do you mind if I chat her up and get an idea of what she's like?" he asked with sincerity. Nicholas loved women, but when it came to fashion, he was a perfectionist and he knew in a flash if someone had that extra something to make it happen.

"Be my guest. I'm sure you'll make her dizzy with excitement, so go easy," said James, not wanting Nicholas to give her any unrealistic expectations.

The four of them got back together, and James started to talk with Stacey while Nicholas talked with Lisa. The evening was now in full swing and James couldn't resist the opportunity to dance, so he yanked Lisa away to the dance floor.

The two of them danced their legs off to all the latest sounds and then returned to the table. Nicholas had taken his girlfriend to do the same thing, and now James and Lisa had a moment to talk.

"James, you're a lord?" asked Lisa with astonishment.

"Yes, I am, but you tell no one, and I mean no one," he said emphatically.

"But why?" she said, not understanding him at all.

"Because it would change the way people see me, and when I've finished my time to become an accountant, then I don't mind, but not now," he said again emphatically.

"I knew you were a mystery man, but that's what I love about you. You've got that other girl half-bananas over you. I can see why you don't want all that attention," she said, completely understanding the whole picture. It all made sense to her now, and she knew why.

"Lisa, I want people to know the real me and a title doesn't make the person. The person has to make the title," he said firmly.

"Are you ever right! You are most deserving of your title. You get out there with people, people who work to live. You're one of those who lives to work, and that's what I admire about you," she said, leaning over and giving him a big kiss.

"Wow Lisa, you just go there. I like being with you," he said, amazed at her boldness.

"Let's wait until there's a slow one. I'll show you how a woman can dance, Lord Lover-boy," she said, laughing her head off. James laughed too.

The slower music started to play and he took the opportunity to dance with her. She was very warm and nestled up close to him. It was hard not to like Lisa. She had sex appeal and she had her mother's delightful personality. James knew it was just a fun evening, and he was going to make the best of it. She spoke about her interview with Nicholas and sounded excited about a new job opportunity and possibly some modeling. She was so grateful for the introduction.

"James, in one evening, you light up my life with opportunity, and yet you ask nothing of me," she said, knowing he had put in a good word for her.

"Nonsense, it was just timing. You were in the right place at the right time. I know Nicholas enough to know he doesn't waste time. If he sees a potential, he goes after it. You'll like him. He's obviously well educated, he's come up through the ranks in his father's business, and he knows his trade inside and out. His makeup salon and beauticians are top-rank as they work on his models. At the very least, you'll have an entertaining job, a much broader cross section of people, and some very good-looking models to work on."

He thought it would be a step in the right direction for her. He knew her mother had been very patient in teaching him, and in this way, he could return the favor.

The gong went off and they shuffled to the last dance. He felt Lisa becoming very intimate, but he was careful not to overstep the boundaries and put himself in a position he couldn't correct easily. As he was leaving, he could see at a distant table his sister Flick with Gordon Petersen. He didn't wish to intrude, but he felt sure Gordon knew he was there.

James thought he was working his sister over to learn more about him. He would let it go for now, as he knew Flick had other boyfriends. He thought better of it and didn't want to cause a scene, which is exactly what Gordon would have wanted.

As they stopped a cab to go back to his place, she asked, "James, I normally stay at my girlfriend's flat at Battersea, but if you had a spare bed or some room, I won't impose. I know it's an imposition, but I don't think I should go back to Wimbledon this late at night with this amount of booze in my system," she said, knowing that she had an ulterior motive and that men, on the whole, were weak with a woman. She didn't mind how weak he was with her.

"Look Lisa, it's not that I don't want you to stay with me. You are a very attractive woman, and I don't want to do anything that would jeopardize my relationship with your family. So, if we have that understanding, yes, you're more than welcome," he said, knowing that if he looked at her too closely one more time he would cave.

They arrived at his mews home, and again, Lisa was amazed.

"So, this is where you hang out. What a pad! Anyone would give their right arm to live here," she said, looking around.

"So, let's have a night cap. I want a cigarette and then we can hit the hay," James said, wanting to unwind after a fun evening.

"Bring it on, sailor; I'm your woman."

They both had a brandy with some black coffee and smoked a cigarette while they chatted for a good hour. Then Lisa asked, "What's holding us up?" as she purposely crossed her legs so that James could see now that her skirt line had risen higher on her beautiful legs. She was using all her cunning to seduce the man she wanted. "James, you can have your way with me if you want. I know you want me, and I know I want you, so what's holding us up?" she said again with even more force.

"Lisa, any man on the planet would want you; you're irresistible, but I won't go there. It's not right to take advantage of a situation like this, and it would cheapen the relationship between us." He knew she wanted him, but he had a responsibility to her family, and he wasn't going to start something he couldn't finish. The temptation was enormous, but the prize wasn't worth it for a man in his position.

Then she said, "James, I'll keep your secret if I can just have one night with you."

"Lisa you're worth more than that! You'd better keep my secret. Otherwise, we won't be seeing each other again," said James looking very forcefully at her.

"You know I would never do that," she wailed before bursting into tears. She was only showing her true feelings now that she'd fallen headlong in love with him.

The couple decided to call it a night, and James showed her to her room. After they shared a long kiss and hug, James retired to his room.

In the early morning hours, James awoke but still remained half asleep. He felt this person next to him that smelled like Sandra. He was still dreaming, but this very amorous and available partner was starting to work him up between his legs, and the need for him to hold this beautiful woman became magnetically erotic. He leaned over to kiss this beautiful maiden of his dreams as he felt her hand guiding him into a place of pleasure. As things began to become more intense, he started to wake up. To his astonishment he was looking up at a very voluptuous woman who was eagerly pleasing him and herself. She was moaning, "Oh My Lord, My Lord, this is the most beautiful experience of my life. Forgive me please, forgive me, but I couldn't resist you any longer." Lisa had become so infatuated with the young lord that she didn't care what he thought; she lay awake all night wondering how to have the experience she was now having. She had punished so many would-be admirers in the past by not allowing them to have sex with her, and here was a man that decided he didn't need her. This was her moment and she was going to make the best of it, even if he did sling her out of his bed.

"Lisa, my God. What are you doing? I thought I was making love to an angel. You have such a beautiful body. I had no idea how gorgeous you are without your clothes."

Her long hair falling down across his face as she passionately kissed him again and again was now sending him into overload. The two ravaged each other to the early hours of the morning and then fell back asleep till midday. James woke up, and much to his anguish, he realized that he'd made love to Lisa. As he saw her lying blissfully asleep on the pillow next to him, he didn't have the heart to chastise her. She was beautiful and he'd been a very lucky man to have this beautiful woman love him with total abandon.

He slowly got up to put on the coffee and fully take in all that had happened. She had gotten her way. He liked her, and to hell with what anyone thought! She had made beautiful love to him; what more could a man ask for?

Lisa slowly emerged from her slumber and made her way down to the kitchen.

"James, you gave me the most beautiful night a woman could ever have. I will hold these memories in my heart forever," she said with tears rolling down her cheeks. She hated the way she had taken him, but she didn't regret the invasion into his bed for one moment.

James looked at her and thought that even in the morning after a night like they had, she looked so beautiful.

CHAPTER 25

AN ITALIAN WEDDING

Everyone was excited about the upcoming wedding. James was busy with work and exams, so he decided that he would fly to Florence on the Friday evening before the wedding and return on Sunday. He had an important audit coming up. He had been with the firm almost two years, and his final exams were in June. Now he was an important member of the team, and it was only after tax time later in the summer that he would really be able to take time for himself. Still, he hadn't written to Sabrina since her last letter over two weeks ago. He knew he would be seeing her and was excited at the prospect of being with her again.

James landed late that Friday evening in Florence, and a taxi dropped him at the hotel villa where his mother and sisters were staying. He was tired, so he unpacked his morning suit and hung his clothes up. He then took a shower before going to bed.

The next morning, the family met up for breakfast at the ho-tel villa lounge to discuss the events of the day.

"James, glad you made it in last night. Did you have a good trip?" his mother asked.

"Yes, I did. Unfortunately I have to leave on Sunday night; I have a large audit job on Monday."

"I understand. Now I have something I need to tell you. I know you're anxious to see Sabrina, but you need to know that she has another boyfriend whom she is seeing, a young man whom Antonio highly approves of."

"It's understandable she would have a boyfriend. We don't exactly live next door to each other, but at least we'll all be fam-ily after this weekend. I will at least have a chance to sit with her at the wedding and after the service."

"James, Antonio has her sitting with Marco, who is the son of the largest wine grower in Tuscany. They have been seeing each other for quite a while now, and I believe they want to get engaged."

"I think I know Sabrina well enough to know she would want to be next to me." He was feeling hurt by his mother's remarks.

"You have to understand that if Marco and Sabrina marry one day, it would be a very proud moment for their families. The marriage would considerably enhance their future in the wine business." She thought her son was being unrealistic. Yes, they felt an attraction when they met, but it would be impracti-cal for them to think of a future together.

"I don't care who this person is. I am the person whom Sa-brina loves because that's what she's written to me." He was con-vinced of her intentions and knew that someone, probably her father, was manipulating her future behind the scenes.

"How recently has she written of her love for you?"

"Within the last month. We have stayed in touch, and I have a locket of hers that she gave me. We both know we are too young to get married, and we will have other relationships in the meantime, but if I know Sabrina, she will never change her mind, and neither will I." James was emphatic about the way he felt, and his mother looked at him, a little shocked.

"I didn't realize how serious you were. I have to say, she's not been too happy these last few days. I thought it was because she felt she was giving up having all the attention of a doting father. Now I see that Antonio wants this relationship for the betterment of the family. She has asked me countless questions about you, so I know she cares for you greatly, but I don't want to start a family feud before we're even married."

"Mother, I don't want to upset your wedding day, but I think I should at least talk with Sabrina and find out the truth. If she loves Marco and wants to marry him one day, I will accept her choice. However, I know she doesn't. Arranged marriages in this new world of ours will only end in pain and anguish for everyone."

"I know, but I also know Antonio is dead set on Sabrina being with Marco, and this is going to be difficult. I'm going right now to meet with Sabrina and ask her what her feelings are. If she's with this man just because it's what her father wants, I want to have it out with Antonio. I'm not marrying a man that forces his children to marry someone they don't love. One way or another, I'm going to get to the bottom of this, and if she truly feels this way towards you, James, then this forced engagement is all wrong. I can see you're hurt, but be prepared to take it on the chin if she's fallen in love with someone else."

"Of course. I don't want to spend one day of my life with a woman who doesn't love me."

The Countess asked for a taxi. "I'll see you all in a while. I'll be back for lunch, and girls, remember there is a practice ceremony at three o'clock this afternoon."

Throughout the rest of the morning, James anxiously awaited the return of his mother and paced endlessly around the gardens. Finally, she returned, and as she walked into the hotel lobby, James could see she was visibly upset.

She spotted him and walked over. "That didn't go down too well." They began walking toward the lounge, and she ordered a coffee for both of them.

"Mother, are you all right?" asked James nervously.

"Just before I get married, and now this. Well, the truth is the truth, and it appears that Sabrina is in love with you. She's fanatical about it. Her father is so furious with her, he's about to banish her from the wedding."

"Doesn't he want what's best for his daughter? I don't understand."

"It's these Italian customs where, apparently, the father gives his daughter certain choices. In return for all that he's done for her, she must follow her father's wishes and what is best for the long-term interests of the family. Apparently, they did have a relationship going until you entered the picture, but she still says that she was never in love with him in the first place. Antonio doesn't want to upset Marco's family. I can see that the whole situation has now been planned. It's too complicated to change."

"What situation?"

"Antonio was going to announce their engagement at the wedding. Marco was going to be there to make it known to everyone, and for Antonio, it was going to be a very proud moment."

"But it's your wedding," James exclaimed, not understanding why the wedding would be turned into some sort of opportunistic occasion.

"Antonio is adamant about his decision, and I've told him that I don't want to start out this way. I've called the church and put off the rehearsal ceremony until five o'clock to give him time to make up his mind. If he doesn't change his mind, I want out of here." She opened her bag to get a handkerchief to wipe the tears from her eyes. James got up to give his mother a hug, and then she added, sobbing, "No man I marry is going to treat two people that love each other like that. Sabrina's very unhappy. She's such a beautiful, caring child that's done nothing but wait on that family hand and foot. If her father wants to use her for his own personal gain, I want nothing to do with him."

"Mother, if he truly loves you, he'll think better of it, although I know he won't be very happy with me."

"I know you love her. I can see it in your eyes. Antonio saw it as well. Whether you're together or not in the future, that's up to you two. I truly believe you will be, somehow—with or without my marriage to Antonio."

"Mother, I'm proud to be your son. I can never say you don't stand up for your kids. As a young boy, I never realized how much you cared." James thought about what Sarah McKenzie had said about his mother and realized he'd had the wrong opinion of her as a child.

His sisters walked in, and Phillipa told them that the rehearsal had been put off. James recounted the situation to get them up to speed. Their mother decided to go to her room to rest and to think about the future. James was about to go to his room to get his book when Antonio came walking through the lobby. "James, just the person I wanted to see. Let's go out on the veranda and have a cigar and a glass of Chianti."

"Yes, sir."

"You know the situation with Sabrina. It seems that my daughter is in love with you. I recognize that you are young and things can change, but I can't deny my one and only daughter the love she has for you." It was clear he had thought the whole situation through carefully.

"I'm happy you recognize the sincerity of what I feel for Sabrina," James said with relief at Antonio's words.

"Now I want you to come to the rehearsal. Sabrina will be there, and you two can talk. Marco will not be there, as he will be an usher with Piero tomorrow. When he learns of the change of plans, he won't be happy. I want you to understand that they have known each other for a while, and they do care for one another, which I'm sure you can appreciate. I want him to understand that we in no way wish to offend him or my longstanding relationship with his family. James, we Italians of my generation, especially those of means, often married within our circle, and that's how we have grown and protected the growth of our industry. I understand that in this modern age, these old values are changing. We must handle these matters delicately, as I know Marco does love Sabrina. So don't be upset if she spends time with him tomorrow. It's the correct protocol, and with time, Sabrina will gently ease her way out of the situation."

"Sir, it is your day, and I'm sorry this matter had to come between my mother and you. However, my feelings toward your daughter are so strong that it would be painful not to be sitting with her."

Antonio laughed. "Do you always get your way? I admire your conviction."

"Sir, I would fight like this for anyone I love."

"Even if you're not my son-in-law someday, I'll always love you like a son." He gave James a warm hug and went to look for his bride.

Later that afternoon, James was excited to see Sabrina at the church. When she saw him, she ran toward him to give him a kiss. "You're here, you're finally here! I can't believe it. It's like a dream come true to be in your arms once again."

"I've missed you so much. You look even more beautiful than how I remembered you."

"I have to go and prepare, but I want to tell you so many things afterward." She reluctantly left his embrace as her father motioned her to the rehearsal.

"I'm not going to leave or take my eyes off you. I want to watch the whole ceremony."

After the ceremony was over, they went back to Antonio's villa. James was quite taken by the beauty of the vineyard and its setting amongst the surrounding hills. The whole place spoke to him of romance and warmth.

After everyone was settled, Sabrina said, "James, come with me. I want to show you around, as tomorrow is going to be hectic, and we might not have a chance." She held out her hand. They walked amongst the vines arm in arm. Sabrina stared into his eyes and said, "I knew you would stand up for me. It told me our love was true, and I was not fooling myself. Marco has style and looks, I have to admit, in his late twenties. I've known him for nearly five years and had always looked up to him, but now that I'm older, I find him too self-centered. With all that he has, he's become spoiled and intolerant. If he doesn't get the right service or someone doesn't do exactly as he pleases, he throws a fit. Even though you're only twenty, you are more mature than he is. But it's more than that. The first moment I laid eyes on you, I knew you were the one."

"Sabrina, I think about you every day, and although I see other women, my heart beats for you. I will finish my accounting in the late summer, and I promise to see you more then. I can't possibly go this long again without being with you."

"I hope you won't think me too forward, but I want you. I can't bear not holding you in my arms. I have taken all the precautions, and I feel there is nothing we can't share."

"Nothing could equal the experience of making love to you."

"Tomorrow evening, my papa and your mother will be flying off to Capri for their honeymoon. We can be alone to share a beautiful time."

"There's only one problem. I've booked a flight out tomorrow night. But I'll change it. Work can do without me for one day. I will send a telegram from the hotel tomorrow morning first thing. I've dreamed of this moment with you, and I want this time together."

"We better get back. Otherwise, they'll be thinking the worst." She started to run, and he ran up behind her and picked her up off her feet. "You're so strong! Will you carry me over the threshold one day?"

"I'll do more than that! I'll hold you in my arms and carry you to bed every night. As long as it's not upstairs." He pinched her and they both laughed.

The next day, the ceremony at the church was beautiful, full of color and flowers. James sat next to Claudia and Sir Thomas. Sabrina and his sisters looked beautiful in their bridesmaid dresses. When the Padre asked the traditional question of whether anyone objected to the marriage, a woman stood up for a moment, as if to make a statement, but she said nothing. She was wearing black, and her face was shrouded by a lace veil, so it was hard to see who she was. After a moment, she sat back down, and the ceremony continued. James decided he was going to find out who she was after the service.

After the service, James spotted the woman in black standing alone. He made his way over to her to speak. "Madam, I hope you speak English. I would like a few words with you before you leave, if I may?"

She turned slowly but was slow to respond. "Sir, I have no wish to interrupt your day, other than I came to pay tribute to a man I love very much." As she lifted her veil, James could see that she was a very attractive woman who reminded him a little of Claudia. She was Italian but spoke excellent English and was dressed immaculately.

"Madam, I couldn't help notice that you stood up in the service, and I felt sad for you. I would just like to understand your sadness if that is something you would like to share."

"You are the son of the Countess, I assume," she asked, starting to smile.

"Yes, I am."

"Sir, I appreciate your concern, but I belong to the past. My feelings, whatever they may have been, belong there also. Whatever I shared with Antonio is gone, and I must learn to let the pain of my love go." She started to weep.

"I understand, even at my young age, the pain of loving someone, and I know how hard that is to let go of. However, looking at you today, I'm sure a pretty woman like you will find that right person. Sometimes we become so wrapped up in the person we love that we don't see what's right in front of our own eyes. I do know that we can't move on until we let go, and then God opens up a new door for us to see a whole new journey."

"Thank you for your kind words. I'm glad I came today, if only to meet you. You helped me to see myself again."

"Madam, it was a pleasure. I can't bear to see a woman so unhappy. I wish you every success in your journey."

She strolled down the lane toward her car, but she constantly turned to look at James. He had opened a door to her heart, and as tragic as this day had been for Antonio's former bookkeeper and lover, she somehow felt lifted and rejuvenated.

The newlyweds were driven home in a Mercedes limousine while the others slowly wound their way back to their cars to follow the procession to the reception at Antonio's villa. The veranda had been beautifully decorated for the day, and the tables were laid out with nametags for all the attendees. James rode with his sisters, Sabrina, and Piero.

The afternoon was a great success. Marco spent the entire afternoon staring daggers at James. He and Sabrina talked and laughed with an intimacy that was clearly obvious to all who were seated at the neighboring tables. Finally, Antonio's best man—Marco's father—got up to say a few words. "Ladies and gentlemen, this is the happiest I've seen Antonio since he was a young man working in London and spoke of a woman called Phillipa who had won his heart. He was so sad when she got married. Now he has found the love of his life again."

The speech went on for a while, and many more speeches and toasts followed. The whole affair of about sixty people was intimate and friendly. After dinner, the band started to play, and

Antonio and Phillipa got up to dance.

Sabrina leaned over to James and said, "I must dance with Marco, as it is etiquette. After all, we did depose him from his seat, so I must show him some consideration."

James noticed his sister alone, but Piero was quick to take her hand, so he looked around for another suitable dance partner. He then noticed Claudia sitting alone. "May I have the honor?" asked James.

"I would always dance with you, James."

"So how's that boy of yours doing?"

"Thomas? Oh, he's doing just fine," Claudia said with a smirk, which made James chuckle. "No, he's doing magnificently. He's into everything, and you'd think Thomas was a schoolboy, playing with him and making baby noises on the floor."

"If he inherits any of your good looks, you'll have to keep a tight rope around him."

"Sabrina looks stunning, as usual, and seems to have quite a following. I notice that Marco has his eye firmly stuck on her."

"When there's a pretty woman, there's always competition, but in the end, it's all about chemistry. It either works or it doesn't."

She teased, "My, oh my, you have become tolerant for a young man. Just remember, faint heart never won fair lady. I never thought you to be a person to become that philosophical so easily."

"You're right. I'm just bluffing. I'm so crazy about the girl I could marry her tomorrow, but we're too young. Still, she's the woman I want."

"Don't leave it too long. These Italian men can become quite convincing, so make sure you keep the relationship alive, and don't become too distant."

James changed the subject. "Will you see your parents while you're here?"

"Yes, we're off to Rome first thing tomorrow. They've already been over to see Alex, so it's a return match."

"When I get home, I'm going to come see how you and the bank are doing. We must make decisions on Nigel Thompson."

"Yes, I know. You've been busy with your accounting, but it's time to make a decision. We are saving a huge amount of money with the new accounting firm." The music stopped, and James escorted Claudia back to her seat.

"Stealing my beautiful wife when my back's turned?" Sir Thomas, who had returned from visiting with Nicholas, stood up to give James a hug.

"Why not? She's the most beautiful woman in the room."

At that moment, Marco walked up to introduce himself to James. "Your Lordship, my name is Marco, and my family and Count Antonio have been very close for years. I welcome you to our valley and hope you have a very enjoyable stay. It's so nice to see that your two families get on so well. I know Sabrina was captured by her visit to your estate in England. She and I plan to come back to England together later in the year. We would be so happy to visit the Throne Room that she speaks about with such great reverence. We are considering plans for our engagement soon."

"Well, sir, you would be most welcome at our home, as you have indeed shown us such great hospitality here. I can only say that you have a beautiful part of the world to live in. The English climate couldn't come close to what you all enjoy here." He tried to be cordial, respecting the relationship held between the two families.

"It was a pleasure to meet you, and I look forward to talking with you again."

James turned and walked up to the bar where a very pretty young lady was standing alone. "Would you like to dance?" he asked courteously.

"I would love to, sir."

"What is your name?"

"Gina. I'm Marco's sister. I'm sure you know the feelings my brother has for Sabrina. However, I notice that Sabrina is quite taken with you. How do you see the future engagement of Sabrina to Marco now that you are a member of the family, so to speak?"

"I'm not aware of the depth of their relationship, so it would be impossible for me to answer."

"Well answered, James. Personally, if I were to place a bet on whom she likes best at this moment in time, it would be you. That being said, I don't know your intentions, and Marco has the edge, as he lives closer and has known her longer."

"You do play tough, but you get to the point, and I like that," James said with a smile.

"Thank you, James, for asking me to dance. I hope one day to visit your home and talk more with you." He escorted her back to the table, and then she whispered in his ear, "My bet's on you." Then she winked and sat down.

James danced with his mother and sisters, and then the moment came for the couple to depart for their honeymoon. The Mercedes limousine pulled up at the front door, and everyone formed two lines to throw the confetti and flower petals at the couple. Then came the defining moment as Phillipa turned her back to the bridesmaids and threw the bouquet of flowers. Sabrina, being that little bit taller, stretched out to grab one end as it fell. Without hesitation, she turned to look straight into James's eyes.

The party soon broke up, and around ten o'clock, Sabrina told the staff that they had cleared away enough for the evening and could finish in the morning. Now Sabrina and James were alone.

James picked her up and carried her up the staircase to the bedroom she pointed out. Her bedroom had a lovely private veranda where she had laid out some finger foods and an ice-cold bottle of champagne. She had planned the evening, and everything was in place. James went outside to open the chilled bottle of champagne while she went to refresh herself after a long and hectic day. She returned to the veranda wearing a white chiffon garment that had gold embroidery around her neck and at the base of the dress. Her hair was brushed out and pulled down to lay gently on her shoulders. She looked like a Roman goddess, and as he looked closer, he could see through the dress to the outline of her naked body. He poured her a glass of champagne as they sat enjoying the moonlit night.

He took her by the hand and led her toward the bed. They were naked within seconds in a passionate embrace. The experience for James was so overwhelming. She was so soft and calm and yet deeply intimate. She gently made love to him, in no hurry. It was as though the experience for her was surreal and spiritual, and it took her some time before she started to become extremely intense. He felt that she had some experience in making love, but it didn't bother him. He felt she was more in control than he was, and when he overcame his desire to ravage her, he started to learn something that was deeper and more consuming than he could ever imagine.

After nearly half an hour of heated lovemaking, James finally released himself to the appreciative screams of a well-satisfied woman. "James, that was beautiful, and I have to say the first time that I have experienced a climax with a man."

"That was a beautiful start to the real meaning of us."

They went outside to sit again on the veranda and let the night breeze cool them off.

"James, when I sat on the throne that day and learned all that I did, I knew there would never be a question in my heart again as to the one I love. I know you are the one I love."

James got up and took her by the hand and said, "I think about you every day, and the thought of leaving here tomorrow makes my heart ache." They went back to the bedroom and made love all night until they fell asleep with exhaustion.

The next morning, James was awakened by an anxious Sabrina. "James, wake up. The staff has arrived, so get your stuff and go into the adjoining room and get dressed, okay?"

James hurriedly went through the side door of the bedroom. He waited until he heard Sabrina go downstairs and gave her time to talk to the staff before heading down himself.

He joined her on the veranda for breakfast. Sabrina talked quietly as she poured the coffee. "James, that was the best night of my life. When I go to university in Milan, we must see each other more regularly. I don't know how I can bear not seeing you for periods at a time, but we must, as I must get a profession, and you must finish your accounting."

"We can plan something once a month, where one weekend you come to me, and the next month, I come to you."

"That would be fantastic, but I don't have the money to fly to England, and I don't want Papa to know everything yet."

"Don't worry. I can afford to do it for now. When you can, that's great, and when you can't, I'll pay. Nothing will keep us apart."

They took one more walk through the vineyards, and then he knew he had to return to the villa, pack his suitcase, and catch his plane. Sabrina drove him to the airport. She had tears in her eyes as they parted, but as she drove home, she knew she would be with him again soon, and that pleased her tremendously.

CHAPTER 26

THE KEY OF THE DOOR

The day James had been waiting for was finally near. The time was drawing toward his much-awaited twenty-first birthday. His family had planned a big New Year's Eve celebration in combination with his twenty-first birthday, and a huge list of guests had been invited. James had been kept in the dark and wasn't supposed to know the plans of the evening's events. His mother and sisters had made all the arrangements with the staff.

James had been busy checking on the farm and its progress with Keith. He took time out to ride Foxy and think about his plans for the future. He had passed all his exams and was accepted as an associate chartered accountant. To become a fellow chartered accountant would take more years, but he was happy to have what he had worked so hard for.

The Throne Room was a success; more and more people visited each year. Word was traveling fast about the intriguing history and mystery of the throne. It was now completing its third year and was showing a fine return on the investment. Sarah McKenzie had been a huge part of its success, and her school had up to a four-month waiting list. She had expanded the building but couldn't recruit trained people fast enough, as in most cases, they had to be taught from within the school. The extra income was helping with the restoration of the cottages around the estate, of which they had rented out over half of. The last project would be to upgrade the properties they held in the village of Penbroke and the small Anglican church that the Bishop of Lincoln sent a vicar to once a week for the sermons on Sunday.

The special week finally arrived; a large marquee was erected on the lawn at the rear of the house and had an adjoining awning that connected to the main house. The plan was to have all the food and catering services in the marquee. Tables had been laid out to hold at least six people, with larger tables for the family, close relatives, and friends in the center. The idea was to have easy access for the caterers and all their equipment for the evening dinner and to host the dancing in the large ballroom in the main house.

A group called the Adjectives had been hired as the entertainment. They could play music from all the great rock stars of the era. They were well known for their versatility, expensive electrical sound system, and musical instruments. Their equipment would work well with the high ceilings and create phenomenal acoustics in the ballroom.

James took a moment to wander through the marquee and ballroom to examine the layout. It was Wednesday afternoon, and the guests would be arriving on Thursday. They could arrive early at the hotels that had been booked for them and visit the Throne Room. It had been closed for the winter but would be open free of charge to any guests that wanted to see the great collection. Friday was New Year's Eve and James's birthday party.

As he was viewing the ballroom, Kate snuck up behind him. "James, I finally get to see you after all this time." She gave him a kiss and a hug.

"I see you girls have been very busy. I think you've done a tremendous job, and I can't wait to hear this band when they get into action." He noticed Kate had matured and was looking very appealing.

"So I will get to dance with you, I hope?"

"Of course. I want to see how well you can rock 'n' roll. Knowing you, I'm sure you'll show me up."

"I'm racing a full-blown race car now, so you need to come over sometime, and I'll teach you how to be really quick at the wheel. I know you're a competitor, but I'd like to teach you all my tricks."

"I'll definitely take you up on that, but I doubt I'll ever be as fast as you are."

Friday evening arrived, and at seven o'clock, the crowds of invited people started to enter the main entrance hall. Some had never been to Penbroke Court before and were in awe of the size of the house. James stood at the front entrance to greet the crowds of people. He wanted the affair to be personal. It was an opportunity for many people from the village and management staff to pay their compliments to His Lordship and shake his hand. James was shocked to see Sally and her whole family as well as Ron and Dennis Smith from the accounting firm. He realized that some guests had probably arrived earlier, and the people he knew better had obviously been ushered in a different way without his knowing. He thought this was definitely Becky and Flick's doing, so now he didn't know what he was in for. He politely stood at the front entrance until the numbers started to dwindle and Becky came up in her beautiful ball gown to tell him that he was needed in the main ballroom. James looked very dashing in his untraditional but appropriate dinner jacket with tails and medals that were family heirlooms of the estate.

He followed Becky into the ballroom and saw that it was full of all the people he knew. He was motioned toward the front podium where the band was set up. When he arrived, Sir Thomas took the microphone and announced him. "My Lords, Ladies and Gentlemen, I, Sir Thomas Arthur Ringstone, present to you James Edward Bannerman, the Tenth Earl of Penbroke. Happy twenty-first birthday, My Lord. Please raise your glasses to toast His Lordship on this most auspicious occasion."

After the toast, the band started playing "Happy Birthday," and the entire room sang along. James was overwhelmed by the attendance and felt extremely proud to officially accept his inheritance.

After the birthday wishes, the crowd started murmuring, "Speech, speech!" So James took the microphone to say a few words. "I'm truly amazed that so many of you are here to share this special day with me. I know we're not just up the road from London, so your attendance is all the more appreciated. Sir Thomas, Mother, and Claudia, I thank you greatly for being my guiding light in my teenage years and for trying to keep me on the straight and narrow. Your experienced advice has been of extreme value. Also, my thanks to my family for all the hard work they have done on my behalf for this special occasion. Thank you all for being here; I hope to have a chance to talk with you during the course of this evening. So let the party begin!" The crowd cheered and clapped, and the band began to play.

The band played for about an hour and then announced that dinner was ready. People started to make their way toward the marquee. James waited and was one of the last to enter the marquee. He was amazed to see all the people who had come. He could see that Sandra, her brother Michael, and her mother and father had come, so he made his way over to their table to greet them. Sandra got up to give him a kiss.

"I'm so glad you've all come. I've been kept in the dark, as my sisters have arranged all this."

"You've got your hands full tonight," said Sandra's mother.

Sandra then asked, "Who's the beautiful woman you have sitting at your table?"

James replied, "Which one?"

"You know perfectly well who I mean," she laughed.

"They're all family. I'll explain later."

"It better be good."

James made his way over to his table, and everyone stood to acknowledge his arrival. He went around the table shaking hands and kissing the ladies. James couldn't help noticing that while Becky was sitting next to Piero, Flick had brought to his twenty-first the last person he could ever have imagined. James walked over to say hello to Piero and Becky, and then he went over to see Flick.

"James, I'd like to introduce you to Gordon. He's studying journalism, and it's a career that fascinates me for my own future."

"Gordon and I have met before; we went to school together."

"Oh, really? I had no idea," said Flick innocently.

"Hope you're on your best behavior, Gordon. My sister is important to me," said James coldly.

"Your wish is my command Your Lordship," said Gordon with his evil smile, enjoying every second of the moment.

James sat down between his mother and Sabrina. "Well, James, what do you think?" asked his mother proudly.

"Mother, you've all done a fantastic job, and I can't believe how many people have come all this way."

"Sir Thomas certainly gave you a fine introduction. He's so good at that sort of thing."

"James, who was that very pretty young lady you were talking to before you came over here?" asked Sabrina.

"Oh, that was Sandra. We went to school close by in Scotland, and like you and Marco, we became very close because we shared similar circumstances. If it's any help, she thinks you are very beautiful too." He quickly changed the subject. "So how's life in Milan going?" He wondered how many boys were hitting on her already.

"I love it, but I miss you so much. Let's see each other again in a month or two, please. I keep your photograph by my bed, and I look at it every night before I go to sleep."

James leaned over and whispered, "I'm wearing your locket, and I do the same thing." Her eyes teared up, and she smiled with delight. He continued, "Sabrina, I've got a busy night in front of me, and I don't want you to feel that I've neglected you. I will be with you later, and we have tomorrow. Please understand that I must try and get to as many people as I can.

"James, I do; just don't forget me completely."

"That would be impossible!"

After his meal, James started to circulate and told Sabrina he would be back soon to dance with her. He went over to Ron Smith's table to talk with him and Dennis, and then he went over to Sally and Lisa and the family.

Sally greeted him. "James, you're a dark horse. I didn't know I was training a lord. When I found out who you were, it all took shape. I love you for putting up with me and being at my beck and call so many times. I like a young man who's prepared to get out there in spite of who he is and do what you've done. More people in your position should set an example like that."

"I wouldn't have missed it for the world. I'll miss your sense of humor. Every day was a riot, and I loved it."

Lisa then asked, "Are you going to dance with me tonight? I spent all day making myself look my best for you."

"Lisa, how could I not? You're one of the most beautiful women in the room. I can see all these other men looking at you."

Bobby jumped in and said, "James, mate, I know you're a lord and all that, but to me you'll always be a mate. Just remember, any night you want to come down to the Jolly Rodger and just be one of the lads, I'll be there for you."

"Bobby, I'm actually getting a bit short of cash, especially after this bash, so I may need to do that so I can get another fiver off you."

The room was starting to empty out, so James moved over to Sandra's table to visit with the Coles for a bit.

"So the food was all right?" asked James.

"Excellent," said Mary and Francis.

Francis then asked, "Did you finish your accounting?"

"Yes, sir, I did my two-plus years and worked for an accounting firm in Putney, and now I'm a chartered accountant. Best of all, I got paid to become one!"

"That's the only way to do it. Now I can have you come over and teach Sandra a few things so I don't have to pay all those accounting fees."

"I'm actually going to China soon, where we have banking interests in Hong Kong, but I'm going as a simple auditor, and they won't know who I am. In that way, I can see if they're up to no good."

"Smart. It doesn't pay to stand in the spotlight, even if they think otherwise."

Out of the corner of his eye, he saw the Lloyd family, so he told the Coles he would be right back and went over to speak with Sarah's family. "Victor, I've got someone for you to meet." He motioned to Peter, Sarah, and Kate to follow.

"Francis, I'd like you to meet Victor Lloyd and his family. I believe you've got a lot in common being in the same industry." The families were delighted to meet, and they all sat down together to visit.

As James got up to leave, he bumped into Sir Nicholas. "Fantastic party, old boy. We don't have all that ceremonial stuff with my family, but it suits you. Congratulations."

James realized that since Sir Nicholas was in manufacturing, he would enjoy meeting Francis and Victor, so he took him and his latest girlfriend, Davina Sampson, over to meet them as well.

James took the opportunity to have his first dance with Davina. He thought choosing a supermodel for his first dance would make his choice a little easier than choosing Sabrina over Sandra. "So, My Lord, how honored am I to have the first dance with the Tenth Earl?" She was in her mid-twenties, but every eye in the room was fixated on a person everyone knew. She had been plastered over magazines everywhere and had become one of England's most famous apparel models.

"Well, I know you're no stranger to rock 'n' roll, and to ask anyone else would have been too political," he said, eyeing her swift and gracious movements.

"Such a young man with all this can certainly have his pick of the day, I'd think," she said teasingly.

"I have to give Sir Nicholas a hard time. He's always doing it to me," said James as he returned her to her seat.

"I hope it's not too long before the next time we meet," she said, enjoying the limelight.

"Indeed," said James politely.

"Sarah, you must come and dance with me," said James.

"You have all these beautiful young ladies who'd love to dance with you, so why would you choose me?"

"Because I want to talk with you."

"Well, if you are so insistent, how can I refuse?" The music was slow, so they could talk. "James, you have a very complicated evening."

"Tell me about it. No matter whom I dance with, I'm going to upset another," he laughed.

"So have you chosen the young lady of your heart yet?"

"I'm in love with Sabrina, but I'm still too young to get hitched."

"Wise words, James. Sabrina is very beautiful, and I can understand the attraction between you. She has a beautiful soul, and out of all the women you presently know, she would make the best homemaker and mother for the busy world you're about to enter."

"I love Sandra, but I think she will want to be a professional woman or even a business woman.

"I think you are very right in your choices, but the most important thing is what you're about to do, and then destiny will play its part. You know the person who has a lot of time for you?"

"No, who?"

"Kate. She would so love to run your horse stables for you, and she could ride over with me and get a break from her father. She's a sharp young lady, and she knows how to save. She could be a valuable friend to you, James. Talk with her. She won't get in your way, I know."

"You're right. I will talk with her. With all this accountancy, I had completely let it go from my mind that she wanted to run the stables." He felt bad about forgetting, since Sarah had done so much good for the Throne Room. "Sarah, I want to thank you so greatly for all you've done to make this Throne Room venture a success. I want to reward you for things that I think you help us with but you personally don't benefit from."

"I know you've been preoccupied, and I've been happy to make things work. I'm used to start-ups after being with Victor. We can discuss it more in the new year."

"Well, that'll be in a couple of hours."

"Lisa, my dear, I believe it's your turn to have a dance with me."

She was so excited and jumped up immediately to give him a hug. "I wondered how long it would take you. Thank you for your advice to see Sir Nicholas. He has given me a wonderful job, James. I really enjoy working at his place, and I do have some modeling work he's training me for. Thank you for the introduction."

"You look fantastic tonight. You always choose the most unusual clothes and have a way of standing out. You're a very beautiful woman."

After the dance, he took her back to her table and then went over to ask Sandra to dance.

She looked irritated and said, "I want to go somewhere and talk. Then we can dance."

"Your wish is my command." He took her to his father's study and poured her a glass of champagne. "What is it, my dear? You look unhappy."

"We've scarcely been together in the last two years, apart from a cocktail here and there. Is there any hope for us?" Her eyes started to tear up.

"Sandra, I will always love you, but you have to realize I've been working my ass off and have seen very little of anyone. I've had one goal, and that's to get my professional license as a chartered accountant."

"I know you well enough, and I know you're not the type of person that goes running after women all over town. You are sincere and true, and that's what's so lovely about you. I also know when I see you with Sabrina that you're in love; it's in your eyes and your whole demeanor. You can't lie about those things. A woman can feel that."

"Yes, circumstances have brought us together due to my mother's marriage to Antonio. Yes, she's very attractive, and a person can't lie about those things, Sandra. I'm still young and am not ready to totally commit to anyone yet. I, just like you, want to have some sort of social life, as I've had next to nothing in the past two years." She had trodden on a sensitive subject that he truly didn't want to address that evening. Then he asked, "Are you thinking of someone else?"

"After two years, of course I am. You've always been my first choice and still are, but I have to know what expectations I should have, if any."

"Look, I will be back in London soon. Let's go out and spend the evening together. We've spent too much time apart, and you're far too important to me to let you go like that." He wanted to take the time to tell her the truth, but he also knew that this was not the appropriate moment. He would always care for her, as she was his first love. It was only right that she should know the true feelings of his heart, and she deserved to have that said in the best way possible.

"That's all I want to know. So let's go dance."

They began to dance, and Sandra said, "James, you know you're my first love, and I know it's not easy."

At eleven thirty, he went looking for Sabrina, as he wanted to see the New Year in with her. He found her in the awning, holding hands with Sir Nicholas. "Sabrina, where have you been?"

"I could ask you the same question." He noticed she sounded a little tipsy.

"Come with me. It's about to be midnight, and I want to see the New Year in with you."

He felt her reluctance to join him, but she did so. "Sabrina, if you don't want to dance with me, I understand."

She butted in, "How can you say that? You've been with everyone else all evening, and I've been waiting for just a little of your time. How do you think I feel having to dance with all sorts of men when all I wanted to do is dance with you?"

"I'm so sorry, but like you and Marco, I have people I know, and I must spend time with them. We have the whole weekend together." He was a little frustrated by her lack of understanding.

"I know that, but couldn't you have taken me with you some of the time to visit with them?"

"You're right, and I apologize. Please, let's dance."

They moved to the dance floor and held each other closely. "James, don't you know how much I love you? I can't bear it when, right before my eyes, you walk off and leave me standing there. At least introduce me around. I can take care of myself. I know you have old girlfriends; it's normal and to be expected."

"I know that was wrong. I just didn't think."

She squeezed him tighter and said, "Just to be in your arms is all I need. Nothing more, just you."

The clock countdown began, and all the people on the floor counted down the seconds. The streamers went up in the air, the whistles blew, and hats were thrown everywhere. The couple moved around the room together to hug and kiss others to the sounds of "Auld Lang Syne." Sabrina felt connected to him for the first time that whole evening. Her smile returned, and she radiated with happiness.

The band then stopped, and James was asked to come to the center of the room. All his friends gathered around; they handed him a glass of champagne, and the whole room sang "For He's a Jolly Good Fellow."

After everyone finished wishing him a happy birthday, James looked around for Kate because he knew he needed to talk with her after her mother's suggestion. He explained to Sabrina that he needed to dance with Kate, and he would tell her the reason later.

"So finally, His Lordship dances with one of his great admirers," Kate joked.

"You're an admirer? I've always admired your guts when your ride a horse or drive a car. You have an allure, although I'm not smart enough yet to put my finger on it."

"How could any woman compete with Sabrina? She has movie-star looks, and on top of that, she's very sweet. She definitely has her eyes set on you."

James got to the point. "Would you like to run the stables? I really feel you could make a difference."

"I'm up for the challenge, and if my talents prove worthy, would you consider me for other positions?"

"Absolutely."

She thanked him, gave him a hug and kiss, and congratulated him on his twenty-first birthday.

Sabrina and James hooked up again and went to sit in his small drawing room. "What an evening!" he said as they sat on the sofa arm in arm.

"I know it wasn't easy for you. You have a lot of people who look up to you, and it's not easy to reach out to everyone. I'm sorry for my outburst earlier. I understand I can't get in your way. So forgive me. It's just that I love you so much."

"I like you being a little jealous. It makes me feel you really care. Think nothing of earlier. We're here now, and I'm sitting next to the woman I love. That's all that matters." He looked at his watch and saw that was almost two o'clock. He suggested they call it a night.

The next morning, everyone got up late, most feeling a little hung over. Antonio and Phillipa were already in the kitchen when James came down, and one by one, his sisters, Piero, Sabrina, Sir Thomas, and Claudia came in for coffee. They all visited for a while, sharing stories from the night before.

James took Flick to one side and said, "You know that person you were with last night had one of the worst reputations in the whole school? His brother and Gordon were absolutely hated by many of my friends and students; they were notorious bullies, and I put an end to their behavior. How on earth did you meet up with such a person?"

"I met him at a party in London with a close school friend of mine, and we immediately hit it off. He's been a great influence on helping me chose a career, as he is at university studying journalism to go into his father's business. He wants to be an editor, and I think he's very smart," said Flick.

"Well I know you have other boyfriends, so be careful with that one; that's the only advice I can give you," said James.

"James I never knew you could be so protective, I'm flattered to have a brother like you who cares about his little sister," she said in her typical teasing way.

James then suggested to Sabrina that they go for a walk. They put on their winter coats and headed out.

"Where are you taking me? A little hideaway where you can make passionate love to me?"

"You read my mind. I have the keys to a little cottage where we can spend some time together."

"I'll do anything you want."

"Anything? Now that's saying a lot. I'd be careful with a wolf like me."

They opened the door to the little cottage where Claudia used to live. "James, I like this. It's very romantic."

He put on the fire in the bedroom while she heated up some more coffee. They sat together sipping their drinks and looking at one another with heated anticipation. Her eyes were electric, and the smell of her perfume was intoxicating. He stood up and grabbed her in his arms. They kissed and then went up the tiny staircase to the bedroom. He couldn't believe he was holding her in his arms again. They undressed each other and then made love with an intensity neither had known before. They felt free to be themselves and make love with total abandonment. He took his time to slowly work his way up her body, adoring every part, from the tip of her toes to between her thighs. He gave her all the passion he could until he heard her erupt with ecstasy. He now slowly caressed her ample breasts and her upper body, smelling the unique fragrance that only a woman can exude. He then passionately kissed her and penetrated her body as they held each other tightly. He worked hard again toward giving her another intense climactic experience, remembering what Vivian had taught him in his teens. They lay together afterwards and fell into a light slumber in each other's arms.

When they awoke, it was nearly three o'clock. James said, "It's getting late." All around them was silence. The light snowfall had muted all the neighboring sounds. The sun now setting on a short winter's day made the little cottage the perfect setting for what would always be a memorable occasion in both of their lives.

"That was so beautiful. Being with you makes me feel complete," she sighed, then added, "We're leaving tomorrow morning, as you know, so we won't have too much more time together. I just want to say that today has made the whole visit very special. When I get back to Milan, I'll call you in London and give you my number so we can plan our next visit."

They got dressed and went downstairs to have some more coffee and a cigarette. James sat there thinking about the whole weekend and how beautiful this encounter with Sabrina had been. It was a perfect start to what was now the real beginning of his adult life. After a while, they strolled back up to the main house in time for tea.

The next morning, Sabrina slipped a small note under James's door and then ran down to get in the car with the rest of her family.

CHAPTER 27

RETURN TO THE STARS

James had special plans for the first Sunday after New Year's Day. It had been seven years since he last spoke with his master, and today he was going to do it again. He had made plans with Rodney to open the Throne Room especially for his visit.

He walked quickly down to the Throne Room, entered, and then sat on the throne. Within seconds, he was sucked up through the vortex and sitting on the beach where he had been before. This time, there was a group of people to greet him.

Czaur stepped forward and said, "Welcome, James. It's been a while. And here you are now, about to set foot on the journey of life. You have achieved much since the last time you were here that we're so proud of."

"I've longed for this day and look forward to learning more from you."

"Let me introduce everyone here with me. To my right is the Seventh Earl, who has watched your progress with great interest and is so proud of what has been done with the Throne Room. When I'm not available, he will serve as your immediate guide. To his right is another guide called Morphus, whom you knew on Atlantis and is your technology expert. To my left is Serena, who is your guide to your heart and spiritual development, and to her left is Rachel, who is your guide to your health and well-being. Between the five of us, we complete your circle of evolvement toward the fifth dimension. They will leave for now. I will bring you up to date with any questions you may have, and then you will have personal time with each of your four guides."

The others departed, and Czaur began to answer James's questions. "In general, do you agree with the plans I have for the future development of our business?"

"Yes. The consolidation of your business is most wise. The ideas you have for building properties in the location of your shipping fleet are also very good. During the next twenty-five years, property values will increase beyond imagination. The management of your affairs will become easier and allow you to do other things, which we will go into at greater length with Morphus, who will take you to the Hall of Thoughts to show you some of the designs of the future. The Seventh Earl will give you his thoughts on the development of the Throne Room. Serena will work with you on evolvement and how to leave behind the three-dimensional world you live in. Rachel will help you by doing things to increase your energy field so that you can see and understand more of what you don't see now."

"I don't see everything now? Please explain."

"You have developed intuition, but your sight is mainly three-dimensional, and only when you are in thought do you see and understand more. Now you will be aware of much more. You will see people's auras only when you exercise the need to know something more deeply about them. You will come to learn whether they're just feelings they have at a particular moment or if those thoughts are a particularly dark part of their soul that is not out for the greater good. In other words, there are souls that continue to return to the cycles of your planet; they don't have the upward spiritual journey you seek. You will slowly learn this as you speak with various people. Your communications will either improve their aura or intensify it against you."

"So now I only feel that a person doesn't wish me well, is jealous, or is unsure. With increased energy, I will be able to see by the colors of their aura what I need to learn about them?"

"Precisely. You will be aware of the souls that we have, to some degree, kept you away from so you could focus all your efforts on mastering your education and trade. Now we will open you up to the world of experience. You will be in a world where good does exist, but a darker force is also more apparent to you."

"So there are people who choose to constantly live in the three-dimensional world and not advance spiritually?"

"Absolutely. Some of these more self-absorbed people have become very adept at their arts and trades and don't wish to leave a world that satisfies all their physical needs. They don't advance and cross over; after one life, they wait to incarnate again and continue to need more, have more, and so on. Some of these souls are very clever at what they do."

"So what becomes of them, eventually?"

"They continue to create Karma. It's inevitable, and so they get trapped in the karmic wheel. At the end of an age, they have to start all over again due to climatic change and many natural causes, over which they have no power. The dark side feeds off peoples' fear, and that gives them more and more energy. It is, in a sense, a parasite of the positive, but it creates your three-dimensional reality."

"So how does one deal with those forces?"

"By avoidance and not giving into fear. Sometimes one has to fight, but only for the very best of reasons. The one force they don't have is love. If you love, they have no power over you. So when a person is calm in the storm, all can be restored. Fear is what the opposite wants you to feel so it can reduce you and weaken you by causing you to surrender your faith, your love, and all that you value; in this way they can increase their powers. It sounds simple, but it takes great strength of character to resist."

"How do you know this force if it can be so subtle to start with?"

"There are many ways it can start: by temptation, a beautiful woman, easy money, promises that are unfulfilled. The list is endless, but your intuitions will guide you. Have your antenna up and listen well to the words of deception and lies. As your Bible well states, 'Be wise as the serpent.' Even though the children of the light are more innocent, they are also more protected."

"So I will be able to see people that have passed over? Ghosts and apparitions?"

"Yes. Only if you desire to see that, but we will give you an energy level so they can't see you. To them you'll just be a being of light, and they won't perceive that you can see them. We don't want you to be bothered by those matters. Seeing people who have passed over is only something that will take place if there is a specific message or reason. We have angels that are assigned to those duties, and it is not for us to interfere unless it crosses our path, which in this case is yours. It will take you a moment to get used to these new abilities, but don't be afraid. They're gifts that need much practice to learn, and you have Sarah who can teach you how to manage these insights.

"The last thing I want to discuss with you again is the Law of Karma. Read up on the Indian culture to understand this more deeply. Life in your dimension is very challenging, and the one thing you don't want to do is make mistakes that build up karmic debt. This is done by knowingly taking action against another that causes them pain or hardship. This traps you into a circle of events where what you have done to another will be visited upon you. This is not a punishment; this is a lesson, and it teaches us that all our actions have consequences. So know your direction well, before taking actions that result in consequences that may eventually have a price you may not want to face."

James sat silently thinking about all that Czaur had said, then he asked, "So how does a person escape an injustice they may have caused to another?"

"By asking for forgiveness. This very action shows recognition of your error and an attempt to put matters right. It may not always be well received, but then the burden is placed upon the other person. This is how we learn to forgive and evolve. Easier said than done!" said Czaur, dropping his head and raising his eyebrows with a smile.

"That's a subject that I must analyze and be very aware of, especially when my emotions get involved." James started to analyze himself and wonder just how many inconsiderate things he'd done in his own life by not thinking of others.

"Don't worry. You are well on your way. Let your conscience be your guide, and believe me, we'll give you a firm nudge when you're getting off track." They both laughed out loud knowing how easy it was to not always see another person's point of view.

"Now I'm going to hand you over to the Seventh Earl, who will tell you how to address him in the future. I will see you at the end to answer any questions you may still have."

In an instant, he was gone, and the Seventh Earl appeared. "James, my name is Arthur, but call me Art. I've watched you since you were a young lad and am very proud of you. The next part of your journey will be challenging, but we all think you're tough enough to handle it. The Throne Room is a great success. I will always be there to guide you on my thoughts as you expand this and other historic treasures you'll find in the business. Watch out for the ladies. Many, but not all, like position and power, and you'll have a lot of both. You'll be able to see through them now; you'll know the ones that love you for you and the ones who are there for opportunistic reasons. Women, on the whole, have a greater sense of awareness, and it's this characteristic that's so necessary to giving birth and protecting their children. A good woman looks for a mate whom she can trust, and she is not so critical of the physical appearance as a man. You must keep a moral code; once you lose that, you lose your compass and the respect of the community, which is hard to regain. People of the dark side will enjoy that; it gives them pleasure to see someone of stature torn down. You'll be less innocent when you return, but what you will now learn will amaze you."

"What happened to my father, Art? Do you know?"

"Yes, he's preparing for his new life. If you have a son one day, don't be surprised if you are the soul mates that you were before. I know you miss him, as your time together was short. We had to make you tough, and he'd had a full life; it was part of his script. He knew his time was up, and that's why he backed away from the business in his mid-forties to enjoy his estate."

Suddenly, he was gone and Morphus appeared. "James, you have not been aware of my presence until now. I have been working with you on your thoughts that you now have for the business and also on the reconstruction of the Throne Room. My skills lie in architecture and business development. We knew each other on Atlantis, and I have not returned to Earth since that time. I will take you now to the Hall of Thoughts, where we work to evolve planets like yours."

"The Hall of Thoughts? I don't get it. You're saying that my thoughts are not my own?"

"Not at all. You always have choices. We just lead you to the best possibility based on the way a project or invention is evolving. We go through may steps before releasing an idea—like that of the motorcar, the airplane, a building and its structure and shape—into the physical reality of the third dimension. The list is enormous, and we have many people who are working to progress ideas that come from advancement, necessity, and so on, like the electric light bulb. Our one goal is to move your planet away from fossil fuels. It was an abundant source for the planet after the dinosaur age, but it results in pollution, which is heating the planet you're living on. Fossil fuels are inefficient and wasteful compared to the technology we had on Atlantis. It will take time to move away from this, but it will happen as resources dwindle and big business finds other ways to produce better results with less waste."

"What about the planet in the meantime? Will this form of energy hurt the air we breathe, people's health, or the lives of animals and vegetation?"

"The planet will adjust, as it has through countless cycles of environmental change. The planet you live on is extremely resilient and knows much more about protecting itself from environmental change than any scientist. If the use of this fuel persists well into the next century, it will become harmful, but we are sure the necessary adaptations will take place with other forms of energy that will be discovered through us."

"So when we reach a roadblock in our thinking and we stand back to seek answers, you are there to provide them? You give us choices based on the particular profession or situation we find ourselves challenged with?"

"Yes. It is your choice, in a sense, but when you either wake up with an idea or you're deep in thought with a challenging situation and an idea pops into your head, it comes from us. It doesn't mean you're all robots; it's how we help each other to evolve and understand the galaxy and the universe we inhabit. We are more evolved beings, not better, and in the same way, when we are challenged, we need answers from a higher source than us."

"So we are all in a giant classroom trying to understand the dynamics of this incredible universe, and we are taught as we strive to learn."

"You have it. There are those of you who are writers, inventors, aviators, doctors, musicians, and so on. We are all different, but it's working in unison that brings about the advancement of all of us, including those of us who are here. Now let me show you some of the technological things you will see before the next century."

James followed Morphus to the Hall of Thoughts. They floated effortlessly through the atmosphere between buildings of glass and light. They reached a large stadium-like structure, which glimmered with the colors of the rainbow, and then they entered the building. "There are various levels in this building. We, here on this planet, deal with a number of different planets that are all like Earth and have evolved in a similar way, with similar mutations and looks in a primarily oxygenated atmosphere like yours. In this building we handle eleven different planets. We have separate floors for each planet, except for the new planets, which are still in what we call the 'genesis stage,' where human life has not evolved from tiny cell forms, and the consciousness level isn't ready to receive more evolved entities."

"So we in spirit form choose a body or such to inhabit in order to experience life?"

"Yes. In the lower dimensions of physical form, you require food and personal needs for the body you have entered. In the higher dimensions, you don't need those things. You know your stage of evolvement by the energy you have, which is directly related to the experience of knowledge you have learned so far in the universe. This is spiritual knowledge. Here, there is no profit, no personal gain; it's all about evolvement. We have no need of those things. We rest, we drink herbs, and we have our own form of entertainment in the arts and ideas we help to create. Anything you have on Earth we can recreate here if we want to, so the need to have more is only important to the particular spirit form that's here. It's a whole new learning process but a very rewarding one. As you'll learn, the more energy you have, the more fascinating and illuminating the universe we live in becomes. You will see things in a completely different way."

"Do you have sex and relationships between males and females?"

"Absolutely, and the energy level of love that is experienced is something you couldn't begin to know in the physical realm."

"So how do you know whom you are attracted to and whom you want to have a relationship with if you have no physical body?"

"It's easy. We know each other by the Hall of Records and our own intuitions as we know all of our previous incarnations. We can choose and actually see the soul that totally fits with our own. The attraction is so true and uncomplicated that it's total. We don't have to analyze it; we feel it in an instant. It's of such beauty that it literally takes your breath away. We don't have a physical body to complicate matters. However, we can lower our energy levels to a point where our form is more visible, as I have done in my meeting with you. We blend, and in that moment of love, our energy increases tenfold. In the same way, your heart beats faster when you're with a woman you're attracted to. Imagine that force being so powerful you couldn't contain the force of attraction in a physical body. The laws of the planet you live on come from a divine source. Therefore, it's a reflection of the true essence. Physical relationships are quite secondary in experience to the intensity that's felt in the universe. You have that expression 'when stars collide,' do you not? Well, it's true."

"Really? I am always amazed at what I learn when I'm here. I realize in the larger scheme of things, I have a long way to go."

Morphus showed him all around the earth-level floor. He saw the computers that would replace adding machines and typewriters. He also saw phones that would hold all sorts of information and allow people to both talk to and see each other. He saw the designs of new architecture to come, the advancements with health and disease as well as advancements in the arts, music, and fashion world. He learned how souls could tap into this library of information. It was indeed exciting.

"James, I think I have given you enough for now. We will return, and Serena can rest you for a moment. Then you can talk with her."

James followed him to Serena's place. She had a house that overlooked the sea but was high in a mountainous region of the planet. When he arrived, she could see he was tired, so she put him into a trance to restore his energy level. When James awoke, he felt fully energized, more than he'd ever known.

"Who are you?" James was still in a daze.

"I am Serena. I am here to tell you about your feelings and your spiritual soul."

"How is it you look so beautiful? I can't take my eyes off you. You're not like anything I've ever seen before." James knew his attraction was nothing like he'd felt for Sabrina. It was the kind of love that came from his heart, yet being a new experience, he was unable to define it in earthly terms.

"Morphus told me you had asked about how we make love on this planet, so I've lowered my energy so that you can see me more clearly. I've known you on Atlantis in many incarnations, and you and I have loved each other before."

"So we were married then?"

"Yes, many times. I have loved you and been with you in many of your incarnations, and after that, I have been your guide every time you have taken physical form."

"I know that I could never leave a woman who gives the love that you are showing to me now."

"James, when you come to this side, I will be here waiting for you. I am part of the feminine side of your life, and we are connected in a way you could never understand until you come here."

"When I saw you on the beach, I didn't feel like I do now. Why is that?"

"That's because I didn't want to show you who I was yet, and that's why you didn't meet me when you came as a young boy. I didn't want to distract you from your journey and make you have daydreams about me. Another soul could arrive here, and they wouldn't have the same feelings about me as you do." She then shifted topics. "So let's get down to business. You are here to learn about your heart, something that you don't pay enough attention to. You are always thinking about what to become, who to be, and working to be better and have more. These things have separated us from being with one another."

"Well, it's the way of the world we live in. If you don't make something of your life, what possibilities do you have?"

"Yes, that's true, but you have to listen to your heart more. That's the way to spiritual growth. The things of physical form are very attractive when you are in that state, but as you are experiencing here and now, they're not so important, are they?"

"Yes, you're right. Looking at you in this moment changes the way I feel."

"So when you return, hold onto that thought. As much as you feel it's your duty to sacrifice for a way of life you believe in, know that love comes first. No matter how much you have or how much you think, it's all empty without the person or persons you love."

"You'll always be here for me?"

"I'm not an apparition. I'm real, more real than your physical body will ever be, and yes, I will be here for you always."

"I'm so glad to have had this experience. It makes me realize that the spiritual energy is much more powerful than the physical."

"You will feel the same way about Rachel. She's every bit as beautiful as I am but in a different way. I've said to you before, we are not that way for just anyone. It's you who feels this way because you're seeing and feeling with your soul. For another person, it would be completely different. For example, when Sabrina or Sandra or whoever comes over to our way of life, they will shine more brightly, and their beauty will be tenfold to what it is in the physical body."

"So what you're saying is that we have more than one woman who loves us? So do you have other male forms that you love too?"

"Yes. But in the physical form, you are territorial and jealous. I understand in life on your planet, it would not work for the purposes of child-rearing and the development of a civilization. In your life on Earth, you will be attracted to the very person that has incarnated for that lifetime and is with you for that purpose. Your world is three-dimensional, and by its very nature, is more structured. In our world, no one fully completes another; we all partially complete each other, and that's how the universe works toward a oneness that is the divine. Each one of us is a small but immensely important part of that complete whole or oneness. We are souls that come from God or the divine, and in that, we are all different in our entirety. We are all part of the divine in our own individual way. We wander out into the universe to learn according to the essence that is you and me, to experience and grow, and it is in this way that we become one with a greater knowledge and understanding. It is a vast and all-encompassing journey, and love is at the very center of it all. That's why we all have feelings toward one another."

"I would feel pain at the thought of you loving another, as I'm sure anyone would. I can only understand so much. That's a tough one to get my head around."

"James, I feel your thoughts. You must understand I don't love you any less. In the same way you feel for me, you too can feel for others who also fulfill your needs. None of us has it all for any one person. It will be a challenge, but you will grow to understand when you reach a higher level of energy. Your desire to fulfill and be fulfilled for different reasons will be driven by the exact need you have at that time. I think I've tried as best I can to open your eyes, and in time, you'll grow to see it. Come and walk in my garden and see a little of our planet before you go to see Rachel."

Her garden was beautiful; the flowers were luminescent in their colors. The grass was greener than he could ever imagine. He thought that it had to be heaven. He looked out over the hills to the sea and up into the sky where he could observe the two suns. He thought it was funny that he could look at them like planets, but it was because his energy level was at a much higher state. Looking up at her balcony, he noticed a large, almost globe-sized, crystal ball. She had birds flying around, and pets were everywhere. It was like living on Earth but at a different frequency, where everyone moved so fluently, just gliding.

"What is the crystal ball for?"

"So I can see you and watch over you. I'm always there. All you have to do is think of me, and I'll be there. You will soon develop the ability to hear my words."

"I'm going to miss you. I don't understand everything yet, but the kind of love I feel for you is so real, I don't think I can ever forget it. It's the most powerful experience I think I've ever had."

"Here comes Rachel. She'll take you to her place now, and she'll have a few things to teach you too." He could feel her heart pouring out love to him as he left.

Gliding over the hills, he followed Rachel to her home. He was surprised to find it was larger than he expected. There was a huge fountain in the front garden full of birds of every imaginable variety and size. Their colors were so brilliant and healing.

"James, come out to this corner of the garden where we can sit and talk in private."

"Rachel, you're also very beautiful. How is it that I meet two of the most beautiful women I've ever seen in the same day?"

"I, like Serena, was your partner in life and lived with you on Atlantis, but since then I too have become a part of this new dimension. My love for you has always been there and always will be. In this dimension, the very essence of who we are is magnified. Serena has probably told you it's you who finds me beautiful, as I too find you the same way. To someone else, that same connection may not be there, and hence that beauty which resonates between our souls would be different in the eyes of another. In this world of no territory and structure, which exists in the animal kingdom you now live in, we have advanced beyond that. We enhance ourselves with those souls we love, but each of us brings our own unique quality, and not any one of us has it all. It's in the unity of who we are; we combine to have the force to become one. It's something that's not easily grasped in your dimension, but you'll find no jealousy, control, and need for someone over another. It will be plainly obvious who we want to be with when we want to be with them."

"I'm slowly grasping the fact that you obviously have love, and as a result, the type of insecurities we feel are not present here. I can't believe how beautiful you are, and yet it's completely different to Serena. So it is possible to love more than one person for different reasons and different qualities?"

"Exactly. You'll get there, but don't try practicing that on Earth. Not too many people will grasp the reasoning, as the level of evolvement is not there yet. Progress will be made. I am here to watch over your health and see, based on your aura, the foods you need to eat to ensure your longevity. You carry genetic weaknesses, like the cancer your father suffered with. Your predisposition to heart disease can be managed through healthy habits like exercise, good nutrition, and staying away from carbohydrates, dairy products, and too much sugar. Cholesterol is a huge problem that can cause blockage to the heart. By the next century, the medical profession will have made great advances to address these genetic faults, which exist in all human bodies. I recommend that you exercise and keep a positive state of mind every day to reduce the stress you will face. Sarah can help you achieve that healthy balance."

"I feel your love. It's something that we do feel on Earth, just not to such a degree. It's such a beautiful feeling to be loved and in turn to love. It can be so painful on the planet I live on."

"You have been told by Czaur and Morphus of the increased energy you will receive. Although this will require getting used to at first, it will give you far better insight into whom to love— for all the right reasons. The body can lie, as can the tongue. The aura speaks for itself, and as you learn the energies around people, you will expose yourself to less pain and more wisdom." She smiled at him with such warmth and compassion and then said, "I believe you must leave now. It will be quite a time in Earth hours that you've been gone, and when you return, you will be very tired and aware of the heavy gravitational pull of your body and the heaviness of other people's feelings at first. Go to bed straight away, and sleep as long as you can; then you'll be ready to go forward." She got up to lead him back to Czaur, who was waiting on the beach to see him off. "Just remember, James, as with Serena, you can connect with me anytime, and you'll hear my thoughts for the questions you may have." With that, she was gone.

"Well, James, I hope this return trip has been meaningful to you and will help you on the next leg of your journey. Remember, we only give you extra energy when a situation requires it; you are, in a sense, a receiver that we can use to empower only for the right reasons. We release this power not for personal profit or gain, only to help."

"I understand. Czaur, thank you for all the kindness you've shown. I will miss all of you very much, but I will think of you all and communicate, as I can now see you all so clearly in my mind."

With a parting look at his old father, Czaur, he was sucked up into the vortex and back on the throne. It took him several minutes to recover from the journey. He felt very dizzy, and the room was turning in circles. He finally got up, and he could feel the full weight of his body again after the free movement he had experienced with his spirit. He was tired and wanted to sleep. He'd been away for nearly an hour—his longest visit yet.

When he reached his room, he immediately dropped on the bed and fell into a deep slumber. He awoke the next day at nearly lunchtime. It was only then that he saw the letter Sabrina had left and opened it. He read:

> *James, Amore Mio,*
> *I leave with a heavy heart and a longing to see you again. Each time we meet, I feel closer to you and understand you more. Your party was an unbelievable success. I know you're loved by others, but don't forget the one who loves you the most. Until we meet again.*
> *Amore Bellissimo,*
> *Sabrina*
> *P.S. I leave you my handkerchief with my perfume to remember me by.*

He brought the handkerchief to his face and smelled her perfume. He was pleased that she had left him with something that would make him feel she was with him.

James went downstairs to see if his family was still around. He knew his mother would be headed back to Italy, and he wanted to see her off.

"James, where have you been?" his mother asked, concerned. She was already packed and ready to leave.

"After the party, I was so exhausted that I had to rest, so I've spent most of the time in my room." He didn't want to get into the whole story, and what he said was basically true.

"Well, we didn't want to disturb you, as we thought you looked very tired. Anyway, now you're the man of the house. I would like you to take over all the check-signing obligations, as in a sense, I'm now your tenant and live here at your pleasure." She looked at him with a sly grin. She was actually very excited, as she and Antonio could now travel more and see the world. In a sense, she was free of her responsibilities.

He laughed and hugged his mother goodbye. He then said goodbye to Becky and Flick, who were headed back early to finish school at the Institute Alpin Videmanette in Switzerland. He would be heading to London himself the next day, so the house would be, for the most part, empty, at least for a while. James was saddened at the thought, but he knew it was necessary.

James felt an incredible sense of freedom, but in another sense, he felt very sad. It was the end of the family in a way. Things would never be quite the same. Someday, James would marry, and only then would the house come alive again with the voices of young children clamoring down the corridors.

James spent the afternoon with Keith Pruett going over business matters and then talked to Rodney about keeping a watchful eye on the house and property. He then went home and packed. He was planning to head to the city early the next morning. He wanted to be at the bank soon after lunchtime to meet with Claudia and go over the new agenda he had prepared.

James arrived at the bank shortly after lunch. He walked into his father's office and put down his briefcase. Rose quickly came in to see if he would like a cup of coffee. He sat there for a moment, thinking about all he had learned. He was about to put the next plans for the business into action and transform what had been a traditional merchant bank into a modern-day international conglomerate.

He leaned back in his chair and said to himself, "Well, I'm finally here, and now we're really going to make a difference and become the Bannerman's international business I've dreamed about." At that very moment, Rose called him on the intercom. "Sir, I have a call from your mother, and it sounds urgent, on line four."

"Okay, I'll take it."

"James, thank God I found you. Something dreadful has happened."

"What is it?" he said anxiously.

"Marco and Sabrina have met with a terrible accident in Milan. Marco is on life support, and his prospects don't look very good. Sabrina has suffered a lot of bodily injury. It's not known to what extent. She's in a coma and is heavily medicated. When she becomes conscious, which is only briefly, she calls out your name, so I think it's extremely important that you come here immediately. If it's possible, catch the next flight out of London. When you know your arrival time, we'll pick you up at the airport. Antonio and I are staying at her apartment here in Milan."

"What happened?" asked James in a state of shock.

"James, it was a car accident. I'll tell you all about it when you arrive, so call me and let me know," she said before hanging up.

My God, I hope she's all right, thought James as he went to Claudia's office to share the news.

"Rose, book me a flight immediately!"

EPILOGUE

For years I've known that a book was inside me. When I finally set about writing it, the process felt natural. I wrote for days and days on end—and then for months.

My inspiration for this particular book was life itself. I wanted the challenge of integrating the pragmatism of everyday life with the unseen world beyond. The world we cannot see has a structure. For example, what is a miracle? It's something that happens; yet we cannot quantify it. We can't explain it in the practical, real world. However, if we were able to transport ourselves into the future, say two thousand years ahead, would it be just an everyday event?

It is my hope that this book—and the entire *Legacy* series—provokes you, the reader, to dig more deeply into your everyday lives—to look at what lies beyond our reach. This first book is an all-encompassing story of business, love affairs, human relationships, intrigue, an expression of human nature, and all our facets. From the past I have brought us to the present.

Our history may not be as it appears or has been written. I have attempted to make the reader see things from a different perspective through this transcending of an intense story.

I would like the reader to "suspend disbelief," let go, and enjoy the possibility that this could have been a reality in the civilization preceding us. So open your minds and know that this may be possible for all of us one day.

I wish all my readers to have a great experience and know there's more to come. Happy reading to you all, and know I'm always available to answer any and all of your questions.

Inspirationally,
David Francis

David Francis

David Francis was born and educated in England. He was raised by a long line of entrepreneurs who date back before 1890. In 1917 his grandfather started in the aerospace industry, and today his brother still runs the family business. In 1967 David immigrated to the United States. At the age of twenty-three, he completed his apprenticeship in machining and gained certificates for workshop processes and mechanical engineering from Guildford Technical College in England. He started his own business in 1982 after having worked for major aerospace manufacturers to gain experience within the industry.

In November 2003 he sold his business, which became the largest wing forming company in the world, to a Belgian consortium.

In 2006 he built his own two and half mile road racetrack in North Texas, where most of his family and grandchildren now reside. He also spends time at his home in Canada, where he likes to write.

Throughout David's life he has been a prolific writer and public speaker within the industry in which he worked. He has taught and learned from many writers to fulfill his dream of writing:

The Legacy

As the former owner of an international enterprise, vast experience in dealing with high-ranking people in governments and different countries has given him the knowledge to write this series of books. He has always had faith and belief in the amazing universe we live in. In his travels all over the world, he's been able to capture thoughts about other cultures. His working years allowed him to make notes. He has applied those experiences to this all-encompassing set of books he has written. He plans to expand on that knowledge in future books.

It is David's hope that his work will provoke the reader to contemplation, introspection, and thought. He would like the reader to come away with a positive experience . . . and perhaps a revitalized way of seeing our world.